Also by Matt Dickinson

The Death Zone
High Risk

BLACK ICE

MATT DICKINSON

St. Martin's Paperbacks

First published in Great Britain by Hutchinson
an imprint of the Random House Group Limited

This is a work of fiction. All of the characters, organizations and events portrayed in this novel are either products of the author's imagination or are used fictitiously.

BLACK ICE

Copyright © 2002 by Matt Dickinson.

Library of Congress Catalog Card Number: 2003052602

ISBN: 0-312-98932-6
EAN: 9780312-98932-3

Printed in the United States of America

St. Martin's Press hardcover edition / December 2003
St. Martin's Paperbacks edition / October 2006

St. Martin's Paperbacks are published by St. Martin's Press, 175 Fifth Avenue, New York, NY 10010.

10 9 8 7 6 5 4 3 2 1

for my son
TOM

ACKNOWLEDGEMENTS

Research for this Antarctic novel would not have been possible without the kind invitation of explorers Julian Freeman-Attwood and Skip Novak to join their expedition to Terra Incognita. I don't think I've ever laughed so much—or been more terrified—in my life, and the wonders we witnessed there have left me with a longing to return. I would also like to thank the personnel of the Argentine base on Deception Island and the Commander of the British Base Faraday on the Antarctic Peninsula for their warm welcome and their patient efforts to explain the mysteries of spectrophotometers, ion chromatographs and lakes beneath the ice.

You are welcome to visit the author's website at:
www.mattdickinson.com

PART 1

Antarctica

1

Enchanted as a child by tales of the last unexplored continent on earth, Carl Norland had fallen in love with Antarctica. Now, not far short of his twenty-seventh birthday, the Norwegian explorer was beginning to appreciate that it was a love affair which might—quite soon—end with his death.

'Great God! This is an awful place . . .' Robert Falcon Scott had written as he dragged his dispirited and starving team into second place at the South Pole in 1912. Now, Carl knew exactly how he felt.

Carl turned his face to the north. Somewhere beyond that dark horizon, there was a world of warmth, of light and the love of a wife and daughter. But if he didn't act fast, he was never going to see that world again.

Carl crawled into the tent and pulled the emergency beacon from the side pocket of the rucksack. He cradled the device in his hands, ignoring the searing pain in his fingers, the crackle of the frostbite blisters as his skin flexed and broke. Many days earlier the last battery on their main radio had failed, leaving this transmitter as their final lifeline. This box of tricks had to work, he prayed, or no one would ever find them.

The unit weighed 2.1 kilos and had been manufactured by a specialist communications company in Maine. Mostly they were bought by yachtsmen in case of capsize, but it would do its job just as well here in the heart of Antarctica.

The casing was yellow plastic, a stubby black rubber aerial protruding for six inches or so from the top. Next to it was a red switch marked *Activate only in emergency.* The switch was protected by a plastic seal to prevent it being fired by an accidental knock.

Once activated, the beacon would emit a constant radio pulse on the international distress frequency of 121.5 mhz. The pulse would be picked up by a passing satellite, the signal relayed instantly to a permanently manned station in New Hampshire. Their position would be fixed, and a rescue plane would be dispatched from Tierra del Fuego—the landmass closest to Antarctica.

More than anything he had ever desired before, Carl wanted to rip open that seal and throw the switch.

He stumbled out of the tent and stood swaying on his swollen feet as a bitter gust of wind ran through the camp. There was a haze of frozen fog lying a few metres above the glacier, but above it Carl could see as far as the Madderson Range, almost two hundred miles distant.

What were they trying to prove here? Carl squinted through windbeaten eyes at the immensity of the landscape that surrounded them and realised he was no longer sure.

Three and a half months earlier, he and one other had set out from the far side of this continent, men of supreme motivation and commitment, men who could endure phenomenal levels of pain. Their plan was an audacious one—a crossing of Antarctica at its *widest* point, a trek of more than two thousand miles, which would establish their names alongside the great legends of Antarctic exploration. It was a noble quest, they had thought, a prize worth fighting for—an opportunity to join the most rarified club in the world.

They were manhauling, each starting out with a sledge carrying five hundred pounds of gear. The weight had been crucifying, the straps chafing running sores into their flesh, their bodies deteriorating with every passing day until they were on the very point of collapse.

They were unsupported. Totally alone.

Now—eighty miles short of their objective—they had failed. There was no food left on which to survive. The rolling ocean of ice had sucked the flesh from their bones, sapped the very essence of sinew and muscle away until they were reduced to the stumbling progress of a child. Carl reckoned he had lost about fifteen kilos, his skin tightening against his skeleton the way that vacuum-packed plastic clings to supermarket meat.

Winter was closing in on them. Daylight was down to just a few gloomy hours a day. Soon the permanent night of the Antarctic winter would fall across the ice sheet, and then there would be no escape.

It was time to get out. And fast.

2

Before him, slumped in a despondent heap against his sledge, was Julian Fitzgerald, crosser of continents, planter of flags, conqueror of the heights and depths, and member of that elite band of media-friendly explorers whose faces are as familiar on TV chat-show circuits as they are in the hallowed corridors of the Royal Geographical Society of London and the Explorers Club of New York.

Fitzgerald was as close as an explorer could ever get to a celebrity with a truly global profile, an obsessive expeditioner for whom the expression 'been there, done that' might have been invented. He had dived the deepest trenches of the oceans, walked alone across the deserts of Australia and Namibia and put his marker on the summits of Everest, K2 and Kanchenjunga. When it came to playing the media, Fitzgerald was a grand master: just as the press tired of mountain exploits, he would announce his intention to explore the deepest cave system on the planet; if seafaring was in vogue, he would enter a round-the-world yacht race, and no sooner had the oceans begun to pale than he would pop up in the colour supplements with a plan to conquer the poles.

The fact that a significant number of Fitzgerald's expeditions had ended in failure never seemed to diminish the media's appetite for more of the same.

Fitzgerald had his fans, but they wouldn't have recognised the faded figure lying on the ice in front of Carl. He was staring into the white beyond, his bloodshot eyes oblivious to the glare, his face locked into what could almost have been a death mask so devoid was it of expression.

He showed no sign that he was aware of Carl standing next to him and no sign that he had seen the emergency transmitter in the Norwegian's hand.

Carl watched him for a while, noting how Fitzgerald's reddening beard was matted with ice where fluid had dribbled from his mouth and nose, how his cheeks were sunken, his powerful frame reduced to fractions of its former strength. Even the aristocratic sweep of Fitzgerald's nose was encrusted with the blisters of radiation and frost.

Carl sat, easing the pain in his legs, wondering if he had the courage to tell Fitzgerald what he had decided and wondering, also, how this adventure had ever gone so wrong.

The two men had met a year before, a chance encounter at the Alpine Club, where Fitzgerald was holding a launch party for the publication of his latest expedition book. Carl had been in awe of the great man, a little embarrassed even, tongue-tied in the presence of this legend who had been something of a childhood hero. Fitzgerald was initially offhand, but on learning that Carl was an expeditioner himself—and that he had recently skied across the Greenland ice cap in record time—his attitude changed. The explorer gave Carl his card, asked him to make contact to arrange a longer meeting and then moved gracefully on to apply his legendary charm elsewhere in the room.

Three days later, the two men lunched at Fosters—a traditional English restaurant steeped in old-fashioned charm, where fare such as jugged hare and spotted dick was treated with due gastronomic reverence.

'My favourite restaurant,' Fitzgerald confided. 'I dream of it while I'm out on the ice.'

He went on to tell Carl of his planned Antarctic journey and asked the Norwegian—quite bluntly—to explain his background.

Carl told Fitzgerald about his home town of Trondheim, on Norway's western shore, and about his current role as fisheries researcher on a three-year postgraduate attachment to London University. He told him of his English wife, Sally, about his six-month-old daughter, Liv, but mostly he talked about what Fitzgerald was really interested in—his passion for polar travel and overland expeditions.

Like many of his countrymen, Carl was a natural on cross-country skis—a skill which enhanced his passion for the extreme limits of the earth. Nansen and Amundsen had been his early inspiration, and their tales of polar exploration had led him to seek places on expeditions whenever the opportunity arose. His crossing of the Greenland ice cap had been a great triumph, and now he had his sights set on bigger things . . .

Carl had done his Antarctic research, had read the expedition accounts of Scott, Shackleton, Amundsen and Fuchs. He had attended lectures by contemporary explorers, been inspired by the extraordinary achievements of modern Antarctic stars such as Reinhold Messner, Robert Swan and Ranulph Fiennes.

If he was offered the opportunity to go south, Carl told Fitzgerald, he would jump at the chance.

Fitzgerald had been impressed with the young Norwegian's enthusiasm and proposed—straight out—that they might team up for the attempt.

'Publicity is vital on these things,' Fitzgerald had told him. 'A Brit and a Norwegian teaming up will get the press stirred nicely. They'll want to know if it's going to be a race between us!'

Carl smiled, disguising the slight unease Fitzgerald's

comment had roused inside him: the idea of capitalising on
the ancient South Pole rivalries of Scott and Amundsen was
not in the least attractive to him.

Nevertheless, Carl was flattered by the approach, and realistic enough to realise that such an opportunity was un-
likely to come his way again.

'Just one thing,' Fitzgerald had added. 'Even though
there'll only be two of us out there, I'm still the leader of this
expedition. You accept that my decisions will be final?'

'Yes, sir.' Carl gave a mock salute in a failed attempt to
make the moment a humorous one.

But Fitzgerald did not smile.

'Just so long as it's understood.'

3

'I can't take another step,' Carl told Fitzgerald, 'and that's all there is to it.'

Fitzgerald stared right at him for long moments before he spoke, the booming, operatic voice of which he was so proud reduced to a plaintive croak.

'You want to quit?' he asked. 'When we're so close?'

'I don't want another fight,' Carl told him quietly. 'We're talking life and death now, and I think you know it.'

Fitzgerald pulled a map from his pocket and stabbed at it with a finger.

'Eighty miles, Carl. It's nothing after what we've been through. Eighty miles and the widest crossing is ours. Write our names in the history books once and . . .'

Fitzgerald's voice fell away. Carl would have laughed if he could have found the energy. Instead he felt the stab of tears prick at his eyes as a vision of his wife and daughter flashed momentarily through his mind. He breathed deeply to recover.

'You think anyone gives a damn?'

'Just three or four more days . . .'

Carl felt the familiar frustration well up inside him.

'And if the weather closes in? Think about it, for Christ's sake. We haven't eaten for a week. Winter is just around the corner. If that plane can't get to us, we'll both starve to death.'

'I should have gone solo.' Fitzgerald retreated to his habitual mantra. 'I'd have been faster without you.'

They sat in silence for many minutes, looking out across the unending expanse of ice, while Carl pondered the manner in which his relationship with Fitzgerald had deteriorated. Locked into each other's presence, Fitzgerald's hoped-for balancing act of the master and his apprentice had been way off the mark. The concept of Carl deferring to Fitzgerald's greater range of experience had been sorely tested by a number of bitter arguments between the two men: rows over navigation, over food, over Fitzgerald's use of the radio for endless media interviews even when their battery supply was dwindling fast.

Carl had tried to make it work, tried so hard he sometimes felt the rigours of living at close quarters with his fellow explorer were sapping more of his energy than the physical demands of the sledge journey itself.

But his attempts came to little. On an emotional level, Fitzgerald had been reserved, taciturn even, giving little away. Carl's mission to peel back a few protective layers resulted in little by way of revelation. On the subject of his single status, Fitzgerald's only comment was a brief 'Marriage? Never had the time.' About his family background he was similarly tight-lipped, adding nothing to what Carl had already gleaned from press cuttings and biographies about a restless, globetrotting childhood spent moving from one embassy to another with his diplomat father.

The one subject on which Fitzgerald *could* get emotional—and Carl had seen him flare up into a rage more than once—was on his past failings, whether imagined or real. Criticism, particularly by the media, of any of his previous expeditions could leave the explorer apoplectic with fury. When he heard on the radio that an investigative reporter was putting a damning documentary together about his recent disastrous Tierra del Fuego Youth Expedition—a trip which had ended with several of the participants hospitalised with serious injury—Fitzgerald went ballistic, going into a sulk which lasted for weeks.

Faced with a virtually silent travelling companion, Carl sought solace with his diary. He wrote for hours in the tent each night, venting his frustration at what he saw as his companion's increasingly irrational decision-making and his growing fears that the trip would end in disaster.

The crux had come at the South Pole, halfway point and effectively the moment of no return. According to Carl's calculations, their food would run out before the challenge was over. He was tempted to call a halt.

Fitzgerald had turned to Carl and fixed him with a look he had not seen before.

'You can't pull out,' he said quietly. 'I won't let you.'

Carl had experienced a curious stab of emotion which, at the time, he was hard pressed to recognise. Was it apprehension? Or a new wariness about what lay beneath Fitzgerald's protective layers?

Only later, way too much later, would the young Norwegian come to realise that what he experienced in that moment was fear.

But now it was too late to turn back the clock. They *had* tried to achieve the impossible, and, as Carl sat there, he knew that he should never have continued beyond the pole.

'The saddest thing of all,' Carl told Fitzgerald, 'is that I used to love this place. Now I think of it as the enemy.'

'We can still do it,' Fitzgerald repeated. 'It's your mind which is letting you down.'

Carl tugged at Fitzgerald's arm, forcing him to turn towards him.

'Look at me,' Carl pleaded. 'I've lost too much weight. I can taste ammonia in my mouth . . . do you know what that means? Our bodies are consuming themselves.'

Fitzgerald turned away in disgust. 'If you're so desperate to get out, why didn't you just push the ruddy switch anyway?'

Carl sighed.

'Because I'm working to the principle that we should take all the important decisions together.'

'Very noble, I don't think.'

They sat in strained silence for a while, both exhausted by the expenditure of nervous energy.

'Do it if you want,' Fitzgerald told him, finally, 'but I want it to be understood between us that it's you who is calling the expedition to a halt. Not me. It's not in my nature to quit.'

Carl took the emergency beacon and ripped the protective plastic seal away.

'I'm doing this for both of us, Julian, and I hope in time you come to appreciate that.'

He clicked the switch to 'on'. A faint bleep could be heard emitting from the tiny loudspeaker.

It was done. Carl looked up into the sky, fantasising that he could already hear the drone of an incoming aircraft.

There would be food on board. Carl felt the craving deep inside him as he thought about that.

4

Richard Leighton was in his hotel room in Ushuaia, play-ing a little pre-lunch patience on his laptop, when the telephone rang. It was Julian Fitzgerald's radio operator, Irene Evans, calling from the expedition control room at the airport.

'We just got a call. They let off the beacon. Get down here as fast as you can.'

'Thank Christ for that. I'll be right with you.'

Richard stuffed his thermal clothing into a kitbag and packed his laptop and camera. Please God, he thought as he walked the now-familiar dusty road down towards Ushuaia airport, don't let this be a false alarm. If he had to spend one more day in this dead-and-alive hole, he'd start talking to the penguins. Kicking his heels in Tierra del Fuego wasn't what Richard Leighton had expected when he'd been offered the reporting job of his dreams.

Just a month earlier he'd walked into the offices of the *Daily Mail* feeling ten feet tall. This wasn't just the beginning of a job, Richard felt, this was the beginning of an illustrious media career. Getting the royal tour to Brazil had been a great excitement, his first foreign assignment. Granted, it wasn't exactly the Gulf War, or a Washington posting, but it was a start.

He filed his daily reports, diligently stayed awake during the interminable official meals and slipped easily into the reporters' 'club' which followed the British royals around the globe.

It was five-star all the way.

Then the bad news, just as he was packing his bags for the business-class flight home: the call from his editor back in London.

'Ever heard of a place called Ushuaia?'

'Can't say I have.'

'I want you down there as soon as possible. Seems that explorer Fitzgerald has gone missing in Antarctica. They haven't had any radio contact for ten days.'

Richard listened to his brief with dismay. He had heard of Fitzgerald and his overblown exploits, but as far as he was concerned the man was a dinosaur. What the hell was the point of trying to walk across a bloody continent when you could fly? It all seemed a bit of a farce.

Still, he couldn't say that to the editor.

'How long's the assignment?' he asked.

'Can't say. They should have reached the edge of the continent some days ago. Their control people are pretty sure they're in trouble . . . so get your ass down there.'

There was no business class to Ushuaia. Richard sat in an economy seat with a stale chicken sandwich and a cup of fake Pepsi, watching miserably out of the window as hundreds of miles of Altiplano rolled endlessly by.

Where the hell is this place? he thought. It feels like we're flying to the ends of the bloody earth.

They were, as Richard found out when he finally got round to seeing a map. Ushuaia is the southernmost human habitation of any size on the planet, a frontier town cursed with a year-round wind so cutting and intrusive it frequently drives inhabitants insane.

'A gold-rush town without the gold,' Richard wrote in one of his first scene-setting pieces, 'a place which feels like it is being punished for some forgotten crime, where even the dogs look like they are contemplating suicide.'

He made contact with Irene, Fitzgerald's stressed-out radio operator, who filled him in on the nuts and bolts of the story. The two explorers had been out there for well over three months and should have been making radio contact every day or two. In fact there had been silence for eleven days.

'What does that mean?' he asked her.

'It means I don't sleep until we get that emergency signal. Those men are dying out there now, and winter's about to strike.'

'Winter?'

'It's the southern hemisphere,' she snapped impatiently, 'upside-down land. The Antarctic winter happens in our summer.'

'Oh yes. Of course. Gets a bit chilly down there, does it?'

Irene gave him a frosty look. 'Once winter sets in,' she explained, 'there's no daylight at all. The temperature gets too low for a plane to land.'

That was the beginning of the wait, the beginning of Richard Leighton's forced exile at the southernmost tip of South America. The days had dragged so slowly he actually began to believe time had a different pace to it down here in nowhere land. He bought himself thermal clothes. He visited the nearby penguin colony. He took a boat trip around the Beagle Channel. He learned a few words of Spanish from the almost-attractive girl at the reception of his hotel.

He masturbated. And he played patience on his laptop.

Now Irene's call had broken the spell, and the waiting was over. Richard bustled into the tiny expedition control room at the airport, where Fitzgerald's radio coordinator and a local pilot were consulting a large map.

'What's the news?' Richard asked.

'They're here,' Irene told him, tapping a position on the map, 'at the far end of the Blackmore Glacier. I'm just discussing the rescue with Captain Villanova here.'

Richard shook the captain's hand.

'Think you can get them out?'

'There are many crevasses in that area,' Villanova told him, 'but we can try.'

'How about the weather?'

'There's a big storm front coming in from the west, but that's normal for Antarctica. We'll try and get in and out before it hits.'

Richard made a quick call home. He knew his fiancée would be excited to hear the news, but all he got was the answerphone.

'Sophie, it's me. We got an emergency signal from Fitzgerald and his mate; we're leaving for Antarctica right now to pick them up. I'll call when I can, OK? Love you.'

The co-pilot, Ariza, escorted him out to the aircraft.

Finally, some action, Richard thought as he buckled himself into his seat. Desperate explorers, tales of derring-do, skeletons on the ice: maybe this story was going to get his byline on the front page after all.

Hope they've got some food on this old crate, he mused, his stomach hollow after the missed lunch.

The co-pilot came to check he had mastered the lapbelt.

'Got any food for the flight?' Richard asked him. 'I'm starving.'

Ariza's English was not as good as Villanova's.

'Starving? What is starving?'

'Don't worry,' the reporter told him, patting his substantial stomach. 'Just my little joke.'

5

The two men lay side by side in their sleeping bags, suspended in that miserable hinterland between sleep and despair.

For the moment, the wind was light, playing lazily about the fly sheet of the tent, rustling the fabric in that soothing way, as if apologising for the days—the weeks—in which it had been so hard.

But from the hunger there was no respite. Carl was astonished at how painful starving to death was proving to be. He had considered the early days hard—those days when he had fantasised endlessly about roast meats, sweet chocolate, plates of fried rice, peaches and strawberries, and butter and curry. But those days had been nothing, a pathetic prelude to what he was experiencing now.

Now, after seventeen days without a single scrap of food, he was hunger, he had become it. Every cell of his body was putting out chemicals which were causing him pain. His kidneys throbbed and ached in his sides, and urination had become a dreaded event. His head pulsed permanently with a brilliant sharp pain, his teeth had loosened and fractured in his jaw, tiny unknown infections deep in their roots flaring into abscesses which wept with pus.

They had run out of antibiotics long ago.

Carl had done his research; he knew in perfect detail what was happening to him, how his systems were breaking down. He knew his muscles had been robbed of their sugars and fats, that his liver was being forced to give up its own reserves.

They still had gas to melt ice, but no one can keep going on water alone. There would be a point at which he would not recover. Carl was terrified he was already there.

'We have to put out the flares,' he said, switching his thoughts to the rescue. The pilots would need a landing strip to be identified and marked out.

Fitzgerald grunted. 'You do it. I'll melt down some ice.'

Carl slowly unzipped himself from his sleeping bag and dressed in his cold-weather gear, every painful movement costing him a few more precious calories of energy, bringing him a few tiny chemical steps closer to the point where his body would cease to function at all.

He found the flares and went out on to the glacier, scanning the terrain for an area with potential to mark out a strip. His progress was erratic, wandering backwards and forwards, looking for a good enough site, trying to ignore the constant stars in his vision, the sensation that at any moment he might faint. Each time he found a possible stretch of ice, he would slowly pace its length, counting his steps laboriously before coming to the next obstacle and realising that it was not enough.

The Twin Otter needed a minimum of four hundred metres. Nothing less would do. Carl reckoned that was about six hundred and fifty of his shuffling steps.

So far he had failed to find any strip of ice longer than half that. Not for the first time on the journey, Carl had the feeling that the terrain was conspiring against them; surely there was *somewhere* to land a plane in this godforsaken wilderness?

He sat, despairing, on a hummock of ice, his head cradled in his hands as the wind began to rise. Even in his exhausted state, Carl had registered the further deterioration in the weather. Last time he had looked, the determined-looking clouds on the horizon seemed to have moved a little closer.

Fear brought him back to his feet. If he couldn't give the pilots a place to land, they would have to return empty-handed to South America. Would they come back and try again? Carl wasn't at all sure.

'Come and help me!' he shouted back towards the tent. But there was no sign that Fitzgerald had heard him. Carl was sure that the rising wind had swallowed up his words.

6

Captain Manuel Villanova walked out across the tarmac at Ushuaia airport, his leather flight jacket hunched up against the bitter wind which was ripping off the waters of the Beagle Channel.

Co-pilot Juvenal Ariza had already completed the pre-flight checks, and the starboard turbo-prop was coughing into life as Villanova climbed up the steps into the ageing Twin Otter aircraft.

The captain sealed the door, nodded briefly to the journalist, who was sitting in the back, and made his way into the cramped cockpit. He strapped himself in, not bothering to question Ariza on the pre-flights, the two men had flown so many hours together, they trusted each other implicitly.

Both men were ex-Argentinian air force, veterans of the ill-fated Guerra de las Malvinas. Between them they had more than forty thousand logged hours, much of it on supply runs to the numerous Argentine bases which were scattered around the Antarctic Peninsula.

Their civilian employer, Antarctic Air Service, was one of the most unusual airlines in the world; its sole trading purpose was to place, supply and retrieve people, fuel and equipment on the Antarctic continent. It was a lucrative niche; in an average year there were dozens of scientific and other expeditions heading south, and they paid big money to do so. The minimum fare per passenger was thirty thousand US dollars. Each way.

Villanova took the controls for the take-off, easing the Twin Otter smoothly into the air and putting in a right-hand turn to avoid an incoming Aerolinas Argentinas 737. It was not a view to tire of easily: to the north he could see the permanent ice cap covering Tierra del Fuego, with the towering summit of Mount Sarmiento glinting on the horizon. To the south was the tail end of South America and the myriad islands marking the ends of the earth.

Beneath them the red-and-green-painted houses of the outpost town were quickly slipping away. They circled over the port and headed for the wooded slope above the bay.

Villanova knew he wasn't supposed to do it, but hell, he thought, if you make a promise to your six-year-old son, you'd better keep it.

He picked out the woodbuilt house on the hill and flew directly towards it. He could see his wife Lola standing in the yard in a red dress, little black-haired Luis jumping and waving excitedly by her side.

Villanova passed over the roof at about a hundred feet, dipped his wings and rolled back out over the Beagle Channel.

'That's a nice kid you got there,' Ariza told him.

Villanova put the aircraft into a climb, keeping to the left of the channel to avoid straying into Chilean airspace. The disputed border between the two countries ran loosely down the middle of the naturally straight passage and had been the scene of numerous skirmishes and minor wars. Crossing the line would be an embarrassment, to say the least.

The Beagle was a remarkable sight from the air, a feature so straight and deeply cut it could have been a Norwegian fjord. Named after the ship which had so famously carried

Charles Darwin to his discoveries, the Beagle had been the gateway to the Southern Ocean for as long as men had sailed, or flown, to the south.

The water of the channel was as dark as night, the land to either side densely forested, the higher slopes home to hardy shrubs which had learned to resist one of the windiest environments on the planet. A couple of ranches had been carved out of the flatter ground, tough estancias producing scrawny cattle and a few malnourished chickens.

Tierra del Fuego was a very hard place to scrape a living. Better experienced from the air, Villanova was sure.

After a while the islands of Lennox and Wollaston came into view, brown heathery outcrops of salt-lashed rocks, home to pelagic birds and not much more. Then, to the right, the distinctive camel hump of Cape Horn, absolute south to centuries of mariners, graveyard of ships and dreams.

Villanova raised the Cape Horn station on his radio, telling them his callsign and asking them for the latest weather.

Their report confirmed the earlier satellite map: a huge depression was sweeping up from the west, one of the seemingly endless storms which race clockwise around the bottom of the planet. They would be in for a battering as they fought their way back.

Cape Horn passed on the starboard side, the cockpit compass set to one hundred and eighty degrees. The water beneath them now was the Drake Passage, the turbulent one-thousand-mile ocean corridor separating the landmasses of South America and Antarctica.

Far away, deep in the continent across that most intimidating of seas, the two explorers would be anxiously waiting for them. Villanova figured they would bring them back successfully, as they had done on every other emergency call over the years. Villanova and Ariza were a 'lucky' team, according to their fellow pilots; somehow they always seemed to bring off the rescues, no matter how dangerous the location.

Villanova was proud of that one-hundred-per-cent record.

After a couple of hours in the air, Ariza left Villanova at the controls. One of the advantages of a lightly loaded run was that they could take turns to steal a little sleep on the stretcher in the passenger area.

In the cockpit, Villanova was ever observant. Unlike some of the other pilots, he was not in the habit of reading newspapers or completing crosswords to pass the time. Instead, he let his body tune to the pitch of the engines, alert for any change which would indicate a problem.

Fifteen thousand feet beneath him, he could see whitecaps rolling across the Southern Ocean.

Nine hours flying time to the target. Villanova lit up a Chesterfield and switched the heater onto full.

7

Out on the glacier, Carl was cursing his bad luck. An hour had passed, and he still hadn't found a suitable landing strip. The area was more fractured with crevasses than he had thought, and where there were no fissures the ice was ridged and pocked with sastrugi—the rock-hard ridges like miniature dunes of ice.

He scrunched up his eyes, viewing the glacier with increasing frustration, trying to remember the pilots' briefing. 'It doesn't have to be flat,' he recalled them telling him back in Ushuaia, 'but it has to be smooth. We can land on a slope, but we can't land with too many sastrugi.'

He forced his body to move, this time skirting round the end of a huge crevasse and exploring the area to the west of the tent. He was taking risks on this terrain, walking on his own; a snow bridge across a crevasse could collapse as he walked across it.

Finally, one possibility emerged: a long, slightly curving

swathe of ice between two parallel crevasses. It was wide enough, he was sure, but was it long enough?

Carl looked at the stretch of ice, trying to gauge its length. Was that four hundred metres? Or was it less? It was certainly going to be a tight spot to land an aircraft, but that was what these pilots were good at, wasn't it?

He rested for a while then began to pace it out, concentrating hard so as not to lose count as he ticked off the steps in his head. He had reached six hundred and ten steps by the time he came to the end of the available ice. It was an uncompromising fall into one of the biggest crevasses he had ever seen.

Carl kept well away from the edge, he had already tripped and fallen a couple of times during this search, and he didn't trust himself to get too close to that gaping mouth.

Making his way back to the front end of the strip, Carl found another problem: there were two large sastrugi directly in the line the pilot would have to take as he landed, each more than a metre high. Carl kicked at one with his boot, but the impact didn't leave a mark. There was nothing he could do to remove them.

Could the pilots hop over these mounds of ice and still bring the plane to a halt before that monster crevasse? Carl felt hopeless; he simply didn't know.

Perhaps there was a better place. Groaning with the pain the effort brought to his atrophied muscles, Carl managed to climb up onto one of the sastrugi to give himself a better vantage point over the surrounding terrain.

The answer was what he expected: no matter where he looked, he could see no run of ice which offered more than this one.

Carl knew the strip he had found was far from perfect, but what else could he do? They certainly couldn't move out of the crevasse field—neither he nor Fitzgerald had the strength for the two or three days of effort that that would involve.

He didn't feel good about it, but Carl made the decision, putting in the first of the flares, twisting the sharpened base into the ice. Then he stumbled for one hundred and fifty paces and placed the second. Thirty minutes later he had completed the task, the four flares in as straight a line as he could achieve.

He put in a ski pole to mark the spot and tied a scarf to it so it could be seen from a distance. When they heard the aircraft approach, one of them would have to find the strip and light the flares.

It would have to be Fitzgerald. Carl knew he would himself barely be able to exit the tent again once he lay down. He had given everything to complete this task.

He took one last look at the landing place, a mixture of hope and dread filling his heart. Then he began to pick his way back through the maze.

By the time he got back to the tent he was crawling on his hands and knees.

8

To relieve the boredom of the flight, Richard flipped open his laptop and watched the flickering rows of data as it booted into life.

Next to him the co-pilot was still sleeping.

Richard selected Word and brought up his Fitzgerald file. What was he going to call this piece? He thought for a while, then typed:

> Mercy flight plucks explorers to safety.

Too tame. He erased it and replaced it with:

> Rescue at the ends of the earth.

Then he erased that too and made it:

> Escape from a frozen hell.

That would do nicely, he thought: perfect for the front page. He consulted his notes, constructing the first paragraph with care:

> One hundred and eighteen days after they set out on their historic attempt to make an unsupported crossing of the Antarctic continent at its widest point, explorers Julian Fitzgerald and Carl Norland have finally been plucked from the ice in a dramatic rescue bid.

On consideration he replaced 'plucked' with 'airlifted'.

> I was the only reporter allowed to board the mercy flight . . . just a tiny twin-prop plane with two pilots at the controls. We knew the explorers would be in a weak condition, but nothing had prepared us for the two skeletal figures which greeted us as we landed by their camp. Their faces told the story of this journey through hell . . . in their eyes the pain of frostbite, of starvation, the uncertainty of rescue in a land where storms and blizzards are almost daily occurrences. In their handshakes the feeble grip of men who have tested themselves to the limit and beyond.

Richard was pleased with the mood of the piece; it was starting to come together quite well.

He typed for an hour, padding out the article with whatever his imagination could provide—he knew that when it came to filing the story he would have to get it to London fast, and the more he had written in advance, the better. He would slot in some suitable quotes from the two explorers once they had picked them up.

After some time, the co-pilot came out of his sleep and went forward to take the controls. Villanova joined Richard in the passenger cabin.

'Are you hungry?' he asked the reporter.

Villanova fetched some things from the back of the plane.

'Cheese sandwich and cake,' he told Richard. 'Not exactly British Airways business class, but we do our best.'

Richard smiled and ate the contents of the cardboard box. Later Villanova produced a flask and poured them both a cup of strong black coffee.

'You see that?' The pilot pointed out of the window.

Richard looked hard but could see nothing but the grey ocean.

'We are crossing the Antarctic convergence,' Villanova told him. 'Can you see how the sea ahead is a different colour?'

Then Richard *could* see it, the ocean was changing colour as he watched. Beneath them all was grey, a silty-looking sea like most he had seen. It could have been the English Channel. But in front was a different colour altogether—darker, more dense somehow, the type of black-blue water that speaks of serious depth. It looked like ink, he decided, and it looked deathly cold.

'What does it mean?'

'This is the point where the Southern Ocean meets the Atlantic. They don't mix; the Southern Ocean is much colder.'

'How long would we survive if we had to ditch?' Richard asked.

Villanova considered the question. 'A few minutes at most.'

'Not very good odds then?'

'Let's put it this way. I know of at least fifteen airplanes which have ditched in the Southern Ocean. I have never heard of a survivor.'

From then on, Richard's heart tripped a beat every time the engine pitch varied.

Villanova went back to the cockpit, and Richard slept for a while. When he awoke, the scene had changed once more. Now the sea was filled with chunks of ice, each one perhaps the size of a small car, he guessed. Every now and then a bigger iceberg would loom into view, tabular bergs with squared-off edges. Some seemed to be hundreds of metres high, he could see the spray where their walls were pounded constantly by the waves.

They passed an island, no more than a shattered spine of rock completely encrusted with ice. Richard could see where avalanches had peeled great fields of the stuff away from the walls, he could see fathomless depths to the crevasses. He imagined—and he was right—that no human being had ever stood on the high point of that island, that no ship could ever risk tying up beneath those teetering cliffs.

The sea solidified; he could almost swear he was watching it turn to ice before his eyes. There were cracks and faults which looked like they had been forced open by passing ships. He looked for them in vain. Then the sea ice ended abruptly, great mountains began and they were flying over the Antarctic continent itself.

Richard had seen glaciers before, once or twice in the Alps, but nothing like the ones they were now flying over. These were not like rivers, they were hundreds of miles across, so wide it seemed they had no end.

He experienced a stab of loneliness—a sense of his own insignificance perhaps in the context of this place. He felt the longing for a beer, a Heineken would do, but he was pretty sure there would be none on board.

Still the little aircraft plodded on.

'We just switched to the second fuel tank,' Villanova told him some time later. 'We should reach our destination in about four hours.'

Richard was beginning to appreciate that he was a very long way from home.

9

The drone of the approaching aircraft seemed to Carl to be the most beautiful sound he had ever heard. Contained within that reassuring buzz was the promise of salvation . . . of a continued life . . . of an end to this self-imposed purgatory he had so willingly entered.

There had been false alarms in the hours before, whistles of wind which had tricked them cruelly. It is astonishing how the human ear can hear what it wants to hear even if the truth is merely a guy rope vibrating in a light breeze.

But this time the engine noise was too persistent. This time it was real. Carl crawled out of the tent in time to see the aircraft enter its first great arc. Where were they going? Couldn't they see the tent?

Fitzgerald got the flares running.

Carl watched, his heart soaring, as the pilot flew directly over them. They'd been seen!

He was shocked. The Twin Otter seemed so small and

vulnerable, like a child's toy against the sheer walls of ice and black rock which hemmed in this glacial mass.

The pilot came in for a pass at the strip. Carl felt his elation give way to a piercing anxiety. Would the place he had chosen be big enough to put it down safely? Please let him land. Please God let him land, Carl prayed.

The engine note cut stronger as the pilot climbed over the tent and circled around once more. This time his approach was slower, and for a second or two Carl held his breath as the skis kissed lightly against the polished surface of the glacier.

A test, Carl realised. Testing the ground. The pilot was right to be cautious. Carl hoped he had liked what he had discovered.

Again the Twin Otter entered the circuit, and it seemed to Carl that, for a while, the tiny aircraft was flying in a straight line away from them. He noticed that the wind was picking up, that the line of clouds on the horizon seemed to be getting closer with every passing minute.

'Don't go,' he whispered. 'If you go now, we're lost.'

The adrenaline pumping through him brought Carl, shakily, to his feet. He staggered forward towards the strip, wanting to feel the warmth of human flesh pressed into his hands, wanting the embrace of those men who meant rescue and life and a return to his wife and child.

They would leave the tent and all their gear. Carl never wanted to see any of it again.

Slowly, so slowly it seemed it should fall out of the sky, the pilot brought his craft round and straightened up on the strip. He was low this time, really low. Carl was sure this time it was going to happen.

10

Villanova put the Twin Otter into a wide, sweeping turn as they reached the target area. He knew from experience it could take time for the flares to be lit. He didn't even bother looking for the tent, in that huge tortured mass of ice, the chances of seeing such a minuscule speck were as good as nil.

He throttled back the engines, keeping a keen eye on the controls, adjusting the trim as a turbulent spiral of air caught the port wing.

Ariza was the first to spot the orange flares.

'Over there.' He pointed to the north. Villanova followed the line of his hand, spotting two feeble trickles of smoke in amongst the crevasses.

As they straightened out and headed over, a third, then a fourth, flare was lit. They buzzed over the landing area at three hundred feet, clearly seeing a dark figure waving at them from the ice.

'There's the tent,' Ariza said, spotting the circular splash of dacron. Another figure could be seen lying near it.

Villanova went into a tighter turn, this time coming down the line as if on a final approach. He brought the Twin Otter down to fifty feet, slowing it as far as he dared to give them the best possible view of the proposed landing strip. It was turbulent this close to the ice; the pilots were fighting with the controls to keep the craft level.

'These two are jokers,' Ariza said. 'Look at the state of this place.'

Villanova felt his chest constrict as he saw how exposed the strip was. It was straight enough, and probably just about long enough, but, by God, it was surrounded on all sides by monstrous crevasses.

'This is the worst one we've ever had,' Ariza said. 'Why didn't they find somewhere else?'

'I don't think they had much choice,' Villanova replied. 'Can you see anything better?'

It was true; for miles—perhaps tens of miles—in every direction, the glacier was equally broken up.

'Let's take another look.'

Villanova went round again, flying down the line once more, lower still. This time he let his skis touch down for a few metres, the technique all polar pilots use to judge surface texture.

The impact was hard.

'No powder,' he said, as they powered back into the climb.

Ariza knew what that meant: there was no soft surface snow to help them to brake.

'I don't like it,' Ariza said. 'I say we abort.'

'What about that?' Villanova gestured to the west and the line of evil-looking clouds which heralded the incoming depression. 'That storm front is coming in fast. I think we get them out now or not at all.'

Ariza eased forward in his seat, suddenly aware that his shirt was sticking to his back with sweat. Every time he glanced down at that strip, it looked smaller and smaller.

'Why don't we drop them a note?' he said, trying to keep his voice calm. 'Tell them to find a better place, and we'll come back in a few days.'

Villanova overruled him.

'Winter's too close,' he said. 'We're going in. Prepare for finals.'

11

Carl could see from the approach that the pilots were cutting it incredibly fine. Judging from the angle, they were planning to glide in with the landing skids just inches above the sastrugi. They were obviously hoping to maximise the strip available to them, Carl realised, and, with that monster crevasse at the far end, it wasn't hard to understand why.

He heard the engine note change as the turbo-props throttled back, the flaps on each wing lowering as the pilots held their course for the strip. They were fighting to keep the aircraft stable. Carl could see how each wingtip was seesawing as eddies and gusts caught the plane.

Just as it seemed they would skim above the ice mounds with a hair's-breadth to spare, the Twin Otter appeared to be gripped by a new force as a sudden rip of wind raced across the strip. As it did so, the port wing seemed to dip and the aircraft lost height. Carl saw the tip of one of the skids smash into the ice mound.

There was only a few centimetres in it, but this time luck

was not on the pilots' side. The leading edge of the port-side skid crumpled as it impacted into the iron-hard ridge of ice, the starboard wing swinging immediately round as the aircraft slewed out of true.

Carl heard the engines rev louder as the pilots applied more power, the Twin Otter shaking with the violence of the blow as they tried to correct.

Now they were fighting to gain height, he realised, trying desperately to get the aircraft back up into the air. For a moment it looked like they'd succeeded, as the nose began to rise, but a further vicious cross-wind caught them, this time sending the port-side wingtip crashing down.

The Twin Otter belly-flopped onto the glacier with a sickening crunch, the engines screaming as the pilots applied reverse thrust. But they were already running out of control, virtually at ninety degrees to the correct approach angle. The 4,800-kilo aircraft was still travelling at more than one hundred miles an hour.

The pilots tried once more to correct—Carl could see the nose veer as they attempted to steer out of the spin. But the remaining right skid caught on another low ridge and that was when both pilots lost it completely. Now the plane was slewing crazily, skating across the polished ice; a sideways glissade which took it—fast—towards a series of other hard ridges of ice. One hit the starboard propeller, ripping into it with a splintering shower of metal shrapnel and sparks.

The aircraft spun in a fast pirouette, the port-side wing sending a shower of ice crystals into the air as it ploughed a furrow into the glacier. Eighty miles an hour—the entire engine was ripped off and flung to one side with a rending shriek of metal.

Still the aircraft did not stop. It had too much momentum for that.

Carl saw the face of a man—one of the pilots—pressed against the glass in a silent scream.

Then the Twin Otter fell headlong into the crevasse.

There was a muffled impact from the depths.

Carl walked to the lip, numb with shock, waiting for the

fireball, for the explosion which would surely follow. Fitzgerald, ashen-faced, was soon beside him.

They could hear an electronic buzzing from the crevasse, like a swarm of bees heard far away. A light cloud of acrid blue smoke was lingering in the fissure.

Then the buzzing stopped. The two men stood there, looking down into a void in which they could see nothing but black depth.

They barely noticed the rising wind which had come with the approaching depression, the clouds which had followed the pilots rapidly across the wastes.

But it was with them soon enough, and so was the storm it contained.

PART 2

Capricorn Base

12

Capricorn Base. 00.43.06 degrees west, 87 degrees south. A collection of huts anchored to the ice on a desolate high plateau of Antarctica. To an outsider this place could look like hell, a site of frozen exile, a punishment posting in which one dark winter would be enough to turn even the most stable mind insane.

A visitor—if such a thing were possible—would wonder what purpose such a base could serve, for in every direction, for literally thousands of square miles, there was not a living plant or creature to be seen. Nor was there any prominence or drama to the terrain . . . just rolling undulations of glacial ice stretching off to the horizon and beyond.

What could human beings hope to achieve in such a sterile place? And what type of person would willingly volunteer to spend one year of their lives in that quest?

On first inspection, Capricorn seemed small, feeble even. Home to just five personnel, it promised little enough protection against the savage forces which played around it. In total it was just five buildings, three of them modular units, which were interconnected, and two others—shed-like structures—which sat some fifty metres to one side. From one of the sheds a rhythmic thud-thud-thud spoke of a large engine at work.

A radio mast stood proud above the main block, the tubular steel of its structure covered with a thick coating of rime.

Closer inspection would reveal that Capricorn was well—even beautifully—designed, the modules constructed of carbon fibre and wood, the shells triple-insulated against the all-embracing cold. Aerodynamic curves on each corner offered smooth passage to passing storms, a subtle ramp at the base of each wall denied loose snow the opportunity to drift. Each roof was lightly domed, each doorway scalloped to prevent jamming, each ventilation shaft ingeniously designed so that the precious flow of fresh air was never blocked by ice.

Someone had put a great deal of thought—of love, even—into the creation of this place.

Above the door was a plaque of polished wood: 'No Free Newspapers'. Someone here had a sense of humour. Push open the door, savour the aroma of freshly percolated coffee, of frying bacon and newly baked rolls, the calming, homely smells of a new working day.

A day in which everything was about to change.

13

Lauren Burgess was Capricorn base commander, at twenty-eight the youngest occupant of such a post in the history of the continent. This was not her first Antarctic posting; in fact, she had spent a total of seven years at other bases, working in her research speciality of glacial biology.

But Capricorn was different—Capricorn was *hers*. This newly built drilling station was not merely Lauren's brainchild, it was the beginning, middle and end of her universe. One of just two truly independent bases on the Antarctic continent—the Greenpeace base was the other—Capricorn was not an outpost of some far-away land, it owed no affiliation to any government or state. This was the manifestation of a lifelong dream and home to a scientific programme which—if it worked—would, in about five months' time, pull off an astonishing coup.

That morning—as every morning of the seven weeks in which the base had been operational—Lauren was in the place she loved best, the laboratory, analysing samples of the ice cores which drilling engineer Sean had delivered from the overnight bore session. The lab was small but well designed: a work bench fitted with electron and conventional microscopes, a suitcase-sized spectrophotometer mounted in the roof for measuring ozone content and an ion chromatograph for quantifying anion concentrations in the ice samples.

Lauren put on her sterile gloves and took out core number 141 from where it was stacked in the lab freezer. Each of the perfectly cylindrical sections was about the size of a drink's can, and Lauren's first task was to carefully cut a transect ready for analysis on a pre-chilled surgical slide. This was secondary work to the main scientific objectives of Capricorn, but it was no less fascinating to Lauren, even though she had performed these tasks thousands of times before in other bases.

Lauren slipped the ice sample beneath the microscope and adjusted the focus until the crystals were sharp. Every passing day brought cores from deeper in the ice sheet, and it was thrilling to Lauren to think that she was looking at crystals which had first fallen as snow many millions of years before. She recorded the crystallite structure and size, noting that these deeper cores were now producing bigger crystals under the increased pressure of the ice above.

Next she ran a microparticle analysis, searching for anions such as sulphates and nitrates—the by-products of the volcano which was situated some seven hundred metres beneath the base. Lauren was absorbed in the work, the knowledge that a storm was raging outside not worrying her one bit, and by midday the tasks were done, the log books completed and the newly discovered data inputted into the computer.

Lauren picked up her empty coffee mug and walked the carpeted corridor towards the mess room. To her right was the small gymnasium; she could hear the rhythmic mechanical swish as a weight machine was pressed into action.

She put her head round the door, finding, as she had expected, the Capricorn medic Mel halfway through her morning fitness session. Mel was from Auckland—and, like many of her fellow New Zealanders, had a deep affinity for the frozen south. She'd acted as base medic at three previous bases, including Scott base, the main New Zealand station in Antarctica. Mel had a perennially cheerful personality and rarely got depressed . . . a perfect qualification for surviving the rigours of an Antarctic winter.

'Morning, Mel.'

Mel didn't break her bench presses.

'Hi,' she puffed. 'Four hundred and ten . . . four hundred and fifteen . . .'

Lauren continued to the mess room, pausing long enough to take a quick glance at the noticeboard which hung on the wall outside.

'Murdo's joke of the day,' read the Post-it Note. 'How do you stop your girlfriend giving you blow jobs?'

Lauren lifted the flap which concealed the answer:

'Marry her.'

Lauren smiled in spite of herself. Next to the punchline a weather fax was pinned. Lauren removed it carefully and entered the mess room, where she joined radio operator Frank at the breakfast table. Someone had put a Van Morrison CD on the stereo system, the lyrical progressions of *Hymns to the Silence* adding to the mellow mood of the room.

'Have you noticed how Murdo's jokes of the day are getting more and more obscene as the weeks go by?' Lauren asked Frank.

Frank turned away from his copy of *New Scientist*. 'It keeps him amused,' he told her. 'If you fried eggs for a living, you'd probably be the same.'

'You think that's obscene?' Murdo poked his head out of the galley, his rich Scottish vowels accentuated in mock indignation. 'You should work in a rig kitchen. What are you having, boss?'

'My conscience says muesli . . .' Lauren hesitated.

'But your belly says Murdo's bacon and egg special?'

'Add a sausage to that and I'll love you for ever.'

'Actresses and bishops . . .' Frank murmured.

'At this rate we're going to ship half a fucking ton of rabbit food back home,' Murdo observed. 'Unless we can find some penguins to feed it to.'

Lauren smiled as she turned to the weather fax; she loved the morning banter of the mess room—the cosy epi-centre of their world. It wasn't a particularly big room, but it was a welcoming one, with bright rugs on the floor and two huge sofas on which the team could relax. In one cor-ner was a small library, packed with paperbacks, in another was a television and video. Evening films were one of their few entertainments.

This was a happy team, she reflected with some satisfac-tion, a small but cohesive unit of five committed individuals who so far had been getting along just fine. But winter was almost upon them, the days already diminished to the point where all they had to distinguish day from night was a few gloomy hours of half-light. Winter, Lauren knew, was when the team dynamics would be put to the real test; for seven months they would be locked into the darkest and most in-timidatingly cold place on earth.

'That front is quite something, don't you think?' Frank observed, nodding to the weather fax.

'Ninety-six millibars,' Lauren noted as she looked out of the window into the storm. 'Doesn't get much worse. Not the type of conditions to be out on a field trip.'

Lauren finished her breakfast.

'Where's the grease monkey?' she asked.

'Where do you think?'

'That boy works too hard. I'll take him out some coffee.'

Frank was whistling the theme from *Love Story* as Lauren filled up Sean's thermal mug. Lauren pretended not to notice—the team teased her mercilessly about the imagined chemistry between her and the roustabout who was in charge of the Capricorn drilling rig.

Her featherdown windsuit was hanging on the hook by the door. Lauren zipped the quilted wind protector over the top, donned a woollen hat and pulled on her 'bunnyboots'—the plastic boots which had been invented by oil line work-ers in Alaska and were still the warmest footwear in the world. Lastly, the gloves; Lauren was ready to commit herself to the frigid exterior, into a wind which was going to try its hardest to whip her off her feet.

It took her breath away every time, the crisp bite of super-chilled air sending a shock into the centre of her head as she breathed in deeply; like a whiff of smelling salts, one inhalation of Antarctic air was enough to wake the dead.

Others might have found it intimidating, detected something malevolent, life-threatening even, in the intensity of the invading cold, in the driven snow which felt hard against her face. For Lauren the air was like nectar, she breathed it in deeply, savouring it as if it was the breath of a lover.

14

Lauren's fascination with Antarctica—like Carl's—had begun when she was a child, fired by the slides and stories of her father.

Her father was a geologist, 'a deep-rock man' as he called himself. He'd spent most of his life in the oil industry, scooting from the Gulf of Mexico to Nigeria, from the South China Sea to Texas. In 1956, when he was in his mid-twenties, he had spent a year in Antarctica, part of the massive scientific research project called the International Geophysical Year.

He had five yellow boxes of Kodachrome slides from that expedition, still retaining their fresh colours thirty years on.

Lauren loved the paraphernalia which went with a viewing; the projecting equipment was exotic and thrilling to a child. There was the screen; the luminous sheet which rolled miraculously from a cigar-shaped metal tube which then—magically—sprouted legs. Then there was the projector itself, with its whirring fan, its brilliant bulb filling the living room with heady aromas as it cooked old dust and baked long-suffering resistors into a frenzy of hot ceramic smells.

The curtains would be drawn, the lights extinguished. Lauren and her brothers would sit, blinking with excitement, as the images snapped through the projector one by one.

There were whales, their glistening black backs breaking through water which was green like bottle glass. There were icebergs, huge fangs of powder-blue ice which dwarfed the tiny red ship sitting alongside. Then there was their father, astoundingly young and bearded, perched uneasily on a pair of skis, a pipe clamped between his teeth as he laughed into the camera.

Lauren hung onto his words; 'You can see for hundreds of miles in Antarctica,' he had said. Hundreds of miles? Lauren's young mind tried to imagine how far that would be— like seeing to Scotland, maybe?

Lauren had seen pictures of mythical lands in books of fairy tales, but Antarctica seemed so much more beautiful— a place filled with more pristine wonders than any human imagination could ever conjure. When the equipment was put away, Lauren would curl up in her bed, her mind racing with images: orange-breasted penguins guarding their fluff-ball chicks—'You have to watch those beaks,' her father had said, 'give you a nasty snap'—a leopard seal, sleek and mean, barking Rottweiler teeth at a shaky lens which had moved in too close.

And one more: her father standing with a raised flag and two fellow scientists next to a tent filled with strange machines. He held a roll of paper in his hand, a jubilant expression on his overtanned face. 'That was the day,' he told them proudly, always lingering over the shot for longer than he needed, 'the day we found the underground lake.'

His words confused Lauren. What lake? How could it be under the ice? Wouldn't it be frozen? Lauren struggled and failed to imagine how such a bizarre thing could happen.

Still, her father had discovered it, and that made her proud.

Lauren ached to see Antarctica for herself, but she knew

she would have to be patient. In the meantime, she did the next-best thing—seeking with that perfect logic of childhood the biggest expanse of ice she could find. That place was the ice rink at the local mall, Ambassador Ice and Bowl to be precise, located, unpromisingly, in a subterranean complex beneath a car park, approached through concrete tunnels littered with torn sweet wrappers and crushed drink cans.

Inside was another world, a world so thrillingly cool, so refrigerated, it literally took Lauren's breath away every time she queued to hire her skates. Then she would take to the ice, daring a touch with her hand from time to time, loving the way her skates carved elegant grooves into the surface. When she fell, she would let her cheek rest for an instant, enjoying the numb sensation it gave her flesh.

By the time she was eleven she was at the ice rink every weekend. To onlookers she was just another kid, her dark hair a mass of ringlets, pushing herself around the rink, never trying any fancy moves or routines.

For Lauren it wasn't about the skating, it was about the ice. The rink was a place to let her imagination fly. In her mind the ice became the surface of some great glacier—she saw herself skating for hundreds of miles across the frozen wonderland of Antarctica.

Years later, for her fourteenth birthday, her father fixed her up with a treat—a journey to Switzerland, where, in the Alps, she saw her first real glacier. It was the Eigergletscher, sinuous, fissured, filled with unexpected power.

'It's beautiful,' Lauren said with wonder as they stood looking down on the glacier. 'Look at the colour of the ice.' A new light filled her eyes: glaciers would be the new love affair; they were dynamic, exciting, somehow alive.

She began to devour Antarctic literature, consuming Cherry-Garrard's *Worst Journey in the World* in one weekend session. She soaked up the privations of Scott, shivered at Shackleton's narrow escape from the pack, stacking the precious tomes side by side until she had so many South Polar editions you could almost feel the blast of chill air seeping from the bookcase.

Some of the things she had learned about Antarctica were truly amazing: that a boiling cup of water thrown into the air will instantly freeze into a shimmering cloud of ice crystals, that winter temperatures of seventy degrees below freezing are regularly recorded.

Antarctica, Lauren now knew, was the coldest and highest continent on the planet—an environment so obstinately hostile to human life that it might have been created in the mind of some sadistic science fiction author. In total it was covered by fourteen *million* square kilometres of solid ice, constituting almost ten per cent of the total land surface of the earth.

Lauren was hooked, and now she interrogated her father on every minuscule detail of his Antarctic expedition— particularly about the lake which she had first learned about all those years before. Now her curiosity had a scientific edge: was there a way to measure the size of the lake? What type of life could be down there?

'We'll go there together one day,' he told her, 'but first get your A levels out of the way.'

But as Lauren revised for her exams a tragedy befell the family. Her father, who had been troubled by stomach pains for some months, finally went to have himself checked out; he was wheeled into a CT scanner on a bleak Monday morning and learned, twenty-four hours later, that he had cancer of the pancreas—the fastest and most deadly of all the intestinal cancers. It was inoperable, and five weeks later he was dead.

His last words to Lauren were: 'Sorry we won't be going south together.'

'I'll go for you,' Lauren told him, 'and I'll find out more about your lake.'

Her mother begged her to postpone her exams, certain that grief would destroy Lauren's chances of doing well. In fact the opposite happened; she found herself fired by a fierce determination to do her father proud. She got four straight A's and won a place at Cambridge to study Glacial Biology. Why Cambridge? Simple: the Scott Polar Research Institute was there.

Lauren knew that the Scott Polar would, one day, be her ticket to the south, and she was right. After completing her degree, she joined the Scott Polar and was posted to Rothera, then Halley base, then seconded to the US Department of Science facility at the South Pole. She completed her postgraduate studies and moved on to her doctorate, but the lure of her father's lake stayed with her throughout.

One day, Lauren knew, she would raise the money to build her own base, right above the subterranean lake he had discovered.

15

Lauren leaned into the wind, trying not to spill a drop of the coffee as she made her way to the drilling shed. Inside, drill extension number 58 was being attached to the head of the gantry. Sean was swarming all over it, tending to the massive Perkins diesel and the rig which stood in a tripod above it.

Sean Lowery had proved to be a brilliant addition to the team, coming to Lauren's attention after a series of sparkling recommendations by several of her colleagues. The young American engineer had spent three seasons up in Greenland working with a Scott Polar Institute team drawing cores from the ice cap, and his references were first rate.

'Sean's your man,' a fellow scientist had told Lauren. 'He's a brilliant mechanic, and he understands ice. He loves being out there in the wild too, any spare time we gave him he was out there climbing in the mountains all on his own.'

'Can he get along with a team?'

'No worries. He's really laid-back. A little weird

sometimes—like he talks to his machines—but he's basically sound.'

Lauren had flown Sean across from his Colorado home
for an interview at her London laboratory. He was younger
than she'd expected, still weatherbeaten from his most recent Greenland contract, his blond hair tied back in a pony-
tail that made him look more like a climber than an engineer.
Lauren liked him instantly: there was something in his no-
madic existence that echoed her own restless progression
from one base to another.

Sean said yes to a coffee and pulled out one of the lab
stools to sit on as they got the small talk of weather, flights
and the extortionate cost of London taxis out of the way. He
watched her carefully as she poured steaming water out of
the ancient kettle, deciding that his previous theory regarding the undesirability of female scientists was now blown
firmly out of the water. Dressed in a simple white T-shirt and
a pair of faded denim jeans, Lauren had the unmade-up
beauty—and certainly the figure—of a model. With her
dark, naturally curled hair and her earnest brown eyes, she
looked a bit like a young Sigourney Weaver, Sean decided,
back in the *Alien* days when a million male fantasies had
been fuelled by the single scene on the spaceship when she
strips down to her underwear.

If she knew what I'm thinking right now, Sean mused,
giving himself an internal rap on the knuckles, I'd never get
the job. Then he saw the half-smile in Lauren's eyes as she
looked at him appraisingly and thought: Or maybe I would.

'Tell me about the expedition,' Sean said with a cough as
he reddened slightly. 'Are you drilling a core like the Greenland team?'

Lauren handed him the coffee.

'Drilling a core . . . with a twist,' Lauren told him, wincing at her own pun. 'At the far end of the core is a lake. I
want to pull up a water sample, and it has to be completely
sterile.'

'A lake? Beneath Antarctica? I thought the whole place
was frozen.'

'So did scientists,' she told him, 'until the early 1970s. That's when aircraft from various scientific missions began running airborne sounding radar over certain stretches of Antarctica. That type of radar can penetrate ice and find a reflection off the underlying rock or whatever's beneath it.'

'I got you.'

'They found something pretty staggering in Eastern Antarctica—a fresh-water lake about the size of Lake Ontario, and twice as deep, was sitting four kilometres *beneath* the ice. They called it Lake Vostok after the Russian base situated above it. Some cynics doubted the data, but in 1996 the European Remote Sensing Satellite confirmed that it really was what we thought it was.'

Sean leaned forward, his attention caught. 'So why doesn't it freeze?'

'We believe it's because it's sitting in a kind of tectonic rift, a valley—the type of fault that Lake Baikal and the Red Sea occupy. The heat from the earth's interior is sufficient to melt down the lake, and there it is—perfectly locked away from the rest of the planet—a source of pristine water . . . and potentially a source of new life forms.'

'So you want to drill down and explore that lake?'

'Not Vostok. Vostok has too many problems, as I'll demonstrate.'

Lauren crossed to a flip chart. 'This is a cross-section of the ice cap, right?'

Sean nodded as he watched her draw two lines—the lower one representing the earth's surface, a higher, wavy one representing the thickness of the ice above it.

'Lake Vostok is believed to be just below sea level. And the surface of the ice is at three thousand nine hundred metres. To reach it, those scientists will have to drill a colossal four kilometres or more through the ice.'

'Four kilometres!' Sean was astounded. 'But that's just about impossible. Ice moves—it's always moving. The risk of the drill core bending and breaking is too high. Up in Greenland we were pushing it to achieve five hundred metres.'

Lauren flipped the chart to find a blank sheet.

'Exactly. And that's why I've got a different proposal. About a thousand miles away from Vostok, there's a volcano locked beneath the ice. We're talking about a location just about as remote as it is possible to get.'

Lauren drew the same lines as before, but this time she added a cone-shaped mountain jutting high into the mass of ice.

'How do you know that volcano is there?'

'It was discovered by British scientists back in 1956. They were working in Antarctica as part of the International Geophysical Year. But since there are plenty of under-ice volcanoes in Antarctica, no one paid this discovery much attention.'

'So how come you're so interested in it?'

'Firstly because my father was one of the scientists who discovered it, and second because this volcano is the one closest to the surface. The crater is just two thousand feet beneath the ice. That's about seven hundred metres compared with four kilometres to reach Vostok. Much less chance the drill bit will break, much better chance of getting a probe down into a lake.'

'Wait a second. I'm confused. Why should there be a lake connected with this volcano?'

'It has a true crater, we can deduce that from echo location. And it's an active volcano. There *has* to be heat. Where there is heat, ice becomes water. It really is as simple as that. I believe there is quite a large mass of fresh water down there, and where there is water . . . there is life.'

'But how did this life get down there?'

'Millions of years ago perhaps. Before Antarctica existed. We may be talking about life forms that have actually evolved completely independently. Or life forms from an era when the continents were in different places. That's the challenge for science—these lakes are like a time capsule—we can push our knowledge of how life forms far beyond where it is now if we can just get to them.'

'What are the practicalities?'

'I want to set up a tiny, independent base, perhaps no

more than a handful of scientists and a couple of supporting personnel. I'll hire a Hercules C130 to fly everything in. I want to rent or buy a drilling rig and put seven hundred metres of probe down into that lake and find creatures no one has ever dreamed of before. Can you imagine what a thrill that would be?'

Sean laughed at her raw enthusiasm. 'When you say creatures, are we talking things big enough to see?'

'Almost certainly not. The most likely life forms are diatoms—simple single-celled organisms. But just because they're microscopic doesn't mean they're any less important. Some of the greatest advances in life sciences have come from studying creatures which can only be seen through an electron microscope.'

'I like the project,' Sean told her. 'I've been looking for a chance to get down to Antarctica for years. You can count me in.'

16

Setting up Capricorn had been the most thrilling experience of Lauren's life—a roller-coaster logistical ride so packed with highs and lows she sometimes felt that it would be easier to set up a base on the moon than in the wilds of Antarctica.

The money had been tough to find, particularly as her project was regarded as risky by many of the bigger grant-giving scientific organisations. But by sheer power of persuasion, allied with her fast-growing reputation for getting results, Lauren pulled it together.

There was £300,000 from the Scott Polar and a quarter of a million from the National Foundation for Science. Charitable trusts came in with a further £150,000, and Lauren won grants from several leading scientific publications who were keen to gain first access to the expedition findings.

There was still a one-million-pound hole in the budget when Lauren got a call from Alexander De Pierman, chief executive of Kerguelen Oils. De Pierman was a billionaire oil prospector with a serious image problem: his company had encountered the wrath of the green lobby for its oil prospecting in the waters around the Falkland Islands, and his share price was suffering as a result. His PR advisers had decided to look around for a worthy project to 'adopt' as sponsor and—luckily for Lauren—had stumbled across her expedition.

Lauren was uneasy with the association with a less-than-squeaky-clean oil exploration company, but she agreed to meet the sixty-year-old De Pierman to discuss the idea. To her surprise, the two of them got on extremely well. De Pierman immediately grasped the scientific objectives of the base and impressed her with his insight into some of the technical problems the drilling operation would face.

De Pierman, likewise, was very happy with the meeting. As an entrepreneur, he had always admired those who had the conviction to push risky ideas into existence. Lauren was a winner, De Pierman decided, and agreed to back her project—anything that got rid of the placard-waving earthies outside his Park Lane offices was worth a million to him, and Lauren finally got her cash.

Lauren and De Pierman posed together for press photographs when the sponsorship was announced, and De Pierman's new public role as scientific benefactor lifted Kerguelen Oils' share price nicely off the floor. He got to choose the base name too, christening it Capricorn after Lauren's star sign.

With the money in place, and Sean on board, Lauren had selected the rest of her team.

Frank was her first recruit. Lauren had worked with him on three different Antarctic bases, and he'd become a friend, even a father figure in some ways. Lauren liked his unflappable personality and his gentle sense of humour, and his experience of constructing bases in the field was second to none. Murdo was an obvious choice too, mainly because in addition to being the best base chef Lauren had ever known, he had skills in plumbing and electrics which would be invaluable when it came to the rapid construction of Capricorn. Mel was—like Sean—a new face for Lauren, but the Kiwi doctor had come so highly recommended from her previous overwintering at Scott Base that Lauren was prepared to take the risk on her.

And that was Lauren's famous five—but for the design stage it was really Frank that she depended on. Together they devised a CAD program which would enable them to create a three-dimensional computer model of the proposed base, a virtual blueprint which would produce the final construction plan.

The two of them spent many hundreds of hours poring over the options, designing the base in a series of different modules—heavily insulated against the cold yet lightweight enough to be air transportable. Five personnel would need to live in Capricorn for one year; they would have to be fed, they would need hot water to shower, they would need a relaxation area with sofas and videos to watch during the long winter night.

There had to be a laboratory for Lauren, a clinic for Mel, a radio room and more. Their virtual design became more complicated by the day as drilling gear and cooking areas were incorporated.

The program allowed them to enter the three-dimensional graphic and explore the rooms and corridors of the base at will. In this way, problems could be rapidly resolved. A click of a mouse moved the accommodation quarters so they would be further from the cooking smells of the galley, a further click installed triple-glazed windows in every room.

There was a lot of guesswork involved: how thick would the walls need to be? What was the likelihood that drifting snow could block a crucial air intake? How many toilets did they need?

The internal workings of Capricorn were surprisingly complex—the plumbing, the electrical wiring, the heating ducts all had to be incorporated into the plan.

'It's like looking at the veins and arteries of some creature,' Lauren told Frank as they threaded the pipes and cables along virtual walls and ceilings.

Lauren began to think of Capricorn as a living thing.

The other team members came in and had their say: Murdo the cook wanted more storage space for the many tons of food, Sean proposed a heating duct and better ventilation for his engine shed, and medic Mel pointed out that she couldn't run a functional clinic without a wall-mounted X-ray machine and a hot-water supply to a sink.

Finally, they had Capricorn nailed down to the last light fitting, the last nut and bolt.

In January, the middle of the Antarctic summer, precisely one year after De Pierman had delivered his cheque, Capricorn was boxed up and ready to fly. A lumbering Hercules C130 cargo plane stopped at a military airfield near London, and the prefabricated base—all forty tons of it, complete with supplies—was loaded into the cavernous interior.

From there they flew across the Atlantic, landing in Colorado where the giant freighter swallowed up the fifteen tons of engine and drill rig which Sean had carefully crated up. Next stop, South America, where the aircraft was fitted with skids, and then on to Antarctica, where they touched down on a smooth ice plateau exactly at the position Lauren had wanted.

Seven weeks later they had it built; Capricorn was bolted together, anchored against the wind and ready for work. Lauren was pleased with the design: it was warm, functional and sturdy enough to resist the ferocity of the elements. The official opening ceremony was simple: a red ribbon pinned across the doorframe of the mess hut, a magnum of champagne kept in an insulated bag to prevent it from freezing.

Lauren cut the ribbon with the scissors on her Swiss army knife.

'I declare Capricorn base well and truly open,' she said with a beaming smile as the others looked on proudly. 'It may be small, but from here we're going to do great things.'

The day held more excitements: late that evening, Sean got the Perkins engine running for the first time, earning a big cheer from the team, which had assembled for the great moment. He engaged the gears which powered the rig and gently let the rotating drill bite into the ice. The cutting surface buried itself smoothly, carving its way into the frozen ground with slow but steady progress. It produced a distinctive crackling noise as it went, the sound of sharp metal grinding into ancient ice.

Lauren was struck by the fragility of the exercise; the drilling apparatus, which had seemed so bulky and impressive when she had seen it operating before, now seemed dwarfed by the landscape in which it had been placed.

Everything depended on the journey that bit was about to make through the ice. Could it resist for those seven hundred metres, or would it eventually shatter under the pressure?

It would take five months or more to find out.

Back in her room, Lauren collapsed, exhausted, onto her bed, the months of nervous tension catching up with her now the crucial construction stage of Capricorn was complete.

She opened her diary, thinking to write some momentous words to commemorate the great day, but all she could come up with was 'Capricorn lives! V. happy.'

Lulled by the rumble of the big Perkins, lightheaded from the champagne, Lauren fell back on her bed and slipped into a deep and dreamless sleep.

17

'I brought you a coffee.' Lauren had to shout to be heard above the engine noise which filled the drilling shed.

Sean's oil-stained face turned to her as he heard the shout, his features lighting up as he saw the drink.

'How's she going?' Lauren handed him the mug.

Sean consulted the screen which sat beside the rig, the green display registering the progress of the bit.

'One hundred and forty metres and sounding sweet.'

'No breaks?'

'Nothing. She's running fine.'

'Still on target?'

Sean wiped gear oil off his hands and picked up a progress chart on a clipboard.

'We've lost a week or so,' he told her, 'thanks to losing that head. But if all goes well, we'll be done by the end of winter.'

Sean slipped the clutch on the huge rig gearbox, and the universal joint began to spin. Less than six hundred metres to go. Lauren felt a delicious shiver of excitement at the thought. Five years of planning and dreaming and now they were really making progress.

And what would the breakthrough bring? That was the biggest risk of all. Maybe there would be no life at all in the lake which lay undisturbed beneath the ice.

Maybe the whole enterprise would prove to be a total waste of time. Then her competitors would have a field day. Lauren already had her fair share of critics in the competitive world of glacial biology—and they would not be slow to pounce on a failure.

Somehow, Lauren was confident that would not be the case.

A call from the doorway. 'Lauren! Radio call. Urgent!'

Curious to know what could possibly be important enough to make the normally placid Frank sound so stressed, Lauren followed him out into the storm and back to the main block, where she hurried to the radio room. There was interference on the connection, whistles and crackles from the storm. Lauren had to concentrate hard to hear the woman's voice.

'This is Trans-Antarctica expedition control. We have an emergency, Capricorn. I repeat, we have an emergency. Do you read me? Over.'

The connection faltered as a storm of static erupted.

Lauren stared at the radio handset in surprise, wondering if she was hearing right. Who could possibly be reporting an emergency, and why on earth were they calling Capricorn? She raised a quizzical eyebrow at Frank, but he shrugged to indicate he was as lost as she was.

'Let's start from the beginning,' Lauren replied calmly. 'Who are you, and what is the nature of this emergency? Over.'

The voice paused to try and compose itself. Frank tuned in the radio reception, adjusting the digital control by a fraction to squeeze a little more quality out of the incoming signal.

'My name is Irene Evans,' came the reply. 'I'm the radio and logistics coordinator for Julian Fitzgerald's Trans-Antarctica expedition. I'm up in Ushuaia. Forty-eight hours ago we got a signal from their radio beacon. I sent an AAS Twin Otter down to the Blackmore Glacier to pick them up . . . it had a reporter on board as well. But the plane hasn't returned, and we fear the worst . . .' The voice diminished again so that Frank and Lauren had to strain to catch the words. 'We think the plane may have crashed. Over.'

'I hear you, Irene, and I remember reading a press report about Fitzgerald's expedition. But why don't you send down a second AAS plane to check out the situation? Over.'

'That's what we're trying to arrange. But the weather's too unstable now we're so close to winter. As soon as they get a window, they'll go down, but, unless this storm drops off, they won't be able to land. Over.'

Lauren and Frank looked out at the conditions, through a window which was shuddering with the impact as the wind and snow blasted against it. Frank mouthed, 'No way' at Lauren and she nodded at him.

'I understand,' Lauren told her. 'We're sitting in the same storm here. Tell me, how many people are involved? Over.'

'In total, five. The two pilots, a British journalist and the two members of the expedition. Over.'

'What do Antarctic Air Service say about the situation? Over.'

'They're increasingly concerned, particularly as the daylight window is down to a few hours a day. Their first thought was that the plane may have got damaged on landing, or that the pilots had put down then decided to wait out the storm. That's happened to them before . . . so day one and two they were confident we would get some radio message from the pilots to say they were OK. But we got no such message . . . all we have is the emergency beacon, still transmitting from the same place . . .'

Irene hesitated, perhaps fearing in advance what response her question would elicit.

'I suppose what I'm really asking,' she continued, 'is what your state of readiness would be if a land rescue was the only option. You are the nearest base. Over.'

Lauren looked at the massive map of Antarctica which

was pinned to the wall of the radio room, her heart sinking to her stockinged feet as she contemplated the implications of such a rescue.

'Stand by,' she told Irene, then clicked off the handset to talk privately to Frank. 'Has she any idea what she's asking? It's forty degrees below freezing out there and barely enough daylight to see a damn thing.'

Frank tapped a finger against the side of his head as Lauren clicked the handset back on.

'Where are they, Irene? Give us the coordinates. Over.'

There was a pause as Irene checked some papers, then the figures for fixing latitude and longitude came down the radio link.

Frank looked at the coordinates he had scribbled on his pad, making a quick calculation. He consulted the huge map, stabbing a point with his pencil.

'They're here,' he told Lauren.

Lauren paled. 'Stand by, Irene.'

She turned again to Frank. 'I thought she said we're the nearest base? What about the Chileans at Cape Mackenzie?'

'They've already pulled out for the winter,' Frank reminded her. 'Right now we are the closest human beings to them by . . . oh, what would it be now . . . about six hundred miles.'

'And how many miles from here to their location?'

'You really want to know?'

'Try me.'

Frank took an expert look at the map.

'Well, you'd have to do a detour around the Simmons range, of course, and there's that massive crevasse area at the entrance to the glacier. More or less three hundred miles, I'd say, and a bloody dangerous three hundred miles at that.'

'Three *hundred* miles? Each way? Jesus.'

Lauren resumed the radio communication.

'Irene, every instinct inside me wants to help, but I still think that an air rescue is your best option. We are not one of the big national bases, we are a private research facility, five people, a handful of huts and a drilling rig. Total. A rescue at that type of distance would stretch our resources to the limit, not to mention putting my own personnel at extreme risk. It's a six-hundred-mile round trip to get to the location, through very hazardous terrain, in some of the worst conditions I've ever seen. I'm not even sure we have the snowmobile range to do that. Over.'

Irene's voice was bitter when she responded. 'I suppose that was the type of answer I expected. I know there's no love lost between explorers and scientists in your world. Don't you care that there are people dying out there on that glacier? Over.'

Lauren and Frank exchanged a frustrated look.

'Irene, of course I care about that,' Lauren told her, 'and I'm not one of those people who think Antarctica should be exclusively for scientists. Explorers like Fitzgerald have just as much right to be here as we do. All I'm telling you is that I am not at all confident in our abilities to pull this off without further loss of life. By far the best and fastest solution is for AAS to get in there and pull them out. Over.'

Three thousand miles away, Irene was trying, unsuccessfully, to suppress her anger.

'I've already told you they don't think they'll be able to put down. Winter's too close and the temperature is already too low. A land rescue is probably the only answer. And Capricorn is our only hope. You have to come to our aid, Lauren, or those men are going to die. Over.'

Lauren took a deep breath as she considered her options. 'Hold the line, Irene; I need to talk to my colleague here. Over.'

'Roger that.'

Lauren turned to Frank. 'Give me the meteo for the next seven days, will you?'

He consulted a weather fax. 'Deep low sweeping across from the Bellinghausen Sea. Average wind speeds forty to fifty knots. Estimated temperature forty below. Plus the wind chill.'

Lauren put her head in her hands. 'Why now, Frank? Just when everything's going so well.'

'If it has to happen, who's going to go?' Frank asked her.

'I will. Plus one. We have to keep this rescue small or the logistics will get ridiculous. As it is, we'll have to load up the snowmobiles with so much fuel they'll barely be able to move.'

'Won't you need a doctor out there?'

'I can handle that. I did three months in a casualty ward in central London before my first Antarctic posting. It's enough to keep any survivors alive until they're back here; then I'll hand them over to Mel.'

'I'll volunteer to be the second driver if you want.'

Lauren half smiled at the offer; Frank was way too old for this one, and he knew it.

'That's sweet of you, Frank, but I'd rather you were here on the radio.'

'So who will you get to go with you?'

Lauren looked out of the window into the teeth of the blizzard. Through the driving snow she could just see the faint yellow light of the drilling shed.

'Who do you think?'

She picked up the handset again. 'Irene? All right, here's my decision. It will take us twenty-four hours to organise a rescue expedition. In that time I think you should try every avenue to find out what has happened to the plane. I'm not giving the rescue a green light until I have positive identification from AAS that it has crashed or is incapacitated. Otherwise I might risk my people's lives and get down there to find it was just waiting out the storm and has flown happily back with your team. Is that clear? Over.'

'Affirmative. I'll put as much pressure as I can on them to fly down and recce the site. But they're terrified of losing a second aircraft. Over.'

'We need some more details before you sign off,' Lauren continued, taking the pencil from Frank. 'Give us the names of everyone involved and what you know about their condition. Over.'

Lauren scribbled the information down and terminated the call.

'This is the last thing we need,' she told Frank.

'They might still get a plane in.'

Lauren gestured to the window, to an exterior world which was black with the raging storm.

'In this?' she asked him. 'I wouldn't hold your breath. I think it looks like me and Sean are going on a little trip.'

'And the drilling?'

'The drilling?' This time Lauren couldn't disguise her misery. 'For the moment, the drilling will have to stop.'

18

José Antonio Romero and Claudio Vargas flew the second AAS Twin Otter out of Ushuaia some fourteen hours after the radio call which had alerted Capricorn to the situation. It was a full three days since Villanova and Ariza had disappeared. They were exploiting a predicted lull in the storm, a met survey which had spotted a possible window of clearer weather that might enable them to get a sighting.

Even if the met men were right, it was a precarious enough journey, but both pilots agreed it was worth the risk. These men would do anything to try and determine the fate of their two friends.

The disappearance of Villanova and Ariza had been a big shock for the other AAS pilots. They were a small company—just eight aviators and a few office staff.

They had discussed it endlessly in those days, returning home, muted and sombre, to their families.

Romero had been to see Villanova's wife and child, prayed with them, held the boy tightly when he cried and

told the kid his father was the best pilot who ever flew to
Antarctica—that he must surely have landed in a storm and
would be back just as soon as it passed.

He came back home with tear stains on the shoulder of
his jacket.

Privately, Romero had a bad feeling about this one. Villanova was good, he would concede that, but he was a touch
arrogant too.

All pilots hated to concede defeat—to turn back because
a landing place was too tight, too uneven, too close to a crevasse. But they had all done it—except Villanova. In the canteen, the pilots had discussed this subject urgently, sipping
gourds of bitter maté and sharing around their cigarettes.

No one could recall, in all their years of flying, Villanova turning back from a bad landing place. Romero
didn't like that. It felt wrong to him. You had to fail sometimes, didn't you?

Romero's wife had given him a crucifix on a golden chain
as he left the house for the airport. He could feel the metal
against his skin where it lay beneath his shirt.

Conditions were bad, the freezing storm still raging
across the northern flanks of Antarctica. Both pilots knew
they were in for a rough journey, but they could not delay
this reconnaissance flight any longer. The thought that their
fellow pilots were waiting, perhaps injured, with a wrecked
plane, was enough to make the two men volunteer.

They flew at midnight, over Cape Horn and out across the
Drake Passage, a tail wind chasing them at eighty miles an
hour. Like Ariza and Villanova, they took turns to sleep in
the back. Unlike them, their rest was troubled by bad dreams
and by the constant buffeting of the high winds.

Just before nine that morning they reached the target area
where the storm was raging ever stronger. Thick, near-black
clouds were obscuring the ground, giving them just the occasional frustrating glimpse of the glacier surface.

What they could see filled them with foreboding. The
glacier was alive with airborne ice. They saw no place which
would give them a realistic chance to land.

For fifty minutes the two pilots doggedly maintained their search, sometimes getting a few seconds of visibility, but mostly with nothing beneath them but the seething tops of clouds.

Then, as the grey mass briefly parted, Vargas cried out.

'I saw something black!' he cried. 'Go around.'

Romero executed a three-sixty and headed back on the same bearing. The clouds were thicker; Vargas held his breath—had he really seen something down there, or was it a trick of the ice?

The clouds held back, both pilots could see it, almost invisible to the eye: a solitary tent with a waving figure beside it. Next to it, etched into the ice in uneven black lines, were three large letters: SOS.

As clouds ran across, obscuring the scene, Romero saw something else—a black object, perhaps one hundred metres from the tent. It was large—a boulder, perhaps? Sometimes rocks were carried on the surface of these glaciers.

No. An engine.

'That's what he's used to write the letters,' he told Vargas. 'Engine oil. Villanova crashed on landing.'

'And the plane?'

Romero did not reply; he was concentrating on keeping a level flight path as more vicious turbulence bounced them through the air. He knew these conditions; it would be easy to get disorientated, lost. They could fly into one of the nearby mountains and never know what they had hit.

'How much fuel?' he asked.

'Right on the limit. Tank three half full.'

They came around once more, but now the clouds had engulfed the glacier again. Two circuits later and the decision was made for them. Unless they could land, there was no assistance they could give the survivors . . . and in those conditions such a landing was completely out of the question.

'There's nothing more we can do,' Romero said, his voice choking as he spoke. 'It'll have to be a land rescue. Let's go home.'

He put the Twin Otter into a climb, breathing a sigh of relief as they broke through the dense cloud into lighter cover.

He set the compass and began the fight, against the wind, back towards the north.

'You think those guys from the base can get there overland in time?' Vargas asked.

'Maybe. But I reckon Villanova and Ariza are dead anyway, you saw the wreckage.'

'What are we going to tell their wives?' Vargas asked, distraught. 'What about Villanova's kid?'

Romero did not reply.

Save the odd radio call, the two pilots passed the rest of the ten-hour flight back to Ushuaia without sharing another word.

19

Lauren summoned the team to the mess room.

'All right,' she told them. 'This rescue has to happen, so let's make it good. Every day Sean and I are away from base is a day of drilling lost, so I want this to be as fast and painless as possible.'

She referred to a clipboard in her lap.

'I've split the logistics down into five categories: communications, transport, provisions, medical and special equipment. Frank, what can you do for us on comms?'

'I'm going to pack you up with two Argos hand-held transmitters running on one-eighteen-point-five megahertz. I'll give you plenty of back-up batteries and a lead so you can run them off the twelve-volt cigarette socket on the snowmobiles if you need.'

'Should we take an aerial? We'll be six thousand feet lower once we get down on to the Blackmore.'

Frank nodded. 'Those Argoses are pretty punchy; you

should be OK. But, fair enough, I'll throw in a five-metre aerial and an extension pole.'

Lauren turned to Sean. 'What do we need for the snow-cats, Sean?'

'How many miles are we talking about?'

'Six hundred and ten, give or take.'

Sean scribbled some figures down on a scrap of paper.

'Well, assuming we've got a full load in both directions, I'd estimate even in the worst case those Yamahas are going to be averaging at least five miles to the litre. That's roughly one hundred and twenty litres of petrol. If we throw in a contingency for deviations, getting lost and so on, we should be packing one hundred and fifty litres. Per machine. Minimum.'

'Very well. I want you to sort that out as soon as you can please. Now, Murdo, how about provisions?'

'How many days? How many people?' he asked.

Lauren thought quickly.

'Sean and myself for six days max. Plus a maximum of five more on the return trip if by some miracle the pilots and the journalist are still alive. That's an extra fifteen man-days.'

'How many are you *expecting*?'

'From the plane crash? I doubt there will be any survivors. My guess is we'll be coming back with Fitzgerald and his partner and no one else.'

Murdo sucked on his pipe. 'No problem. I'll pack you up with four gas stoves and the coleman pans and cutlery. I'll give you fifty man-days of high-energy rations plus a ten per cent contingency. That way you've got enough whatever happens.'

'Thank you. Moving on to medical. What can you spare, Mel?'

Mel read from her list. 'I'm not expecting that you can do much more than the basics out there in the field, so the whole operation is geared to keeping the victims alive and as free from pain as possible until you can get them back here to the base. We're talking broad-spectrum antibiotics, saline drips, sterile swabs and assorted bandages, excision kit with

syringes and gloves, iodine, painkillers, morphine and pethi-
dine for oral and intravenous application, four stretchers
with fastenings for the sledges, inflatable splints to cover
fractures to the arms and legs, neck braces, one back brace
for spinal injury . . . we've only got the one here, unfortunately. Finally, medical oxygen. You might be dealing with
someone in a coma.'

'Anything for burns?' Lauren asked. 'There might have
been a fire involved.'

'Good point.' Mel added a few items to her list.

'To what extent are we depleting our own medical supplies?' Lauren asked. 'Let's not lose sight of the fact that we
are all going to be locked into this camp for the winter. I
don't want to get into a situation where we have another
medical emergency further down the line and we don't have
the drugs to deal with it.'

Mel nodded her head. 'Obviously, we haven't got unlim-
ited supplies; this batch I'm sending with you represents approximately a third of our drug cabinet.'

'Just so as I know.' Lauren made a note on her pad. 'Now,
how about special equipment?'

'I'll throw in some ropes, ascendeurs and pulleys in case
we need to perform a crevasse rescue at some stage,' Sean
told her.

'Have you thought about cutting gear?' Frank suggested.
'I know it's a hell of a long shot, but what if someone was
trapped inside the fuselage of the plane down a crevasse?
How would you get them out if you couldn't cut into the
metal?'

'I'll add some cutting gear to my tool kit,' Sean told him.

Lauren checked her watch. 'Anyone got any last sugges-
tions?'

Frank raised a hand. 'Sorry to be a pain, but no one has
talked about the possibility of laying down a couple of depots en route.'

'Like Scott?' Lauren had to smile. 'On what basis?'

'Well, being a natural pessimist, how about you lose both
skidoos, both radios and all your supplies in a crevasse fall?

Then you're completely stuffed. But if you lay down a barrel of supplies every fifty miles on the outward leg, then you've at least got a fighting chance of survival until we can get out and find you.'

'What would you propose the barrels contain?' Lauren asked him.

'Keep it simple. A tent or two, a few days of emergency rations, cooking gear, a couple of sleeping bags.'

Lauren looked over to Sean.

'You think we can carry that extra weight?'

Sean looked doubtful.

'It's going to make the snowcats awful slow. How about we lay one depot at the hundred-mile marker and another at two hundred miles? That's easier on the machines, and it still gives us a margin.'

Lauren nodded. 'That sounds like a good compromise. You happy with that, Frank?'

'Yep. I'll supervise the preparation of the barrels for you.'

Lauren scanned the room.

'One last thing. While I'm absent, I appoint Frank as deputy base commander. If . . . if it so happens that I don't return from this rescue mission for whatever reason, Frank becomes base commander. Is that clear?'

There were mumbles of agreement.

'Anyone got anything to add?'

No one spoke.

'Go to it. Sean and I leave in one hour. I want everything packed and stowed on the sledges by then.'

As she watched the team disperse, Lauren couldn't help but feel a quiet stab of pride. Not only was this the happiest base she had ever worked on, it was also the most efficient. She shuddered to think how many committees the bigger bases would have required to achieve a similar result—how many faxes back to London and Washington seeking permissions and advice.

Capricorn was different, smaller, much slicker.

Lauren walked through to the laboratory and began to stow her equipment. She put the microscopes in their storage boxes and made sure the electron micrograph was covered with its dust jacket.

It broke her heart, but for the moment there was no option but to put the science on hold. Out there, somewhere in the wasteland, men were dying. And the Capricorn rescue attempt was their only hope.

20

Ice had sealed the door in its frame. Sean had to push his shoulder hard against the wood to get access to the interior of the shed.

This was where the snowmobiles were housed, an un-heated shack approximately thirty metres from the main accommodation buildings of Capricorn. There were four in total, brand-new 600cc Yamaha snowcats sprayed up with dayglo go-faster stripes.

They were rugged, powerful machines, winterised with special lubricants and seals by the manufacturer for the extreme lows of Antarctica. Each had heated hand grips and a heated seat—a small concession to comfort to anyone crazy enough to want to drive one in minus sixty degrees or less.

In the early days of Capricorn, the snowcats had been clocking up two or three hundred miles a week as Lauren and her team searched with their echo locators for the best position to sink the bore. Since then they had been more or less redundant, a transport contingency in case of emergency rather than an essential part of the day-to-day operation.

They were Sean's responsibility, a duty of care he was happy to perform. Once a week he would warm up a few litres of engine oil and introduce it to the frozen engines. He could literally hear the alloy casing crackle as the warm oil met the supercooled metal.

He would fire them up one by one, letting them idle for ten minutes, and then take each for a gentle twenty-minute run around the camp.

After the drive, when the Yamahas had cooled suffi-ciently, he would perform a basic service, checking the spark plugs for correct clearance and signs of damage, ad-justing the fuel mixture and tipping each snowcat on its side to put a torque wrench on the thick rubber belt which gave traction against the ice.

The sledges were stacked in a pile next to the snowcats, each sturdy—and long—enough to carry two incapacitated bodies if someone had to be evacuated in a hurry. Shackled together, snowcat and sledge provided a highly versatile unit; light enough to cross over snow bridges, gutsy enough to cover a hundred miles a day even on bad ground. They could be loaded with up to three hundred kilos of payload, and thanks to extra-large fuel tanks and a couple of spare jerrycans, each had a maximum range of up to a thousand miles.

Sean had never anticipated that they would be used in anger. But now, thanks to Julian Fitzgerald, they were.

So. Which two machines to take on this journey? Sean savoured the decision rather as a trainer might deliberate which of his horses to take out of the stable for an early-morning canter. For four supposedly identical pieces of ma-chinery, the Yamahas were astonishingly different.

'You want to go for a run?' Sean picked out his favourite and began to prepare it for the trip. 'No point rotting in here when there's fun to be had.'

The subject of Sean's conversations with engines had

been debated often in the base canteen, Sean getting the rough end of his colleagues' humour for his eccentric habit.

'What would you think if I started talking to my cooker?' Murdo had laughed. 'Like, Hello, my darling, may I say what a gorgeous couple of dumplings you've baked up for me this afternoon?'

Sean ignored their laughter, sticking to his beliefs.

'Machines have a personality,' he told them. 'They're more than the sum of their parts. An engine is a life form. It understands you when you speak to it.'

Some weeks after this, an incident occurred which shut Sean's critics up for good.

A small petrol generator had been included in the base supplies. It was a battered old 50cc unit about the size of a large suitcase, a veteran of at least one other Antarctic base, if not more. It was intended as a portable power unit for odd welding jobs around the base.

That was Frank's department, but, try as he might, the base construction manager could not get that generator running. He spent a morning etching two sores in his palms trying to pull-start it. Murdo came to his aid, together they stripped the engine down, blew out and adjusted the carburettor and checked all the jets.

They put it all back together again.

Pull. Pull. Still nothing. Pull. That generator was as stubborn as a dead mule. Not so much as a cough of life. Hour after hour went by, until both men were sweating with frustration.

When Sean came out of the drilling shed for a break, he found them sitting furiously by the generator, consulting the manual for the umpteenth time.

'You got a problem?' he asked them.

Frank snorted. 'You might say that. This damn machine is never going to start.'

Sean looked at him curiously. 'Now, why would you believe that? That's an engine—it wants to run more than it wants to stop.'

Murdo gave a cynical laugh. 'And I suppose you're going to lay hands on it and it's going to roar into life?'

Sean knelt by the generator. 'I'll take a look at it if you want.'

Murdo was delighted. 'All right. All right, you do that. Let's see what type of conversation you can get out of this little bastard, shall we?'

Frank laughed with him, and they retreated to the steps of the main shed, where they sat sharing a smoke.

For a few minutes Sean didn't do much other than kneel on one side or another of the generator, rubbing the back of his hand against the metal casing. After a while Frank and Murdo thought they could hear him talking in a low voice. Then he looked out across the ice for a while.

Sean placed his hands carefully beneath the unit, cradling it for a moment. Then he gently lifted it and turned it on its back so that it was completely upside down.

He took the black bakelite handle of the pull start and held it in his hand for a further passing of time. Again, Frank and Murdo thought they could hear him murmuring something.

With one smooth, unhurried draw of his arm, Sean pulled the cord back to its full length. The engine coughed once, apologetically, then began to run, purring beautifully like a cat.

Not quite believing what they had witnessed, the two men walked across and stood above the humming generator in stunned silence.

Sean turned it back upright.

'You won't have any more problems with her now,' he told them and walked off to the mess room for his lunch.

'Who was that masked man?' Frank stammered.

That was the last time anyone at Capricorn laughed at Sean's tendency to talk to machines.

Now Sean shackled on the sledge and pressed the starter on the second snowmobile, enjoying the throaty burble of the engine as it quickly warmed. He slipped the clutch and drove it the short distance to where the first was already being loaded.

'All set?'

Lauren was dressed in her cold-weather gear, her face hardly visible through the balaclava and goggles, worn beneath a motorbike helmet with a full face visor.

Sean checked the straps securing the loads to the first sledge, noting that Frank had done a good job.

When the second was ready, Sean slipped his ski goggles on and gave Lauren a nod.

'I've got the bearing,' she told him, indicating the prismatic compass mounted on the front of her snowmobile. 'We shouldn't have any problems for the first sixty miles or so.'

Lauren looked quickly around the assembled team.

'So,' she said, a little breathlessly, 'no speeches. We're out of here.'

Lauren climbed onto the snowmobile and accelerated away from the base in a dead straight line. Sean gave her a few seconds' start and followed on. In her rear-view mirror, Lauren could see Capricorn receding quickly as she picked up speed, the buildings rapidly disappearing from view as the blizzard swallowed them up.

For an instant a feeling of sadness swept through her, a half-sense that she might never see that precious place again.

'Focus on the task,' Lauren reminded herself, banishing that pessimistic feeling to the back of her consciousness as she steered the snowmobile on, into the teeth of the storm.

21

The first thirty miles were straightforward enough, a dead flat run of ice with little in the way of obstructions. Lauren stayed in front, navigating by way of the compass she had mounted on the front of the snowmobile and checking constantly in her mirror to confirm that the yellow beam of Sean's headlight was still following on.

The conditions were diabolical, visibility down to five or ten metres at most, ice collecting on their goggles so rapidly that they were forced to stop and clear them every mile or two. Lauren kept the speed low, throttling back and fixing her attention on the terrain ahead, ever alert for any change in the surface texture which would indicate a trough or crevasse.

Competing with the windrush of the storm, the snowmobile engines were revving hard, the engine note mixing with the sound of the wind until the two were virtually indistinguishable. Sean kept an eye on the temperature gauge and the revometer, his senses tuned to the brittle roar of the exhaust as the 600cc power unit struggled with the seven-hundred-kilo payload of the sledges. They were pushing it to carry so much weight, Sean knew, and the probability of a mechanical problem was high.

Thirty-seven miles from base. Two and a half hours into the journey. The ground began to change, the flat surface breaking up into something much less predictable. There were sudden dips, the snowmobiles crashing down without warning, holes which threatened to rip off a belt. Lauren called a halt.

'It gets a little rougher from here,' she shouted to Sean. 'Stay as close as you can and watch my back light. It'll give you a clue what's ahead.'

Lauren had an insulated pack strapped on top of the petrol tank. She pulled a thermos flask out and poured sweet coffee into a mug.

'Sure wish we could see some scenery,' Sean told her, raising his face visor so he could get at the fluid. 'It gets a bit wearing on the nerves to be driving into this whiteout.'

'You think the machines can take it?'

'If we treat them right.'

'How about you?'

Sean grinned at her. 'Actually, I'm enjoying it. But I wouldn't want to try this without the heater packs.'

Lauren agreed with him. The heated seats and handgrips were essential, transferring just enough warmth to their hands to enable their fingers to operate . . . and just enough warmth to their asses to prevent them from freezing to the seats.

They set out again, Sean tailing Lauren as close as he dared, staring hard into the gloomy light as the blizzard—and the lateness of the hour—conspired to reduce the world to black. It was a rough ride, the snowmobiles bucking and sometimes becoming airborne as they hit hidden ridges and pits.

Facing into the spindrift, the headlights were largely ineffective, the tiny beam of light casting such a small pool of illumination that the ground was apt to play tricks on the eye. They both had falls: Lauren when her sledge suddenly slewed sideways as she crossed a pressure ridge, causing her machine to tip over and dump her in the snow, and Sean when the nose of his snowcat suddenly dived into a small crevasse, catapulting him over the handlebars to land with a crash on some hard ice.

Lauren stopped her machine and went to his aid.

'That one took me by surprise,' Sean told her as he picked himself up. 'Didn't even see it.'

'You OK?'

'Nothing broken. More worried about the snowcat: a dive like that could break a front runner.'

They turned their headtorches on the small crevasse, just a thin black indentation, no wider than a couple of feet. It looked like it had been cut with a knife, Sean thought.

'It's just a baby,' Lauren told him, 'probably no more than a few metres deep.'

They unshackled the sledge and pulled it back from the coupling so they could manoeuvre the snowcat out from the slot. It took some heavy pulling, and they were both breathing hard when it was done.

'Hope we don't get a sledge stuck in one of these,' Sean observed. 'That would really slow us up.'

They pushed themselves on, tensing fingers and toes inside their gloves and boots to try and prevent them from freezing altogether. Lauren had already lost all feeling in her nose and was dreading the moment when she would have to thaw it out. She made a mental note to try and seal the bottom of the face visor with another scarf when they set out for the following day's ride. Frostbite was a real danger, and she knew from bitter previous experience how painful it could be.

Now they hit sastrugi, roughing up the ride even more. Sometimes they were small, creating a surface like the furrows of a newly ploughed field; more frequently they were big enough to bring the riders to a halt. Some were shaped like sails, some rounded like motorway bollards. One area they got into was sculpted by the forces of wind so that every sastrugi resembled a breaking wave. Like a frozen sea, Sean thought, a force-ten tempest frozen in mid-flow.

The place was like a maze, one dead end leading to another. Lauren patiently explored every possibility, detouring round the impassable obstacles, revving the machine over the lighter ridges, always keeping an eye on the faithful glow of the compass. Thank God Frank had thought to rig up a small light for it, Lauren thought; progress at night would be all but impossible without that small touch.

The sledges took a pounding, the runners subjected to a constant battering, the loads shifting beneath their tarpaulins as the snowcats powered through the miles.

Be easy to lose something off the back, Sean thought, taking care to shine his torch back every once in a while to check the fuel barrels were in place. Lose one of those and the whole rescue would be off.

Gradually, the terrain became worse, the sastrugi piled high as upturned cars, the pressure ridges jumbled with chaotic blocks of dense ice.

At nine p.m., Lauren called a halt.

'We're getting near to the mountains,' she told Sean. 'This mess is getting worse. What do you say we set up camp, get some warm food and sleep? We can leave at first light.'

'I'll go with that,' he told her. 'We should rest up the snowmobiles anyway.'

Lauren found the dome tent in one of the kitbags, and they worked together to thread the kevlar poles through the loops. It was no easy task with the wind threatening to rip it out of their hands at any moment.

Finally, they had it constructed, Lauren crawling inside to weight the tent down while Sean banged ice stakes into the glacier to anchor the guy lines.

Lauren unpacked the cooking gear while Sean put the canvas covers over the snowmobiles to protect them from freezing in the night. When he was finished, he threw in the kitbags with their sleeping bags and crawled in after them to join her.

'How many miles you reckon we cracked today? I forgot to check the milometer when we stopped,' Lauren asked him.

'Mine was reading fifty-six.'

'That bad ground really slowed us up. I figured we'd be over the eighty mark by now.'

That first night camping together was an awkward one, both Lauren and Sean experiencing the natural self-consciousness of two relative strangers forced into a space not much bigger than the average refrigerator.

Since arriving at Capricorn, the two of them had had little contact—Sean locked as he was in the drilling shed for ten hours a day and Lauren wrapped up in the lab work and the thousand and one small administrative tasks which are part of running an Antarctic base.

Before that they had spent just a few days in each other's company—forty-eight hours on the search for the drilling rig and a day in London when Sean had flown across on a whistlestop trip to meet the rest of the team.

Now the rescue had thrown them together and Lauren realised, as they tried to get the tent in some semblance of order, that she didn't really know much about him at all. She was attracted to him, her Capricorn colleagues had got that right, but Lauren had seen how messy base relationships could get—a complication she wanted to avoid at all costs.

'I suppose I should ask you—you being the boss and all—do you like sleeping on the left or the right side?' Sean asked her with a cheeky smile.

'I'll take the left side,' she told him. 'That way you get the prevailing wind.'

'Thanks a lot.'

They unpacked the things they would need for the overnight stop, fumbling like a couple of adolescents on a first date, a performance punctuated by plenty of 'sorrys' and 'whoopses' as they clashed shoulders and hips in their efforts to unroll the unwieldy sleeping bags out of their stuff sacks. The clumsy ballet had an unspoken sexual subtext about it, the awareness that this shared expedition could end in a *much* more intimate relationship between them . . . if they chose.

For a second or two, Lauren caught herself wondering if

the sleeping bags would zip together. Then she put the idea out of her mind.

Lauren peeled off her outer layers of protective clothing and stored them neatly in her kitbag. It felt good to be out of the bulky cold-weather gear, but even in her fleece and thermal layers she couldn't help shivering at the chill air inside the tent.

'We've got to warm this place up. I'll get the cooker going.' Lauren knelt in the entrance and sparked the little epigas into life, the blue flame licking around the bottom of the aluminium pan as she poured in water from a thermos flask.

They drank hot chocolate, then boiled up some prepacked meals of casserole and potatoes. The warm food was gone in minutes, the heat it conveyed seeping quickly and welcomingly into their bodies.

'So what more can you tell me about this Fitzgerald character?' Sean asked her as he lay back in his bag. 'Since we're busting our asses to save him, it might be nice to know who he is.'

Lauren let out a curious laugh. 'You really want to know?' she asked him. 'I'm almost reluctant to tell you in case you decide to head back for base.'

'Come on,' Sean responded. 'He can't be as bad as all that.'

'Well,' Lauren told him earnestly, 'that would depend on who you talked to.'

22

In the UK, he's a legend. An exploration superstar. A successor to Scott and Shackleton . . . at least in his own eyes.'

'We're talking about someone with a big ego?'

'Ego?' Lauren snorted with laughter. 'It's hardly an adequate word. He's got an ego the size of Antarctica. He's got charm too, coming out of his ears.'

'Do you know him?'

'When I was young, he used to be a sort of idol of mine, embarrassing though it is to admit it. Maybe I even had a crush on him. I can remember going to a few of his lectures when I was a child.'

'You can? So he's pretty old?'

'He has to be in his mid-fifties.'

'Isn't that a touch ancient for the task? I mean, crossing the entire Antarctic continent on foot is not what you'd call an old man's game.'

'He's still fantastically strong. Everyone who's ever been on an expedition with him says the same thing. He's got that type of natural fitness that means he can just keep going and going.'

'So how come he's failed on this one?'

'Oh, I imagine the same reason just about half of his other expeditions have failed. He's got the dream, but he hasn't always got the attention to detail that these things require.'

'But he still gets sponsorship?'

'Sure. He's a genius when it comes to getting press attention. He's everyone's favourite tame explorer. Including mine. Or he was until last year.'

'What happened?'

'He put a trip together called the Tierra del Fuego Youth Expedition—there was a girl from Senegal, a boy from Siberia, a few Europeans and Americans. The purpose was to cross the Patagonian ice cap on foot, a sort of international peace expedition; he got the UN and all sorts of other foundations to fund it.'

'Sounds OK,' Sean replied. 'A bit holy for my tastes, but I guess the kids had a great time.'

'His critics say it wasn't really about the kids,' Lauren told him. 'That he was in it for the reflected glory, for the kudos of flying this great humanitarian flag. They say all that one-world stuff was just another way of getting his smiling features in the colour supplements.'

'What do you think?'

Lauren paused as she considered her response. 'I suppose I'd like to give him the benefit of the doubt. He's always encouraged kids to have an appreciation of the wild places of the world, and I don't see anything wrong with that.'

'But?'

'But on that Tierra del Fuego trip, things went seriously wrong. They got halfway up this mountain, the kids were already exhausted and badly scared, then a storm ripped in. Fitzgerald was the only one with a compass. He was the only one who knew where the camp was and the only one with any real idea of how to get off the mountain. The whole thing was caught by a documentary camera team filming a one-hour special about the expedition.'

'You've seen the film?'

'Sure, it's pretty strong stuff. Anyway, Fitzgerald must have taken a wrong route off the mountain, because they ended up wandering through this ice fall, the kids almost on their last legs, a few of them already suffering from frostbite and exposure. It went on for hours, right into the night, blundering around in circles with Fitzgerald screaming at them to keep up. In the end Fitzgerald forced the camera team to stop filming.

'By the time they finally found the camp, three of those kids were in a serious state. They were helicoptered off the next day and taken to hospital at Punta Arenas. The girl from Senegal lost a hand to frostbite, one of the American kids lost both his feet . . . can you imagine the horror of that when you're sixteen? Fitzgerald was deeply fortunate no one got killed.'

'What was the response when he got back to London?'

'Initially, he was fêted as a hero. As far as the media saw it, he'd saved those children's lives in the face of a potentially fatal storm. The film went out at peak time and got phenomenal ratings.'

'So how did things go sour?'

'A couple of the kids' parents began to look a little closer at the story, started to piece together what had really happened that day. As far as they were concerned, the whole incident was Fitzgerald's fault from start to finish: he deliberately led the kids up the mountain when he knew that a storm was on the way.'

'Why on earth would he do that?'

'The parents reckoned he did it to pump up the film. He needed some drama along the way so he could end up being the great all-conquering hero of the moment.'

'That's a pretty serious allegation.'

'Yeah. And two of the kids backed it up, said that climbing the mountain had never been a part of the original plan, that Fitzgerald had sold it to them as a sort of fun excursion.'

'How did Fitzgerald react?'

'He did a big damage limitation job, cranked up a charm

offensive. He spun the press a story about how it was a freak storm, conditions beyond his control and so on.'

'They swallowed that?'

'At first, but the tide's definitely turning against him. There was a critical radio documentary about him last month; I caught a review of it on the BBC's Internet news site.'

'Maybe his fans will desert him.'

'Don't be so sure. Most people think of him as a lovable eccentric, he does a lot of chat shows and radio stuff . . . always telling amusing stories about how he narrowly cheated death in some scrape or another. Millions of people are genuinely fond of him. It would take a lot to change that.'

'How about you? You still got a soft spot for your childhood hero?'

'I think his heart's in the right place, but I think he's losing the plot. This Antarctic expedition is a case in point: he's bitten off more than he can handle, and now it's us—and Capricorn—that's having to bail him out at the cost of precious time and resources.'

'How many survivors do you think we'll be taking back?' Sean asked.

'Depends on what happened with the plane. If it crashed on takeoff with the two explorers on board, we could come back empty-handed.'

'I pray they're all still alive.'

'Me too, Sean. And if we can save them, we will.'

Lauren and Sean brewed up a final cup of chocolate and fell silent as they drank it, lost in their own thoughts as they listened to the wind ripping at the outer shell of the tent.

23

Now the mountains were before them, revealed suddenly as the clouds parted in a rare moment of calm. Sean and Lauren paused as they drank in the scene, awestruck at the imposing ramparts of the Heilman range soaring many thousands of feet out of the glacier. The peaks were sharp, the frost-shattered rocks jutting like the shoots of early spring flowers from beds of winter ice, stark black towers competing side by side for prominence.

'These are brutal when you see them close up,' Sean told Lauren, deeply impressed by the untamed beauty of the craggy peaks.

'Depends on your definition of "close",' she told him. 'By my reckoning they're still fifteen miles away.'

'How many of these have been climbed?'

Lauren laughed. 'As far as I know, not a single one has ever been attempted, let alone climbed.'

'Seriously?' Sean was astounded to think that so many

tempting summits could remain untouched. 'But how many people have been here?'

'This region is hardly researched,' Lauren told him. 'It's only been mapped by satellite, and I can't think of a single scientific expedition which has come out here. What you have to remember about Antarctica is that there are literally hundreds of mountain ranges like this . . . some are the size of the Alps, and most of them are virtually unexplored.'

'But Fitzgerald and his buddy must have passed this way?'

'Sure. And they'd have crossed the range on the shortest route. You don't do a single metre more distance than you have to when you're on foot out here.'

Lauren pulled her map from her windsuit pocket and folded it to the relevant section.

'We got two choices here,' she told Sean. 'We can continue parallel to the range for another eighty miles or so and sneak round the far end onto the glacier. Or we can tackle it head on and save a few hours.'

'I say we go for it,' Sean told her after he'd scanned the route with the binoculars. 'That pass doesn't look like it'll give us any major problems. It'll be much more interesting to cross the range,' he added. 'All this flat terrain can get a little dull, don't you think?'

Lauren smiled. 'OK. We'll go for it. But don't forget we have to put down the first depot before we hit the mountains.'

Just after three p.m., Sean checked his milometer and gave his snowmobile a burst of speed to catch up with Lauren.

'That's a hundred miles since we left the base,' he called over as she slowed. 'This would be a good place, on that tall sastrugi.'

Lauren considered the terrain. 'You're right. Not much in the way of landmarks around here, so we might as well make it as high as possible.'

They silenced the engines and untied the first of the emergency barrels from the back of Lauren's sledge. They rolled it to the top of the sastrugi and set it upright. Sean screwed two ice anchors into the walls of the mound, and they lashed the handles of the barrel down so it wouldn't blow away.

Lauren fetched the marker pole, and that too was tied to the barrel, the red pennant at its top fluttering in the wind at the end of the two-metre aluminium pole.

They viewed their handiwork from the snowmobiles. The finished result was about as good as they could hope for, as visible as they could make it under the circumstances.

Lauren brought out her mobile GPS unit, a Magellan device not much bigger than a cigarette packet. She switched it on and waited for the transmitter to lock onto the satellites which would give the precise latitude and longitude.

'Three satellites,' she read out from the LCD display, 'good fix.'

Lauren wrote down the figures on her pad and replaced the precious unit back inside her jacket.

'Sure hope we don't need to rely on finding this depot *without* the GPS,' Sean said. 'All it needs is a real good blow and that pole could snap like a twig. Then we could end up like Scott, wandering around in circles trying to find the damn thing while we starve to death.'

'Don't talk like that,' Lauren told him. 'There's no reason we should ever need this depot. And no reason why we should end up in a situation where we haven't got the GPS.'

She pressed the starter on the snowmobile and drove off across the plateau, trying to clear Sean's words from her head. A few miles later she stopped, just out of interest, to see if she could still see the marker flag.

Even though she knew exactly which bearing it was on, she could only just make out the tiny barrel and its marker pole. A few miles later she stopped again. This time it was completely impossible to see, obscured by the ice mounds in front of it.

After a heavy snowfall that thing would be pretty well invisible amid the many hundreds of sastrugi which dotted the plateau. Without the GPS it would be worse than looking for a needle in a haystack. For the first time, Lauren wondered why she had only brought the one positioning device with her when there were three others lying redundant back at the base.

Anyway, she reasoned, it would be a pretty catastrophic set of circumstances which would see them stranded without their snowmobiles *and* without the GPS.

Very unlikely to happen.

She pushed her shoulders back to stretch the muscles of her back; sitting on the snowmobile for so many hours had built up a persistent ache in there which didn't feel like it was going to go away any time soon.

Lauren straddled her leg over the seat and looked to the horizon, where the Heilman range was waiting for them, the peaks jutting through the swirling storm. That would be the first real test for the snowcats.

The sooner they were through it, the happier she would be.

24

'We'll keep to the middle of the glaciers,' Lauren had explained to Sean. 'That's where the ice is at its smoothest.'

Sean had to smile at her use of the word 'smooth' as they rubbed their noses into the first of the huge ramps of ice. Nothing he had seen so far could qualify for that word; the snowcats were continually beating across small weathered rocks and stones which had been eroded from the surrounding peaks by frost shattering. Worse were the large collections of moraine at the glacier snouts, the runners of the sledges grating horribly as they tracked across gravel and shingle. Then they were back onto ice, accelerating hard as they bit into the climb, the engines straining as the sledges bucked and jumped behind them.

The wind was still blowing intermittent storm force, rocking them on their seats as they leaned into it, but at least the visibility had improved. They had forty to fifty metres of clearway before them, and sometimes more as sporadic gaps in the cloud gave them tantalising glimpses of the mountainous landscape through which they were travelling.

Crossing the range was largely a matter of following the natural weaknesses in the terrain, the rising valleys and cwms which glaciers had eaten into the mountains over millennia of passage.

With every thousand feet of height gained, they lost another degree or two of temperature. Soon, Sean was shivering inside his many layers of protective clothing, his fingers beginning to freeze even though the gauge in front of him indicated the heated grips were still working. On the insides of his thighs Sean could feel sores starting to spread, the chafing from the snowcat seat eroding his flesh in the same way that a horse saddle will do after a long day's ride.

He put the discomfort to the back of his mind, knowing that only by the highest level of concentration would they beat a trail through these mountains without an accident. In front of him, Lauren was driving with considerable skill, rising from the seat to throw her centre of gravity forward on the steepest parts of the ascent and never failing to take the best line through the many dangerous icefalls which littered the route.

They continued to climb, five miles' progress taking them almost to the heart of the range, but eight miles into the traverse they found themselves out of safe options, creeping tentatively round the flank of one of the highest peaks and wondering if they could take the risk to continue.

'If we can crack this one, there's nothing between us and the saddle.' Lauren pointed out the straightforward trail which lay enticingly on the other side of the lethal slope. 'Think we can do it?'

'I don't see any other way,' Sean confirmed. 'Either we try this or we go back.'

There was one truly heart-stopping section: a polished face as smooth as glass, on which they were forced to traverse. The incline was working against them, tipping the snowcats—and the sledges—out to the point where it seemed likely they would roll. Beneath the slope, revealed from time to time when the clouds allowed, was a three- or four-hundred-metre fall to a plateau littered with sharp rocks.

They inched across, their hearts in their mouths, ready to leap off the seats in an attempt to save themselves if the worst happened. Both were painfully aware that if one of the sledges lost its grip and began to slide sideways there would be little they could do to recover the situation.

The runners held. They reached the better gradient of the far side and stopped to celebrate with a shared bar of chocolate.

Lauren showed Sean the altimeter. 'We're very nearly at the high point.'

They kicked into gear and powered onward, choosing a direct line up the final obstacle, a forty-degree ice wall which they took at speed before gunning the engines for the last steep burst up onto the saddle, which was the only realistic crossing point of the range.

This place was more exposed than the lee slope they had been climbing, the wind howling across the col so strongly that they had to crouch in the shadow of their snowcats as they considered the view. It was a dramatic vision, banks of rushing cloud scudding across the horizon as the black heart of the storm front continued on its path. Here and there they could see individual snow clouds bursting out from the mass, while beneath the cloud they could see small patches of the glacier which they were now to cross.

'The Blackmore. Biggest glacier on earth,' Lauren told him. 'You could fit France and Germany into the space this thing occupies.'

'How far do you reckon we can see?' Sean tried to fix his eyes on the horizon.

Lauren shrugged. 'Five hundred miles at least.'

'Awesome. And no sign of man.'

'Not that you can see.'

'How do you mean?'

'The air.' Lauren gestured into space. 'It's polluted even here.'

Sean gave her a sceptical look. 'No way. This air is the cleanest I ever tasted.'

'Sorry, you're wrong. Just a few parts per million, but we're breathing sulphur, carbon monoxide and a whole batch of other pollutants right here at the end of the earth.'

'I find that hard to believe, this place looks so pristine.'

'You don't believe it? You can even see it in an ice core. You drill a core into any part of the glacier and you can see the taint of man-made pollution as clear as day. Hundreds of metres of crystal-clear ice, going back through time, then you get these dark rings appearing in the last six inches of the sample . . . that's the Industrial Revolution.'

The few moments of rest had left them bitterly cold; this was not a place to linger.

'Which way do you think we should take for the descent?' Lauren asked.

Sean considered the options. There were three different possibilities, all quite steep, all seeming to pass through areas where crevasses were likely to lurk.

'I think we should keep to the left.'

'What about that smooth gully down the middle?'

Sean shook his head. 'That's an avalanche chute. See where the ice fall at the top feeds into it? Not a good place to be caught if something decides to come down.'

They committed to the descent, using the inherent braking potential of the snowcat engines to keep the pace down to walking speed. Many times they were forced to retreat, spinning the machines at the edge of uncrossable crevasses and powering back up the slope to try their luck on another trajectory.

But by eight they were down, stiff and bruised after thirteen hours of almost continuous driving.

'Camp?' Lauren asked him. That was the only word she needed to utter; Sean was as ready to rest as she was.

They had the tent erected in less than twenty minutes, a

meal cooked and eaten in just an hour. Then they put up the aerial for the nightly radio call back to Capricorn, the calm voice of Frank a reassuring—if faint—presence as they gave him an update of progress.

'How about tomorrow?' Sean asked as he helped Lauren to pack the radio away.

'Tomorrow,' Lauren replied, 'will make today look like a picnic. We're heading for one of the most evil crevasse fields in Antarctica.'

'That's nice to know.' Sean could barely mumble the words before he fell asleep.

25

It was the uncertainty which was so wearing, the never-quite-sure of whether a snow bridge was going to hold or not . . . the will-it-or-won't-it of the process which shredded even the steeliest of nerves in the end.

Lauren had crossed crevasse fields before in other parts of Antarctica. She had skied through them on the way to research sites, even once or twice run through them with ski-doos like now.

Then she had been a passenger. Others had been making the decisions on which zig-zag line to follow through the maze, more experienced eyes than hers had been weighing up the odds between one route and another.

This time was different: now she was the leader, and Sean was *her* responsibility.

'The technique is pretty simple,' she had told Sean when they reached the first of the big ones. 'You take a good look at the snow bridge, pick what you think is the strongest part and drive as fast as you can across it before it collapses.'

'And the penalty for getting it wrong?'

'There's a word for it . . . let me see now, I think it's called "death".'

Sean held up his hands. 'OK. Stupid question.'

'Look how solid this snow bridge is; you can see it clearly if you come over and take a look from the side.'

Sean did as she suggested, moving down the crevasse to look side-on at the place where snow had congealed across the gap.

'How do they form?'

'By the wind. Imagine it blowing hard from the south, snow gets impacted against that far wall there and it begins to stick together. Over the years it congeals and hardens, growing outwards to the other wall until eventually it forms a seal—like an arch—over the top. Some crevasses get covered completely.'

'This one looks strong.'

'We hope.'

Lauren revved up her snowmobile and blasted across the fragile span of snow, trying not to look down into the inky drops which beckoned on either side.

Sean followed on a few moments later, holding his breath as he felt the weight of the snowmobile press down on the central—most vulnerable—part of the arch.

'It felt like it sagged as I got to the middle,' he told her as they rejoined on the far side.

'Sagging we can cope with. It's the breaking we don't want.'

'So how many more of these are we going to have to deal with?' Sean's face was flushed with the excitement of the prospect.

Lauren squinted into the distance, trying to assess the scale of the crevasse field they were about to weave through.

'Hundreds certainly,' she told him. 'Maybe even thousands.'

By the halfway stage, Sean had taken over the lead, quickly assessing each crevasse crossing as it came along and invariably choosing the same route that Lauren would have done. Gradually, she relaxed, secretly pleased that he was taking the reponsibility off her for a while.

They came to a smooth section, crisp, even snow offering maximum purchase for the snowmobile tracks. Sean pushed the speed up to fifteen, twenty miles an hour.

Then Lauren saw it.

'Stop!' Her scream was loud enough to cut through the rip of the engines. Sean did as she said, and she pulled up by his side.

'You see that?' she said.

Ahead of them was the merest hint of shadow, a long line which they were about to cross, something so subtle that Sean could not be sure it was there at all. It could have been a sagging in the surface . . . but then again, it might just have been a trick of the light.

'I'm . . . I'm not sure,' he told her. 'I think it's solid. It looks like a fault line from an old pressure ridge.'

'But look how wide it is,' Lauren told him.

Sean looked again. Then he saw what Lauren was saying: it really *was* wide—the darker shadowed area was a good thirty metres across. Looking to each side he could see it snaking for hundreds of metres, perhaps even kilometres, in both directions. A cold shadow of terror crossed him as he recognised its true scale.

They stopped the engines.

'You think there's a crevasse under there?' Sean asked. 'Because if it is, it has to be the biggest mother of them all.'

Lauren shrugged. 'I don't know, but I think we should check it out before we try and drive over it.'

She took a snow probe from her rucksack, a thin section of aluminium with a sharpened tip normally used for locating buried avalanche victims. Now she used it to test the solidity of the snow in front of her, edging forward on her knees until she was right on the lip of the shadowed area.

To her horror, the probe slipped into the snow as easily as a hot knife through butter. She put her fist into it and moved it around, easily creating a hole. Whatever she had found, it was hollow; there was no doubt about that.

Lauren bent her face to the snow and looked into the hole she had just made.

'No way!' she whispered in awe. 'Sean, you are not going to believe what I'm looking into here.'

'What do you see?'

'Well, imagine you're lying on the high point of a cathedral dome and you can slide one of the tiles off and look down into the interior.'

Sean inched forward to join her, bending down to look into the hole as Lauren had just done.

His eyes took a while to register the scale, but, when they did, he could hardly comprehend what he was seeing. It really *was* the biggest crevasse he had ever looked into, a cobalt crack which might have plunged four kilometres down to the true surface of the continent, for all he could guess.

On the far wall he could see stalagtites of sharp ice, each one as thick as a factory chimney, each one pointing a frozen finger into the oblivion he had so narrowly avoided.

Sean pulled his gaze away from the hole with difficulty, looking across the deadly trap with a dread feeling clutching at his guts.

'You think that snow would have held if I'd kept going?'

Lauren chose not to answer verbally but instead broke a piece of ice off a nearby sastrugi.

'How much you think this weighs?' she asked him, showing him the book-sized chunk.

'Couple of kilos.'

Sean watched as Lauren tossed it right into the middle of the snow bridge, the area around the impact immediately caving in to create a hole about a metre square. The ice was swallowed out of sight, and an instant later it plummeted to the depths of the crevasse.

They listened, like two children waiting for a stone to hit the bottom of a well, for any sound from the interior, but there was none.

'It's just like a skin,' Lauren said, deeply shaken. 'That

snow bridge is a few inches thick in the middle and no more . . .'

'This one has to have a name,' Sean said. 'I'll christen it Deep Throat.'

They remounted the snowcats in silence and found a way to route around the giant crevasse, Lauren leading the way. The detour was a big one, but when it was over she felt they had overcome the worst.

'Don't feel bad about what just happened,' she told Sean as they paused to drink tea from the flask. 'It could happen to anyone.'

Sean shook his head, subdued after the near miss. 'I was getting too cocky. I've done that before on big climbs sometimes; you know, you just get to the point where you think you got the whole thing worked out? Then—bam— something creeps up and slaps you back awake.'

'You're doing great. Just slow down a little, and we'll get through fine.'

Lauren looked ahead, experiencing a surge of relief as she saw the changes in the terrain. Now the glacier shrugged off its stresses and strains like a river reaching middle age leaves its rapids behind. It became docile and quiet, free from the traps and pitfalls of the first crevasse field, level enough to hit thirty miles an hour in short bursts.

Although they never discussed it formally between them, Sean let Lauren lead the way from that moment on.

How she had seen that slenderest of visual clues, he would never know.

26

That afternoon they hit the two-hundred-mile point, the agreed position for the second depot. This time the location was an easier choice: a huge black boulder which sat, incongruous and alone, on the surface of the glacier.

'What's this thing doing here anyway?' Sean asked. 'Where did it come from, unless it fell from outer space?'

'It's a wanderer. Or at least that's my name for them. This one will have come from the mountain range forty miles behind us. It got eroded off one of the peaks by frost action, fell onto the glacier and has been travelling down towards the sea for probably the best part of a few thousand years.'

'A travelling rock?' Sean was delighted with Lauren's description. 'That's weird. I like that.'

'Sometimes they travel for hundreds of miles.' Lauren smiled as she watched Sean circle the boulder in awe.

They placed the barrel in the lee of the boulder and lashed it down as they had at the first depot. Like before,

Lauren made a note of the GPS position in her pad, and they had some food while they checked the map.

'We've got another fifty miles of flat ground, then we're into the next crevasse field,' Lauren told Sean. 'And it's bigger than the last.'

'What I don't understand,' Sean said, 'is why the hell Fitzgerald and his buddy kept going when they hit more crevasses. They must have known by then they'd have to call in a plane . . . so why didn't they do it here, where it could land realistically?'

Lauren shrugged. 'That's Fitzgerald for you, the man just doesn't know when to quit. He would have kept going right up to the time he physically couldn't put one foot in front of the other.'

Three hours later they were driving the snowcats into the labyrinth, progressing cautiously as huge drops fell away beneath them on every side. If anything, the objective dangers were even greater than the first crevasse field, the snow bridges weaker now they were loaded with snow from the storm. They kept to a crawling pace as the hours ticked by, never taking chances unless they could be sure no monster crevasse lurked ahead.

The transit passed without incident, and they found themselves in the middle of the crevasse field. Lauren checked the GPS.

'This is it,' she told Sean. 'According to my calculations, we're right on top of the coordinates for the spot where the beacon was fired.'

Sean looked around. 'I see nothing. How accurate do you think that beacon is?'

'It definitely won't be as precise as the GPS,' Lauren replied after some thought. 'Maybe accurate to within four or five hundred metres either way.'

'Which means we could have an area of a couple of square kilometres to search.'

'Or more.'

They looked out over the glacier, realising the task of

finding the tent was going to be no easy feat in that minefield of crevasses. Worse, there were numerous ridges where pressure from within had pushed up great mounds of ice.

If the tent was hidden from view by one of the larger pressure ridges, they could easily pass within ten or fifteen metres without spotting it.

They began the search, keeping together for safety, slowly crossing and re-crossing the glacier in a grid pattern, stopping every ten minutes to scan the surrounding terrain with binoculars. The weather conditions were fickle and changeable—for ten minutes it might snow heavily, preventing them from moving at all, then it would clear without warning, giving them another chance to see.

Suddenly, Sean spotted the tent.

'There's someone standing next to it! He's heard the engines.'

27

The lone figure raised a hand as he saw them approach, a gaunt spectre of a man standing by the half-collapsed tent. Not far off, odd-shaped bits of metal were strewn across the ice field—the remains of the crashed aircraft, partly covered in snow.

They killed the engines as the man stumbled forward.

'Who are you?' he managed to say. 'Where are you from?'

If Lauren hadn't known she was being addressed by Julian Fitzgerald, she would not have guessed it was him. Fitzgerald was proud and erect, with a ramrod back; this creature was stooped and hunched. Fitzgerald was well built, almost stout; this man was emaciated and hollow.

'We're from Capricorn base,' Lauren told him. 'We came overland.'

Fitzgerald screwed up his eyes as he looked at her.

'You,' he said, searching his mind for the name, 'I've met you, you're . . .'

'Lauren Burgess. And you're right, we have met before . . .'

'Welcome to our camp,' he told them and fell forward onto his hands and knees.

Lauren and Sean helped him to sit and gave him hot chocolate to drink from a flask.

'Have you got food?' he asked them urgently. 'We don't seem to have eaten for some time.'

'We've got everything you need,' Lauren told him. 'But what happened here? Why did the rescue plane crash?'

'The landing site was too small,' Fitzgerald replied. 'They tried to bring it in, but it was just too tight. They hit that sastrugi at the far end and lost control. That big lump out there is one of the engines.'

'Where's the rest of the plane?'

'Down here.' Fitzgerald stood with some difficulty and led them to the edge of the nearby crevasse. 'And it's not a pretty sight, I can tell you. The fuselage is broken in two.'

'Those poor men.' Lauren was distraught. 'They wouldn't have stood a chance.'

Sean spotted a red rope dangling over the edge of the lip.

'You've been down there?' he asked Fitzgerald.

Fitzgerald unclipped the rope from its anchor.

'Of course I've been down there. How do you think I got the journalist out?'

Sean was astounded. 'You pulled a man out of there on your own? How deep is the wreckage?'

The explorer shrugged. 'Deep enough. Not the first time I've carried out a crevasse rescue. We had a pulley with us.'

'What type of condition is he in?'

'In a lot of pain. Both legs broken, I think.'

Sean was expecting the explorer to pull up the rope, but instead Fitzgerald tossed the end of it into the crevasse.

'Won't be needing that again. Both the pilots are dead. Nothing we can do for them now.'

Lauren went to the tent to check on the condition of the other men. The interior was squalid, reeking of human waste.

The man on the left was the Norwegian Carl Norland, she imagined, the more skeletal of the two. His condition looked bad, his nose damaged by frostbite, his mouth bleeding. He appeared to be close to coma, unconscious, starving and extremely dehydrated. In his right hand he held the emergency transmitter, his bony fingers locked around the yellow casing.

Lauren prised the unit from his grasp and de-activated the switch, there was no point in having the emergency bleeper sounding into the airwaves with the land rescue underway.

She tossed the transmitter amongst the jumble of equipment at the back of the tent and turned to the other man. This was the journalist, she realised, awakening from sleep as she bent over him.

'I heard a noise,' he croaked, 'Is there another plane?'

'We're here to rescue you,' Lauren told him. 'You're going to be all right now; we've got drugs and food. What's your name?'

'Richard. My legs . . . you've got to do something about my legs.'

Lauren pulled back the sleeping bag, trying not to retch at the stench.

'Sorry about the mess . . .' Richard began to sob.

'That's nothing,' she told him. 'We'll have you cleaned up in no time.'

The legs were in a terrible state. Lauren shuddered to think of the pain the reporter must have gone through in those days.

'You need morphine,' she told him. 'I'm going to give you an injection now.'

'Thank you.' The reporter looked at her with such gratitude, Lauren thought for a moment that she would cry.

'I'll go and get my medical kit,' she told him.

Lauren left the tent.

'How are they?' Sean asked her.

'Worse than I'd hoped. The reporter has two nasty fractures on his legs. The other man is extremely weak. I'm going to do what I can to stabilise them both, but the priority has to be to get them back to the base, where we can look after them properly.'

Lauren assembled the radio and raised Capricorn base. She confirmed that they had found the explorers and gave Frank an accurate account of the survivors' condition to pass on to Irene Evans at Ushuaia. Then she signed off and turned to Sean.

'Sean, I want you to get these machines refuelled and ready to leave as soon as possible.'

'Sure. But don't you think I should go down and check out the wreckage?'

Fitzgerald stepped up to him. 'What do you want to do that for? Can't you see every second counts in getting those two men to medical attention?'

Sean was surprised at Fitzgerald's tone. 'Well, I was just thinking that either Lauren or myself should see the wreck. There's obviously going to be an inquiry into the crash and the deaths . . . Perhaps we can help the investigators.'

'I can tell an inquiry anything they need to know,' Fitzgerald told him. 'I saw the crash, and I can inform them as to the exact situation down in that crevasse.'

'Did you take any photographs?'

Fitzgerald stepped closer still to Sean. 'Photographs? There are two men dead down there. You think I'm going to go snapping holiday pictures, desecrating the dead?'

Lauren stepped in.

'Sean. Maybe Fitzgerald is right; we don't have time to lose now. These two men are in a very serious state, and we know we're in for another storm on the way back. Forget about the plane, stick to the snowcats.'

Sean held up his hands. 'Anything you say. I'll have them ready.'

They turned to their tasks, Sean servicing and refuelling the two machines, Lauren administering painkillers, putting both of Richard's legs in splints, and boiling water to begin the process of rehydrating the three men.

Fitzgerald made himself useful, warming up soup on the small gas stove and helping Richard to drink before feeding himself.

'What about your gear?' Lauren asked the explorer, gesturing to the tent. 'We're running overweight, so be selective about what you bring.'

'Just our personal packs,' Fitzgerald told her. 'The rest of the stuff's beyond repair anyway.'

Sean entered the tent and found the two small rucksacks. He left the soiled sleeping bags and the jumble of harnesses and cooking gear which was scattered at the back. Then he spotted the yellow emergency transmitter.

'What about the transmitter?' he called to Fitzgerald.

'Leave it,' the explorer told him. 'It's dead weight.'

'Expensive thing to leave behind,' Sean told him.

'The suppliers give me a new one for every expedition.'

Sean left the transmitter in the tent and helped the others as they loaded up. They left the explorers' tent where it stood and put the two sick men into clean sleeping bags. Sean arranged the kitbags so that they could lie in relative comfort on the sledges, and tied both men on. Fitzgerald rode behind Sean on his snowcat.

They made slow progress through the crevasse field, weaving their way carefully to avoid the harder bumps.

As the effects of the morphine faded, Richard began to cry out in pain with every shudder of the sledge. No matter how delicately Sean drove, the rough surface was transmitting shocks to his shattered legs.

'He needs more drugs,' Lauren decided. 'We'll pitch camp for a few hours' sleep once we get out of the crevasse field. We could all do with some rest anyway.'

By the early hours of the morning they had their three tents erected and had melted down enough ice to hydrate some more food. Richard ate like a man possessed, spooning the fruit compote into his mouth so fast that Lauren had to tell him to slow down. Carl Norland had to be spoonfed and still showed little sign of recovery.

Lauren put in a radio call back to base, then—utterly exhausted—fell into a deep sleep as soon as her head touched her inflatable pillow.

Sean lay awake by her side, there was too much running through his mind. Finally, he dressed quietly and went out onto the glacier, where a sliver of moon was occasionally visible through gaps in the clouds.

The next storm would be with them within a few hours, he realised, the incoming front was already lifting ghosts of powder snow off the ice.

Sean turned on his torch, watching the wind scouring the glacier. Their tracks would be erased within a few hours. He knew he would never find the crevasse again if he could not retrace their route.

He looked back at the tents. All was quiet. He climbed onto the snowmobile and fired up the engine, letting the machine idle as he arranged his balaclava and gloves.

Suddenly, a hand gripped his arm. Fitzgerald was next to him, standing on the ice in just his socks.

'Where do you think you're going?'

'I lost one of the kitbags off the back of the sledge,' Sean told him, easy with the lie. 'I'm going to backtrack and see if I can find it.'

He shrugged off the explorer's hand.

'Wait! I'll go with you. It's not safe on your own.'

'I'll be fine,' Sean told him. 'Get some sleep.'

Fitzgerald watched him set off into the crevasse field, the snowcat quickly accelerating away into the dark night.

28

Sean pushed the snowmobile hard, squinting through his goggles as the headlight picked out the tracks which were his guide.

Unladen, the machine was fast and responsive. It took him less than one hour to cover the same ground they had so painstakingly driven in three hours that evening. Sean relished the speed.

By two a.m., he had located the crevasse. It wasn't going to be a problem identifying where the Twin Otter was—the skidding aircraft had cut a trench a foot deep into the glacier as it crashed, a gently curving line running for two hundred metres and ending right at the crevasse lip.

Sean thought about what those final seconds must have been like: the panic in the cockpit as the pilots saw the crevasse looming . . . the desperate attempt to steer themselves out of the skid. Then the crushing finality of the fall.

Sean snapped his crampons onto his boots and walked carefully to the crevasse edge. He leaned as far as he dared over the lip, shining his headtorch down into the abyss. The bulb was a quartz halogen, the most powerful available, but it still picked out no detail in that blue-black void.

The Twin Otter was too deep to be seen.

He pulled a fifty-metre rope from the rucksack and uncoiled it as he looked for a suitable anchor point. He found a patch of unbroken ice and scraped it clean with his axe. Next, he twisted a fifteen-centimetre ice screw into place, snapped on a carabiner and secured the rope to it with a figure-of-eight knot.

A few steps away, a glint of metal caught his eye; it was another ice screw. Fitzgerald's belay was still in place. Sean wasn't going to use it, but he inspected the titanium device out of professional interest, noting that the explorer had done a good job.

But why had Fitzgerald tossed his rope into the crevasse like that? It went against the grain to waste any resource out here. That bothered Sean in a way he could not quite define.

Sean threaded the double loop of his waist harness and fastened the leg straps. Then he clipped his descendeur onto the line and stepped off the lip backwards into the frigid green interior of the crevasse.

Straight away he found himself swinging in free space, the wall of the fissure undercut. He began to lower himself cautiously down, abseiling in one continuous movement into the dark chasm below and shivering involuntarily from the rapid drop in temperature.

Forty metres down, he began to pick out the broken outline of the Twin Otter, the shattered wreckage shining dimly in the light of his headtorch. Sean let himself down gently onto the flattest section of metal and checked on his line. He had descended forty-five metres—almost the entire length of the rope.

He took stock, sweeping the twisted debris with the headtorch beam, each breath sending a puff of frozen vapour to catch in the light, the sharp smell of aviation fuel still detectable in the air.

The aircraft was tilted at an angle, the nose down, the

fuselage crushed by the vice-like jaws of the glacier. Directly beneath it the crevasse narrowed dramatically, becoming little more than a metre-wide slit falling away to an unknown depth.

Sean walked down the fuselage, still holding the rope for safety. Metal crampons are not made for clambering around on aircraft, and an unprotected slip would certainly be fatal.

He saw that one of the wings had been ripped off to a fractured stump, the control wires and cables spewing out like the nerve endings of a sawn-off arm. The other wing had been folded down beneath the plane. Both engines had been lost.

One thing was certain: the Twin Otter was not broken in half as Fitzgerald had described. As far as Sean could determine, the only major part of the structure which had been severed was that wing.

He swung down further and found the gaping hole where the door had been ripped from its hinges.

He entered the passenger area, wondering how, from this mess, the reporter had ever survived. Almost all the seats had been torn from their anchoring points and were jumbled in the front end. A fire extinguisher had been ripped from its clip and had embedded itself in the front bulkhead. Several of the windows had cracked, the glass crunching beneath Sean's crampon spikes as he moved.

There was a pool of frozen black blood near the front. Close to it, two dark green boxes were lying amongst the debris. Sean read one of the labels: *Fuerzas Aéreas Argentinas: Comida de Emergencia.*

The plane had been carrying emergency food, he realised. Sean checked the boxes, finding them empty, as were the many tins and wrappers scattered all around. That was how Fitzgerald and the others had kept alive while they waited for rescue, he thought; lucky for them that the plane's operators had thought to include the food as a contingency.

There was a medical supply box too, and to Sean's surprise he found it had barely been touched.

Then he noticed something had fallen beneath one of the

squashed seats. It was a small packet of biscuits, wrapped in green paper. Sean put it in his pocket to eat on the way back to the camp.

Next he pushed through the narrow gap in the front of the fuselage and entered the cockpit. The headtorch beam picked out the two pilots.

The scene was not as he had imagined it. He had expected the stench of death, but there was none; both victims had been frozen where they sat before decomposition could set in. He had imagined them in uniform; in fact, both wore civilian clothes.

He looked closer, trying to make some sense of the tangled mess of metal and flesh. Both must have been killed instantly, he surmised, crushed by the enormous impact as the front of the cockpit had been driven into the ice wall. The instrument panel had been thrust forward with incredible violence, and parts of the rudder controls were embedded into the chest of one of the men.

The other—the one wearing a leather flying jacket—had lost half of his head, his skull pulverised, the blue-grey pulp of brains clearly visible through matted hair and dried blood.

Suddenly, a loud crack cut through the silence. The wreckage shifted slightly. Sean stood there, his heart beating wildly, realising that the walls of the crevasse must be closing in, crushing the aircraft ever tighter.

What should he do? Sean was overcome with a terrible sadness at the fate of these two men and for the families which must be grieving for them. There was no way he could extricate their bodies for a proper burial. He took out his compact camera and switched on the flash. He took a series of photographs of the bodies and their wounds—maybe a crash investigation would need this evidence later.

Then he held onto the frozen hands of the two aviators and whispered a prayer he had not spoken since childhood. The words sounded strangely comforting in the midst of such violent death.

Next he checked the pockets—there would be belongings, identification; perhaps someone would be grateful for the return of these things.

In the flying jacket he found a wallet. He flipped it open and saw the name on a credit card: Capt Manuel Villanova—that was the one with the head wounds. There was a photograph inside the wallet, a pretty woman standing in front of a woodbuilt house, a smiling black-haired boy by her side.

Sean placed the photograph in Villanova's hand. It seemed the right thing to do.

Then he tried the pockets of the other man, finding nothing save a few coins and a cigarette lighter.

Another crack, louder, more resonant. The aircraft fuselage gave a metallic groan.

Time to go. Sean zipped the few items he had retrieved into his jacket pocket and clambered out of the wreck. He fixed his jumar ascendeur onto the line and began the ascent. He settled quickly into the rhythm—sliding the jumar clamp up, pushing up on his foot sling, letting his harness take the weight, metre after metre, up towards the lip.

Halfway up, feeling himself breaking into a sweat, he stopped to rest. The wreck was already almost invisible beneath him, lost in the turquoise embrace of the ice.

What a place to die.

An image flashed to his mind as he began the climb once more—Fitzgerald manhandling that reporter out of the plane, using the crevasse pulley to winch him to the surface.

My God, he must be strong, Sean thought, marvelling at the feat.

One hour later he was back at the camp where he found to his relief that everyone was asleep. He covered up the snowcat and crawled as quietly as he could into the tent he shared with Lauren.

'You went down to the plane?' she asked him sleepily.

'Yeah. Not a sight I want to see again in a hurry.'

'Tell me about it tomorrow,' Lauren told him, 'and get some sleep yourself. We're leaving at six to try and get these men back to Capricorn.'

'Going to be a tough one towing these guys on the back of the sledges. They're going to go through hell.'

'I think they've already been there,' she told him, 'to hell and back. And there's a different type of hell waiting for them back at the base.'

'How come?'

'Because tomorrow's the last day of daylight. From then on we're officially into winter. No flight will be able to reach us until September at the earliest.'

'These guys are going to be stuck with us for the whole *winter*?' Sean looked at Lauren, aghast at this realisation.

'I'm afraid so.'

'But that's going to be a nightmare. What if the mix doesn't work? We don't know them at all.'

'We're stuck with it, Sean; there's nothing we can do. Those men are going to be with us now for the next two hundred days, so we'll have to accept it. Maybe it won't be so bad.'

Even as she spoke the soothing words, Lauren knew that she didn't believe them for a moment. She knew too much about the unique pressure the Antarctic winter exerts on the human psyche.

Nightmare might not be a strong enough word.

PART 3

The Big Eye Blues

29

Frank raised the binoculars to his eyes and began a leisurely sweep of the northern horizon. The oppressive gloom of winter was permanent now, and the only clue to the existence of the sun was a dull, barely detectable orange and blue glow in the sky. This was the fifth or sixth time that morning that he'd forsaken the warmth and security of the mess room to venture out onto the ice, scanning for the headlights of the two snowcats.

The previous searches had revealed nothing, but, this time, he locked onto two crystal pinpricks of light.

He rapped on the window of the mess room where the others were enjoying their mid-morning coffee break.

'Incoming! Lauren and Sean on the horizon!'

Minutes later Frank's colleagues were with him, hastily donning their protective clothing as they gathered in front of the base.

'Let me see.' Mel took the binoculars. 'How long before they're here?'

'Twenty minutes at a guess,' Frank told her. 'Switch the floodlights on, will you? Give them a target to head for.'

The inhabitants of Capricorn waited in a state of nervous anticipation as the two specks of brilliance gradually crept towards them. As usual, the business of judging Antarctic distance had proved fickle; the snowmobile headlights had been much further away than Frank had estimated. His guess of twenty minutes proved to be far off the mark, and it was almost an hour before the first of the machines came roaring up, Lauren blinking with the intensity of the base floodlights, beaming with delight to see her comrades.

'Welcome back and well done!' Frank gave Lauren a big hug as she stiffly dismounted the snowmobile. 'I can't say how delighted we all are to have you back!'

The second machine pulled in, Sean driving with Fitzgerald riding pillion behind him. The two men dismounted, Sean greeted and hugged by the team members, Fitzgerald warmly welcomed with handshakes and smiles.

'Welcome to Capricorn!' Frank told the explorer. 'This place must be a sight for sore eyes, I imagine.'

'You could say that,' Fitzgerald conceded. 'I can't say we've had the most comfortable journey.'

Mel turned to the two sledges, on which Richard and Carl had been transported for the last three days.

'How are the patients?' she asked.

Richard poked his head out of his sleeping bag, blinking in surprise at the intensity of the artificial light which struck his face.

'Are we here?' he asked groggily. 'Is this the base?'

'It certainly is,' Mel told him. 'You're safe now.'

'That's good,' he said, simply, 'that's really good.'

'They're both heavily sedated,' Lauren told the medic quietly. 'They've both been in a lot of pain, and lying in those sledges for three days is no joke either. They're going to need quite a bit of care.'

'What about the other one?' Mel gestured to Carl, who showed no sign of movement.

'He's worse than the journalist. I haven't managed to get much out of him at all; he's extremely debilitated.'

'OK. Let's get them into the clinic right away.'

Lauren and Mel began the delicate task of transferring the two injured men onto stretchers and the others hurried to help them. Sean, meanwhile, unhitched the snowmobiles and ran them over to the maintenance shed, where he immediately began to service them. Lauren watched him go with pride; typical of Sean, she mused, to think of the machines before himself.

Personally, she was looking forward to two things now the six-hundred-mile journey was over: a decent warm drink and a shower. From the doorway of the base, enticing aromas wafted, the familiar reassuring smells which were a part of the fabric of the place. Lauren could detect the distinctive tang of freshly ground coffee, the hot, yeasty fog of Murdo's morning baking session. They called her, made her want to be back inside the mess room of Capricorn—to reassure herself again that it was still real, to enjoy the camaraderie of her team, the jokes and good-natured piss-taking which were a part of the character of the place. Instead, like Sean, she got stuck into the tasks at hand.

Carl and Richard were the obvious priority, and they were quickly transported into the clinic where both were rapidly assessed by the doctor.

'You patched them up pretty good,' Mel told Lauren as she examined the temporary splints and dressings. 'I'll deal with the journalist first. Why don't you take some rest?'

But Lauren refused to leave, staying to assist Mel through the hour-long operation to X-ray, administer anaesthetic and then set and plaster Richard's two broken legs.

'He was lucky these weren't compound fractures,' Mel observed. 'He's escaped serious infection by the looks of it, but I'll still put him on a course of penicillin to be sure.'

The skeletal Carl was next, his frostbitten face and hands bandaged and treated with zinc cream and iodine before he collapsed without a word into a bunk.

•

'He's lost a dangerous amount of weight,' Mel observed quietly to Lauren, 'and he seems in shock. Has he been like that since the rescue?'

'He hasn't said a word,' Lauren told her. 'It's like his mind has closed down with the stress and trauma.'

Lauren made sure that both men were given soup and tea, and only then did she make her way to the mess room, where she flopped gratefully into one of the easy chairs. The luxurious sensation of sitting on the soft fabric was heaven after the six days of constant jarring motion on the snowmobiles. The room seemed particularly colourful after so many days of unrelenting ice. The simple patterned rug on the wooden floor—opposing quadrants of yellow and red weave—now looked extraordinarily exotic, whereas before she had hardly noticed it.

Across the room Fitzgerald was helping himself to tea from a flask. Lauren couldn't help noticing that he poured his drink into Mel's personal mug—clearly marked with her name—even though Murdo had put out plastic cups for the new arrivals. Then he crossed to the long table and began to demolish the huge plate of sausages and potatoes Murdo had served him.

'D'yae wanna eat?' Murdo called over from the galley.

'Not right now,' Lauren lied. 'I'll wait until Sean comes in later.'

'You really should come and join me, my dear,' Fitzgerald called over to her. 'This is simply delicious.'

'I'll hang on for Sean.'

'Coffee?' Frank broke her reverie, standing before her with the percolator steaming in his hand.

'You bet.'

Lauren sipped the coffee slowly, wincing a little as the hot liquid brushed against her wind-chapped lips.

'So,' she asked Frank, 'what's new?'

Frank handed her a sheaf of papers, tightly packed with names and fax numbers.

'What's this?'

'Calls from the press while you've been away,' Frank told

her. 'Your little rescue mission has stirred up more media interest than you'd believe. The radio's been red hot all week, and our sponsors have been taking a lot of heat back in London. I tell you, there's nothing quite like a rescue to get the ratpack jumping up and down.'

'I'll deal with these in the morning.'

Sean came in and flopped down next to Lauren, every bit as tired as she was.

'Hey, Sean,' Lauren told him warmly, 'you were really tremendous on the rescue. I wouldn't have wanted to be out there without you.'

Sean smiled back. 'Oh. Well, I enjoyed it too. Now we're back, I guess we're going to start with the drilling right away?'

'If you're up to it,' Lauren told him. 'I'd like to fire up the plant this afternoon. I want to try and claw back the days we've lost, so it might mean some twenty-four-hour sessions if that's all right.'

'Fine by me,' Sean told her. 'I'll keep her running all winter if you want.'

'Thanks . . .' Lauren handed Sean a coffee. 'You want some food?'

A stab of memory hit Sean. He still had that packet of emergency biscuits from the plane. He patted his right-hand pocket, feeling the bulge.

'Hey . . . I've got some biscuits. I clean forgot about them.'

He pulled out the distinctive military-green packet and sipped his coffee, opening up the biscuits as he did so. He gave one to Lauren, and then began to eat one himself, only then noticing that Fitzgerald had fixed his attention on him with unusual intensity. Sean tried to ignore the stare, but it quickly became irritating.

'What's up?'

'Nothing . . .' Fitzgerald returned to his normal inscrutable smile as he watched Sean toss the green paper of the biscuit wrapper into a nearby wastebasket. 'Nothing at all.'

30

'You'd better talk to De Pierman,' Frank reminded Lauren. 'Our sponsor's getting a little hot under the collar, I'm afraid.'

'Oh God. I really don't need a lecture from Alexander right now, but I guess he deserves an update.'

Lauren followed Frank through to the radio room where he patched her through to London. By good fortune, De Pierman was in his office. His secretary put Lauren through.

'Alexander, it's Lauren calling from Capricorn.'

'Lauren! I've been waiting for you to get in contact.'

'Sean and I got back this morning. The rescue was a complete success. We brought back the three survivors—namely Julian Fitzgerald, Carl Norland and Richard Leighton, the *Daily Mail* journalist. How's it been your end?'

'It was fine to begin with—the first few days gave us quite a bit of positive publicity as you set out on the rescue. Then the lack of news set the media looking for a spin on the story . . . and the spin happened—unfortunately—to be me and my oil operations.'

'Oh.' Now Lauren could hear the clipped anger in De Pierman's voice.

'This is rapidly becoming a pain in the neck, Lauren. I've got press men camped—and I mean literally camped—outside my offices here, I've had photographers on motorbikes tailing me through the streets. I don't think I've had a straight hour I could concentrate on my work since this bloody rescue scenario came up. My involvement with your project was on the understanding that I was promoting serious science, not feeding some sort of tabloid frenzy.'

'Can't you explain to them that you're nothing to do with the day-to-day running of the base?'

De Pierman tutted in frustration. 'You think I haven't tried that? But that's not the way the media work; my name's on the Capricorn website as the sponsor, and that makes me fair game in their eyes, especially with a profile like mine. When they can't speak to you, they turn to me . . . and, because I've got no new news for them, they begin to get pissed off. Listen to this little gem from *The Times* at the weekend. It's only a diary piece, but you can't imagine what trouble it's caused me . . .'

Lauren could just hear the rustle as De Pierman opened a newspaper.

'It's a piece called "The Slippery Slope": "Oilman Alexander De Pierman is treading on thin ice with his latest venture, a drilling operation in the very heart of Antarctica. According to the Antarctic Treaty, only genuine scientific bases may be established, but some scientists both here and in the USA have already questioned the objectives of Capricorn commander Lauren Burgess, suggesting that her project has only a slender chance of success. De Pierman is no fool, he knows that Antarctica is the last great reserve of mineral wealth. If Capricorn's scientific objectives prove to be a front, De Pierman could find himself in contravention of the Antarctic Treaty and looking at a fine of up to fifty million dollars." '

'God, I'm so sorry, Alexander; the last thing I ever wanted was for your name to be dragged through the dirt.'

'There's more . . . there's a feature on the front page of the *Mirror* today: "Scientists pull off daring rescue in Antarctica". Your name's all over it . . . and, unfortunately, so is mine. Again. They know you're expected back at Capricorn today so I guess you're about to be deluged.'

Lauren looked down the seemingly endless list of journalists' calls which Frank had fielded in her absence.

'We already are,' she told him wearily. 'It would take me a week to respond to the list I'm looking at here.'

'So, let that explorer—what's his name, Fitzgerald? Get him to sort out the press while you get on with the science. That's what it's all about after all.'

'My feelings entirely.'

'When are we likely to get some results? Something to put these rumours to rest.'

Lauren sighed.

'We can't hurry it, Alexander. If we push the drilling too hard, we run the risk of screwing it up completely. We're scheduled to reach the lake sometime in August, and even that is assuming we don't get any technical glitches.'

'August? That's months away.' De Pierman sounded despondent. 'Look. Do the best you can. Give me some good news to play with, a progress report in a few weeks' time, anything positive. I need ammunition to keep the environmental lobby off my back.'

'We'll do our best.'

'I'm depending on you, Lauren; don't let me down.'

'I won't,' Lauren told him earnestly, 'and thank you for hanging with this, Alexander; it will all be worth it when we break through to the lake.'

The radio line went dead.

Lauren stretched her arms in the air, turning her head to try and ease some of the stiffness in her neck. The pressure. Lauren could feel the tension running through every fibre of her body.

'Frank?' she asked. 'Do you sometimes feel like you want the rest of the world to roll over and die?'

Frank contemplated this with a puff on his pipe.

'I think I got to that point by about the hundredth radio call from the press,' he told her. 'I was almost tempted to pull the plug, it got so bad. And today's no better; we've had more than twenty calls this morning.'

Right on cue, the radio signalled an incoming transmission.

'This is Sarah Armitage at Reuters in London. Can you give us an update on the rescue of Julian Fitzgerald?'

'I can do better than that,' Frank told her as he saw the explorer arrive at the doorway. 'The man himself has just arrived at the base.'

Sarah sounded like this news was about to give her a telephonic orgasm.

'Marvellous! Just fantastic! Are we the first to speak to him? Has Associated Press talked to him yet? Put me on to him now!'

The explorer hastily took the handset from Frank and sat at the transmission desk. 'This is Julian Fitzgerald speaking.'

'Good morning, sir. I'm delighted to hear you alive and well after your ordeal. Can you tell us more about the rescue?'

'The rescue?' Fitzgerald found his voice cracking with emotion.

'Well, I only did what anyone would have done for his fellow man under the circumstances . . .'

'Let me stop you there . . .' The journalist's voice was confused. 'I was thinking about the rescue that Lauren Burgess and her teammate have just carried out to bring you back to Capricorn base.'

'That? A simple matter of driving a snowmobile . . . it's a bit like tootling round the M25, my dear. No, the rescue I'm talking about was the one in which I managed to retrieve the *Daily Mail* journalist when his plane had crashed down the crevasse.'

'Well, that *does* sound dramatic. Tell me more about that . . .'

'It will be a pleasure . . .'

Lauren couldn't listen to any more; she went to her room, suddenly feeling more tired than she could ever remember.

One thing was for sure, Lauren reflected as she lay in her bed, Capricorn wasn't going to be the same place now. The three new additions would change the demographic mix, altering the chemistry of the place for good. All three would have to remain at the base for the duration of the winter; there was simply no way a plane could get in and rescue them during the following months. How long would it be? Lauren didn't like to think about it. Two hundred days? Two hundred and fifty? The three newcomers going crazy with the inactivity.

Winter was hard on any base personnel—it turned this fairytale land into something altogether darker and more intimidating. Storms were almost constant, temperatures obscenely low. A simple walk outside could cost a life if a whiteout swept the base from view.

A base was like a pressure cooker in the winter months, a slowly simmering human melting pot waiting for someone to snap. Antarctic veterans called it 'Big Eye': the gradual retreat of an individual into a dark—and sometimes violent—world of their own. Lauren knew of incidents from other bases: the Russian scientist who killed his fellow crew member with an axe after an argument over a game of chess, the Argentine medic who deliberately burned down the Almirante Brown station to force his own rescue in 1983. That was why she had worked so hard to choose the right mix of people. And that was why she was beginning to worry now, as she contemplated what this winter would bring.

It was Fitzgerald who gave her most concern; even though he'd only been at the base for a few hours, Lauren could instinctively sense that his long-term presence might mean trouble. There was something about the way he'd snatched the radio handset from Frank, something irritating about the way he'd cradled Mel's personal mug in his hands. Tiny details like who drank from which mug were surprisingly important in the day-to-day running of a base like Capricorn; they defined personal territory, personal space, and somehow, Capricorn space already felt violated with Fitzgerald in their midst.

There was a proprietorial aura about him, Lauren realised, almost like he owned the place.

I'll have to watch him, she resolved, resigned to the fact that Capricorn, her cosy, personal little dream domain wasn't quite the same now and wouldn't be the same again until the three men were airlifted out.

She would have to double her efforts in the research, Lauren decided, sink herself into the science as she always did.

31

'Can't we try one last time?' Richard pleaded, his voice desperate. 'There *must* be a way to get out of this place. I can fax my editor if it's a question of money. I've got too much to do, there's so many things I'll miss . . . I don't even know if my job will still be there waiting for me after all that time.'

'Let alone your girlfriend,' Fitzgerald added.

'Precisely.' Richard's gloomy expression took on an extra seriousness as this new thought struck home.

'These two know the reality,' Lauren told him, referring to the grim-faced explorers sitting on the bed. 'Once winter strikes in Antarctica, there really is no way in . . . and no way out. Capricorn is going to be completely unreachable by air for at least two hundred days and maybe more.'

'Because there's no daylight?'

'Partly, and there's the added complication of the high likelihood of gale force winds or blizzards. But the real clincher is the temperature. Hercules C130s have an operating range down to a minimum of sixty below freezing; Twin Otters can only handle forty below. We're already below that, and this winter will take us down to minus seventy, even minus eighty or worse . . .'

'Worse?' The journalist tried, and failed, to imagine what could possibly be worse than that.

'Vostok Base gets the prize. Minus ninety-four point five degrees.'

'And the RAF? What about the US Air Force? Haven't they got a base at the South Pole? Surely they've got the know-how to fly in and out regardless of the conditions?'

'Amundsen-Scott base is in the same situation, even in a medical emergency they can't get a winter flight onto the ice there. Just a couple of years back a doctor called Jerri Neilsen was forced to perform biopsies on herself to analyse a suspect breast tumour. When they found it was cancerous, they *still* couldn't find a way to evacuate her, she had to administer her own chemotherapy.'

'That's it then.' The journalist blinked back tears. 'We really are trapped.'

'I'm sorry,' Lauren told him gently. 'I know this is going to be tough on you. We'll give you all the support we can.'

'And you're not the only one,' Fitzgerald reminded him. 'This is just as much a disaster for me.'

Carl said nothing, but just rocked slightly back and forth in his bed.

'Anyhow, you're all a part of Capricorn now, so we have to find a way to make this work. The first thing is to familiarise you with the base. Mel and I will take you on a quick tour and give you some of the base rules.'

They helped Richard to dress and lifted him into a wheelchair, then turned to Carl, who had already returned to his bed.

'Are you coming with us?' Mel asked him.

Carl's response was to pull the covers over his head.

'It's OK,' Lauren told him. 'If you want to rest, we'll take you on the tour when you're feeling stronger.'

They wheeled Richard into the mess room, Fitzgerald

shuffling behind in a pair of slippers he had borrowed from Frank.

'This is the heart of the base,' Lauren told them. 'It's our meeting place, playroom and dining hall all in one. There's always coffee on tap here, and Murdo keeps these cookie jars full when he's not hungover. You can put any music you like on the stereo so long as it's not Dire Straits or The Carpenters.'

'Those are Frank's favourites,' Mel told them with an apologetic smile.

Lauren opened the television cabinet.

'Mondays and Fridays are movie nights, don't blame me for the selection, that was down to Mel. There's chess, go, backgammon and plenty of packs of cards here, and the dartboard's open to all comers.'

They crossed to the bar, where Murdo was busy cleaning away the previous night's beer stains off the formica top.

'This is the sacred temple,' he told them, 'and it opens from eight to eleven sharp every night. No alcohol at *any* other time or we'll run out of booze long before the fat lady sings.'

'Everyone chose their alcohol allocation before we left Europe,' Lauren explained, 'so if you want to drink you'll be dependent on the generosity of your fellow man.'

'My advice with the tobacco,' Mel told them, 'is smoke Murdo's not mine.'

'The galley's out of bounds except when you're on duty with Murdo. We're strictly rationed on food supplies, and we don't have the surplus that you can just cook what you want when you want. Meal times are set so that we all eat together. Unless you're sick, we really want you there at every meal; often it's the only time we get to see each other.'

Back in the corridor they stopped at the noticeboard.

'This is the duty rota.' Lauren read down the list. 'Laundry, bathrooms, galley, drilling shed, ice cutting for the water maker, balloon duty. As soon as you're both fit enough, I want you signed on and sharing it with us. It gives you one task a day.'

'Balloon duty?' Fitzgerald queried.

'All Antarctic bases act as weather stations. We send up a radiosonde every day,' Lauren explained. 'It measures temperature, pressure and humidity at different altitudes and radios the data back to us.'

She showed them into the laboratory, the microscopes neatly dressed with their dust covers, the shelves lined with research manuals.

'This is where the real work happens,' she told them happily, 'but the serious drama's going to come later in the winter when we break through to the lake that's sitting seven hundred metres beneath us.'

'A lake?' Richard asked, not quite sure if he'd heard right.

'Don't get her going,' Mel warned him. 'She'll never stop.'

'I'll tell you another time,' Lauren said. 'As for now, I'm running two small-scale projects, both at the request of other agencies. The first is to construct a microparticle analysis of the ice core that Sean's bringing up. I'm looking for anions such as sulphates and nitrates, helping to fill in data on volcanic activity in Antarctica.'

She patted a suitcase-sized instrument which was built into the roof of the lab. 'And we also have a small spectrophotometer for measuring ozone content above us. Want to know how that works?'

'Another time, maybe.'

They left the lab, and Lauren opened the door to one of the bathrooms.

'You can take two showers a week, but never more than three minutes at a time. Every litre of water we use in this base has to be melted down from ice and that takes precious energy, so go easy on it.'

They continued down the corridor to the next room, where a sun bed occupied most of the space.

'This is the sun room. You have to spend two hours a week in here on doctor's orders.'

'It's compulsory?' Fitzgerald asked.

'Certainly is,' Mel told him. 'If you don't, you'll end up the far side of winter looking like a cave-dwelling lizard. Oh, and you'd probably have anaemia and vitamin D deficiency thrown in.'

Lauren pointed out a red alarm button on the wall.

'The one thing we can't take a chance on here is fire,' she continued. 'There's smoke detectors in every bedroom, and the rule is no smoking whatsoever unless it's at the table in the mess room. If you do find a fire, the fire alarm buttons are never more than a few steps away. We'll be running fire drills every week through the winter, and you'll all be required to participate.'

'Every week?' Richard questioned. 'Isn't that overkill?'

'Fire is the biggest single cause of loss of life in Antarctica,' Lauren told him. 'There have been six major bases burned down in the last three decades, so we can't afford to take any chances.'

In the radio room, they found Frank manning the machines.

'Good timing,' he told Fitzgerald. 'There's another newspaper wanting to talk to you.'

He gave the handset to the explorer, who gladly quit the tour. Lauren and Mel wheeled Richard to the dressing area and explained the importance of the thermal weather gear.

'You *never* leave the base unless you're properly dressed,' Mel told him. 'Take a look out there, and you'll see why.'

Richard peered out of the window into the pitch-black world which surrounded them. Ice granules were flying through the air at surprising speed. A small way distant he could see two sheds, each spilling light out of frosted windows. A rope connected each shed to the base via a series of waist-high poles.

'That's Sean's department. The shed on the left is the drilling operation and the generator. The right one holds all our fuel supplies. When you're fitter, you'll be over there to help him out as part of the rota. The rule is you use the hand-line at all times, even when conditions seem good. People have been lost from bases when they ignored that rule and got caught in a whiteout.'

'How many days did you say we'll be trapped here?' the journalist asked.

'Two hundred. At least. The earliest you'll be out of here is late September . . . the end of the Antarctic winter.'

Mel and Lauren watched a tear roll down Richard's cheek.

'I'm supposed to be getting married in July. How the hell do you think I'm going to tell my fiancée?'

32

The days that followed were a period of adjustment, a shakedown stage during which Lauren and Sean got back into the rhythm of the base and the new arrivals began the monumental task of adjusting to a fate which was, in effect, not far removed from a prison sentence.

Richard had broken the news to his fiancée in a radio call which he later described as 'the worst conversation of my life'. Then—partly to distract himself—he set about writing an account of the plane crash and the rescue.

'I have to file my story,' he told Lauren stubbornly. 'My editor will be waiting for it, and it's a type of therapy.'

They took him into the radio room and kept him stoked up with tea and painkillers as he recounted his incredible tale via satellite to the waiting editor.

'I know a lot more about pain than I knew two weeks ago,' he dictated, reading from his notes, 'and I also know a great deal more about the spirit of my fellow man.

'Imagine, if you can, the sensation of coming out of unconsciousness, only to find that the plane I had been travelling in had crashed. Of the crash itself I remember nothing, only coming round to find myself frozen as if in a deep freeze, stuck somewhere in the bowels of a crevasse. In front of me I could see the two pilots had been killed, and I soon realised that my own injuries meant I could not move.'

Richard paused emotionally. 'I prepared myself to die, prepared my mind to accept that I would never see my fiancée again and that my story would, indeed, never be told. But then a knock on the fuselage told me that help was at hand. Tears of relief fell down my cheeks as I saw the heroic figure of Julian Fitzgerald swinging through the door of the shattered aircraft. That valiant man saved my life, hauling me—God only knows how—up a single rope to the comparative safety of the glacier surface above.'

Later Richard got the news that his story had been run on the front page of the next day's edition.

'That was my first front-page byline,' he told the others at the evening meal. 'That's something at least.'

'You earned it,' Frank told him, sincerely. 'Big time.'

Carl was not so quick to recover; in fact, Mel confided in Lauren that she was deeply worried about his mental state.

'It's almost like he's lost the will to fight back,' she observed. 'He shows no interest in eating, no interest in fighting the infections he's got, like the ordeal he's been through has put him into a state of deep shock. He just lies in his bed, sleeping twenty hours a day.'

'Let's patch a call through for his family to talk to him,' Lauren suggested. 'His wife's been on the radio several times wanting to make contact. That might snap him out of it.'

'I'd rather not,' Carl told them weakly when Lauren proposed the plan.

'But why?'

'Because I know I have to be stuck here for the whole winter, and I won't see them for another seven months,' he said plaintively. 'It's easier on my mind not to think about them.'

'I can see your point,' Lauren told him gently, but added,

'I think it's worth doing; if nothing else it will remind you there's a world out there which is waiting for you. You have to get yourself healed to be ready to go back.'

But no amount of cajoling could change Carl's mind. He merely turned over in his bed and resumed his silence.

Fitzgerald, meanwhile, was spending his time in the way he liked best, virtually living in the radio room as he conducted one interview after another. The passing days did not seem to have diminished the media's intense interest in the story, and, a week after they had returned to Capricorn, it was still going strong.

'The man's starting to bug me,' Frank confided in Lauren. 'Every time he tells the story he adds a few embellishments. One day the plane is sixty metres down the crevasse, the next it's a hundred.'

'Just another way of keeping the story alive. Now he's the hero of the hour, he's trying to keep his face on the front page.'

But Lauren's relaxed attitude changed when she saw the satellite bill. In ten days, Fitzgerald had managed to rack up more than two thousand dollars of satellite time.

Lauren waited for an opportunity to speak to the explorer alone.

'We've got to get some things straight,' Lauren told him.

'Go on . . .' Fitzgerald was wary.

'It's about your radio use. The first thing is that it's costing a fortune. Every minute eats up satellite time at seven bucks a go. That doesn't sound much, but, the amount you've been using it, it soon racks up. Basically, I don't have the budget to pay for it, and you're costing us a packet. The second thing is that I'm aware from certain feedback I'm getting from the UK that your stories are getting more and more sensational. We are a serious scientific base, Julian, but at the moment we're not much more than a sideshow to the Fitzgerald media circus.'

'I don't see what that has to do with you,' Fitzgerald retorted. 'I'll tell my story how I want. And if you think this publicity is bad for Capricorn, then you're wrong. All publicity is good publicity.'

'That's not necessarily true,' Lauren objected. 'I want the world to be focused on the science, and not on the exploits of Julian Fitzgerald.'

'I'll use the radio as and when I bloody well like!'

With that, the explorer stormed off to his room.

33

Sean went back to his room for a shower at the end of a long session in the drilling shed, happy that the operation was going well. He'd left Frank in charge and announced he was taking half a day off.

In the sixteen days since returning from the rescue mission, his time had been devoted almost exclusively to the drilling operation, but now, with the bore sinking smoothly day by day into the ice, he could afford some time for the many personal tasks he'd had to postpone. The film he'd taken on the rescue, for example, was still waiting to be processed. Sean had been looking forward to seeing the pictures.

Sean dried himself off, dressed and went straight to his bedside locker, where he found the canister of exposed film.

He took it to the darkroom and prepared the chemicals he would need for the processing. The film was Fujicolor, chosen by Lauren for all the base photography because it was one of the few colour films which could be processed quickly and easily by hand. The developing procedure was one Sean knew well. It would take him about an hour in total.

He mixed the chemicals and cleaned out the lightproof bath in which he would soak the film. Then he extinguished the lights, working from that point in the infrared developing light which would not fog the film.

The top of the canister came off easily with a little help from his Swiss army knife. Sean extracted the length of negative, wound the film onto the spindle and slid the result into the lightproof cylinder. He agitated it gently to ensure the film was evenly coated, then screwed on the top of the processing chamber.

He switched the light back on and, satisfied with the work, left the film to sit in the bath. Thirty minutes should do it, he calculated, enough time for a quick coffee in the mess room.

Half an hour later, he was back, ready to extract the film, wash off the outer residue of chemicals and dry the emulsion.

But as soon as he unscrewed the lid of the lightproof chamber, Sean knew that something had gone wrong. He held the film up to the light, hoping he was mistaken.

He was not; the film was blank, every frame black, as if no picture had ever been taken.

Sean swore beneath his breath, wondering how the hell he had made such a mistake. Perhaps the film had never engaged on the sprocket inside the camera? But he could clearly remember the tension as he had rewound it before extracting the film. Or maybe the camera shutter had a fault?

Sean took the strip of duff film back to his room and checked out his camera. The shutter seemed to be working fine. So what on earth *had* gone wrong?

Perhaps he'd processed the wrong film.

He had to make sure. He searched again, taking out the books and notepads which filled the drawer, but he couldn't find another roll of film. He sat, perplexed, on the bed, going back over the events of the last few days to try and remember if he'd moved it for some reason, but he was absolutely certain he'd placed the film in that drawer.

Sean examined the canister itself, looking for the tiny cross he habitually scratched with his knife into the bottom of the casing when he took the film out of the camera. It was an old habit, learned from a professional photographer he'd once travelled with, a trick to ensure that an exposed film would never be mistaken for a fresh one and reloaded into a camera.

The cross wasn't there. The bottom of the canister was unmarked. Sean shook his head, totally perplexed, then decided he must have made a mistake somewhere along the line.

'Midwinter madness already,' he told himself, then turned to other tasks.

34

Julian Fitzgerald waited until three a.m., long after he judged the last of the crew were asleep, before quietly pushing open his bedroom door. He tiptoed down the dimly lit corridor, making his way silently to the medical room where he waited for a few moments with his ear to the door. Satisfied that there was no untoward noise or murmured conversation from within, he entered the room as stealthily as he could and stood there for a minute or so to let his eyes adjust.

The room was a simple medical ward, equipped with just two beds and a curtained examination area. Richard was sleeping in the nearer of the berths, his head buried deep beneath the covers, his two plastered legs raised on pillows. Carl was in the berth nearer to the window, snoring lightly, with his head turned to face the wall.

Fitzgerald took a few steps towards Carl's bed, then froze in midstep as a sudden noise broke the calm. At first the explorer thought it was Carl moaning in his sleep, then he realised it was the window, reverberating as volleys of wind pounded against the base. He waited until the thrumming noise died down, then crouched down next to the bed, cursing the slight clicking of his joints as his knees bent.

The kitbag was pushed back against the wall. Fitzgerald had to extend his arm quite a way beneath the bed to get a grip on the fabric and slide it out. He waited a few moments to consider what was safest: open the bag here and risk the noise of the zip? Or take it out into the corridor where he could search it at leisure?

He decided on the latter, padding back out of the medical bay and rummaging through the bag until he found what he was looking for. Then he zipped the bag shut and returned it to its position beneath Carl's bed, slipping safely back into his own room less than a minute later.

Fitzgerald switched on the sidelight and lay back on the bed with Carl's diary in his hands. He flipped it open and scanned the pages, noting with some relief that it had been written in English. Carl had told him it was a habit of his to write his expedition diaries in English so that his wife Sally could share in the journey on his return, but Fitzgerald had feared the Norwegian might have lapsed back into his mother tongue if he wanted the contents to be secret.

But he hadn't, and Fitzgerald now turned to the first page and began to read:

> *Thursday 11 Jan. Day 37.* JF cuts back rations today. Five hundred calories less per day from now on. Cannot say how angry I am with him. Already losing weight at alarming rate. Not getting enough fats. JF has not thought this diet through properly. Bitterly regret not planning food myself.

Fitzgerald leafed through the pages, picking another at random:

> *Sunday 27 Jan. Day 53.* Radio batteries running low already. JF spending endless hours every night talking to the press. He ignores my reminders about how few bat-

teries we have. If he keeps going like this, we may have
to rely on emergency beacon alone. Not happy with this
at all. Increasing sense that JF isn't thinking about what's
ahead.

Fitzgerald had to read that part again to believe what he was
seeing, then he flicked to another page:

> *Monday 13 Feb. Day 70.* Big row with JF over route. Can-
> not get through to him. Big frustration. JF insists route to
> east of the Harper range will be faster. I point out that
> westerly route is thirty miles less, but JF overrules—his
> theory says that this way we miss big ice fall at the east-
> ern bottleneck. Grit my teeth and concede. Only other
> option is to split up—but I cannot leave him alone here.

The explorer read on, sick with the grim certainty that
what he was seeing was going to get worse:

> *Friday 28 Feb. Day 85.* Administer third course of antibi-
> otics to JF. His frostbite now infected. All my points about
> Harper range have been proved correct. This way has been
> hell for crevasses and much further than west route. We
> have lost several days with this cockup. JF increasingly iso-
> lated. Has not spoken to me for four days. Rations now cut
> to emergency level 2K calories per day. Extreme fatigue
> now. Fear malnourishment will cause us to end this soon.

A few pages on:

> *Wed 12 March. Day 97.* Made only three miles' progress
> today, but JF will not stop. We are both now starving, but
> he refuses to discuss rescue. Food now completely fin-
> ished. Ate last chocolate bar today. Desperate hunger
> now constant. Missing Sally and Liv terribly. Why won't
> JF end this torture? Are we talking death wish? Complete
> breakdown of communications between us. I will have to
> activate beacon soon or fear the worst.

Fitzgerald snorted at the words 'death wish'—he could just see the tabloids lapping that up. He continued to read:

> *Saturday 15 March. Day 100.* Flat terrain. V smooth. Point out to JF this would be good place to bring in rescue plane. Refuses and insists we continue through next large crevasse field. Barely have strength to argue with him. Constant nausea now and fear liver damage now inevitable. Both eyes now losing vision steadily.

Fitzgerald stopped reading at that point—he had to because his hands were shaking with anger. Now he was in no doubt: Carl would betray him with this diary and make a fortune in the process. Fitzgerald could just imagine the relish with which certain newspapers would serialise this diary, the pleasure his competitors would get in witnessing his reputation torn to shreds.

And so unfairly. This mess was not of his own making; it was Norland who had been so slow. But who would listen to that when this document was printed?

What action to take? A confrontation might antagonise Carl further. He could destroy the diary, but how much of this stuff would be in his companion's head—recreatable if he so desired? Fitzgerald held the book of lies in his hand, caught in an agony of indecision.

Perhaps the threat of legal action would be enough. He wished he had a copy of the pre-expedition contract he had made Carl sign. He could check the clauses, make sure it had specifically prohibited him from publishing a diary. It had certainly mentioned a book—and magazine articles—but a diary? He wasn't so sure.

Fitzgerald lay awake all that night, his mind racing as he chewed on the problem. Eventually, he consoled himself with the thought that Carl was really too sick at present to be thinking of the diary at all. Fitzgerald decided to return the document, confident—for the next few weeks at least—that Carl wouldn't be in a fit state to act on it.

But after that? Who could tell?

One thing of which Fitzgerald was absolutely sure: there was no way that he was going to permit his fellow explorer to go public with these lies. That was most definitely not going to happen.

35

Lauren burst into the generator shed in a state of high excitement, her eyes glittering beneath the swaddling fur collar of her parka.

'Sean. Leave the engine and come with me. You have to see what's happening in the sky.'

Sean shucked on his thermal outerwear and walked out to join her. It was the end of their third winter week, an unusually calm night with virtually no wind to speak of—one of the first occasions in this winter sojourn that Sean had seen it so still.

'Come away from the base. We have to get away from the lights and the engine noise.'

Lauren took Sean's hand, and they walked together for a while, their rubber bunnyboots squeaking on the fresh scattering of dry snow which had fallen earlier in the day.

When his eyes had adjusted, Sean whistled in amazement. The moon, platinum brilliant, was surrounded by a number of concentric circles of coloured light which shimmered and pulsed as if fired by some internal force. The effect was as if a rainbow had somehow gatecrashed the winter night and decided, for the fun of it, to play rings around the moon, each bangle a fusion of iridescent reds and greens.

'Moon halo,' Lauren whispered, 'but wait a while, there's more happening . . .'

Moments later the luminous rings began to fade as a new phenomenon superceded them; this time it was a coppery curtain of luminescence stretching in a languid spider's web of light from horizon to horizon. To Sean the light looked liquid, metallic, as if a shower of mercury droplets had been atomised into the heavens and left to play. The intensity of light shifted sensually, gliding endlessly from one glittering array to the next, illuminating sections in the same way that a laser fired from earth will play among the clouds.

'It's like it's raining light,' Sean whispered. 'I've never seen anything more wonderful.'

'Want to know what causes it?' Lauren offered.

'You know, I think I'd rather take it for a miracle.'

They stood for many minutes, watching the lights play across the deep jet black of the night sky.

'Have you heard of Reinhold Messner?' It was Lauren who broke the silence.

'Sure. Didn't he cross Antarctica on foot?'

'He did. And he wrote something that always comes to mind when I witness something like this. He said that he felt when he was travelling here that he was in a time and state where "nature alone is God".'

'Nature alone is God,' Sean repeated, still gazing up at the shifting heavens. 'He got that right.'

Then Sean took Lauren in his arms.

'You know, this winter would be a hell of a lot warmer if we were together,' he told her.

'We are together. With six other people.'

'You know what I mean. If I kiss you now, do you think our lips would be frozen together for ever?'

'Try,' Lauren laughed. 'I bet no one else has at minus sixty-four.'

They slowly kissed, the warmth of their mouths shocking in the freezing temperatures.

Suddenly, Sean was laughing. 'I just got this vision of the two of us creeping into the doc with our faces welded together. You think we'd get any sympathy?'

'We'd never live it down.'

They turned their attention back to the night sky, but the southern lights had melted away. The moon was also sitting alone, naked without its haloes. They returned to the warmth of the engine room where Sean poured Lauren hot chocolate from a flask and watched her drink.

'How do you feel about it?' he asked her.

Lauren kissed him again, the chocolate sweet on her chapped lips.

'There's nothing I want more,' she told him. 'Since the rescue, I guess we both felt the same . . .'

Sean pulled back and looked at her quizzically. 'And I sense an Antarctic-size "but" coming along.'

'This base is everything I've ever wanted,' she told him softly, 'and being the commander brings special responsibilities. I have to be equal to everyone, and I definitely can't be seen to be having a relationship with one of my crew. It would change the whole dynamic.'

'I see. So the dynamic's what's important, is it? More important than what I might feel for you? Or what you might feel for me?'

'Hey, Sean, I didn't mean that . . .'

Sean held up his hand to stop her. 'Please. I know what you're saying. Forget we ever mentioned it.'

He turned his back on her and busied himself with the engine as Lauren, flustered, left the shed and crossed back to the main block.

Back in her bed, she struggled to find sleep, reliving the beauty of the moon halo and the southern lights and the gentle kiss which she had torn herself away from with God only knew what regret. When she heard Sean going to his room some hours later, it was all she could do to prevent herself racing along the corridor and throwing herself into his bed.

But she didn't. And she doubted she had ever hated herself more.

36

Mel cut Richard's legs free from their casts on 6 May, the forty-fourth day of winter. Lauren used the event as an excuse for a party, knowing from experience of other bases that each and every milestone of the passing winter should be celebrated as vigorously as possible.

They gathered in the mess room at eight p.m., all bar Carl, who, despite the best efforts of his fellow base members, had failed to emerge from the medical bay. Murdo had decided on an Indian theme for the food, conjuring up a mouth-watering selection of samosas, spiced chicken and popadoms. Pride of place went to a substantial foot-shaped cake, piped with Murdo's subtle icing legend: 'Let's get legless.'

To the chef's irritation, Fitzgerald immediately began picking at the food.

'We were planning to eat together,' Murdo told the explorer icily.

'Oh yes?' The smiling Fitzgerald languidly popped another morsel in his mouth.

'Leave it.' Lauren flashed Murdo a warning look. 'This is a party not a food fight. Richard's been locked in those casts for six weeks, and he's itching to get out of them.'

'Itching's the word,' the journalist agreed with feeling.

Mel used a pair of Sean's tin cutters for the task, slicing with some difficulty through the stubbornly tough cast and creating a mini dune of powdered plaster beneath the journalist's seat. As Richard's legs were revealed, the watching team burst into a spontaneous round of applause.

'Those are the ugliest pins I've ever seen,' Frank remarked, 'and, believe me, that's quite an achievement.'

Richard looked at the atrophied limbs in horror, shocked at the pallid chicken-skin flesh and the blotchy blisters where the plaster had irritated the skin.

'Take a walk,' Mel told him. 'Carefully.'

Richard rose from his seat, picked up one of his crutches and took a few cautious steps around the mess room.

'How do they feel?' Lauren asked him.

'Weak. Stiff as hell. And light, like someone switched off gravity.'

'Your legs have lost about thirty per cent of their muscle mass,' Mel told him. 'It'll take a while to get that back.'

'We'll get you into physio first thing tomorrow,' Lauren said. 'Three hours a day on the bike machine, and you'll be as good as new.'

The team sat to eat, relishing the exotic spices of the Indian meal after six weeks of relatively bland fare. The beer rations were distributed, Fitzgerald and the *Daily Mail* journalist receiving an equal share of cans, even though this meant the others were not getting their full allocation. As the alcohol kicked in, the babble of conversation picked up, voices rising to be heard above the Radiohead album Sean had put on the CD player.

Lauren was at the head of the table, with Sean, Frank and Fitzgerald seated closest to her.

'Let's tackle the big one,' Frank said as he stuffed another samosa into his mouth. 'Scott or Shackleton, who was the greatest?'

Lauren laughed. 'I wondered how long it would take you to get round to that old chestnut. I think my answer would be neither—it was Amundsen who was the greatest; he was a polar explorer par excellence.'

'Better than Shackleton?' Frank was surprised at her response. 'On what grounds?'

'Attention to detail. Amundsen was a man who knew his subject intimately; he was the first polar professional if you like. Unlike Scott, one might say.'

'What's this I hear?' Sean joined the conversation at this point, putting on his crustiest British accent. 'Slagging off one's fellow countryman? Not the pukka thing, what?'

'It is when you look at the amateurish way Scott put the whole project together,' Lauren told him. 'Amundsen was in a different class.'

'Examples,' Frank demanded. 'Support your argument with facts.'

'All right.' Lauren thought for a while. 'How about the question of clothing? Scott relied on cottons and wools, warm enough until you sweat, at which point they freeze as stiff as a board, reducing you to little more than a human icicle. Amundsen, on the other hand, did his research, he spent time with the Inuit up in Greenland and realised that their loose-fitting animal furs were vastly superior. He kitted his entire team out in fur—and it was a great success.'

'What about the animals?' Sean asked. 'Amundsen had the edge with that too, didn't he?'

'He did. He had more than two hundred dogs and a great deal of experience of how to handle them. Scott only had a couple of dozen inferior dogs, putting more of his faith into ponies.'

'Ponies!' Sean scoffed. 'I'd forgotten that little detail! What kind of madman would bring ponies to Antarctica?'

Frank and Lauren could think of no answer to this, but after a pause Lauren continued: 'And to give you a further example of the way Amundsen planned ahead, he'd even calculated the precise day on which each of the dogs would have to be slaughtered to feed the others.'

'Brutal!' Sean was outraged. 'Those animals worked themselves to the bone for that guy, and he thanked them with a bullet?'

'Scott's team did the same. One of the few advantages of their ponies was the amount of meat they could get out of them.'

'Amundsen might have had the planning expertise,' Frank commented, 'but the man didn't have any charisma. Shackleton was a born leader, wasn't he? And don't forget, he never lost a man . . . brought them through that shipwreck, the open boat journey, the crossing of South Georgia, without a single fatality.'

'Aha!' Lauren was quick to challenge him. 'That's a myth. It's not true that he never lost a man. He lost three men on that expedition, and that's a fact.'

Frank gave her a sceptical look. 'You sure? I was brought up as a schoolboy believing that Shackleton was the greatest expedition leader because he never lost a man.'

'He didn't lose anyone from the half of the team that was with him, but that expedition was in two parts,' Lauren corrected him. 'It was split on both sides of the Antarctic: Shackleton and one half of the team preparing for the crossing in the west, the other half travelling down by ship to lay depots and meet them on the eastern side of the continent. That group had a dreadful time, were pretty ill-prepared for what was in front of them, and they *did* lose three men. So there.'

Frank was crestfallen. 'So. In those few brutal words you've destroyed the myth of my childhood hero.'

'And how about Scott?' Sean asked. 'What really killed him in the end?'

'I don't think there's too much doubt about that,' Lauren replied. 'It was the disappointment of being beaten to the Pole. When he saw that Norwegian flag flying there, something died inside him, and in his team mates too.'

'You mean they might have survived the return trip if they'd been first to the Pole?'

'Quite possibly, yes; they were returning as failures, and,

for someone with Scott's drive and ambition, that would have been an unbearable cross to bear.'

Frank turned his attention to Fitzgerald, who had been ignoring the conversation. 'What about you, Julian? What do you think?'

The explorer toyed with his beer glass for a while before responding. 'I don't think any one of you has the faintest idea what you're talking about.'

With that he downed the last of his drink, rose from the table and left the room.

The conversation went quiet for a while.

'That man is beginning to get on my nerves,' Frank said. 'And to think we have to suffer him for the rest of the winter.'

'We don't have a choice,' Lauren told them, 'We're stuck here with him, and we've got to make the best of it.'

'Then you should do something about his behaviour,' Murdo protested. 'That's your job as base commander, right?'

The party resumed, but the mood never regained the carefree spirit of celebration it had had at the start of the evening. Lauren was particularly preoccupied, aware that Murdo's words echoed the sentiments of everyone at the base. It *was* her job to do something about Fitzgerald; there was little doubt he was getting increasingly bad-tempered, flaring up over trivial irritations. Each passing week was making him more withdrawn and isolated, classic symptons of 'Big Eye'.

Lauren resolved she would confront him about the problem, next time an opportunity came up.

37

Mel and Lauren were out on the glacier, cutting ice, on the sixty-fourth day of winter. This duty was the toughest of the daily tasks, a one-hour session with axes and a two-man saw, slicing into the specially created ice quarry and carving chunks for transport back to the water maker in the generator shed. Unlike most of Capricorn's crew, Lauren welcomed the heavy physical work, the chance to break into an honest sweat was a relief from the uncertainties of the drilling operation and the ever-shifting human dynamics of the crew . . . even if the sweat did freeze against her skin the very instant it formed.

She particularly liked sharing the rota with Mel, the cheerful Kiwi medic keeping her entertained with base gossip and her own thoughts on how things were going.

'I'm still dead worried about Carl,' Mel confided in her as they lifted a suitcase-sized block of ice into the wheelbarrow. 'We're only two months into this winter, and he's going downhill fast.'

'Don't think I haven't noticed. I haven't seen him in the mess room for weeks. What's going on?'

'Physically he's weak as a kitten,' Mel told her, 'and he's way underweight. A man his height should come in at seventy-five kilos, but he's twenty-five per cent under that.'

'Doesn't he eat?'

'I try my best, but he hardly touches his tray. He's lost all interest in it.'

'How's his medical condition?'

'That's the perplexing bit. There's nothing clinically wrong with him; all the medical problems he had when you brought him back here have cleared up . . . but he still isn't getting any better. It's definitely a mental thing, he's just deeply depressed.'

'We've got to take some action on this,' Lauren said. 'I want him out of that medical room and into the mess as much as possible. And from now on he gets no meals on his own, he eats with the rest of us.'

Each morning, Lauren and Mel would bully Carl out of his bed, coaxing him onto his feet and taking him by the arms for the shaky walk to the mess room, where he would spend the day lying listlessly on the sofa beneath layers of blankets. He rarely spoke and, if asked a question, would often lose the thread of his answer, his face crumpling in confusion as his mind struggled to pick up the wayward thought.

At meal times he reluctantly took his seat, pushing food around the plate with a fork but eating little.

Richard tried to interest him in chess. Murdo challenged him to darts, but Carl's heart wasn't in it and they soon gave up trying to involve him. Instead, he just lay there, silent and unresponding, staring at the television screen regardless of whether a movie was playing on it or not.

'He's toasted,' Frank said. 'He's got the thousand-mile stare.'

The only time Carl became animated was when Fitzgerald was in the room at the same time. Then he would make a point of sitting as far away from the explorer as he could.

Finally, Lauren found an opportunity to talk to him alone.

'This winter is going to be hard on all of us, Carl, but it'll be much worse for you if you carry on like this.'

Carl nodded his head weakly but did not look her in the eye.

'You need to get your strength back, physically and mentally. You have to start to contribute to the day-to-day running of the base, and I suggest you find something to occupy you over the next five months.'

'That's easy for you to say,' Carl told her bitterly, 'but I never asked to be locked up here for the winter. This is a bloody nightmare for me, and nothing you can say is going to make it any easier.'

Lauren had a sudden brainwave.

'What if I gave you a laptop?' she proposed, 'that's what keeps Julian busy.'

Carl's interest was spiked. 'Fitzgerald's got a laptop?'

'Sure. He asked to borrow one at the start of the winter.'

'Writing his fictional account of our great Antarctic expedition, no doubt.'

'Are you taking the name of the great Julian Fitzgerald in vain?' Lauren smiled as she faked the indignation. 'Can you possibly be doubting the veracity of the greatest explorer on earth?'

Carl returned the smile, the first time Lauren had seen his face register anything other than despondency for a very long time.

'He'll do his normal whitewash,' Carl told her, dropping his voice so they couldn't be heard out in the corridor, 'and he'll probably blame me for the fact we failed.'

'But why would he do that? Surely you share the responsibility?'

'No, no. It was his blundering that screwed our chances. If he'd planned the whole thing properly, we could have pulled it off.'

'So what did he do wrong?'

'You want a list? I'll tell you if you've got a few months to spare.'

'That bad, eh?'

'I put my heart and soul into that expedition, Lauren.

Crossing Antarctica on foot was a dream I'd had for years. I'll never get another crack at it, but Fitzgerald probably will. And what sickens me the most is that he'll fool the public with his official book, make out I was the weak link.'

'Why don't you ask him to let you write a couple of chapters of the book? That way you get to put your case.'

Carl snorted with laughter. 'No chance of that,' he told her. 'I doubt he'll show that manuscript to a damn soul. He'll just come out with the lies and post it off to his publisher without a second thought.'

With that, Carl reached into his bedside drawer and brought out his diary. 'This is what the public should be reading. I've got the real story here.'

Lauren took the battered notebook and flipped through a few of the pages. 'This is a lot of work.'

'Yeah. Not that I'll ever be able to publish any of it.'

'Why not?'

'Fitzgerald made me sign a pre-expedition contract.'

'Well, if I gave you a laptop, at least you could get all this down as hard copy. It would be worth it just for your own records.'

Carl thumbed through the diary as he thought about the offer.

'All right. I'll do it. It'll keep me busy at least.'

The next day, Carl was up from his bed under his own steam, making his way to the mess room without assistance and amazing Murdo by requesting a plate of fried eggs and toast. Then he returned to the medical room, locking himself away with the computer.

'I think he's turned the corner,' Mel told Lauren a couple of days later. 'Since you gave him the laptop, he's been getting back on track.'

Lauren watched Carl closely over the next week, noting how—little by little—he was eating more and participating more in the daily social activity of the base. He was still spending large amounts of time in his bed, but no longer merely lying there with his eyes fixed on a blank spot on the ceiling. Now, every time Lauren stuck her head round the door to say hi, he was tapping busily into the computer.

'Still transcribing your diary?' she asked him.

'Something like that,' he told her and went back to work.

38

Lauren was sleeping when the generator-fail alarm went off, the shrill two-tone siren piercing her dreams and bringing her, heart palpitating, fast to her feet. Her first thought was fire—but she quickly realised the alarm was not the continuous bell of the fire system. She tried the light switch, found it was dead, then began to pull on clothes in the dark as Frank rapped hard on her door.

'Get out here!' he called. 'Sean's got a problem in the shed.'

By the time Lauren emerged into the corridor, the rest of the team were out of their rooms. The battery-powered emergency lights had come on in the public areas, giving the team a chance to dress in their outdoor protective clothing as they moved into the pre-rehearsed emergency drill.

Frank was dressed, ready to make for the generator building as Lauren arrived. 'The heat exchanger on the genny's failed,' he told her, 'and Sean can't get the standby going.'

Lauren hit the kill switch for the alarm unit and put a

hand on the nearest radiator. It was already stone cold. The digital thermometer above it was reading fifty-eight degrees below zero for the external temperature, and two degrees below for the internal temperature. The moisture in her breath was freezing as she exhaled and the windows were even now coated on the inside with frozen condensation.

'What time did the heating fail?' Lauren asked Frank.

'I'm not sure. Thirty minutes ago, maybe forty.'

Lauren was shocked. In much less than an hour, the cosy ambient living temperature of sixteen degrees had been stripped down below zero. They were now losing more than a degree of temperature for every two passing minutes. Within the next half an hour the entire water system of the base, even sealed within its triple-lagged protective insulation, could be frozen completely solid. De-freezing it could take weeks . . . if it was possible at all.

Lauren made a quick calculation, realising that it would take less than two hours for the air temperature inside Capricorn to plummet to the same extreme lows as the exterior. Their previously snug world would then be six times colder than an average domestic freezer, cold enough to make their existence a living hell . . . if they could survive at all.

She checked her watch. It was just after five a.m.

'Murdo and Mel, get into the galley and drain down the water systems as fast as you can. Julian, you can help them. Frank, you come with me.'

Lauren hurriedly climbed into her protective suit and pulled the insulated neoprene face visor over her mouth and nose. The walk to the generator shed was only thirty metres or so, but at fifty-eight degrees below freezing, even a few seconds of inadequate protection could mean first-degree frostbite or tissue necrosis. Outside, conditions were clear, pitch black as only an Antarctic midwinter night can be, with a wind gusting at twenty to thirty knots. Lauren held onto the safety handline and bent her body into the blast as she followed Frank across to the generator shed.

As they approached, Lauren flashed her torch towards the shed. Caught in the quartz-halogen light beam was a billow-

ing jet of steam—freezing to water droplets as she watched.
The acid-sweet smell of burning glycol filled the air, instantly taking Lauren back—as dangerous smells have a
habit of doing—to an incident in which the radiator of her
first car had exploded, showering the red-hot exhaust mani-
fold with antifreeze.

Without the thudding intensity of the generator the scene
inside the shed was eerily quiet, the atmosphere thick with
vaporised glycol and frozen water droplets. Lauren felt the
prick of tears as her eyes reacted to the irritating chemicals,
the fluid instantly freezing as it ran down her cheeks.

Sean was standing on an inspection ladder, bent over the
twin tubes of the heat exchanger with a plume of vapour
spraying his lower body from a foot-long split in the metal
tubing. His thermal suit and boots were encrusted with a
thick coating of ice.

As Lauren approached him, she could hear an ominous
bubbling noise from the extensive pipework, which was
plumbed above the engine, and the hiss of incinerated antifreeze as drops fell on hot metal. 'The heat exchanger
sleeve has split,' Sean said. 'I think the duct pipe to the main
building must have frozen up and the whole thing's built up
back pressure until it boiled.'

Lauren knew enough about the design of Capricorn's
technical layout to know how serious the problem was.
Common to almost all Antarctic bases, excess heat from the
main generator was transferred via a heat exchanger into a
closed-circuit glycol system through which conventional
water pipes ran in sealed sleeves. If the system went down, it
would also shut down the ice-melting unit, which would
leave Capricorn not just with no warm water . . . but with no
water at all.

'What about the standby genny?' Frank was already
crossing to the second engine.

'The temperature's fallen too fast,' Sean told him. 'It's
fifteen below in here now, and that old Honda doesn't like
that. Try it again.'

Lauren and Frank tried the starter button on the standby

generator, their hearts sinking as the unit cranked clunkily for a few reluctant revolutions without firing. A further try resulted in an even less convincing performance, the engine not even coughing with an attempt at life. Worse, the deep-cycle lead-acid batteries which powered the starter motor were also beginning to suffer the cold invasion, the output strength falling noticeably with each attempt.

'How long's it going to take you to fix the main unit?' Lauren called to Sean.

'Gonna be an hour at least. You got to get that standby going or we are in serious shit.'

'How?'

'Do it like the truck drivers do in Siberia,' Sean told her. 'Warm the whole engine up with fire.'

'Light a fire underneath it?' Lauren knew that would be a risk too far in a room which held tankloads of diesel, glycol and kerosene.

'Let's try these.' Frank crossed to the store area and produced three butane blowtorches. 'We can fire these up and place them round the sump. That'll get the engine oil warmed up and lower the viscosity. The stuff'll be like tarmac in there.'

'Don't like to worry you,' Sean was checking the internal thermometer for the shed, 'but it's minus twenty already.'

Lauren had a further heart-stopping thought. 'How about the kerosene?' she asked Sean. 'How low can it go before it freezes?'

'It solidifies at fifty-five degrees below,' he told her. 'So we'd better get some heat going in here fast.'

Lauren and Frank got the blowtorches lit and started to heat up the metal sump of the back-up generator. As Lauren worked, she considered how fast their fortunes had changed. Less than an hour ago she had been happily asleep in the warmth and security of her berth. Now the normally smooth-running systems of Capricorn were under serious threat—and the drilling operation was even more compromised: if their kerosene supply froze, they would not be able to maintain the de-icing environment of the drill; the bit would be irretrievably frozen into the glacier. Capricorn would have to start a new bore—an impossibly expensive and logistically nightmarish prospect—or give up the project for good.

By six a.m.—by which time every bone in Lauren's body felt like it had frozen to the flesh that surrounded it—Frank judged that the blowtorches had done their work. The exterior of the engine was a blistered mess of bubbling paint but at least the oil inside would be warm. The temperature inside the shed was now thirty-seven degrees below freezing. They wired up two of the lead-acid batteries in series to give some extra clout to the charge and held their breath as the starter motor whirred once, twice, followed by the sweet sound of the diesel engine ripping into life.

Lauren and Frank smiled at each other in triumph, and, with temporary heat and light back on line, the fight to help Sean fix the main generator began in earnest. This they achieved by midmorning, replacing the damaged section of the heat exchanger and refilling the glycol reservoir with spare fluid to get the master system back up and running.

When they had finished in the generator shed, Lauren, Sean and Frank crossed back to the main block, where Murdo had prepared soup and tea. They sat in silence, sipping the liquid warmth into their bodies, emotionally and physically spent by the events of the night.

There was little incentive for any of them to stay in the frigid mess room, and by midday the team had dispersed back to the relative comfort of their berths. Lauren made her way wearily to her room and peeled off her glycol-soaked clothes. Her hair and face were encrusted with the frozen chemical, but a shower was not going to be possible until the ambient base temperature had risen to above freezing and the water systems replenished. That would be days away, Lauren was sure.

The radiator was still cold, the room completely unwelcoming. Lauren slipped into bed in her thermal underclothes and lay there shivering until her body heat had created a fragile pool of warmth.

From the window she could hear the ceaseless roar of the wind as it raced across the ice, the patter of frozen granules beating against the glass in sharp volleys. They had got away with it this time, she reflected, escaped with a few frostbite injuries and bruises.

Next time they might not be so lucky, Lauren knew; this winter could kill them yet.

39

Richard drew a ring around the date and snapped his diary shut with a sigh. Today was going to be a psychological endurance test, he already knew, even more of an endurance test than Capricorn days normally were. It was ninety-two days since he'd entered the base, with so many weeks of winter left to run that Richard preferred not to think about it.

He quit his room and went to the rota board, to see what tasks he'd been allocated today. Lauren routinely shuffled the rota pack around to keep things fresh.

Getting the casts off his legs had been a huge booster, and a daily two-hour physio session with Mel had got them feeling—almost—as good as new. Now, two and a half months on, he still got an occasional twinge of pain from the newly set bones, but on the whole Richard reckoned he'd got off lightly.

Standing on his own two feet had been a turning point which meant he could participate in the thousand and one physical tasks which were rota'd through the Capricorn week. This he did with an enthusiasm which made him wonder if that plane crash had actually altered his personality. Back home, Richard considered domestic chores a curse, but here he found himself enjoying the laundry sessions, the duties in the galley helping Murdo prepare the meals, the hours out in the drilling shed with Sean, maintaining the engine and generator. It was therapeutic, this mundane cycle of essential tasks; it voided his mind and seemed to banish the tick-tick-tock of the clock which was so slowly marking the hours of winter in his head.

And it gave him a break from thinking about Sophie.

Sophie. During the early days of that Capricorn winter, when he was still weak and dazed from the after-effects of the crash, Richard had been moved and grateful as Sophie's e-mails arrived almost daily. Her relief and joy that he'd been rescued was just what he'd needed, a familiar and sympathetic voice in a world which seemed to him to have taken some pretty vicious turns against him.

Breaking the news that he wasn't going to get home at all for the next seven months had not made things any better between them, particularly as it meant their wedding in her parents' home village in Suffolk—a full church affair with a three-hundred-guest reception—would have to be postponed.

That was when the e-mails started to change, with Sophie writing mournfully:

> It always was too good to be true. Fate has really done a good job on us this time, hasn't it? I'd only decided on the dress the day before you flew to Antarctica, and now it's sitting in the cupboard like a spare rag. Dad says you should sue the newspaper for sending you in the first place. Mum's just as gutted as I am. Anyway, I will wait here for you to get back, and then we'll start again. But, Richard, you can't believe how difficult this has all been, what with having to contact all three hundred guests and explain why we've had to cancel for this summer.

By early June, their correspondence had deteriorated further:

> This is the week we should be decorating the flat together, the week we agreed we'd find the sofa, the bed and all the things we need. I thought about going and choosing on my own, but what's the point . . . it's supposed to be us, doing things together, that was the whole point of us getting married, wasn't it? Now, I walk into the flat and it just feels so empty and hollow. I'm going to stay at home with my parents until you get back.

Richard had sat at the computer screen in the radio room for a very long time that day, searching for the words which would console, the words which would heal, the words which would make everything absolutely one hundred per cent all right. Then he had given up and retreated, deeply depressed, to the sanctity of his bedroom.

Now he made his way to the mess room, where he sat at the bar for a beer.

'What's up, Rich?' Murdo asked. 'Got the blues?'

'Kind of.' Richard toyed with his glass.

'Any particular reason?'

'You could say that. Today's the day I should be getting married.'

'Christ, that's a toughie. How's your dearly beloved taking it?'

Richard sighed. 'How do you think?'

'Oh dear.' Murdo went behind the bar and flipped open the fridge.

'She's had to cancel the church and the reception, her parents have lost money on the deposits for the caterers. You don't realise how much stuff goes on around a wedding until you have to cancel the damn thing.'

'Can't you just reschedule it?'

'That's what I keep telling her. I'll be airlifted out of here by October, so why not a November wedding? But no, that would be too bloody simple for Sophie, wouldn't it? She wants a summer wedding; that's what she's always dreamed of, and that's what she's sticking out for. So now we're looking at waiting a whole year before it can happen.'

Murdo cracked open a Guinness. 'Try and put it out of your mind,' he told the journalist. 'If you dwell on what's happening fourteen thousand miles away, you'll end up talking to the pixies.'

'But it's here. It's in my head. It doesn't matter how far away I am. How about you? You got someone back home?'

'Oh, aye. Got a girlfriend called Jan, she works in the kitchens at one of the big hotels in Aberdeen. We've been together since school.'

'Miss her?'

'To bits. But we're used to time apart, before I got into these Antarctic bases, I was working the rigs, and that's even tougher on a relationship, believe me.'

'You ever think of getting married?'

'Nah. No point really. We're both saving at the moment, getting psyched up for a big trip round the world. Twelve months on the road, no responsibilities, just the two of us living out of rucksacks on the quest for the perfect beach. That's what keeps me going when I get blue down here in nowhere land.'

'The really dangerous thing . . .' Richard continued hesitantly, 'is that I think I'm beginning to have second thoughts. I mean, Sophie and I were going through a hell of a rough patch last year, and then everything got a lot better after we decided to get married . . . but now, well, she's just giving me such a hard time over this bloody mess I've got myself into here. And it's not my fault. It's just not my fault at all.'

'D'you fancy a game of darts?'

'You know what, Murdo? You're really kind. But I'm not in the mood. I'll just take my beer to my room.'

As he passed the radio station, Frank called out:

'Richard. You've got mail.'

Frank tactfully left as Richard sat at the terminal and opened up his hotmail file.

Dear Richard,

I went to the church today. I had to, even though I know you'll be angry with me for doing it. It was a lovely afternoon, the sun as bright as I ever dreamed. The gardens smelled of jasmine and roses.

There was a couple just coming out, they must have taken our slot I suppose. And they just looked so bloody happy it made me want to scream. I didn't, of course. I just drove home, but I had a good scream in the car. And I need your shoulder to cry on now, more than ever before. Why haven't you sent me a message today? I need to hear from you now, not tomorrow.

Richard clicked on the mouse and closed the file, then sat for a long time just staring vacantly out into the dark otherworld of the Antarctic night.

God, I hate this place, he thought. When is this winter ever going to end?

40

Lauren went to the sun room and stripped off to her underwear for her session on the sun bed. The machine was still cooling off from the previous occupant, and she could tell from the sweet smell of coconut sun-tan oil that Murdo had been the last one on. She wiped down the surface with a towel (Murdo wasn't always the most fastidious of the Capricorn crew when it came to sweat removal, Lauren had discovered previously) and climbed onto the machine, the plastic creaking a little as she did so.

She placed the tiny protectors over her eyes and stretched out luxuriously beneath the buzzing brilliance of the ultraviolet tubes, enjoying the tingling sensation as her skin soaked up the rays. She let her body relax, putting all thoughts of work aside and thinking instead of the party that was being organised for that evening—the team's one hundredth day without sun, and the halfway point of the winter night.

From the sun bed it was straight to the sick room, where Mel was waiting with her scissors newly sharpened. Hairdressing was one of Mel's secondary duties, not that she liked it particularly, but she did as good a job as she could do on Lauren before taking the hot seat while Lauren returned the favour.

'We're not talking Toni and Guy, but it'll do,' Lauren said as she admired her handiwork.

'Doesn't matter anyway,' Mel told her. 'I'm not planning to pull tonight.'

'Men not up to your standards?'

'You know what they say, by the middle of winter there are no ugly women in Antarctica. But the darnedest thing is, there are still *plenty* of pig-ugly men.'

Lauren showered to remove the loose strands from her hair and dressed in a light-blue silk shirt and a clean pair of jeans—the nearest thing she had to partywear.

At the store, she found Murdo and Frank hard at work. They had pulled what looked like half a ton of canned and packaged food out into the corridor, and only the rear end of Murdo was visible as he searched the darkest corners of the cupboard.

'We're buggered without the bubbly!' he exclaimed, rummaging ever deeper.

'He's misplaced the champers,' Frank explained, 'and it seems to have made him a little stressed.'

There was an ecstatic yell from the depths of the cupboard, and a moment later Murdo emerged, beaming, with the case in hand.

The meal was a triumph, a 'candlelit extravaganza'—as Murdo put it—'fit for a king'. Assisted by Richard and Frank, the chef had roasted three chickens to perfection, lining them up with roasted potatoes, parsnips and all the trimmings. There were cheers from the crew as each steaming plate was brought in, and the champagne got a standing ovation.

The knowledge that they had successfully reached the halfway stage of winter had put the entire crew in an excellent frame of mind. There was a contented buzz of laughter around the table, eyes alive with candlelight as the champagne bottles emptied one by one.

For dessert Murdo produced caramelised apples with custard and cream, a dish which cunningly made good use of the dregs of their bruised apples. As the last of the desserts were finished, Lauren chinked a spoon on her glass and got the room quiet.

'I just wanted to say thanks,' she told them, 'for the first hundred days. We've had our problems, the genny failure and so on, but on the whole it's been pretty much how we planned it, and that's all down to your hard work. Murdo, you've kept us fed and watered, better than we could have ever hoped. Keep the breakfast pancakes going and we'll love you for ever! Mel, you've done wonders in the sick bay, the way you set Richard's legs was textbook stuff, and no matter how much frostbite and wind-burned flesh we throw at you, you still keep healing us and making us laugh.

'Frank, where would we be without you? Lost in a world without radio calls or e-mails, that really would be hell. And, Sean, well, apart from the genny problem, you've kept those engines—and the drilling operation—as sweet as pie, and that's a hell of a thing in these conditions.'

Lauren turned to Richard, Carl and Julian Fitzgerald. 'As for our three squatters, what can I say? Given the circumstances, you've all settled in better than I could have hoped.'

'Tell the truth, Lauren,' Murdo shouted good-naturedly. 'They're a bunch of wankers!'

A smiling Richard lobbed a chunk of bread across the table, hitting Murdo on the forehead.

'The most important thing,' Lauren continued, 'is that I want all of you to feel a part of the Capricorn team. I know you never asked to be here, I know there's been tension, and a bit of conflict here and there. But I want everyone to put that behind them and concentrate on making the next hundred days as positive and productive as we can. We're halfway through, guys, and it's all downhill from here. So let's raise our glasses and drink to Capricorn!'

'And the sun!' Frank added. 'Wherever the hell it's gone!'

'To the sun!' The team raised their glasses and downed their champagne.

Then Julian Fitzgerald stood.

'I wanted to add a brief word,' he told them, 'more in the way of an announcement, I suppose. I've been thinking about the way that my trans-Antarctic expedition failed, and I've realised that the potential is still there to finish off what Carl and I started. I've decided I'm going to give it another try. At the end of the winter. Go back to the place where I was forced to postpone the expedition, and set off—solo this time—to try and reach the edge of the continent. That way, the enterprise can still be successful, and I will still become the man to have crossed the Antarctic continent at its widest point!'

Fitzgerald raised his champagne glass.

'To adventure!' he exclaimed and sat back in his seat as a muted ripple of applause went round the table.

'I think that's very courageous indeed!' Richard called out. 'And may I be the first to wish you the best of luck!'

Cigars were circulated, and the base's single bottle of vintage port breached and distributed. Then it was over to the dartboard for a tournament which was destined to last into the early hours.

Lauren stayed at the table, and so did Fitzgerald.

'I don't want to pour cold water on your plans, Julian,' she told him, 'but how are you planning to get back to where you left off on the trek?'

Fitzgerald puffed on his cigar.

'Snowmobile, of course. Simply drive back down to the Blackmore.'

'And if I can't spare a snowmobile?'

'You've got four, haven't you? I'll pay you back when we all get back to Europe.'

Lauren was furious.

'Those snowcats cost eight thousand pounds.'

Fitzgerald shrugged.

'I'll talk to my sponsors,' he told her. 'That type of money's a drop in the ocean to them.'

'Don't you think it would have been courteous to *ask* me

first? You're talking about using the base's resources as if they're your own. Well, they're not, and they're in limited supply.'

'You can spare a couple of kilos of food.'

'Maybe, but that's not all you'll need. You'll be asking for navigation aids, drugs, camping equipment, skis and boots, a sledge . . . stuff that's irreplaceable out here and which we might need.'

'It's to the greater good,' Fitzgerald told her. 'I'm surprised you can't see the merit in the idea.'

'There's another thing,' Lauren continued. 'We've already put massive resources into one rescue; how do I know you won't screw up again and call us out for a second time?'

Fitzgerald's face puckered up with anger.

'That's one step short of slander,' he hissed. 'It was Carl that decided to quit.'

'That's not what he says.'

'Oh yes?' Fitzgerald leaned towards her, his eyes glittering. 'What does he say exactly?'

'Maybe you should read his book.'

Lauren regretted the words as soon as they had left her mouth.

Fitzgerald's eyes narrowed.

'So that *is* what he's doing in that sick bay all day? He *is* writing a book?'

'He's transcribing his diary. I gave him a laptop to get him interested in something. When I said a book, I mean he's copying his diary down . . . nothing more as far as I know.'

'As far as you know . . .'

For a while they sat in silence at the table, watching the darts tournament as it began to get heated. Then Fitzgerald broke the pause.

'I know about you and Sean,' he told her. 'You thought you'd kept that one quiet, didn't you?'

Lauren felt the blood drain from her face. 'What are you talking about?'

'I've seen enough. Very romantic . . . but not terribly professional to embark on a sexual relationship with one of your crew. Just the sort of blunder that causes friction, don't you think? I do hope the others don't find out.'

Fitzgerald blew a smoke ring, the rich blue circle drifting perfectly for a few seconds before breaking onto the back of an overturned bottle.

41

'Lauren, can we talk?'

Lauren turned away from the microscope and gave Sean her attention. 'Sure. What's up?'

'There's something bugging me, and I wanted to run it past you.'

'Talk.'

Sean pushed the laboratory door to and pulled a stool up to the workbench.

'Carl showed me a section of his expedition manuscript yesterday. And there's something about it which just doesn't add up at all. He's written this really graphic chapter describing in pretty gruesome detail the pain his body was going through and the starvation he was suffering after the rescue plane crashed.'

'And?'

'So what about the food and drugs which were in the plane? They must have been eating pretty well after Fitzgerald found that stuff.'

Lauren shook her head. 'I'm not getting you, Sean; which food and drugs are you talking about? As far as I remember, after you went down there our only conversation was about the state of the wreck and the conditions of the dead pilots.'

'In the back cabin there was a whole pile of debris, the remains of a big emergency food box. It'd all been eaten. There was a medical kit too, with morphine and bandages and so on, most of that was still intact.'

'Really? Why didn't you mention it to me?'

Sean looked a little shamefaced. 'Why should I have done? I just assumed they'd been sharing the stuff between them and anything left down there was excess to requirements.'

Sean paused as footsteps sounded in the corridor. He waited for whoever it was to pass.

'There's another thing,' he continued quietly. 'You remember how strange Fitzgerald was about me going down the crevasse . . . how insistent he got when I said I wanted to see the plane?'

Lauren nodded. 'You're right. He was pretty adamant about it. Why do you think that was?'

'Maybe there was something down there he wanted to hide. Maybe that's also why he was giving me such a weird look when he saw me with a packet of biscuits I picked up at the crash site . . . that confirmed to him that I *had* been down to the plane . . . and that I knew about the food.'

'You think he kept it all for himself,' Lauren asked, incredulous, 'and let the others starve?'

'Well . . . yeah. I don't see what else could have happened.'

A flash of fear crossed Lauren's face. 'You didn't mention this to Carl or Richard, did you?'

'I've got a mind to. Don't you think they deserve to know?'

'No, I don't! If we alert Carl and Richard that something's wrong, we run the risk of a row that could go on all winter. It could blow up in our faces, and that's the last thing we need. I'll find another way to check this out.'

Ten minutes later Lauren was back, her expression even more disturbed than before.

'I told Richard I was compiling a chart of his daily calorific intake to put on his file. He confirmed that from the moment of the crash to the time we arrived for the rescue he ate absolutely nothing whatsoever. And nor did Fitzgerald give him any medical supplies.'

Sean whistled.

'This is starting to look really bad. How could Fitzgerald do such a thing? He deliberately let those two men starve while he set about saving his own life.'

'Hold on,' Lauren said. 'One thing doesn't add up . . . if Fitzgerald was stacking himself up with calories, how come he was so weak when we arrived? You remember how he fell onto the ice like a baby?'

Sean shrugged. 'Maybe it was an act. Maybe he wanted us to *think* he was at death's door. I'm beginning to think he's capable of that. And he certainly wasn't *that* weak, because he'd been down to the aircraft several times, and that was pretty damn physical. Also, his recovery was astounding . . . he was back on his feet within a day, as right as rain.'

'You're right. He was way stronger than the other two.'

'We can't let him get away with this, Lauren.' Sean went to the door. 'We have to tell them what he did. It's going to eat away at me all winter if we don't.'

Lauren stood, her voice low and insistent.

'Please, Sean. This place is on a hair trigger as it is. There's enough bad blood between Carl and Fitzgerald without us pouring gasoline on the fire. Let it go, Sean, for the sake of the base.'

'All right. But it's not the type of secret I relish keeping.'

Sean turned and left.

42

Mel and Lauren were peeling potatoes in the galley on the one hundred and twenty-fifth day of winter, the doctor obviously itching to get some gossip off her chest. She waited until Murdo was out of earshot.

'You're a dark horse,' Mel told Lauren with a sly smile.

'What do you mean?'

'There's a rumour going round the base that you and Sean are doing some drilling practice of your own, if you know what I mean. Not that I'd blame you, of course; he is pretty gorgeous.'

'Who told you that?' Lauren asked, knowing the answer already.

'Just a little bird,' Mel said coyly, 'but a juicy titbit like that doesn't stay secret for long.'

'The whole base knows?' Lauren was aghast.

'So you admit it! You are shagging him! And I had you down for a number-one ice queen. So much for all your stuff about base discipline, eh?'

Lauren threw a half-peeled potato into the pail and ran to Fitzgerald's room.

'Are you in there, Julian?' She rapped on the door. 'I want to talk.'

She tried the handle, but the door was locked.

'I don't appreciate your lies!' Lauren shouted through the panel. 'You've gone a step too far. Come out here!'

But the explorer remained silent, and for forty-eight hours Lauren did not see him around the base. He remained in his room, no noise audible from within, not even emerging to take his meals.

'You think he's still sulking in there?' Murdo asked her finally. 'Surely he must need food by now?'

'Leave him be,' Lauren instructed. 'I'm sick of his pathetic games. If he thinks he can freak us out by going quiet on us, he's wrong. As far as I care, he can stay in there for the rest of the winter.'

Fitzgerald's mysterious absence resulted in a mood of uneasy calm, but a small surge of optimism ran through the team as Sean announced, day after day, the drilling progress towards the lake.

Lauren and Sean had little time to relax, every waking moment devoted to the drilling operation out in the shed. They kept the engine running twenty-four hours a day, taking it in turns to supervise the power unit which was the heart of the entire venture.

It was after one midafternoon shift that Lauren was accosted by a harassed-looking Frank as she removed her outdoor clothes in the corridor.

'You are not going to *believe* what Fitzgerald's done now.'

'What are you talking about?'

'He's been talking to the press again.'

'So?'

'De Pierman's office just faxed through today's front page from the *Daily Mirror*.'

Frank handed Lauren the document, which revealed a huge picture of Fitzgerald and the headline 'Prisoner!'

'Oh, Christ.'
Lauren read on . . .

A dramatic clandestine radio call from explorer Julian
Fitzgerald has revealed his bizarre plight at the hands of
Capricorn base commander Lauren Burgess. Transmitting in secret at three a.m. Antarctic time, the eminent
explorer revealed how he is now held under virtual *house
arrest* at the remote base.

'The problem started when I announced I was thinking about resuming my solo trek,' the explorer told us in
the whispered conversation. 'These scientists can't bear
the thought that someone else might eclipse their own
publicity. That's why they've *forbidden* me to leave the
base. It's pure professional jealousy and nothing more.
Now I'm a prisoner here, my ambitions thwarted by the
paranoia of the base commander.'

Lauren continued to read, her lips tight with rage:

Fitzgerald also revealed that he suspects other reasons
for the gagging order. 'I know too much about their objectives,' he told our reporter. 'They may be masquerad-
ing as scientists, but their real purpose is to find mineral
wealth. Everyone knows that Antarctica is heaving with
reserves of gold, oil and other minerals.'

'De Pierman's waiting on the radio link for you now,'
Frank told Lauren. 'I think this has pushed him over the
edge.'

'Pushed *him* over the edge?' Lauren stormed. 'What
about *me*? I've had enough of this, Frank, I really have.'

They ran to the radio room, where Lauren picked up the
handset.

'Alexander, I cannot apologise enough for this . . . this
rubbish!'

'Give me one good reason why I shouldn't cut all my

connections with Capricorn,' De Pierman demanded, 'and my funding too. My interest in your project was in promoting the science, but I'm going to have to disassociate myself from Capricorn if this gets any worse. I can't have this type of press hanging over me, it's just not good for business.'

'That's clear, Alexander, and I understand your concerns. But if you pull the plug now, then how can we possibly win?' Lauren told him. 'It would be a tragedy to give up now. We're drilling twenty-four hours a day, and it's going really well.'

'That's as may be. But no one's going to give a damn about the results in the face of this type of sensationalism. That bloody explorer is ruining everything. Can't you shut him up, for God's sake?'

'I thought I had,' Lauren replied.

'Well, you clearly underestimated him. Now the question is what are you going to do about it?'

A sudden idea occurred to Lauren.

'Hold the line, Alexander; I want to confer with my radio operator for a moment.'

She turned to Frank. 'What do you say we ban Fitzgerald from all radio comms? This is getting well beyond a joke, and I can't think of any other way that's going to take the heat off us.'

A broad smile swept Frank's face.

'There's a typed-in password facility on the satellite link,' he said. 'I deactivated it at the beginning of the winter, but I can easily set it up with a new password so that Fitzgerald won't be able to sneak in and use it in the night.'

'OK. Let's do it.'

Lauren picked up the handset. 'We're going to bar him from the radio comms, Alexander, at least until he can give us a guarantee he's going to behave himself.'

'Good plan.' The relief was tangible in De Pierman's voice. 'If they can't get any new lies out of your blabbermouth down there, I guess the press will move on to some other story soon enough.'

'Signing off now. And thank you for sticking with us, Alexander. It'll be worth it in the end, I promise you.'

'I hope so, Lauren; I really do. Over and out.'

'Listen to that,' Frank told her, putting his ear to the silent speaker with an expression of bliss on his face. 'The sound of silence.'

Lauren smiled grimly. 'Give us some peace and quiet,' she said. 'Right now that's exactly what we want.'

Lauren went to Fitzgerald's room, only to find the door still locked.

'You're poisoning this whole operation, Julian!' she called through the door. 'You are banned from using the radio link as of now. We've put an access password on the satellite connection, and you're not going to be given it. If you start behaving yourself, we'll reconsider.'

There was no response from within the room.

'I know you can hear me,' Lauren called again. 'Your shit-stirring is over, Julian, over for good!'

Lauren went to her laboratory to write up some notes, feeling better than she had done for days.

43

Fitzgerald was building up his stash, little by little, night by night. The opportunities were not difficult to exploit, for none of the Capricorn stores were ever locked, and for six to eight hours every night he could cherry-pick the provisions he needed, package by package, tin by tin.

Tonight he was in the food store for no more than a couple of minutes, careful not to disturb the order of the boxes, wary of taking too much from any one of Murdo's supply chests in case he became suspicious. He knew precisely what he needed, long experience of hauling expeditions meant he needed no list other than the one which was in his head.

He placed the spoils in a canvas rucksack and walked the corridor to where his outdoor clothing was hanging on its hook.

The question of what to do with his gains was one which had taxed the explorer for a few sleepless nights. He had thought about hiding them beneath the base, in the gap between the glacier surface and the raised, insulated floor. But that was too obvious, as was the roof cavity and the loft space in the generator shed.

In the end he had acquired a small shovel and gone out into the endless night with the idea of digging a hiding hole somewhere discreet. As it happened, an easier solution had presented itself, and that was where he was heading now as he zipped himself into his thermals and stepped out onto the glacier.

The explorer brought out his compass and waited patiently until his eyes had adjusted enough to the dark to be able to see the illuminated face. He clicked round the dial and set it to due east, and, after a cursory glance over his shoulder to check that no one was watching him from the base, he set out on the bearing. He was counting his steps, ticking them off beneath his breath as he crunched across the glacier.

At five hundred paces he stopped, looking around until he spotted the dark crack across the ice. This was his target, a tiny fissure which would one day open into a crevasse, but which for the moment was just a metre or so deep and a couple of hand's-breadths wide. The ice cap was criss-crossed everywhere with these wrinkles of pressure, and the explorer had spotted this one as perfect for his purposes.

He checked back towards the base once more, seeking a shadow or a torchlight which would betray a follower. Then he began to unload the contents of his small pack. He'd gone for the nutritious foods, the ones which would deliver maximum calorific value when it came to the trek: there were a few different types of pasta, some tinned stews, a half-dozen cans of tuna, dried apricots and prunes. The weight of the tins was worrying, that would add to the load when he came to haul the sledge, but there was little he could do about it under the circumstances.

Fitzgerald packed the items carefully into the bottom of the small crevice, alongside the gas stove, butane cylinders and other essential items he had carefully been accumulating over the previous weeks. Slowly, slowly, a box of matches here, a tarpaulin there, he had built up the stash. No one had noticed, so far as he knew, and no one would if the explorer could help it. This was a good insurance, Fitzgerald reasoned, a hedge against the certainty that Lauren would refuse to supply him when it came to the crunch.

The base commander's reluctance to back his bid to restart his trans-Antarctic trek had struck Fitzgerald as particularly unfair. He deserved her support, and the fact that it wasn't forthcoming had created a smouldering ember of resentment inside him.

That, and the way she had given Carl a laptop. That was even worse.

It was a conspiracy, of course; Fitzgerald had already deduced that it was no accident that Lauren had given Carl the word processor. She *wanted* his lies to be made public; she *wanted* Fitzgerald to be humiliated and cowed. No doubt she had encouraged Carl, egged him on, tempted him with tales of massive publishing advances: that was why he had decided to start typing.

And where would it end? Two rival publications coming out at the same time, each telling a story from a totally different perspective? How would the public react? Fitzgerald wondered if his loyal fans would snub Carl's book. He knew them, the people who bought his books, who hung on his every word at public lectures in halls and clubs all over the land. He smiled and shook their hands; he listened with a smile to their tales of how a nephew, a cousin, a sister or an aunt had once climbed a mountain in the Alps. They were *his* people, not Carl's—and it had taken him a lifetime of exploration, of suffering, to build that loyalty up.

And now everything was under threat.

Fitzgerald patted the snow back into place around the top of the fissure and admired his handiwork with the headtorch. He knew there was virtually no chance that anyone from Capricorn could accidentally stumble across his secret stash, but he wasn't about to make it easier for them if they did. The work was good, he saw with satisfaction, the ice smooth and giving nothing away. Someone could pass a metre away and never know it was there.

Fitzgerald stood, stretching a little to ease the stiffness in his back. Far off, he could see the lights of the base, beckoning and warm, the faint hum of the generator carried to him on the light wind.

Best of all, towards the northeast, he could see the faintest of glows on the horizon. It was the gentlest yellow, so subtle, so pallid it might have been a trick of his eyes, but Fitzgerald knew what it meant: that winter had turned, that the sun would—within the next couple of months—once again pour light into this blacked-out continent. He took a deep breath, the dry, frosted air searing his lungs with small, familiar pinpricks of pain.

Soon it would be time to go.

44

Lauren could feel the muscles in her shoulders tense up as she waited in the drilling shed for the seven hundred and ninety-fourth extension to come up the bore on the wireline. The critical phase of the drilling operation was about to commence—the day on which they would break through to the under-ice lake and attempt to extract a precious water sample.

In the next hour they would de-rig the conventional cutting tool, fit the custom-built final extraction head and send it on its way into the black depths of the ice cap on its one and only journey.

'Here she comes. And not a single break on the line,' Sean said with pride as the metre-long cutting head came smoothly up the bore with a satisfying hissing sound, spewing a little sludgy kerosene onto the floor as it emerged.

'Don't speak too soon,' Lauren warned him. 'The show's not over yet.'

Sean cut the power to the wireline winch and hitched the

cutting head to the block and tackle which was suspended from the drill shed's main gantry. Lauren and Frank put on their thin leather work gloves and helped him with the bolts, working as fast as they could to minimise the exposure of their hands to the frozen metal. When they had the cutting head free, they swung it to one side and onto a wheeled trolley which was stowed in the storage area.

'Time for Big Boy,' Sean said, rubbing his hands together with relish. 'This is going to be fun.'

'Big Boy' was the nickname Sean had given to the next piece of equipment to go down the bore, a one-off, two-hundred-thousand-dollar piece of drilling innovation, which they now lifted from its protective flight case.

Lauren and Sean had struggled long and hard over the design for the final extraction device. Crashing the main drill bit into the lake and pumping out a sample was the simplest option (the technology for this would be the same as for a conventional oil exploration bore), but would lead to unacceptable levels of contamination. The sample had to be pristine or there was no way for subsequent analysis to determine what was from the lake's ecosystem and what was foreign.

'That's a laboratory down there,' Lauren had explained to Sean. 'It's been untouched by the outside world for twenty-five million years, so it would be a bit of an embarrassment if we screwed it up now.'

Back in London they had spent several months agonising over the design for the extractor, dreaming up and discarding dozens of ideas, and consulting with mining engineers all over the world, until someone came up with the comment: 'What you need is not a drill extractor, you need a giant biopsy needle.' The throw-away remark led Lauren into fruitful new terrain, and the more she looked at the technology of biopsy core needles, the more she realised that the problems—and objectives—of biopsies were the same as her objectives with the lake.

A biopsy needle is required to retrieve a completely un-contaminated tissue sample from an organ deep within a patient's body. To achieve this, a relatively large-diameter hollow needle is inserted as close as possible to the organ to be sampled, at that point, a sterile and finer-core sampling needle which rides inside the outer sheath is then fired—normally hydraulically—into the target organ, where it cuts the tissue core. Then the internal needle retracts and the entire device can be retrieved.

If they could engineer a massive sterile probe—in effect a giant biopsy needle—into the middle of a cutting head, Lauren wondered, could they use that to penetrate the lake?

Lauren and Sean had borrowed the biopsy technology, expanded and adapted it and then commissioned a specialist drill bit manufacturer in Norway to turn the designs into reality. The result was Big Boy, one hundred and forty kilos of titanium and chrome, which would shortly be sent on a journey down to the bore end, where it would be less than one metre from the roof of the lake. When they were sure it was in position, the hydraulic 'needle'—several inches in diameter—would be spun out of the cutting head and slowly rammed through the ice, its progress eased by a heated annulus at its tip.

A radio echo sounder was built into the device, and, connected to a screen at the surface, it would enable an operator to judge the instrument's proximity to the lake. The hard, polished roof of the lake cavity would be perfect for this task as its radio signal would be totally different to the solid, compacted ice which surrounded it.

Then came the fine judgement. Inches before the final breakthrough, the sterile inner probe—this one of less than half a centimetre diameter—would be fired into the lake itself, where it would suck out no more than a litre of fluid and then snap back into the sleeve, in less than a second. If all went well, Big Boy would be pulled back up on the wireline with the sample safely intact.

'Let's get it down there,' Sean said.

They rigged up the extractor, and Sean sent the unit down the wire. Lauren felt her stomach turn as she watched it descend, and, as she sat at the radio echo monitor with Frank, she noticed her hands were shaking.

A few minutes passed before Sean confirmed the unit was in position.

'Turning on the heater core now.' Sean activated the switch which sent power down to the tip of the cutting head.

Lauren and Frank focused on the neon-green screen of the radio echo monitor, watching intently as the fuzzy edges converged centre screen, minute by minute, into a well-defined line which was unmistakably a harder barrier.

'That's the roof of the cavity.' Frank pointed to a lozenge-shaped mass. 'We're about thirty centimetres off.'

'Stop the burner, Sean.'

'Heater off.'

Seven hundred and ninety-four metres beneath them, the fragile heated tip of the probe began to cool.

'Give it three minutes to let it freeze,' Lauren instructed Sean. 'When the needle goes in, I don't want any meltwater going in with it.'

They waited, Lauren watching the seconds tick past on her wristwatch, knowing that if the next stage failed they would be going home empty-handed. And, if they had con-taminated the lake, things would be even worse. Lauren knew there were plenty of environmental pressure groups waiting to analyse Capricorn's results. News that the team had inadvertently tainted a hitherto pristine reservoir of life would make future fundraising virtually impossible and could blacken Lauren's reputation for good.

'Go ahead.'

'I think the honour's yours,' Sean told her.

Lauren held her breath and pressed the button which would release the final stage of the probe. There was a hiss of compressed air as the hydraulic ram was activated. Sec-onds later a green light came on on the instrument panel.

'Second-stage probe successfully deployed,' Frank said, unable to disguise the slight tremble in his voice, 'and back in its sleeve.'

'Acquisition?' Lauren asked him.

Frank checked the gauge which monitored the contents

of the probe's sterile internal tank. 'Acquisition confirmed,' he told her. 'The tank is full.'

'That's it?' Sean shouted in joy. 'We reached the lake!'

Lauren stared at the instrument panel in delight.

'It worked!' she cried. 'It really worked! Now get that thing back up here quickly before the whole unit freezes in.'

Sean powered up the wireline and Big Boy began its three-quarter-kilometre ascent back up the bore. These were still anxious moments: if the core collapsed, or the wireline broke, they could still lose the sample.

Four minutes later the unit was swinging free from the gantry, the inspection hatch on the side opened to reveal the titanium container in which the lake sample was stored. Lauren unscrewed the specimen container from its position and held it reverently in her hands. She found herself lost for words, all the tension of the past hours spilling from her as she savoured the moment.

'That's it.' Sean smiled as he took a rag to wipe away her tears. 'Hell of a lot of effort to get your hands on a litre of water!'

Sean disengaged the drive unit for the bore and waited for the revolutions to stop. Then he hit the kill switch for the Perkins. The huge engine shuddered to a halt with surprising suddenness, leaving them in silence bar the rumble of the wind rushing around the exterior of the shed.

'How long will it take you to work out the results?'

'Forty-eight hours to see if we have a success or not, two or three weeks before I'll be ready to announce anything to the world.'

Lauren hurried away, the precious sample tucked into her windsuit.

45

Julian Fitzgerald lay back on the bench and wrapped his hands round the rubber grips of the weight bar which was suspended above him. He flexed his arms, clicked the bones in his fingers and took a deep breath, pushing the forty-kilo load to the mechanical limit of the machine and then letting it slowly down to his chin before exhaling and repeating the movement. The weight felt good, the muscles in his arms warming quickly as he got into the rhythm of push-rest-push, a light sheen of sweat breaking out on his brow as he stared into the ceiling lights above him.

The weight room was a good place to be, the explorer had found, such a good place that he devoted anything up to six hours of his day to the process of honing his body back into shape. It was a familiar business, this test of pain, a way of blocking the frustrations which seemed to be growing daily inside him.

Capricorn. This prison. Fitzgerald hated every moment of this winter endurance, wanted with every fibre of his body this dark, testing nightmare to end. He was missing opportunities, losing money hand over fist; back in Europe, long-arranged lecturing commitments had had to be cancelled, lucrative new sponsorship deals put on hold. By the time Fitzgerald got back, he knew that interest in his Antarctic story would be waning . . . that some other explorer would be capturing the public interest with a fresher, perhaps more successful tale.

And how the days dragged. He had tried to write, spent interminable hours in front of his laptop screen, only to encounter a writer's block as stubborn as any he had ever known. Normally, he was a fast and efficient author, turning his expeditions into gripping factual accounts which rarely failed to make the best-seller lists.

But this time it was different. Despite the fact that this unasked-for winter layover had given him a seemingly ideal situation to put his story into words, Fitzgerald found himself sitting listlessly at his desk, cup after cup of coffee drunk with no progress on the manuscript. Part of it was his own frustration, the knowledge deep down that, no matter how he tried to dress up the achievements of his trans-Antarctic trek, he could never shake off the stigma that it had ultimately failed.

That Carl had made him fail.

Now the weight was really telling, the mechanical swish-swish of the machine pounding up and down as ligaments and tiny internal sinews in Fitzgerald's arms began to ripple and stretch. He checked the clock on the wall, seeing with satisfaction that he had already been bench-pressing for twenty minutes, more than most men his age could manage. He wouldn't give up, not till every last vestige of strength had been tested and probed to its limit.

Carl. His expedition partner was still an unresolved problem. As was the question of the rival book which Lauren had clumsily revealed to him. Carl was writing like crazy, the explorer knew; he spent most of his waking hours tapping away in the medical bay and was rarely seen anywhere else in the base.

What were Carl's plans? Had he e-mailed a publisher already? Perhaps he already had a contract. Fitzgerald felt the sweat running into his eyes as he pushed the pace yet harder. How many words a day could Carl produce? Was he one of those people who could churn out two, three thousand words every day without fail? If so, he might already have the best part of a manuscript complete, a block of digital information which could be sent via the satellite in a matter of seconds to any publisher he chose.

With a final long exhalation of breath, Fitzgerald let the weight bar down. He swung himself back into a sitting position and rubbed the sweat from his face and neck with a towel, waiting for his heart rate to return to its normal resting pace.

It was time for a confrontation, he knew, time to find out from Carl what the hell he thought he was up to.

Fitzgerald made his way to the medical bay, where he found his fellow expeditioner sitting up in his bed, the laptop positioned on his knees.

'How are you feeling?' Fitzgerald asked him.

Carl stopped typing and looked at the explorer suspiciously. 'What do you want?'

'Nothing. Just checking you're doing all right. Hadn't seen you out and about around the base, that's all.'

'Leave me alone,' Carl told him. 'I don't need your sympathy.'

Fitzgerald sat on the bed and tapped the back of the laptop with his hand. 'Working on anything in particular?' he asked.

Carl resumed his typing. 'Just some correspondence.'

'Eight hours a day?'

'I write long letters.'

Fitzgerald stood, crossing to the sink, where he ran some water into his hands. He splashed some on his face, drying himself off with the towel as he looked out of the window at the black winter night.

'You're not writing a book about our expedition?' he asked.

'I don't have to answer that question, Julian, so I'm not going to.'

'Because you know you can't. By law. You signed a contract with me before we set out, remember?'

'What's wrong, Julian? What are you scared of?'

'I'm not scared of anything. I just wouldn't want there to be any . . . misunderstanding between us.'

'Misunderstanding?' Carl managed a bitter laugh. 'Oh, you needn't worry about that.'

'You are, aren't you? That's what you're doing in here, all day, every day. That's why you never come out for your meals, why you lie in here like some goddamn invalid. You're writing a bloody book!'

Carl said nothing, but resumed his typing.

'You won't find a publisher,' Fitzgerald told him. 'My lawyer will see to that.'

'You're talking about your precious gagging clause? That pathetic so-called contract you forced me to sign? Well, I no longer agree to it. It's a fundamental breach of my right of freedom of speech.'

'It's enforceable by law.'

'There is no law here, Julian, or hadn't you noticed that? I can write what I want, when I like, and there's not a damn thing you can do about it.'

There was a pause in the conversation while Carl continued to type. Fitzgerald sat on the bed, itching to rip the laptop from his hands and only restraining himself with some difficulty.

'Is it a question of money?' Fitzgerald asked him after a while. 'Because, if it is, I think I can propose a compromise.'

Carl said nothing.

'I'll cut you in for thirty per cent of the profit from my book of the expedition,' Fitzgerald went on, 'but only on the condition that you abandon any thought of writing a book of your own. How does that sound?'

'No deal,' Carl told him. 'This isn't about the money, Julian, and you know it . . . although I dare say my account— that is, if I *was* writing one—might even attract a bigger advance than your own.'

The two men stared at each other for a while. Fitzgerald broke the silence.

'The law is on my side, Carl. I'll take out an injunction if I need to.' With that, he stood to go. As he reached the door, the tap-tap of Carl's fingers on the laptop keyboard had already begun.

Fitzgerald went back to the weights room, where Mel was midway through her daily session on the rowing machine.

'Good morning,' she said, brightly.

Fitzgerald ignored her, lying once more on the bench-press machine and this time selecting sixty kilos on the bar. He let the weight press down, his already overexercised muscles cracking a little with the stress. Push-rest-push. Fitzgerald focused on the ceiling lights and let his body take the pain, the hot flare of anger burning inside him, brighter than he had known before.

46

Lauren called Mel into the laboratory, where she had been analysing the samples. When she spoke, her voice was unsteady.

'Mel. Can you take a look at this, please? I want to be sure I'm not imagining these.'

Mel put her eye to the viewer on the compound microscope, her reaction immediate. 'What the hell are they?'

'Well, they don't exist in any textbook I've ever seen, that's for sure.'

Mel watched the circular organisms twist and turn. 'They're beautiful.'

'They're more than beautiful,' Lauren laughed. 'They're exquisite; they're gorgeous. We did it, Mel: we found life!'

The two women embraced in their excitement.

'We have to tell the others,' Mel said. 'Do you want me to go and fetch them?'

'Keep it secret for a while. I need to do a further test,'

Lauren told her. 'There's something about these organisms that doesn't add up, and I want to be sure of my facts.'

An hour later Mel returned to find Lauren ashen-faced.

'Can you call the team in now, please? I've got an announcement to make.'

Within minutes the team had assembled in the laboratory.

'Put us out of our misery, Lauren. Do we have life down there or not?' Frank asked her impatiently.

'Oh, we have life, Frank . . . we have life in abundance.' Lauren could not keep the huge smile from her face. 'But not as we know it, so to speak.'

'You mean new species?'

'New species, but with a twist. In fact with the ultimate twist.'

Lauren paused, enjoying the hushed expectation of her assembled team.

'The sample we pulled out of the rig last night is teeming with diatoms. Our theory about the lake was correct. But these creatures are not following the normal rules of life as we understand them.'

'How so?' Sean took a look into the compound microscope. 'What's the big deal?'

'The big deal is that one of the fundamentals of science has been to try and discover what the basic requirements for life actually are. Until the late seventies, we thought that solar power was the deal breaker as it were, that without the energy of the sun there would be no life on the planet. Then, in the late seventies, scientists from the NSF began to investigate hydrothermal vents on the sea bed off Hawaii. We're talking really deep on the ocean floor, so deep there's no light at all. By rights there shouldn't be anything living there, but there was . . . tardigrades and crustaceans, big complex creatures that were harvesting geothermal energy. That discovery changed the textbooks; it meant that life could exist without solar energy by utilising a supply of carbon . . . and energy.'

Mel peered into the eyepiece of the compound microscope. 'So that's what these creatures are doing?'

'Not at all,' Lauren said, 'and that's why we're into exciting new territory here. We already know there's no light down in that lake, and now I find these samples show virtually no traces of carbon at all, less than one part in ten million. This microbial life is breaking all the rules . . . by the standards of our current science, it shouldn't be able to live down there at all.'

'So if it has no light and no carbon, what's its secret?' Frank asked.

Lauren couldn't prevent the excited smile which lit up her face. 'Silicon,' she said. 'The tests I've just finished show these diatoms have hydrated silicon shells.'

'And where do they get the silicon from?'

'The volcano beneath the lake. Silicon comes from igneous rocks, and active volcanoes are a prime source. These single-celled creatures have evolved a method of harvesting it, and they've been successfully doing that in an environment which has been deprived of air, and sunlight, for at least twenty-five million years.'

'So these are new to science?'

'New to the planet, to be more accurate. There's even the possibility that these creatures may have an extraterrestrial origin, that they came to earth on a meteorite or other space debris, got locked into the lake and never looked back.'

'And where will this discovery lead?' Mel asked.

'That's the really interesting part. The sample we're dealing with here comes from the very top stratum of the lake, the furthest from any volcanic energy source. The next step is to come back with a more sophisticated probe, a robot submarine, and explore the sediment layers which we know lie at the bottom. Then we might be talking big drama, and possibly big creatures too. The fact that there's more than one species of silicon-based diatom means there's competition for resources. Where there's competition, food chains evolve, and the closer to the energy source we can get, the more chance we have of finding significant macrofauna.'

'Silicon-based macrofauna?'

'Precisely.'

'Hold it right there,' Sean laughed. 'Are we talking big scary monsters? I mean, I don't want to be a sceptic or anything, but just because you found a few microscopic creatures, that doesn't mean you're going to find anything bigger.'

'Want to bet?' Lauren responded. 'How many links in the food chain do you think separate the single-celled diatoms that float around the oceans of the world, and a one-hundred-and-twenty-ton blue whale?'

'I have no idea. Hundreds, I guess.'

'The answer is one. The Antarctic krill, *Euphausia superba*. Krill eat diatoms, blue whales eat krill. That one-centimetre-long creature is the only link between the smallest and biggest beings on the planet. So it's not the least bit unlikely that there could be significant macrofauna down there in that lake. All we have to do is get a robot sub in there and find it.'

'How much would that cost?' Frank asked.

Lauren hazarded a guess. 'It's big, complicated science. I doubt you'd get much change from fifty million for such a project. Capricorn would have to be quadrupled in size to pull something like that off, and we'd need a far bigger team.'

'Think you'd find the money?'

Lauren held up one of the test-tube samples. 'With these samples we can raise any amount of money we like. We've pulled off something amazing here, and there'll be no shortage of money to extend the science. I think we've guaranteed the life of this research base for at least the next five years . . . and for me that is just a dream come true.'

'I get the feeling this might be an excuse for a few beers,' Murdo said, his face beaming at the prospect.

The party began after the evening meal, the tables pushed back in the mess room to create an impromptu dance floor. Murdo pumped up the stereo as high as he dared without blowing a speaker while Mel dragged one protesting victim after another onto the floor for dancing exhibitions which had them all in stitches.

Frank won the prize for worst dancer of the night, his enthusiastic gyrations to a fifties rock classic managing to beat even Murdo and Lauren's hilariously uncoordinated attempt at a tango.

Fitzgerald was the only one who didn't participate in the festivities. He sat at the bar all evening, downing one can of Guinness after another and making little attempt to converse with anyone else, or even to acknowledge their existence.

'Don't you think it would be better for everyone if you joined in?' Lauren challenged him.

'Not really,' the explorer replied, not bothering to look her in the face.

'And while you're about it,' Murdo chipped in, 'don't forget those Guinnesses you're drinking come from my allocation. Every one of those you down comes out of my stash for the winter.'

Fitzgerald reached behind the bar and pulled out another can. He clicked back the ring pull and began to pour the black liquid into his glass.

'That's it, you bastard,' Murdo screamed. 'I'm going to teach you some fucking manners.'

The chef launched himself towards Fitzgerald, fists raised to strike as Lauren and Sean piled in to restrain him. The scuffle went on for a few seconds before they had Murdo under control.

'Forget it, Murdo,' Sean shouted at him. 'He's not worth it.'

Fitzgerald took his beer and retired to his room.

47

'I've prepared the press release,' Lauren told Frank as she entered the radio room. 'It's time to tell the world what we've found.'

Frank was consulting a technical manual at the bench, a puzzled expression creasing his face. 'Not right now you won't. The satellite unit's down.'

'What's new?' Lauren wasn't initially concerned. Radio telephone links from Antarctica rely on connections with satellites which lie barely above the northern horizon, and a medium-sized storm can disrupt signals for days. There had been many occasions that winter when the base had been unable to reach the outside world for twenty-four hours or more. Privately, Lauren had quite welcomed these brief interludes of peace—at least it kept her troublesome sponsor off her back.

'I don't mean a weather problem,' Frank told her. 'I mean the whole system is dead. I can't even get it to power up.'

'Antarctic gremlin?'

Frank switched the unit on and off. 'Listen to the speakers: there's not even any static. It's most peculiar. I've had the fuse board out of the front panel, but they all seem intact.'

Lauren checked the five fuses and agreed they were fine.

'I've got the manufacturer's fault-finding guide here,' Frank tossed the pamphlet on the workbench, 'but it's as good as useless. It's limited to the basic stuff and pretty much says, if it's anything more than a fuse or a switch falling off, return it to the manufacturer under warranty.'

'Great. Have you had a go with the voltmeter?'

'Sure. I've been checking the circuitry through as far as I can, but my electronics only goes so far. If it was a standard radio, or even if I could recognise a transistor or two, I'd be in with a fighting chance, but we're talking rows and rows of chips, and to be honest I'm not at all confident I know what I'm doing in there.'

'So what can we tell?'

'OK . . . there's power going into it. But there's nothing coming out. Something's gone wrong with the circuitry. I guess one of the components failed.'

'You're sure it's not the satellite dish? Maybe it got dislodged or iced up?'

'The dish is fine. First thing I did was to check it.'

'How's the back-up radio if we have an emergency?' she asked him.

'Well, it's there if we need it.' Frank gestured to the ancient longwave transmitter they had brought as a standby for just this eventuality. 'But you know how fickle it can be.'

'Let's have a look at the guts of this thing.'

Frank pulled back the front fascia of the satellite transmitter and they peered without much hope at the many circuit boards which were stacked within the instrument panel.

'See what I mean?' Frank said. 'We're talking chip city.'

Lauren sighed as she contemplated the workings; like Frank, her electronics was good—but not this good. 'We'll just have to test the power output of each chip,' she said. 'Put the fine probe on the voltmeter, and we'll see if one of these babies has died on us. Do we have any spares?'

'I checked in the electronics reserve kit. We've got dupli-
cates for most of these chips, thank God, so if we do find a
dead one we can probably replace it.'

'While you're doing that, I'll get on the back-up and see
if I can raise a ground station while the weather's still good
enough to get one. We should let our sponsors know we have
a comms problem or they might start to worry about us if we
go completely dead.'

Lauren left Frank to his task and played with the radio
transmitter for ten minutes or so before she managed to raise
a ground station through the waves of static. The receiving
operator was sitting in a New Zealand base at the edge of the
continent almost twelve hundred miles away, and the connection was so distorted and faint that Lauren had to shout to
make herself heard. Finally, she got the message through,
along with Alexander De Pierman's office number in London and the e-mail address of the British Antarctic Survey in
Cambridge.

'Tell them we're working on a problem with our satellite
comms. We've only got the standard radio operational right
now,' she yelled, 'so not to worry if they don't hear from us
for a while. It might take us a week or more to get this
sorted.'

'Roger that,' came the response. Then the connection
faded completely.

Lauren returned to the workbench and assisted Frank
with his task. They attached the voltmeter to the chips on the
motherboard one by one, registering positive output for
them all.

'These all seem to be powered up,' Lauren observed. 'Do
we have a circuit diagram to try and work out what their
functions are supposed to be?'

'I was hoping it wouldn't come to that,' Frank said, 'but
we do have one, yes.'

While Lauren continued with the voltmeter, Frank began
to consult the circuit diagram, patiently ticking off the components as listed against the circuit boards installed and trying to make some sense of the design.

For the length of the afternoon they worked side by side, getting more and more frustrated by the task.

Finally, Frank exclaimed: 'Look at this connector—it's empty.'

Lauren looked at the space he was pointing to, not noticing anything odd about it.

'So? There's always empty connectors in a complicated circuit system like this one. Look, there's empty gaps on the other boards too.'

'I know,' Frank said patiently, 'but I've checked them all off against the circuit diagram, and there's definitely a chip missing from this one.'

'No way.' Lauren looked at him in amazement.

'Believe me.'

'Which means what, exactly?'

'Someone removed it. To disable the comms.'

'My God,' Lauren whispered. 'Someone in the base opened this thing up and *stole* one of the chips?'

'Seems bloody hard to believe, but, yes, that's about the sum of it.'

Lauren shook her head. 'Who in their right mind would do that? You must have made a mistake. Check the circuit diagram again.'

Frank consulted the pamphlet once more.

'One hundred per cent sure,' he said emphatically. 'There should be a chip sitting right there. And now there's not.'

'Which chip is it?'

'A D47K887.'

'Do we have a spare?'

Frank checked the spares kit, his expression of gloom deepening as he compared the contents against an inventory.

'There should be one,' he said, perplexed, 'but it's vanished.'

'Whoever did this was being pretty damn sly,' Lauren observed. 'If we hadn't had the circuit manual, we would never have spotted it.'

'That's what's so frightening.'

Lauren crossed to the window and looked out into the

night. 'Who asked for access today? Was there anything special happening?'

'Sean had a couple of e-mails to send, so did Mel. Oh, and Carl was going to send a chunk of his book to a publisher he's got interested. He brought me the disk last night, but the satellite connection was playing up with some bad weather. I was planning to do it this morning.'

Lauren picked up the floppy disk. It had 'First draft synopsis and 50,000 words' written in pen on the label.

'Did you leave this disk on the desk like this?'

Frank looked a little guilty. 'Well, Carl did ask me to keep it hidden, but I may have left it out overnight by mistake.'

'So Fitzgerald could have seen it, could have known that you were about to send it. Has he been in here?'

'Not that I've seen.' Frank shrugged.

'Could he have been in here during the night?'

'Well, this door's never locked; why should it be?' Frank paused, then: 'You think he sabotaged the unit?'

Lauren closed the door and dropped her voice. 'Listen. I don't want anyone else on this base to know that we discovered the missing chip. As far as we're concerned, the satellite's got some electrical gremlin in the works, and you're in the process of identifying it. If anyone asks, tell them it'll be up and running in a couple of days. OK?'

'OK.'

Lauren opened the door to leave.

'Hey,' he called after her, 'what are you going to do about this?'

'I'll sort it,' Lauren told him. 'Just give me a bit of time.'

'Well, be careful. For God's sake.'

48

Lauren waited until Fitzgerald was well into his nocturnal weight-training session before making her move, her bare feet making no sound on the carpeted floor. She passed Mel's room, then Murdo's, the muffled sound of the chef's distinctive snore just audible through the insulated door.

Fitzgerald's room was at the end of the accommodation block, and, as she had expected, it was locked. Lauren took the replacement key from her pocket and quietly opened the door. She entered the room, leaving the door open a crack in case she needed a fast exit.

As her eyes adjusted to the dark, she began to pick out the details of the room. Like all the others on the base, it was a three-metre-square construction with a sink in the corner and a low chest of drawers for clothes and personal belongings. Some of Fitzgerald's personal survival gear was heaped in the corner, and the laptop sat on the desk.

Lauren thought about turning on the light, then decided against it. There was always the chance that Fitzgerald might leave the weights room for some reason, and the last thing she wanted was to alert him to her presence in his room.

Now. Where to search? Lauren thought about the options and decided to check the most obvious places first. As far as she knew, Fitzgerald would be assuming that no one had discovered his secret piece of sabotage, so there was always the chance he had not taken too much trouble to hide the chip.

She took two stealthy steps over to the drawers and slid open the bottom one with infinite care. Taking out her small penlight torch, she shone the beam into the interior, shielding the light from the rest of the room with her body and running her hand beneath the assortment of clothes which had been placed there.

There was no sign of the missing chip.

She checked the other drawers one by one, and then slid each one right out so she could run her hand around the base to see if anything had been taped underneath. Nothing; the chest of drawers was clean.

Lauren crossed to the basin and checked behind the ceramic plinth, where a useful-sized cavity could easily have held something small, then she went through the items in the mirrored cabinet sitting above the sink, removing the caps of shaving foam and shampoo to check that nothing had been secreted inside.

Then to the bed, running her fingers along every inch of the metal frame, and sliding her hands underneath the sheets to see if there were any incisions in the fabric.

A sudden noise made her jump, her heart racing with adrenaline as she froze to the spot. But it was only Murdo, coughing fit to bust in the room next door.

Lauren continued the search, now focusing on the clothes and equipment which had been dumped in a pile on the floor. She worked her way through the assorted thermal gear, running her fingers along the seams, and then went through the boots and skis, again finding nothing suspicious.

She slid the chair across to the window and stood on it while she searched the curtain rail, then turned her attention to the small circular plastic fire alarm which was bolted high on the wall. Each of the rooms had these alarms, and, shining her torch on it, Lauren realised that there might be enough spare space inside to hide something away. She clenched the penlight between her teeth as she clicked the plastic cover off its mounts.

She shone the torch onto the workings of the alarm, finding that there was indeed something hidden inside the alarm case, but not what she'd been expecting. Lauren reached up and pulled the 35mm canister of film from where it had been jammed.

'Now what the hell is that doing here?' she murmured, replacing the cover of the alarm and stepping to the floor. She looked the canister over, then put it in her top pocket. She had just slid the chair back into place when there was a slight noise behind her, a quiet footfall which turned her blood instantly cold. Before she had time to turn, Lauren felt the blow on the side of her head. It was powerful, feeling more like the impact of an iron bar than a fist, then Fitzgerald was on her, slamming Lauren's face into the top edge of the cupboard and locking a muscular arm around her neck.

'You've made a big mistake,' Fitzgerald hissed, his grip tightening with terrifying force. 'Intruders in the night get what they deserve.'

Lauren tried to struggle, but Fitzgerald had her arms pinned, her hands unable to strike a blow. The explorer increased the pressure, quickly reaching the point where Lauren could feel her windpipe beginning to be crushed. She tried to force her throat into a scream for help but could manage nothing more than a croak. No one was likely to hear them, she realised; the triple-insulated walls of Capricorn made for good sound-proofing, and Murdo, the nearest room occupant, slept like a corpse.

I'm dead, Lauren thought. I'm dead if I don't fight.

Lauren tried to twist her body, attempting to wrest herself free, Fitzgerald turning with her to hold the grip. She tried to kick back at the explorer's legs, to knock him off balance, but Fitzgerald was too fast to be caught out.

Lauren could feel her vision beginning to deteriorate as

oxygen starvation cut in. She was being strangled to death and for long seconds it felt like there wasn't a damn thing she could do about it. Then she began to kick against the cupboard, smashing her foot against the panel so hard she splintered the plywood in her desperation to make some noise.

An age seemed to pass, Fitzgerald gradually increasing the intensity of his grip as Lauren began to black out.

Suddenly the room filled with a brilliant intensity of light. Lauren heard a brief flurry of footsteps and then felt Fitzgerald's weight slump against her as the meaty sound of metal against flesh resonated close to her ear.

Lauren, gasping horribly, forced herself upright, shrugging off the weight of the explorer from her back so that the unconscious body fell to the floor.

In front of her was Sean, trembling, dressed in a T-shirt and shorts, a fire extinguisher in his hand. He helped Lauren to the bed, where she sat, her face bright purple, hyperventilating as her winded lungs gradually got some air and allowed her to breathe.

'I thought he was going to kill me,' Lauren told him, looking down with loathing at the motionless figure at her feet.

'But what were you doing in his room?' Sean asked.

'I was looking for something. Something Frank and I thought he might have stolen.'

'Did you find it?'

Lauren pulled the canister from her pocket.

'No. But I did find this, hidden in the fire alarm.'

Sean took the film and turned it in his hands, immediately spotting the tiny scratched cross on the base of the metal roll.

'Son of a bitch. That motherfucker stole my film.'

Then the realisation hit him.

'God, I am so dumb . . . the pictures of the food and the drugs . . . I took a couple of photos inside the wreck. *That's* why Fitzgerald stole my film.'

49

'What the hell's this God-almighty row?' A sleepy-looking Murdo was at the door in his pyjamas, staring in astonishment at the body of Fitzgerald where it lay on the floor.

Mel and Frank were not far behind him, followed by Richard.

'What happened to you?' Richard asked as he saw the livid red bruising on Lauren's neck. 'Has he gone crazy?'

'He tried to kill Lauren,' Sean told him. 'We have to immobilise him while he's still unconscious. If he comes round, we'll never hold him.'

The Capricorn team bent to the task, lifting the comatose explorer onto the bed. Fitzgerald let out a deep moan as they shifted him.

'His arms,' Lauren managed to croak through her damaged throat, 'we have to tie them, fast.'

Sean scanned the room. 'What can we use? Frank? You got any ideas?'

Frank thought for a few moments and then disappeared to the store room. He returned with a handful of black plastic ties, the type electricians use to bind cables together.

'I reckon these will do the trick,' he said, sliding one of the sturdy ties into its port until it clicked in place in a ring. 'Try and break that.'

Murdo took the bracelet of plastic and tried to pull it apart with both hands. 'You're right,' he said, red with the exertion of the failed attempt. 'These are as good as handcuffs.'

'Put three on each wrist,' Lauren ordered. 'I don't want to take any chances.'

They placed the still-unconscious Fitzgerald in a sitting position against the headboard of the bed and spreadeagled his arms until each wrist was against a bed post. Then they clicked the plastic ties into position, taking care not to pinch the flesh.

'He won't escape from that,' Frank assured Lauren. 'He'll slice through his wrist before he'll break that plastic.'

'What about his legs?' Sean asked. 'He'll kick if he gets an opportunity.'

'Tie them together,' Lauren ordered. Frank produced a length of rope, and a few minutes later the task was done, the explorer well and truly trussed up.

'How bad is his head wound?' Lauren asked Mel. 'Can you take a look?'

The Capricorn medic made a quick examination of the split in Fitzgerald's scalp.

'He'll live,' she pronounced, 'but he'll wake up with a serious headache.'

'Should have hit him harder,' Sean told Lauren.

'That's not helpful, Sean,' she snapped.

Lauren turned to the others, trying to sound rational even though her heart was still racing with shock.

'All right. Someone wake up Carl. I want everyone to the mess room. I want to brief you on what's happened here, and we have to make a team decision on what we're going to do about it.'

They retreated to the mess room table, where Murdo rustled up hot drinks. Mel tended to Lauren's neck, putting an ice pack against the bruised flesh in the hope of reducing the swelling.

'So what was the fight about?' Murdo began. 'Was he trying to rape you or something?'

'Take it from the beginning, Lauren,' Frank told her. 'It's time they knew everything.'

Lauren breathed deeply to calm her nerves, then began.

'We suspect that Fitzgerald might have deliberately sabotaged the satellite comms,' she told them. 'There's a vital chip missing from the transmitter, and I was in his room trying to find it.'

There was a stunned silence as this news sank in.

'But that's our lifeline,' Mel said. 'Whatever was he thinking of?'

Suddenly, Carl was animated. 'I bet this has to do with my manuscript,' he said. 'I was due to e-mail the first fifty thousand words of my book to a publisher yesterday morning. Fitzgerald must have found out and decided to wipe out the transmitter.'

'Bit of an extreme measure, wasn't it?' Mel questioned. 'What's so bad about your book that he'd go to those lengths to stop you sending it out?'

'All I've done is tell the truth,' Carl said, 'but the truth and Julian Fitzgerald don't get along too well. Suffice to say that his glorious reputation will be taking a bit of a knock when my account hits the bookshops.'

'So, if you're determined to get the story out, what's he got to gain by delaying it?'

'He's threatening legal action. He's e-mailed his lawyer in London to get him to put legal pressure on my publishers not to go ahead. It all rests on the pre-expedition contract I signed before we set out. I suppose he's waiting for his lawyer to check the fine print.'

'But surely he must have known Frank would spot the satcomm had been nobbled?' Murdo observed.

'Not necessarily,' Frank told him. 'We had no reason to suspect sabotage, at least not initially. It was only because we checked through the circuit diagram that we discovered the component was gone.'

'And did you find the chip?' Mel asked Lauren.

'Not yet. But as soon as we can move Fitzgerald to somewhere more secure, we'll go back in and do a fingertip search. But I did find a film which Sean lost at the beginning of the winter.'

The team turned to Sean.

'I took a roll of stills on the rescue,' Sean explained, 'and I tried to process them months ago. But the roll was blank, and I put it down to a camera fault. Now it turns out Fitzgerald switched the film for a blank one.'

'Why would he steal your film?' Richard asked.

Sean looked to Lauren and got her confirming nod to continue. 'Because I took some pictures which I believe might incriminate him.'

'Incriminate him? How?'

'There was an emergency box down in the plane. It was packed with food and drugs. One of my pictures showed all the wrappers and stuff.'

Richard was stunned. 'You're wrong. There wasn't any food. We didn't eat a damn thing until you and Lauren . . .'

'Fitzgerald ate the lot,' Sean told him bluntly, 'while you and Carl were starving to death. Every time he abseiled down to the plane, he was feeding himself up.'

'I can't believe it . . .' Richard was dumbfounded. 'No one would do that . . . would they?'

Suddenly, Carl was making a curious muffled sound, a sniffling which Lauren at first took for tears, but when he raised his face she saw that it was laughter.

'None of you have any idea,' he muttered, laughing insanely. 'Fitzgerald only ever cared about himself. The man is not to be trusted, take my word for it. But Sean got a picture down in the plane? How beautiful . . . now we've got the proof. We can destroy him with that.'

'Assuming all this is true,' Frank addressed Lauren, 'what the hell are we going to do with him?'

'He's dangerous,' Lauren said, 'and he's violent. I don't intend to give him a chance to hurt any more members of my team.'

'I think he's paranoid,' Carl told the group. 'I've thought that for months. You can't let him free again . . . he'll really hurt someone.'

'But how the hell are we going to keep him a prisoner in there?' Frank asked. 'What about feeding him; what about when he needs the toilet?'

'We'll have to construct something better,' Lauren proposed. 'Frank, can you strengthen one of the rooms, reinforce it so he can't get out?'

'I could do,' Frank replied after some thought. 'I'd have to weld up some bars for the window, maybe plate up the door with some four-millimetre steel so he can't kick it out. It would take me a day or so, but it's feasible, yes.'

'Do it. As soon as you can tomorrow,' Lauren ordered him. 'We'll keep Fitzgerald tied on his bed until we can move him into something more humane. Meanwhile, I don't want anyone going in there. That room is out of bounds except to me and Mel.'

'I have to tell my editor,' Richard told her. 'Put the record straight about that bastard. To think I was setting him up as the great hero. How soon can you get the satellite link fixed?'

'We're still missing the vital component,' Frank told him. 'It'll take me another week or so to design a way around it.'

'In any case,' Lauren added, 'I'm not sure I want this story broadcast to the world when I'm just about to announce the results of the scientific work. We've already attracted too much sensational publicity thanks to Fitzgerald.'

'But that's totally unethical . . . it's censorship of the worst kind. I *have* to tell this story. You *must* give me that chance.'

'Winter'll be over in less than five weeks,' Lauren told

him. 'We'll fly you out of here, and you can write whatever stories you like. But for now the satellite link, when and if it's fixed, remains for my use only . . . and that's my last word.'

'Maybe Fitzgerald was right about you, Lauren,' Richard told her darkly. 'Maybe you are a control freak.'

'Stop it!' Frank stepped in. 'It doesn't help if we start to attack each other.'

'Sean. Process that film,' Lauren ordered him. 'Let's at least see what was bugging Fitzgerald so much he had to steal it.'

For an hour they waited while Sean went to the darkroom. He returned with the freshly dried prints and handed them to Lauren. The others crowded round as Lauren flipped through them until she found the shots inside the crashed plane.

'There's the food box,' she said. 'Sean was right about that, you can clearly see all the wrapping and the empty cans . . .'

Richard swore beneath his breath as he was handed the prints.

'And here's the drugs,' he said, 'the drugs which would have saved Carl and me from six days of living hell. Presumably he would have let us die out there and kept them for his own use.'

'This will ruin him when the story gets out,' Murdo said, not without relish.

'Yes,' Richard added, 'and the pleasure will be all mine.'

50

Fitzgerald lay spreadeagled on the bed which was his prison and forced his mind to search for a way out.

Early experiments had revealed that his legs were too tightly tied. No amount of movement, of wriggling inside the cords, could loosen the bonds that held his limbs together.

For his left hand, also, there was no hope of freedom; the plastic cable ties were thick enough to resist even the most strenuous pull, the hand held so tightly against the wooden strut of the headboard that any type of movement sent sharp pains into his wrist.

The right hand was different, the cable ties a little looser, enabling the explorer to move his arm a few inches up and down the strut. He considered trying to splinter the wood with his nails, to create a sharp cutting edge with which to saw into the plastic restraints.

Then he made a discovery: just beneath the position in which his hand was locked, a metal plate was screwed into the back of the strut. He figured it was the device holding the headboard to the main frame of the bed.

One of the screws was slightly protruding, the head sharp and burred where a screwdriver had slewed it.

By forcing his arm down, Fitzgerald found he could rub the outside of the plastic ties against the serrated lip of the screw head. Do that for long enough, he told himself, and he could cut through the ties. He worked through the long day, only halting when Murdo came to stuff a sandwich in his mouth.

Many hours' more concentrated work, biting his lip against the pain from his increasingly tender flesh, gave Fitzgerald a breakthrough: the first of the cable ties sprang open.

Two more to go. Sleep was out of the question even though he guessed it must now be four a.m. or later.

If he could bear the pain, he could get the hand free. Fitzgerald began again.

51

Richard took a surreptitious glance along the corridor to check that no one was watching, then entered the room where Fitzgerald was tied up. He closed the door behind him, slightly guilty already that he had broken his promise to Lauren that he would not try to speak to the explorer.

The things he had learned about Fitzgerald in the last hours made it impossible for him to stay away. There were too many questions burning up inside him.

Richard looked closely at Fitzgerald, feeling his skin creep a little at the sight of the trussed-up figure, his face still bloody from the fight of the previous night. Even tied up as he was, there was something undeniably frightening about Fitzgerald's presence, a latent capacity for violence which reached beyond the physical limits of his body.

The extraordinary power of his frame was all too evident, even at rest. Richard was no fighting man, and the thought of all that destructive strength let loose was enough to make him shudder.

'Are you sleeping?' Richard asked him. 'Or is that a sham like everything else?'

'What the fuck are you talking about?' Fitzgerald did not bother to open his eyes.

'They developed the film,' Richard told him. 'They found it hidden in your room. I've got one of the prints here.'

Fitzgerald's eyes flicked open and locked Richard in a hostile gaze. Now he had the explorer's full attention.

'And what does the pretty picture show?' Fitzgerald sneered.

'I think you know.'

'I have nothing to hide.'

'That's a lie for a start. This photograph definitely shows an empty emergency ration pack down in the fuselage of the plane. Kilos and kilos of the stuff . . . and you ate it all while Carl and I were going day after day without food.'

'I deny it,' Fitzgerald told him emphatically. 'The pack might have been empty when it left Ushuaia. I never saw any food down there.'

'And the drugs?' Richard continued. 'The bandages, antibiotics and morphine? How do you explain that, unless you were saving them for your own possible use? You *must* have known they were there, Julian, and you *must* have known how desperately I needed them. How could you have watched me go through all that pain when you could have helped me?'

Fitzgerald let his eyes flicker for an instant to Richard's belt. *The Swiss army knife was there in its holder.*

'Without me pulling you out of that crevasse, you'd still be rotting there now with those two pilots.'

'I know that, I recognise you saved my life,' Richard said wearily. 'But that doesn't stop me from hating you for what you did next.'

'All you have is Sean's fantasy version of what he saw down there. How do you know it wasn't *him* who found those rations and ate them?'

Richard shook his head. 'I don't believe that for a moment. I trust Sean . . . he's not the type of person who could do that.'

'Have you thought about *why* they are filling your head with all this?' Fitzgerald asked him. 'Why they go out of their way to spread all these lies about me? Can't you see it's all a smokescreen to cover up for the fact that this base is a failure?'

'What on earth are you talking about?'

Fitzgerald dropped his voice. 'You're a journalist. You have influence. They're terrified you're going to discover the truth about Capricorn.'

Richard had to resist a laugh. 'The truth? What truth?'

'The whole project is a scandalous waste of time and money. There's no lake down there, Richard; they're drilling down into solid fucking ice. They're spending millions on a false premise, and Lauren Burgess knows it. If you weren't here, they could cover the whole thing up, make it seem like a test exercise perhaps, but what if you decided to write about it? To make that failure public? How do you think her sponsors would feel? It could destroy her precious reputation overnight . . . she'd be a laughing stock, and she'd never raise the money for another base.'

'Nice try,' Richard told him, shaking his head, 'but it doesn't wash. Capricorn isn't a failure at all; it's a fantastic success.'

Fitzgerald seemed to sag, his chest sinking slightly as he exhaled long and hard.

'The problem is this,' Richard continued. 'You've made me feel pretty foolish. In fact, I've never felt more stupid in my life. Back at the beginning of this winter, I wrote a three-thousand-word feature about what a great hero you were, how you saved my life. It was my first front-page byline; do you know how proud that made me? And now I find out that I actually missed the real story . . . that the real story was how a desperate, paranoid individual was saving himself at the expense of his fellow men.'

'How do you know you wouldn't have done the same?'

Fitzgerald asked him. 'Put yourself first? Don't you think when it comes to survival there's something inside all of us which is capable of that?'

Richard was white with rage. 'No, I do not. I would never let someone starve like you did! I was out of my depth out there, Julian; I desperately needed help, and to think of all those days you didn't do a damn thing . . .'

'I wish I *had* left you in the crevasse,' Fitzgerald told him quietly. 'Saved myself all this bother.'

Richard shifted again on the end of the bed, his anger seeping away.

Just a few inches closer . . . Fitzgerald had to restrain himself from making the move.

'I can't ignore this, Julian. I have to tell this story,' Richard told him finally. 'It's my duty as a journalist. As soon as they get the satellite link back up, I'm going to file a piece which will tell the public the truth.'

'You mustn't do that,' Fitzgerald pleaded. 'You'll ruin everything. Let me see that photo properly; bring it closer.'

So close now. Fitzgerald felt the muscles in his right arm tense.

Richard leaned just a few more inches towards the explorer to give him a better look at the print.

Just a fraction more.

'You were prepared to let us starve to death,' Richard said. 'Now I'm going to tell that story, and there's not a damn thing you can do about it.'

Now.

Fitzgerald's right hand snaked forward so fast that Richard didn't stand a chance. The blow was expert, straight to the temple, an instant later Richard was unconscious in the explorer's arms.

A moment later Fitzgerald was reaching for the knife.

52

Murdo and Sean had stayed up late, taking a couple of beers at the bar as they talked through the events of the day, when Murdo happened to glimpse a flash of light out on the glacier. It was an evil night, the wind blowing twenty to thirty knots, and no sooner had his eyes registered the beam of light than it was gone, swallowed up in the driving spindrift.

'That's weird.' He took his beer and stood by the window, peering out into the storm. 'I thought I saw a light out near the vehicle shed.'

Sean joined him. 'Can't be,' he said. 'Everyone's gone to bed.'

'No. I'm sure of it. There! That's it again.'

This time Sean had seen it too, a momentary flickering against a window. 'Looks like it's coming from inside the shed,' he said. 'Let's go and check it out; it might be a spark from a wiring fault.'

They dressed as quickly as they could and were crossing

to the vehicle shed when they heard the sound of an engine from within. 'Sounds like a snowcat,' Sean said, cupping his hand against Murdo's ear to be heard above the wind. 'But who in the name of God would be playing around out here at this time of night?'

Sean stood on tiptoe to see through the window, but the glass was too frozen to register more than the fact that there was a light of some sort inside. Murdo and Sean pushed open the door and stopped in complete amazement at what they found. In the corner of the shed, Julian Fitzgerald was siphoning petrol from the main storage tank into a series of jerrycans. Nearby, one of the snowcats was ticking over, the engine stuttering a little as it warmed. Hitched to it was a sledge, piled with food, equipment and an axe.

Fitzgerald froze, watching the two men warily as they entered.

'Well, well, well,' Murdo said, 'if it isn't Harry fucking Houdini. Complete with half a ton of stolen supplies by the look of it. Help yourself, mate, won't you?'

'Don't get any closer,' Fitzgerald warned them. 'I'm leaving, and there's nothing you can do to stop me.'

Murdo picked up a ten-pound torque wrench from the toolbox.

'I wouldn't be so cocksure about that theory.'

'You're not going anywhere,' Sean added, 'least of all on one of my snowcats. Now put that can of fuel down.'

Sean and Murdo each took a pace towards the cornered man, the explorer's eyes widening with fear as they approached.

'Stay back . . .' Fitzgerald stammered. 'I won't be stopped!'

Suddenly, the explorer kicked out violently, knocking over one of the open jerrycans which were lined up in front of him. Sean and Murdo watched in horror as five gallons of fuel glugged out of the open can, running in oily blue rivers across the wooden floor of the hut and collecting in a pool at the base of the main fuel tank.

Fitzgerald pulled a cigarette lighter from his top pocket and held it with his thumb against the flint.

'Want to put me to the test?' he asked, quietly.

'Now I know you're crazy,' Sean told him. 'Have you any idea what fire can do to us here?'

'Step back.' Fitzgerald made a movement with his hand, as if to throw the lighter on the fuel.

Murdo and Sean retreated a few paces, back towards the door, as Fitzgerald picked up the filled jerrycans with his free hand and placed them on the back of the sledge. He secured them in place with a length of elastic bungee cord and climbed onto the snowcat.

'Open the main door,' he ordered Sean.

Sean swung the door open, exposing the interior of the shed to whirling flakes of snow.

'Stand aside.'

The two men did as he said as Fitzgerald kicked the snowcat into gear. Seconds later he would have been gone, but the rubber of the snowcat belt had frozen slightly to the floor, enough that when he applied the throttle, the machine gave a little lurch forward and stalled.

'Now!' Murdo sprung on the explorer and smashed the torque wrench against his hand, the cigarette lighter clattering harmlessly away towards the open door as Sean grabbed Fitzgerald's parka hood and pulled him backwards off the machine. The explorer hit the floor with a thud, rolling to avoid Murdo's lunging kick as Sean landed a punch to the side of his face. Fitzgerald roared with fury as he pulled Sean down, the two men collapsing into a stackpile of snow shovels which were standing in the corner. Murdo got a kick in, Sean pummelled with his fists and Fitzgerald continued to yell, biting and punching back at his assailants as he tried to break free.

Attempting to regain his feet, Fitzgerald grabbed at the dexion shelving above him. But Sean and Murdo pulled him back down, their combined weight sending the six-foot-high shelving unit toppling over towards the kerosene tank, where it crashed with a resounding clatter of metal tools.

At the time, all Sean and Murdo were aware of was the shed being plunged into sudden darkness, followed a split second later by the flash of a spark and the roar as five gallons of fuel erupted in a fireball. Later they worked out that the spark had come from the inspection light which had been clipped to the side of the shelving, its bulb smashing as it hit the floor and providing the one critical spark which created the blaze that was now raging out of control.

Instantly, the fight was forgotten. Sean and Murdo pulled themselves free from Fitzgerald, staggering to their feet as they contemplated the inferno which was already consuming the shed walls and licking around the base of the main kerosene storage tank.

'Get the extinguisher!' Sean screamed at Murdo as he beat at the flames with a tarpaulin, the chef running to the BCF unit which was clipped to the wall.

Behind them Sean was aware of Fitzgerald starting up the snowcat and driving away. Now the fire had a hold on the floor, thick dark smoke billowing up as it blocked their approach to the tank. Murdo fired the extinguisher into the conflagration, making little impact as the intense wall of heat drove them back.

'It's no use,' Murdo shouted in despair. 'The tank's going to blow.'

'We've still got a chance,' Sean shouted, lunging back once again to try and beat down the flames which had now engulfed the entire front half of the kerosene tank.

Murdo grabbed him by the arm and dragged him from the shed.

53

Lauren stood at her bedroom window, the horror of the vision numbing her for some seconds. Not thirty metres from where she stood, two thousand four hundred gallons of kerosene were burning out of control.

Of the fuel shed there was now no sign; the whole thing had been ripped apart in the enormous explosion which had woken her, the engine shed behind it also virtually atomised by the blast. Pieces of twisted metal were scattered about the ice, fragments of lighter material were still falling out of the flame-lit night sky.

As Lauren watched, the wind picked up its strength, directing the fireball of combusted fuel straight for the main block. Rivers of burning kerosene began to race across the ice. Lauren ran out into the corridor.

'Fire! Everybody out!' She banged her fists against each door as she ran to the hall, where she threw on her clothes in record time.

Outside, she took a step towards the fire, the ice slippery

beneath her boots. There was fuel all over the ground, Lauren realised. Even as she watched, it was acting as a conduit for the fast-moving flames. Then, from a rolling black cloud of smoke, she saw Sean and Murdo emerge.

'Fitzgerald . . .' Sean managed to quell his coughing for a moment. 'He's escaped, and he's got an axe!'

'What?' Lauren's mind struggled with this confusing piece of information even as she saw the explorer accelerating away from the base on a snowmobile, the back of the sledge heavily laden.

Then she snapped back. The flames were spreading, feeding on the fuel, whipped by the wind, leaping aggressively up the walls of the accommodation block and penetrating the wooden frame of the clinic.

Lauren shouted out orders.

'Murdo. Get hold of Frank and Mel. Find Carl and Richard. Get them out of the building. Fast.

'We have to save the snowmobiles,' she told Sean. 'If we lose the base, they're our only chance.' Together they ran to the vehicle shed, pulling back the sliding door. But the interior was already an inferno. The remaining snowmobiles were burning out of control, their fuel tanks exploding one after the other, spraying the interior with petrol and sending flames to the ceiling of the shed.

'Shit!'

Only the right-hand side of the shed was still untouched, the side containing the ski equipment and other gear.

Sean moved quickly into the store, shielding the side of his face with his hand.

'Get the skis. A sledge. Anything we can use if we have to abandon the base,' Lauren shouted.

'Leave me here,' Sean told her. 'I'll save what I can. Help the others.'

Lauren reached the door, saw that the accommodation block was being consumed with astonishing speed. The wind had directed the fireball like a blowtorch into the bedrooms. Lauren ran back to the main block, her heart pounding uncontrollably with a mixture of adrenaline and fear.

She entered a doorway. There was a figure in front of her, coughing with the fumes. It was Murdo.

'Mel's out of her room. So's Frank, but I can't get down to the far end of the block, there's too much smoke.'

Lauren pushed past him, hearing a series of piercing screams at that moment.

'Help me!' came the voice. 'Help me, for God's sake!'

'That's Richard!' Lauren pushed her way down the corridor, falling to her hands and knees as the smoke filled her lungs. 'He's in Fitzgerald's room!'

Murdo shouldered his way into one of the bedrooms and soaked two towels in the sink.

'Wrap this round your head and stay low,' he told her. 'You won't pass out if you stay on the floor.'

Lauren and Murdo crawled towards the room in which Richard was trapped. They could see virtually nothing through the dense smoke and so used his screams as a guide.

They beat down the door. Inside was a desperate scene: the journalist tied tightly to the bed frame, the far wall already alive with a sheet of fire.

'Get me out of here!' he screamed. 'Undo it!'

Lauren fumbled in her pocket, finding her knife. She severed the climbing rope which bound Richard to the metal frame, and they dragged him out into the corridor just as the external wall collapsed into the room, showering them with sparks.

'What about Carl?' Lauren screamed.

Lauren bundled Murdo and Richard up the corridor and out of the doorway, watching as Murdo dragged the nearly unconscious journalist clear of the base. Then she took a big gulp of clear air and ducked back inside to the smoke-filled corridor, heading for the medical bay, where Carl had last been seen.

When she got there, she realised there was no hope at all: the medical room was a wall-to-wall inferno, not even the beds visible through the hungry orange fire. To enter would be fatal, and she knew immediately that if Carl hadn't managed to scramble clear in the first seconds after the blast his chances would have been as good as nil. Perhaps he was somewhere else, she prayed, out on the ice . . . anywhere but trapped in those flames.

A smoke-blackened figure emerged beside her; it was Frank.

'Help me get the back-up radio!' he called as he disappeared into the passage. 'We're fucked if we can't get the radio.'

Lauren took the passage in three long strides, shouldering through the door into the radio room, where the instrument panel was already ablaze. Through the smoke she could see Frank trying to beat the flames down with his hands.

Where was the fire extinguisher? Every room had one. Lauren groped in the corner where she knew it should be. Nothing. The clips were empty.

'Use this!'

Lauren ripped the curtain from the wall and tried to smother the fire. In seconds the curtain too was ablaze, the intense heat driving them back just as the flames began to get a hold on the interior workings of the instrument panel.

The smell of melting plastic intensified as the components began to dissolve.

'Leave it. The radio's dead,' Lauren told Frank. 'Let's try and save the mess room.'

Choking and spluttering on the fumes, they felt their way back along the corridor into the mess room where two figures were fighting a losing battle. Murdo had made his way back into the building and, with Mel, was trying to quell the flames with a fire extinguisher.

The ceiling was already ablaze, the partitions erupting with searing blue flames which curled and snaked as they took hold.

'I'll get water,' Murdo called, heading for the galley with Lauren close behind him. They made for the sinks, but the smell of butane was overpowering.

'Jesus Christ!' Murdo saw flames licking around the butane store.

'The gas!' Lauren screamed. 'That's it. I want everyone

out of the base. Grab anything you can! Mel, take that sleeping bag.'

Lauren began to push them towards the exit, shoving
them forcibly in front of her as they snatched at the bundles
of cold-weather clothing which were hanging in the lobby.
They reached the ice and began to hurry to safety. Then a
sudden realisation hit Lauren.

'Oh my God . . . the sample! It's still in the lab!'

Ignoring the screams around her, Lauren ran back to the
burning building.

54

Now the corridor was a tunnel of flame, the ceiling acting like a giant grill as Lauren tried to get her bearings. She kept low, holding a last giant breath of pure air in her lungs as she counted off the doorways with her hands.

The lab. Fourth doorway on the right. Or was it the fifth? Lauren knocked against something hard, ran her hands over the unfamilar shape in confusion. A weight machine. She was in the wrong room.

Back in the corridor, staggering around the next doorway shielding her face from the heat, she found the lab. Lauren crawled in on all fours, the sharp cutting edge of broken glass lacerating her hands and knees. Visibility was almost zero; she couldn't see her hand in front of her face. Brittle explosions were coming from the storeroom to her left as aerosols of cleaning fluid detonated one by one.

Lauren fumbled her way blindly along the workbench, running her hands along the edge until she found the microscope. She could feel her lungs screaming for air, the desire to take a deep breath almost impossible to resist.

She found the fridge, opened the door, her hands closing round the smooth titanium sample tube. The specimen was still intact.

'Lauren!'

It was Sean's voice punching through the smoke.

'Where are you?'

Lauren tried to call, but felt herself gagging as she spluttered for breath.

Suddenly, his hands were grabbing her by the shoulders. Lauren felt herself pulled to her feet, her legs buckling beneath her as she felt a black wall of smoke run through her body. Then he was pulling her along the corridor, the two of them stumbling as low as they could beneath the flames.

Sean dragged her, retching, out onto the ice and manhandled her away from the inferno until they collapsed amid the others on the safe ground.

An instant later the fire worked its way through to the galley, igniting the gas in an immense fireball. One gas cylinder erupted, then another, consuming the base in a hungry avalanche of combusted butane, which sent dense black clouds of smoke billowing into the dark sky.

The clinic roof collapsed in a flurry of sparks, then the main wall of the accommodation block fell with a muffled crash. The laboratory was next, gone in a pyrotechnic crackle of igniting chemicals and splintering glass.

'Where's Carl? Did he make it?' Lauren gasped.

No one replied.

Lauren lay coughing on the ice, her team gathered around her in shock, feeling the heat of Capricorn on her cheeks as her one and only dream burned itself to the ground.

PART 4

The Trek

55

Lauren and Mel tended to the wounds, checking what injuries each of the team had sustained. The other four sat in appalled silence, unable to tear their eyes away from the terrible carnage which was playing out before them.

To Lauren's relief, their injuries were not life-threatening, although each would be scarred by this day in one way or another. Lauren herself had numerous painful burns to her hands and her scalp where melted plastic from the ceiling had rained down on her during the battle to save the mess room. Murdo and Mel had similar injuries, although Mel had been spared the damage to her head thanks to a woollen hat she had been wearing.

Sean and Murdo were also fortunate in one way: both had been wearing gloves and were thus free from burns to their hands, although Murdo had a number of blisters on his face.

Frank had come off worst: his battle to save the radio had

cost him third-degree burns to both hands. Even as he sat there, the blisters were filling rapidly with fluid.

Having no water to treat him, Mel packed snow around the burned tissue.

'He's the one I'm most worried about,' she confided to Lauren in a quiet moment. 'The other burns will be painful, but they'll heal on their own. Frank needs antibiotics at least if he's going to prevent the tissue necrotising. We could be talking gangrene.'

'He mustn't know that,' Lauren told her. 'Don't even mention that word in his presence, OK? He's going to have enough to deal with with the pain, let alone that shadow hanging over him.'

'I understand.'

As they sat there, watching the smoke curling from the ruins of the base, the sky began to lighten a little, the buried sun struggling, and failing, to clear the horizon. A luminous grey light was cast over the ice cap, not quite daylight, but enough to see the misery in each other's faces.

'You think one of the other bases might see the smoke?' Murdo shivered forlornly.

'The nearest is eight hundred miles,' Lauren reminded him. 'We'd virtually have to set off a nuclear bomb to get their attention.'

As the flames began to subside, Sean noticed that Fitzgerald had reappeared, the headlight of the snowmobile clearly visible a mile or so from the base.

Suddenly, Murdo was on his feet, screaming.

'Murderer! You fucking murderer! Come and get what's owed to you, you fucking . . .'

He picked up a piece of metal and threw it hopelessly in Fitzgerald's direction.

'What's his problem? Why's he sitting there like that, gloating over the dead? You come here, you bastard, and we'll see who's going to burn!'

'Calm down,' Lauren told him. 'He can't hear you. Save your energy for more important things.'

Murdo kept up his tirade.

'I'm going to kill him,' he cried. 'That evil monster is going to die.'

'Murdo, will you please keep quiet!'

The authority in Lauren's tone finally pulled the chef out of his rage. He stared at her in stunned silence, the burn marks already raised into livid welts on his face.

'Everyone gather round me,' she told them, 'and try and be calm. If we panic now, we're certainly going to make things worse.'

'Worse? Make things worse?' This time it was Mel who raised her voice. 'Everything's destroyed, Lauren; we've got injured people here. They need treatment; look at Frank's hands, for God's sake. What do we do about that with no drugs?'

Lauren struggled to keep the tears out of her voice. 'I know, Mel. I know. This is the most screwed up it could ever be. But I also know that we'll find a way out of this one way or another. *If* we keep our heads.'

Sean was also calm. 'She's right. As soon as they find out our radio's down, they'll send a plane out to investigate what's wrong. They'll drop us food, equipment, even if they can't land. We may have to survive a week here, but I doubt it'll be more than that.'

Lauren looked at Frank, seeing the despair in his eyes. He knew what she was about to say.

'That's not going to happen,' she told Sean with infinite regret. 'When the satellite went down, I radioed a message back to London to tell them we had a communications problem. I told them not to worry if they didn't hear from us . . . for a week or so . . .'

There was a stunned silence as the team thought about the new implications of that decision.

Murdo was the first to speak.

'But surely someone will begin to get worried. After a while . . . ?'

'What about the sponsor?' Mel added. 'Won't De Pierman raise the alert?'

Lauren swallowed to clear the sensation of rising nausea

in her mouth. 'I don't know . . . I just don't know. But it's probable no one will start to really worry for at least a couple of weeks.'

'So as far as the rest of the world knows, we're just happily drilling away, day after day, minding our own business in our nice little silent world?'

'That's right.' Lauren could barely whisper the reply.

'And it might be a fortnight before they wonder why they haven't had news from us? Or it might be a month.'

Lauren nodded her head imperceptibly.

'How long can we survive here? Without food? Without shelter?' Murdo asked, gesturing to the empty world which surrounded them.

No one replied.

'That's it then.' Murdo held up his hands in utter despair. 'We can't raise the alarm, winter's still got weeks to run . . . we're going to die here; we're absolutely fucked.'

He walked away from the group and crouched in the snow, the tension of the last hours overwhelming him with tears he didn't want the others to see.

'Not a single one of us is going to die,' Lauren called after him. 'I give you my word.'

She looked over to the smouldering wreckage of Capricorn, no more now than a collection of twisted metal, melted plastic and charred wood.

How she would keep that promise, she had no idea.

56

As soon as the worst of the heat had subsided, Lauren ordered the team into the wreckage—their first priority to find whatever remained of Carl.

The body was not easy to locate, incinerated by the furnace heat of the fire to the point where all that remained was carbonised flesh and scorched bones. When they did find it, the team said nothing, but merely stood with their heads hung low as they contemplated the horror of the scene.

'We've got to get him into a decent grave,' Lauren said. 'Will anyone help me?'

In the end Sean was the only volunteer for the gruesome task. They both retched as they prised the carbonised flesh out of the still-glowing ashes.

The others dug a shallow grave into the ice, and Carl's remains were committed with an improvised prayer from Lauren.

When the burial was over, Lauren turned once more to her team.

'Murdo, I want you to check out the area where the food store was,' she instructed. 'See if there's any way we can scrape something edible out of this disaster. Sean, you see what can be got out of the vehicle shed. I'll work with Mel to try and retrieve what I can in the way of medicine or other supplies.'

Frank and Richard were ordered to keep a watch for Fitzgerald, who, for the moment, had vanished from sight.

Mel and Lauren concentrated on the area where the clinic and laboratory had been, looking—without much optimism—for any locked chests or boxes which might contain still-useable drugs. But the fire had left nothing. Even the most robust of the medicine chests—the one which had contained the most powerful of their painkillers—had only ashes inside.

In the food store, Murdo had also drawn a blank.

'Is there nothing we can retrieve here?' Lauren asked him.

Murdo shook his head. 'It's hard enough to see where the food store even was, let alone find anything intact. This area was right next to the butane supplies, so the tins must have exploded, then melted in the heat. You can see that big blob of molten tin lying there. As for the packet foods and the flour and so on, well . . . you can imagine . . . that was four tons of food reduced to a pile of ash. There is nothing edible in that debris.'

The one commodity they could scavenge was firewood, and Lauren gave each of the team the task of gathering as much as they could. Most of it was heavily charred, but here and there—particularly in the galley area where the gas explosion had blown some of the roof out away from the main inferno—they found the odd small section of structural timber, or roof beam, which would still make a good fire.

They piled the scraps of wood in a stack, and then, utterly despondent, joined together to construct some type of shelter for the night.

Over in what remained of the vehicle shed, Sean picked his way through the debris with infinite care. He found the skidoos, charred skeletons of their former selves, every fuel line and critical engine component melted in the heat to the point at which even he knew they would never run again.

He ran his hands along the still-warm metal, wondering if whatever spirit lived inside those engines would feel the regret in his touch. Then he moved away, finding a few tools to be scavenged, some saw blades and pliers. Finally, hidden behind the metal frame of a workbench, he found one of the sledges still virtually intact.

He pulled it out of the wreckage, calling Lauren over excitedly.

'We got a sledge,' he told her. 'We can do things with this.'

Together they beat the twisted metal runners back into shape, bending the pliable aluminium until they had the sledge back in serviceable order.

Suddenly, a cry went up.

'He's back!'

Lauren and Sean followed Frank's outstretched arm, spotting the distinctive shape of the snowmobile far off on the horizon. They could just detect the thin buzz of the engine blown towards them on the wind.

The movement stopped. The dark shape of a human figure could be seen dismounting and standing next to the machine.

'He's watching us,' Lauren said, 'wondering what we're going to do next.'

'No, he's not,' Sean said, quietly. 'He's wondering how long it's going to take us to die. That's what's going through his mind right now.'

'Why has he done this, Sean? Do you think he's really insane?'

'No. I think he's capable of being perfectly rational. Think about the way he tied Richard to that bedframe. Look at the way he planned his escape. He must have hidden all those supplies, ready for the moment he could get away.'

'And the fire? Was that his plan all along?'

'I'm not so sure. If Murdo and I hadn't disturbed him, maybe he really would just have slipped quietly away. But as it happens, losing the base has played straight into his hands.

Now he can wait for us all to die, go resume his heroic expedition and then come out with some nice story about how he was the only survivor of an accidental fire.'

'You're right,' Lauren said, 'and he's got enough supplies on that snowcat to last for weeks. Maybe months, if he's careful.'

They stood, watching the eerily still figure as the wind picked up around them.

'It's him or us, Lauren,' Sean told her. 'It really might be as simple as that in the end.'

57

Fitzgerald screwed up his eyes as he focused the binoculars, trying to pick out some detail in the half-light as he watched the stumbling figures picking through the smoking wreck which was once Capricorn.

It was risky coming this close to them, he knew, but the question of who had survived the fire was one the explorer was anxious to resolve. He picked out Mel, then Murdo and Lauren, all three seemed relatively fit and mobile. Another figure moved across to join them; that was Sean.

Fitzgerald swore beneath his breath. Of all of them it was Sean he trusted the least. He was strong; he was young and fast, the explorer still had the bruises from the fight to remind him of that. Everything would have been a lot easier if Sean had been killed in the fire.

He was a problem, that boy.

And there to the side? The explorer could see another two figures lying prone on the ice. Was that Frank? Or Richard? Or Carl? It was too dark to see.

Fitzgerald drove back out to his tent, secreted miles away in a small indentation in the glacier surface. Even if they came looking for him, they would never find him here. And if they did . . . there was always the axe he had managed to take from the tool shed. He tested the axe blade with his finger, gratified to find it was razor sharp.

He fired up his cooker and melted down some ice for a drink.

Fitzgerald sipped his coffee slowly, savouring the bittersweet taste against his tongue. One of the successes of the operation, he reflected, had been the amount of food and cooking gas he'd managed to stash away in his secret store. He cast a professional eye over the many boxes and tins, very satisfied with what he saw.

God, it was cold, he thought; thank goodness he had the blankets and sleeping bag, which would guarantee warmth.

Now it was a waiting game. A question of how long they could last before they started to die. They would be burned, he was sure, some of them injured by the fire.

No hurry. Plenty of time. There was nowhere they could go. The explorer had all the time in the world and what a story to tell. He opened up his diary and began to think about the tragic accident . . . an engine fire perhaps, or maybe an accident in the gallery . . . which had engulfed Capricorn in fire.

58

The dim light began to fade. The wind rose steadily. The team huddled in the makeshift shelter hastily put together out of the scavenged iron. They lit a fire with the scraps of charcoaled wood, holding their palms towards it for the precious warmth as thick clouds of spindrift swept in through the many cracks and holes.

An hour later the glow on the horizon was gone, plunging the ice cap once more into darkness and a twenty-hour night which would see the temperature plummet to fifty, even sixty, degrees below freezing.

Lauren could already feel the tendrils of cold biting into her flesh through the inadequate clothing she was wearing.

There were occasional attempts at conversation, Murdo even trying a joke.

'Did I ever tell you the one about the two turtles and the skunk?'

No one responded, and he didn't continue.

They pressed in tighter against each other as the wind

picked up yet more speed towards ten p.m. The fire began to fail, the embers dying away fast, exposing them to yet more chill factor. The powder snow was relentless, drifting against their bodies, packing into the tops of socks and boots, trickling down their necks in frozen cascades.

'Put more wood on, Lauren, don't you think?' Mel begged her.

'We've only got enough for a few hours each night,' Lauren told her. 'We have to conserve it.'

Collectively the group began to shiver, their chattering teeth rattling in their skulls so that they were one shaking mass of tortured human flesh.

'I've s-s-survived some mountain b-b-bivouacs which I thought were c-c-cold,' Sean stammered to Lauren, 'but I tell you, this is s-s-something else.'

They took it in turns to use the single sleeping bag that Mel had managed to save from the mess room, taking one-hour shifts before handing over to the next grateful occupant. Every few hours Mel checked Frank's hands, the blisters growing dramatically as the burned tissue reacted. Frank took the pain in silence, never once complaining, even though the others knew he must be in agony.

Lauren waited until she thought it was three a.m. and checked her watch, grasping her wrist with her hand to steady it enough to see the dial. It wasn't yet midnight. It already felt like the longest night of her life, and it wasn't even halfway through.

By two a.m., the shivering of those pressed against her was so intense that Lauren knew each of them was approaching hypothermia.

'Everybody up,' she announced. 'We h-h-have to move. We need to b-b-body heat to survive.'

There was an outbreak of grumbling protests as she goaded them up and onto their feet.

'Move in a circle. You too, Richard. Frank, you can stay in the bag. I want everyone mobile for one hour.'

The team began to stagger in a rough circle, stumbling frequently on their frozen feet.

'Flex your fingers and toes,' Lauren ordered. 'One after the other. Don't lose the feeling in them.'

Soon the only noise was the crunch-crunch of their boots on the crisp snow and the sound of their laboured breathing as they continued to walk. They might be prisoners in some Siberian punishment camp, Lauren thought as they continued the regime, pushing themselves round and round in circles in the dead of this frozen night.

The motion brought them some relief, the welcome sensation of warmth as their bodies settled into the rhythm. But they couldn't keep going for long, and after an hour Lauren called a halt.

'Back in the shelter,' she told them. 'Get close to each other.'

They retreated back into the pitiful shelter, squatting side by side and wondering how they had ever taken the base for granted. The warmth and security it had offered seemed like a cruel trick of the memory; the very idea that they had been strolling those corridors in T-shirts, that they had enjoyed hot showers and efficient radiators, seemed only to conspire to make the cold more intense.

In no time at all the warmth they had so carefully gained was sucked out of their flesh. The cold was merciless, probing every crack in their clothing, freezing the fabric until it was as stiff as iron, numbing their limbs so that they could feel the muscles crackling as they attempted to relieve cramp.

'How long can we survive this?' Murdo's voice was already filled with despair.

'You mean tonight?' someone asked.

'I mean how long before we die.'

'I don't think it's going to help any of us to . . .' Lauren began.

'Tell us,' Murdo insisted. 'At least give me an idea how much of this we'll have to take.'

Lauren looked at Mel, her eyes posing the question.

'I'd say five days,' Mel said quietly. 'Maybe six or seven for the strongest.'

'And what's it going to be like?' Murdo whispered. 'What's going to kill us?'

'This conversation is not going to help you, Murdo,' Lauren told him gently. 'You have to keep your mind positive, or it'll be worse.'

'Oh sweet Jesus.' Now Murdo was crying, the tears freezing on his cheeks. 'I wasn't planning on dying just yet.'

'And you won't.' Lauren reached out to place her hand over his. 'Just get through tonight, and we'll start to work this out. We'll find an answer, Murdo; you wait and see.'

A little later Lauren found the stub of a pencil. 'Anyone got any paper?' she asked.

The team searched their pockets, managing to find a few scrumpled sheets and a tatty envelope.

'I'll keep a diary,' Lauren told the team. 'Just a few words each day. It'll help keep us sane.'

'And when they find our bodies,' Richard muttered, 'at least they'll know who killed us.'

59

At eight, having not slept a single moment, Lauren pulled together some scraps of wood and lit a fire. She put their one saucepan on it and melted down ice until she had produced a litre of tepid water.

'Everyone has to take some water,' Lauren told them. 'Dehydration will kill us way before we starve.'

They took it in turns to drink the lukewarm fluid, their lips freezing to the aluminium pan even as they sipped. The liquid tasted foul, the pot had been partly carbonised in the fire.

'I would pay every penny I ever earned for a single cup of sweet tea right now,' Murdo commented with a sincerity that could not be questioned.

'And I'd kill for a bacon sandwich,' Sean added.

They sat in silence, passing the pan around, clutching it tight in their hands to benefit from the passing heat of the water.

'I want an inventory,' Lauren announced when they had

finished the drink. 'We have to know exactly what we've got to work with.'

It didn't take her long to jot the list down on Sean's envelope.

'Four sets of skis. Three sets of bindings. One sleeping bag. Assorted tools. One sledge. One half-destroyed cooking pot. One compass. Two Swiss army knives. Several cigarette lighters. Various warm-weather clothes. One blanket. Scrap pieces of wood enough for a couple of weeks of night fires.'

'Anyone got any cigarettes?' Mel asked.

No one replied.

'We've got to keep searching the wreckage,' Lauren said. 'Somewhere in this debris there might be more things we can use. It'll give us a focus to the day, and the movement will keep us warm.'

They began to scour the remains of the base, shifting the movable bits of structure and poking around in the ashes. It was a dismal task with precious few rewards; Lauren called a halt to the search after just a couple of hours, in which time the only useful finds had been a few more pieces of firewood and some odd bits of metal which Sean used to improve their makeshift shelter.

They gathered together, hunger already gnawing at their stomachs. Lauren knew it was time for some decisions.

'So,' she began, 'bearing in mind the fact that we have absolutely no food whatsoever, how the hell are we going to survive this?'

'We'll have to hunt Fitzgerald down,' Murdo suggested. 'Follow the skidoo tracks and surprise him in the night. I'll kill him myself. That way we get the food *and* the snowcat.'

'But he might be fifty miles away,' Lauren countered. 'We don't know where he's gone.'

'And he's got an axe,' Sean added. 'None of us have a weapon at all.'

'It's too dangerous,' Lauren agreed, 'and it'll mean having to split the team. If Fitzgerald sees two or three of our fitter members tracking him down, he might realise that the

weaker ones have to be here on their own. Who knows what
he might do then?'

There was silence for a while.

'The protocol,' Lauren reminded them, 'the protocol is
we stay with the base.'

'For what?' Mel demanded. 'There is nothing for us here.
I say we make for another base. Whichever is the nearest.'

'It's eight hundred miles,' Lauren told her flatly. 'Forget it.'

Sean was the next to speak.

'There's only one way of getting out of here alive.'

The assembled team looked at him in surprise.

'Fitzgerald's emergency transmitter. We turned it off and
left it along with all the rest of their gear back at the crashed
aircraft.'

Lauren thought about it, shaking her head emphatically.

'Sean. That plane is three hundred miles away from
where we are right now. We don't have any snowcats. We
don't have food. Not one of us has the strength for that kind
of journey on foot.'

'I'm not talking about three hundred miles,' Sean told her.
'I'm talking about one hundred. That's how far it is to the
barrel of supplies we dumped at the first depot, right?'

'My God, I'd forgotten about the depots,' Lauren responded, animated now this new possibility had opened up.
'They're still out there from the rescue journey.'

'Didn't you take them down on your way back?' Frank
asked.

'We were too heavily laden; we left them where they
were.'

'Here's the idea,' Sean continued. 'We set out on foot. We
make a hundred-mile trek to the first barrel. That gives us
food to keep us going to the second depot. We feed up again,
crack the last one hundred miles, then get to the plane and
activate the transmitter.'

'How do we know it'll still work?' Mel asked. 'It's been
out there for the whole winter.'

'Those things are like black box flight recorders,' Sean
told her. 'They're guaranteed to survive anything. And the

batteries are lithium, so they're not affected by the cold.'

'Sean's right,' Lauren agreed. 'The transmitter should work. But I'd say the real question is . . . can we get to the plane?'

'Yeah. And that's a pretty big *if* . . . if you ask me,' Murdo added.

'How can we do this?' Lauren asked Sean.

'Well, as far as I can figure, there's really only two ways. Either we split the team and one or two of us—the fittest—make a fast dash on skis for the plane and radio for help. Or we all leave together and make our way there en masse.'

'How many days would the fast option take?'

'Let me think now.' Sean did some quick mental sums. 'Assuming that we find the depots without too many problems, I would estimate we can make twenty miles a day. That's fifteen days minimum.'

'By which time anyone waiting here would be dead. And the other option?'

'We'd definitely be moving slower. We'd be towing a sledge for one thing. In the best case I would say fifteen miles a day. Max. But bear in mind we'll be very low on food . . . and in fact with no food at all for the hundred miles before we find the first depot.'

'What's in those barrels, Frank?'

Frank spoke quietly from his sleeping bag.

'The same in each. Perhaps fifteen, maybe twenty kilos of food. An epigas cooker. Enough gas to last a week. A few pans. I think there were three sleeping bags. And two dome tents.'

'Medicine?' she asked Mel.

'I'm trying to remember. I think we put in some antibiotics, bandages, one splint, a couple of phials of morphine. Not a great deal, frankly, but it might make all the difference to have it.'

'Can we keep six people alive for five days on what is in those barrels?'

'If they weren't burning up any calories, undoubtedly,'

Frank replied. 'But walking a hundred miles on those rations? Hard drill, I'd say, but possible, yes. Men in worse condition than we're in have done much more.'

'Of the two choices, I say we keep the team together,' Lauren told them. 'For the following reason. If four of us wait here, inactive, without any food whatsoever, I don't believe we'd survive more than six or seven days before we died of exposure. This shelter is as good as useless, and we already know there's not enough firewood left to give us heat all day long.'

There was a general nod of agreement.

'There's another factor. We don't know what the hell Fitzgerald is going to try next. If we stick together, we've got strength in numbers.'

'Wait a minute,' Mel interjected. 'Does Fitzgerald know we put those depots down?'

There was an awkward silence as the team tried to recall.

'Shit! I told him,' Sean remembered with a moan. 'I told him about the depots when we were on the way back.'

'Then we're screwed,' Murdo said. 'That madman will drive out there and use those supplies himself before we can get to them.'

'Hold on . . .' Sean's expression suddenly lightened. 'I told him we laid two depots, but I didn't tell him where they were. I didn't even tell him about the hundred-mile intervals . . . just that we'd put down the barrels of gear in case we needed them on the way back.'

'So what's the chances of Fitzgerald finding either of those dumps by chance?' Mel asked.

Sean and Lauren answered simultaneously.

'Zero.'

'For that matter, what's the chances of *us* finding them?'

Lauren thought about it. 'We've got the compass. It'll be tough, but we can do it with dead reckoning.'

'I'd rather do anything than sit here in the ruins of this base, waiting to die,' Murdo said.

'Me too.'

'Does everyone agree we stick together?'

There was a murmuring of assent.

'Then I think we should go now,' Lauren told them.

'Why not wait until first light?'

'Because that's exactly what Fitzgerald will figure we'll do. He won't be looking for us until tomorrow morning. We have twelve hours of total darkness to put some distance between us and the base. With luck, he won't even know we've gone.'

'What's to stop him making straight for the plane himself?' Murdo asked. 'Perhaps he reached the same conclusion about the transmitter.'

'He may not be thinking rationally,' Lauren replied. 'He's out there, alone, not knowing how many of us are dead or alive. He might be thinking about the plane, and he might not. Maybe his plan is to make sure we're all dead and then head for the nearest base on the skidoo. We can't second-guess what he's going to do. That's why I say we go now. From now on we do the things he's *not* expecting. That way we keep at least some of the initiative.'

'But when he finds we've gone, he'll put two and two together.'

Lauren considered. 'We'll leave a decoy note, try and send him off on the wrong trail.'

'And if a real search team *does* arrive?'

'I have an idea for that. I'll arrange it before we leave.'

Lauren made eye contact with every member of the team.

'Anyone not in favour of that plan say so now.'

There were no objections.

Thirty minutes later the team was outside and ready to go. They loaded the sledge with the firewood and the few objects and tools they had managed to retrieve, then Sean rigged up a rope harness which would allow two people to tow the sledge.

Lauren felt the rope dig harshly into the flesh of her hips as she began to ski. Then Sean took up some of the strain and the pain eased a little.

They worked side by side, getting easily into a rhythm,

even their breathing rates gradually adjusting until they were inhaling and exhaling at the same time.

Slowly, they pulled away from the base, moving as quietly as they could.

In her breast pocket, Lauren could feel the smooth outline of the titanium sample bottle. That was another responsibility—almost as overwhelming as the five lives which now depended on her.

That sample had to get out intact.

Lauren held the phial of liquid like a talisman in her hand as the night wore on.

60

Nothing fitted. Everything chafed. Blisters had sprouted on their feet, their hands, their waists in the very first hours of the trek.

The problems came from the boots and the skis; rescued at random in the most chaotic moments of the fire, they were mismatched, odd-sized, missing key components.

There were four complete sets of skis and boots, and by improvising bindings out of rope they managed to make them more or less operational. Lauren, Mel and Frank had the best deal; each of them had size eight or nine feet, giving them access to the best sets. Sean and Richard were less lucky, forced to share a set comprising one size ten boot and one size eleven. They resolved to swap every hour, taking the next hour in the insulated boots they'd been wearing when the fire struck.

Murdo had lucked out completely. His feet were by far the biggest in the base—a size thirteen, a full two sizes bigger than the largest rescued ski boot.

'No fucking way Cinderella's going to this ball,' he cursed as he gave up trying to jam his feet into one of the plastic boots. 'I'll just have to make do with what I've got.'

Lauren nodded, sizing up the leather trekking boots he was wearing. 'They should be OK,' she told him, 'but we'll have to watch you when the ice gets steep.'

Privately, Lauren knew that Murdo was going to suffer. The boots he was wearing could offer very little protection against the cold and would freeze as soon as his feet began to sweat.

Worse still, the Scotsman would have to walk every one of the three hundred miles which lay before them, a factor which would bring down their average speed considerably.

'Never was much good on skis anyway,' he told Lauren, striding alongside the sledge to keep his pace up.

Lauren resolved to spend as much of her own time on foot as she could; it would help Murdo's morale, if nothing else.

That first night, astonishingly, even with the frequent stops to try and adjust their boots and skis, the team completed the first ten miles in a remarkably fast six hours, the spirits of the group lifted by their decision to leave the base.

They were going hard into the night, each team member pushing their limbs faster than a normal walking pace in their desperation to get away from the smouldering wreckage of the base.

And to get away from Fitzgerald.

'Not so fast,' Lauren had to tell them. 'We have to pace ourselves properly. There's no point in blowing ourselves out to do fifty miles in record time if we've got no energy left for the next fifty.'

The team responded to her words, slowing their strides down to a more sustainable pace, searching for, and finding, the rhythm which suited them best.

There was one factor in their favour as they struck out across the plateau: the comparatively easy nature of the terrain. It was not perfect, but it was smooth enough to give them a chance to keep up a high average speed. The sledge ran without much resistance, its passage helped by the polished ice.

As the morning light arrived, Lauren and Sean kept a watch to the rear; this was the time when Fitzgerald was most likely to spot them making their escape.

'You seen any sign of him?' Sean asked her as they stared back in the direction of the base.

'None. And I can't see the base either. That means we've cracked enough distance that the curvature of the earth is working in our favour.'

'What do you think he'll do?'

'I imagine he'll just be biding his time. He'll think we're holed up in that temporary shelter trying to keep warm. With luck, he might not approach until he thinks we're all dead.'

'With luck,' Sean repeated. 'We're sure going to need an awful lot of that.'

'I know,' Lauren told him, 'but for the moment we're one step ahead of him, and that makes me feel an awful lot happier.'

Murdo was proving to be stronger than Lauren had expected, his mood dramatically improved now they were on the move. In the darkest moments after the fire she had feared the tall Scotsman was close to collapse, to giving up the fight. Now he was energised and walking steadily, never complaining even when it was his turn to take a spell at the hauling.

Frank too was trying his best, sliding clumsily on the skis, unable to use ski poles thanks to the burns on his hands. Mel examined him at midday, reporting back to Lauren.

'Those blisters are oozing pus already,' she told her. 'We can't hold the infection off much longer.'

'Nothing we can do about it,' Lauren replied, 'except get to that depot as fast as we can.'

That first night away from the base was horrendous, the firewood reluctant to catch, the improvised shelter flapping and rattling around them in the wind. But at least the spindrift held off; somehow the cold was so much easier to handle when it wasn't bringing driving snow.

Lauren brought in a new regime, rotating the team so that each got two hours in the sleeping bag. It meant there was a longer wait between sleep sessions, but two hours' sleep was a lot more useful than one. Nestled in the cosy cocoon, each of them was immediately able to sleep, the womb-like warmth a blessed relief after the piercing cold.

Lauren put herself last on the list, even though she craved her own turn in the bag as much as any of them.

61

*C*rack. A splintering sound rent the air. Fitzgerald sat up, his scalp tightening with fear as he was jolted from sleep. Someone was pulling his food from the sledge. Even though the wind was beating hard against the tent, he could hear the tins jostling as they stole them.

They were here. They'd get the snowcat.

How could he have been so stupidly complacent? Of course they would try and hunt him down . . . there was no other way for them to survive. Fitzgerald fumbled for the axe, cursing silently as his fingers ran carelessly across the blade.

I didn't go far enough. They've followed the tracks.

His heart was pounding uncontrollably. It would be Sean, of course. And Murdo, the big Scotsman. Too big for comfort. The two of them would be lethal, fighting for their lives. Fitzgerald checked the illuminated dial of his watch: 4:53 a.m., perfect time for a raid. He pulled on his boots, no time for the laces.

Got to get out of the tent and fight.

What would they have? What had the explosion left them? They would have a weapon, perhaps a sharpened metal strut from the debris.

Fitzgerald felt his skin crawling as he crouched in the doorway to the tent. He'd have to be fast or they'd stick him through the fabric of the tent. It rustled loudly as a new blast struck.

That was it. They were slitting the fabric.

Fitzgerald ripped down the zip and sprung quickly from the front alcove, a wave of fear and adrenaline driving him forward. He collapsed onto a snowbank; all was dark. He lashed out with the axe, sweeping great arcs through air which was filled with dense driving snow.

There was no light. Nothing to see his assailants by. He braced himself for the blows, hyperventilating as he blinked into the blizzard.

The sledge. They would take the sledge first.

The explorer felt his way to the side of the tent.

Thank God. The sledge was still there. He could feel the great mounds of boxes filled with food, the rounded outlines of the jerrycans . . . the fuel which would mean the difference between life and death.

He screamed a challenge against the wind, his eyes picking out some detail now, spinning as new eddies of spindrift turned themselves into fleeting figures running towards him.

Had he imagined it? Now he wasn't sure.

Crack. This time it was the ice mocking him, the resonant cry of a glacier under stress. New crevasses opening up beneath him. He paused, listening . . . to what? The palpitations of his own heart, the rumble of the wind.

He had to move this camp. It was compromised. *Had they been there? Did they know where it was?* Suddenly, the night seemed filled with new fear.

Fitzgerald felt his mind come back. He couldn't move while the conditions were like this. He would have to wait till first light.

Crack.

This was a wake-up call. A message he couldn't ignore. Fitzgerald sat alert through that night, knowing that they would come, that they would have to try and kill him . . . all they had to do was find him.

Crack.

They could douse the tent in petrol. Burn him alive.

Now he knew the enemy, Fitzgerald wouldn't take them for granted again . . .

62

'My legs. My fucking legs. Help me, for Christ's sake.'
Murdo was writhing on the ground in agony, both his legs shot out straight, rigid with cramp.

Lauren and Mel pushed on his feet, trying to ignore the tears of pain that this action provoked.

'It'll pass,' Mel told him. 'Breathe as deep as you can.'

Murdo wasn't the only one; they were all beginning to suffer from the harsh struggle to get to the first depot, and Richard was limping with a badly twisted ankle. Lauren calculated they had made forty-eight miles from base and the distance was beginning to tell. So was the lack of food; five days is a long time to ask the human body to perform with nothing but tepid water as fuel, and the miles were stretching into an unending nightmare of pain.

Lauren was hit by dizzy spells, attacks when she was forced to halt, to crouch on the ice with her head low between her knees to avert the threat of a faint. The others were no better: Sean was hobbling painfully on his frozen feet, Mel had developed a constant throbbing headache which refused to go away.

Frank said nothing for hours on end, but stumbled at the back of the group, his burned hands giving him hell. They were all dehydrated, suffering from constant thirst.

'I thought you had to be in a desert to be this thirsty,' Frank commented, talking with difficulty as his tongue had swollen inside his mouth.

Lauren sympathised with him. Her own mouth was filled with a type of glutinous slime, a clear indication that her body wasn't getting anything like enough fluids.

Things had changed in the last forty-eight hours, the early attacking style of the trek now replaced by a miserable shuffling of feet, scuffing across the ice in a despondent line as mile after mile passed at a snail's pace.

The equipment problems had largely been solved; now they'd been hit by the horrific realisation of just how much distance was really in front of them.

'I will never again look at a motorway signpost in the same way,' Frank commented. 'I swear every mile feels like ten.'

Lauren and Sean took on the lion's share of the sledge hauling, giving Murdo, Richard and Mel as much down time as they could. Frank was out of the hauling rota thanks to his injuries.

The haulers had quickly learned to hate the sledge, the way it constantly nudged at their heels, the way the rope around their waists caused friction burns as the hours continued.

There was one positive development: by the third night, Sean and Murdo had the night shelter in much better shape.

Their earlier attempts had been to try and construct a type of wigwam, using three ski sticks and wrapping their one blanket around the makeshift frame along with the few bits of plastic and metal sheet they had managed to bring with them from the base.

There was no room to lie inside, only enough space for them all to sit in a tightly packed circle. The lucky occupant of the sleeping-bag shift—the two-hour highlight of their nights—would curl up in the middle to give the others a chance to warm their feet beneath the fabric.

As an idea, the wigwam principle was sound enough, but the structure was too high and thin, making it fundamentally unstable. A sturdy wind would blow the poles to one side, collapsing the teepee so that one of the occupants—normally Sean—would have to go out and retie the flimsy guy ropes and try to make it erect again.

'We've got to have a better system,' Sean announced after exiting into the night for the tenth time to repair the shelter. 'This one truly sucks.'

During the next day's trek, Sean and Murdo talked it through, discussing the finer points of detail as an effective way of passing the time.

The solution they came up with was for a much lower structure than the previous one. First they took the sledge and turned it on its side so that the flat surface was facing into the wind. It acted as a windbreak approximately two metres long and half a metre high. Behind it, they lined the ice with the metal sheets, then placed the softer, more comfortable plastic sheeting on top to give them some insulation from the heat-stealing properties of the floor.

When it was time to rest, they lay side by side—like sardines in a can—with the blanket suspended over them from the sledge. The sleeping-bag occupant acted as the anchor for the blanket at the other end and also doubled as a foot warmer for anyone brave enough to take off their boots. It was claustrophobic—the blanket sagged just a few inches above their faces—but the lack of space was itself another advantage, giving their body heat a better opportunity to warm the air.

The result—the 'Mark Two Den', as Sean christened it—was a big improvement, an ingenious way of maximising their scant materials and far warmer than the previous shelter. It didn't blow down, it was relatively snowtight in drifting conditions and if snow did collect on the blanket a vigorous heave from below could always clear it. The main disadvantage was suffered by the two team members at the outer extremities of the shelter, their unprotected flanks froze solid without the warmth of another body to close up to. They rotated these positions every hour.

'Like emperor penguins in the winter,' Lauren said. 'The ones on the outside always get the bum deal.'

The Mark Two Den was a success, but it still wasn't enough. Only inside that sleeping bag could any of them find true sleep. For the rest of the interminable hours of the night, there was nothing but the cracking of the frozen blanket in the wind and the chattering of teeth.

In their minds was one thought, and one thought only. When would they get to that depot? And how much food would it contain?

63

Fitzgerald steered the snowcat in a little closer. Now he was just a few hundred metres from the wreckage of the base. It was the closest he had dared to come since the fire.

He paused, looking intently into the ruins, alert for any sign of movement. If someone ran towards him, he was ready to turn and race away.

This was the trap, he knew, and he had to admit it was well done. For three entire days he had seen not a single sign of life from the base. They were luring him in, coaxing him closer, hoping that he would lose his caution and make that one fatal mistake which would lose him everything. If he went too close, they'd be on him like a pack of wolves.

That was where they were. Huddled beneath that charred section of corrugated iron, the remains of the engine shed. Other pieces of debris were placed around it to block out the wind and the snow. He couldn't see inside. But they'd be looking at him, all right, praying for him to kill the engine, to take those few steps away from the snowcat.

They would be desperate with hunger and cold.

'Do you take me for a fool?' he shouted at the ruins. 'I know some of you must still be alive. Show yourselves! Maybe I can help you.'

Nothing stirred.

Fitzgerald looked behind him, suddenly aware that the ticking-over of the snowcat engine would disguise the footfalls of someone running towards him.

He couldn't turn the engine off. Perhaps it wouldn't start again. Then he'd be at their mercy. One man against four . . . or were there five?

He revved the engine, secure in the confident tone of the engine note, then drove in a circle around the base, trying all the while to see into that shelter.

He paused again.

Maybe they were dead? The thought was enticing. Was three days and nights enough to kill them? Christ knows that shelter must be like a deep freeze at night. Fitzgerald shuddered at the very thought.

But Lauren was tougher than that. And Sean too. The others might have fallen with exposure, but Fitzgerald knew enough about those two to be pretty confident they'd still be alive.

And they were waiting for him, had made themselves the bait.

Suddenly, he had an idea. There were a few spare cans of food stashed in the back pannier of the snowcat, a contingency in case he somehow—God forbid—lost the tent or became disorientated in a storm.

'I've got spare food!' he called out. 'I'm leaving some here on the ice for you now.'

Fitzgerald tossed a tin of meat onto the ice.

'Spam!' he yelled. 'No tricks. Just a goodwill gesture. Come and get it.'

He backed off half a mile or so and watched for nearly an hour. No way they would resist that, he thought, no matter how much they wanted to bring him into the trap.

But no one moved. No figure emerged, stiff and frozen, from the shelter to collect the food.

But it wouldn't be there tomorrow, Fitzgerald had never been more certain of anything in his life.

One of them would crack. Or two or three. That meat would be calling to them stronger than they could possibly resist after three days and nights of no food whatsoever.

He drove close again. 'I'll be back tomorrow,' he shouted.

Then he turned the snowcat and drove back out into the wilderness.

64

'm so sorry,' Frank told the others every time they waited for him to catch up. 'I'm getting to be a bit of a liability, aren't I?'

Lauren kept back with him, matching his shuffling steps with her own and trying to keep his morale up by talking as they went. Their conversation was rambling, punctuated by long silences as they succumbed to fatigue.

'You know what I want?' he would say.

'Tell me.'

Frank was invariably fantasising about food.

'Steak and kidney pudding. With thick gravy. And onions.'

'There's food at the depot,' Lauren would tell him. 'You can eat plenty when we get there.'

There was no doubt in Lauren's mind that Frank was gradually losing it. Sometimes he would come to an abrupt halt and stand in a daze for minutes on end, looking out across the white expanse in which they stood as if amazed to find himself there.

Other times he would sing gently to himself, the same words repeated over and again as he tripped along.

'It's good to touch the green, green grass of home.'

By that afternoon Frank was spending more time flat on his back than he was on his feet. Lauren would sit beside him, watching as the rest of the group walked away into the distance in a straggling line, then, impatient and fearful, she would goad him into action; her daily log placed them sixty-three miles from the base—but there were still nearly forty to go.

'Get up, Frank, there's more distance to make before we stop.'

'How far?'

'A few more miles. We've got a target, Frank; you have to hit the target. You've made almost seventy miles; you can do more.'

Sometimes a flash of humour would hint at the old Frank; back at Capricorn he'd been in the habit of imitating an old sea dog, and sometimes, almost hysterical with exhaustion, he would lapse back into it.

'I can't bear it, Cap'n. I'm too weak. Shoot me, for fuck's sake; have you got a gun?'

Lauren laughed.

'I wouldn't waste a bullet on you, Frank. I'd rather leave you here to rot.'

'Not even any bloody vultures to pick at me bones.'

But sooner or later the banter would have to stop and the walking would have to begin. Fifty minutes' faltering progress, ten minutes' rest. Lauren kept Frank to it even when he begged her in tears to let him rest longer.

Eventually, his conversation became stilted and confused, he couldn't hold a line of thought for more than a few minutes without getting disconnected. He took to leaning on Lauren for support, resting an arm over her shoulders and sometimes tipping her off balance.

At that night's stop, Lauren pulled Mel aside.

'I think Frank's getting hypothermic,' she told her. 'He can't stop shivering.'

After examining him, Mel could only agree.

'We've got to get him into the sleeping bag. His body core's getting dangerously low.'

Sean and Murdo prepared the camp while Lauren and Mel persuaded Frank that he had to warm himself immediately.

'I don't want to take up anyone else's slot,' he said.

'Frank. Shut up and get in the bag.'

Frank did as he was told, and after an hour or so of violent shivering, his temperature gradually rose to the point where he was able to sip a little warm water. He was desperate to sleep, but before she would allow him, Lauren insisted that Mel examine his hands. The medic unwrapped the makeshift bandages slowly, taking care not to pull any more of the damaged tissue away from the burned areas of flesh.

The fingers were infected, weeping copious quantities of pus. Around the edges of the wounds, Mel could see puffy, swollen tissue. The smell was slight, but to a trained medic it was enough. The early stages of necrosis were setting in. Gangrene was beginning to take a hold.

Mel cleaned the hands as best she could, causing Frank no little distress as she did so, then they tore up another cloth to use as a clean dressing and let him sleep.

'That's as far as he can walk,' Mel told Lauren later. 'If he gets any weaker, his chances of gangrene are going to shoot up. From tomorrow he's got to be on the sledge. At least until the first depot, where we can get him started on a course of antibiotics.'

This was the moment Lauren had dreaded, and it had come far sooner than she had ever imagined. When they had set out from the base, the fear that one or more of the team would fail to make the three-hundred-mile trek under their own steam was at the front of her mind. Sooner or later, she had reckoned, someone was going to need to be hauled on the sledge.

Now, after just five days, before reaching even the first of the depots, one of the team was already incapacitated. From now on they would have to find the strength to haul the sledge with Frank's dead weight on it. The question was: for how long could they do that? And what would happen if another member of the team became unable to walk?

Lauren didn't sleep that night.

65

The meat was still there. Fitzgerald blinked with astonishment when he saw the can. He climbed off the snowcat and picked it up, examining the seal to check if they'd somehow broken into it during the night and replaced the food with ice.

It was intact. They hadn't eaten the meat. Those starving fools had sat there with a free meal on offer and hadn't come out to get it.

He looked towards the shelter, and, for the first time in those four days, a tiny germ of doubt entered his mind.

Perhaps they really *were* dead. The shock of the fire must have been intense; some, perhaps all of them would have suffered burns. They would be dehydrated, weak as kittens from lack of food.

'I know you're in there!' he yelled. 'Show yourselves, and I'll bring you food.'

How many were still alive? What condition were they in after those four freezing nights? Would they have the strength to attack him? To race to the snowcat and drive it off to raid his camp?

If he could just walk up to that shelter and take a peek inside, all would be made clear. He could remove the bodies, drive them to the nearest deep crevasse and dump them where they'd never be found. Antarctica was not like the sea . . . it didn't give up its secrets easily; a body thrown down even a medium-sized crevasse would not reappear for millions of years.

There was one other possibility. They might not be in the shelter at all.

Fitzgerald rejected that thought as soon as it entered his mind. Impossible. They *had* to be in there; there was, literally, nowhere else to go. The nearest base was eight hundred miles to the east . . . a distance no human could contemplate without food and equipment.

Stay with the base. That was the accepted practice in a case such as this. Lauren would stick to the rules . . . or would she?

'Hello?' he called. Nothing but the flapping of a piece of metal in the wind.

Fitzgerald found himself split. He wanted to believe they were dead . . . oh, how much he wanted that. But at the same moment he could not accept that Lauren and Sean would be defeated so soon. There were always some individuals that had more staying power.

No. They were waiting in there. They knew he would be itching to see if they were dead or alive. They knew how frustrating it would be, not knowing, how the nervous tension would be eating away at him, gnawing at him hour after hour.

Perhaps he should take a bold tack? Just pace right up to the shelter, axe in hand, and attack them outright. But why take the risk? Fitzgerald knew he held all the cards. A few days more wouldn't make much difference.

But it *was* getting tedious, this hanging around. He hadn't imagined it would be like this. He wanted to get on with his journey, to drive the snowmobile back to the crashed plane, find the transmitter, and then set out for the coast . . . and the glory which was his by right.

The explorer knew he could get to the crashed plane comfortably, so long as the snowcat didn't break down. But he had to dispose of the bodies first. And make sure that Lauren hadn't left any note behind that could compromise him.

Before he left the base, he scrutinised the shelter once more. 'Damn you, Lauren!' he screamed angrily. 'I know you're in there, but your plan won't work. I'm leaving now. Leaving for good.'

He revved the snowmobile and retreated for three or four miles, where he parked up behind a big snowbank. They'd never see him at that distance.

'Come on,' he muttered. 'Show yourselves.'

But no one stirred. Fitzgerald retreated, shivering and dispirited, to his camp.

This couldn't go on, he thought impatiently; it was just too much. Tomorrow he'd storm the shelter, come what may.

66

Richard was fighting a losing battle with his feet.

Seventy miles of continuous cross-country skiing across the ice cap had brought the journalist to the point where each excruciating move required a major act of willpower.

Why me? he asked himself a hundred times each day. What have I done to deserve this pain?

When he looked back on the events which had befallen him in the past months, Richard truly wanted to cry. The plane crash, the two broken legs, the endless tedium and tension of the long winter at the base, and then the final shock of the fire. He had fought through so much, always fixing his thoughts on the world—and the warmth—he would return to.

And now it was further away than ever.

It obsessed him, that other world, that world where his day had begun with a tall cappuccino and a leisurely browse through the political pages of the quality press, with a short crowded tube journey and a brisk walk along a rainy street to the buzz of the newspaper office which was his place of work. That was nothing more now than a dim and distant memory. It had been replaced by a new world, one in which each day began with the crackling sound of his ice-encrusted clothing as he unfurled himself from a fetal ball on the glacier. This new world was one in which the moisture on his eyeballs was glazed and frosted as the cutting wind blitzed his face, and where the few drops of dark urine he produced each day froze instantly as they landed.

Thank God his legs had had time to heal at the base, he thought; they ached like hell, but they were still obeying his command . . . for the moment. But his feet? They were beyond belief.

The fast deterioration in the state of his feet had come as no surprise to Richard. He'd always had soft skin, had always been the kid forced to back out of the school cross-country race because of blisters, but this was something else entirely. The first twenty miles hadn't been too bad; his flesh had seemed to adjust to the plastic ski boots quite well, and there'd been little pain other than a few pinches here and there.

The skiing had been straightforward enough, at least where the ice was calm. Despite his lack of experience, Richard found he could mimic the smooth, sliding cross-country action of the others, keeping his skis in their tracks and concentrating on the heels of whoever was in front of him as a way of passing the hours.

But around the thirty-mile point the erosion had begun, a persistent sharp nagging at the back of each heel. His socks—soaked daily in sweat and often frozen—began to act like sandpaper, eating away at the tissue as his heels rocked to and fro with every movement of the skis. By fifty miles the sandpaper effect had become a cluster of red-hot needles, penetrating deeper with the sliding steps, and now spreading from the heels to the soft, flat ball of the foot as well.

Richard felt his toes begin to swell, the pressure building through each agonising day as they ballooned under the bruising impact of the boots. At night—even during his spell in the sleeping bag—he dared not take the boots off, terrified that if he did so he would never be able to squeeze the inflated flesh back into them.

Then the next day it would start again, the pain so intense he was biting his lip with each stride. Concentrate on the depot, he told himself, trying to flip his mind into a mantra as the miles crawled interminably past. But the depot was beginning to feel like an impossible dream, a Xanadu, a mirage which they would never reach. And after that was another hundred miles to the next depot . . . and then another hundred to the aircraft . . .

And the hunger. Well, that was another thing.

After eighty-odd miles, he could bear it no more. When they stopped that evening, he asked Lauren if he could borrow her penknife and a headtorch.

'What for?'

'I want to do some work on my feet . . .'

'If they need medical attention, that's down to me,' Mel told him.

'I'd rather . . .'

'Let Mel do it,' Lauren insisted. 'Take your boots off now.'

Richard lay back as Lauren and Mel removed his boots by the light of their headtorches, stifling a cry as they pulled the frozen sock away from his right foot. There was a collective gasp of sympathy from the team as they saw flesh, which looked more like a plate of bloody steak than a human foot. The miles had exacted a terrible toll, the top layers of skin completely eroded so that the red tissue beneath was livid and raw. The toes were also affected, hammered and distorted by the constant chafing of the boots until the nails were loose in their beds.

'Don't touch it,' Richard urged. 'I'll be all right; put the sock back on.'

'We have to treat this,' Mel told him. 'If these blisters get infected, you won't be able to walk.'

The others were quiet as Richard absorbed this information.

'Leave us for a while,' Lauren told them quietly. 'It doesn't help to have everyone crowded round.'

The others moved off a short distance as Mel took the Swiss army knife and flicked open the scissors attachment. Trying to close her mind to the pain she knew she was causing the journalist, she proceeded to cut away the dead flesh around the blisters, trimming it as deep as she could until he was begging her to stop.

'Can't risk any infection,' she told him. 'You're just going to have to grit your teeth.'

When it was finished, she repeated the process on Richard's left foot, encouraging him with the thought that at least now some of the pressure would be relieved. Then, with the patient still mumbling in anguish, they replaced the socks and jammed his feet back into the boots.

'Don't take these boots off again before we reach the depot,' Mel told him. 'At least there we'll be able to clean your feet up and bandage them properly.'

Later that night, as they huddled together for warmth, Richard gently touched Lauren's arm to get her attention.

'You won't leave me?' he whispered. 'You won't leave me if it gets to the point I can't walk?'

'No way,' Lauren reassured him. 'If we have to pull you on the sledge with Frank, we will.'

'Thank you,' the journalist told her. 'It's just been preying on my mind a bit, that's all.'

Wrapped up in the problems of leading the team, Lauren realised she had spared little thought for Richard and his predicament. Now she thought about how vulnerable the journalist really was—totally dependent for his life on five people he barely knew . . . and with his feet already falling to bits even though they were less than a third of the way to the aircraft.

Lauren reached out and squeezed Richard's hand.

'Think about the story you'll have to tell when we all get out of this,' she told him. 'You'll pick up a Pulitzer Prize for sure.'

'Nice idea.' Richard half smiled, the moment coinciding with a sudden sweeping apart of the clouds to let a few rays of moonlight hit his face. Lauren could see the ice cracking around his mouth.

67

Fitzgerald parked the snowcat a safe distance away and armed himself with the axe. It had to happen now: he hadn't slept a moment that night, and he couldn't take the uncertainty any more.

He strode straight into the wreckage of the base. Don't give them time to think, he reasoned; take them by surprise.

He smashed his shoulder into the outer wall of the shelter, sending the corrugated iron crashing down with a loud clatter into the place where the survivors would be crouching. Axe at the ready, he clambered over the debris, prepared to sink the weapon into the first of them to make a run for it.

'Come on, you bastards!' he called. 'Let's get this over with.'

Nothing happened. The iron sheet had collapsed too far to the ground. It was obvious there was no one sheltering inside. Fitzgerald lifted it, still wary that it might be a trick, still not believing what his eyes were telling him.

They were gone. The space was empty.

Fitzgerald quickly scanned the surrounding terrain, fearful that this was a decoy. Perhaps they had dug in somewhere else in the ruins? Perhaps this was a deliberate dead end, designed to lure him away from the snowmobile?

But there was no figure running for the machine, no sign of life anywhere, in fact.

What the hell was going on? Fitzgerald had never known such a bizarre situation. How long had they been gone, and why hadn't he seen them leave? And what possible logic had drawn them away from their only source of shelter?

He stood, bewildered, his mind ticking through the options.

A rescue plane. A stab of terror ran through the explorer's spine. What if they'd managed to get the radio working? If they'd sent a message, if a plane had come?

No. It wasn't that. The radio room—and the aerial mast—had been well and truly destroyed. And besides, the conditions still weren't good enough to get a flight in, with the temperatures hovering down in the low minus fifties it would be a couple of weeks at least before AAS would risk coming down from South America. Get a hold, Fitzgerald told himself, there has to be an answer.

A note. There had to be a note, somewhere in the ruins. Whatever action they had taken, Lauren would have left a record, to tell searchers where they had gone.

He began to sift through the wreckage, looking for a container, for a box or a burned-up can which might hold the clue.

Where would they put it? It would have to be somewhere obvious. In less than five minutes he found it, a tiny piece of notebook paper, rolled up and placed carefully in the hollow interior of a drilling bit which had been stood on its end as a sign. Sort of logical now he thought about it.

The explorer unfolded the scrap of paper, deciphering Lauren's handwritten note with some difficulty.

31 Aug. Capricorn destroyed by fire following incident in which Julian Fitzgerald attempted to escape the base. Carl Norland killed. Julian Fitzgerald's whereabouts un-

known but approach with extreme caution as is mentally unstable and violent. Six survivors now set out for Chilean base in direction indicated by arrow. Lauren Burgess, base commander.

Beneath the note was a small graphic depicting the points of the compass. An arrow pointed to the northeast, the direction of the nearest base.

Fitzgerald read the note again, wanting to make sure he wasn't seeing things. Heading for the Chilean base? It didn't make any sense. How could they ever hope to make it without food . . . it was physically impossible.

Maybe they *did* have food. Was it possible they had rescued some before the galley went up in the explosion? Fitzgerald immediately dismissed the notion. He had seen the explosion with his own eyes: nothing in that galley—or the storeroom next to it—could have cheated that blast. And besides, logic would dictate that, if they did have food, they would be all the more likely to remain at the base.

It was all too confusing. And yet the evidence was there in his hands. They *had* set out on foot, probably sneaking out in the night when he was not observing them.

He would follow them, wait for them to die. It would all end the same way in any case.

Just as he was about to pull away from the base, Fitzgerald paused. Something had caught his eye. Something strange about some junk which had spewed out onto the glacier.

Seen from ground level it was a random scatter of debris, thrown out onto the ice, presumably by the force of the explosion. But there was something about it that fired his curiosity, a pattern to it, a shape, even, which didn't look random at all.

Fitzgerald stopped the snowcat again and paced out amongst the wreckage. What was it? Something was wrong. Some of the pieces looked almost like they had been placed by hand.

It wasn't until he was standing at the tip that he had it. It was an arrow, the debris was arranged perfectly in the shape of an arrow. Anyone arriving by air—and that was the only way they *could* arrive—would see the fifty-metre-long arrow pointing clearly away from the base. That would be the trajectory they would immediately search.

The explorer checked his compass. The arrow pointed to the northwest, not leading to the Chilean base at all.

So where *was* it pointing? Fitzgerald tried to conjure up a mental map of the region. What was to the northwest apart from the Heilman range and the way to the Blackmore Glacier?

Beneath his feet he suddenly noticed a small strip of metal stuck at an odd angle into the ice. The surface around it had been disturbed. It was lying at the tip of the arrow . . . the very place to put a second note, he quickly realised.

He scraped with his hands, finding the charred remains of a can in just a few seconds. He unfolded the note it contained and read:

> Aug 31. A message from Capricorn commander Lauren Burgess. Ignore any other note found. It is a decoy to throw Julian Fitzgerald off our trail. The survivors of this fire have left today for the Blackmore Glacier on foot. We are heading for the Antarctic Air Service plane which crashed there last month in the hope we can retrieve the emergency transmitter which was left there.

An indication of the bearing followed, along with the coordinates of the plane.

Fitzgerald couldn't believe his luck in finding that second note. The first note had been false. They too were heading for the plane! Like him, they'd remembered the emergency transmitter, left behind in the tent with all the other redundant gear. But how could they make three hundred miles on foot?

Then a half-remembered conversation came back to him. There were depots, food and equipment left by Lauren and

Sean when they came on the outward leg of the rescue! Christ, why hadn't he thought of that? There was food out there, and they might even now be arriving at the first dump.

There wasn't a moment to lose. Fitzgerald scattered the debris so that the telltale arrow was destroyed, then raced to the snowmobile. He would decamp and set out in pursuit as fast as he could.

As he drove, Fitzgerald had to make a conscious effort to calm his rage. Lauren had been clever; he had wasted days observing that ruddy shelter, so nearly been tricked by the false note.

He wouldn't underestimate her again. That much was sure.

68

'How far to go to the depot?' Mel asked.

Lauren scribbled some calculations on a scrap of paper.

'It's day six. Fifteen miles to go. That's a day and a half at our present rate.'

'Let me go ahead with Murdo and see if we can find it,' Sean urged her. 'The rest are just about wiped.'

'The team stays together,' Lauren told him. 'That's the golden rule, and it's a rule I won't break.'

'But that doesn't make sense,' Sean protested. 'Me and Murdo are in better shape; we can be ten miles ahead of the pack by lunchtime tomorrow, pick up the barrel and haul it back by nightfall. It'll gain us a day.'

Lauren sighed. 'Sean, don't think I don't appreciate the offer; believe me, I'd love to take you up on it for my own sake . . . I'm desperate for food too.'

'So why don't you let us do it?' Murdo interjected angrily. 'We're all fucking starving, Lauren, and we need that food now!'

'Because, if you really think about it, it won't gain us a damn thing. You'll both be more tired . . . that's an extra twenty or thirty miles you'll have done. We'll all get some food a day earlier, sure, but that's not necessarily going to help. There's a finite amount of calories at those two dumps, right?'

'Go on . . .'

'So if we break open the rations ten miles early, that means we have to shift the team one hundred and ten miles to the next meal rather than one hundred. On the same amount of food. Do you see what I'm saying?'

'More or less.' Sean conceded the logic but he clearly wasn't happy about it.

'Well, I think you're completely wrong,' Murdo said, jabbing his finger at her. 'You're basically forcing us to wait when we don't need to.'

'I'm keeping the team together,' Lauren insisted. 'We've got a target, and we've got to hit that target together or not at all.'

'Fuck the togetherness,' Murdo muttered. 'I have to eat soon or I'll have no energy left to walk at all.'

'Yes, you will. You'll start walking at dawn like the rest of us no matter how shattered you are. And why do you think you'll do that? Because you'll know that you have to to get to that depot before you can eat.'

'You're treating us like one of your bloody laboratory experiments.' Mel now joined the conversation, exasperated. 'People have limits, Lauren, and you have to recognise that.'

'And what if Murdo or Sean falls into a crevasse while they're out there?' Lauren asked. 'Or what if a blizzard blows up while they're trying to make their way back to us with that heavy barrel? We'll miss each other in the whiteout and then that really will be the end.'

'I still think it's worth the risk,' Murdo persisted.

'We can't accept any more risk. Can't you see that?' Lauren flared. 'It's going to get harder, Murdo, a damn sight harder than you can imagine. Sean and I have driven this terrain, we know what's ahead. There's a bloody mountain range waiting for us! This is going to be the toughest physical challenge any of us have ever faced, and every single calorie is going to count. We might need that extra strength of yours to haul the sledge later on. With someone on it.'

This time no one responded.

'There's one more thing,' Lauren added quietly. 'Fitzgerald might be out there somewhere, waiting. He won't attack us while we stay together.'

With that the team fell quiet, and within an hour or so the ashes of the fire had died down to a dull glow.

69

From the start of the seventh day, Lauren's nerves were in a heightened state. They were approaching the first of the equipment dumps, and it was her responsibility—and hers alone—to locate it. She went through the calculations over and over again as they plodded wearily along, checking her compass every ten minutes for the bearing and calling a halt as they made it to the one-hundred-mile mark.

'This is it,' Lauren told them. 'By my reckoning we should be close to the equipment barrel.'

The tired team scanned in all directions but could see nothing unusual. The terrain was undulating, the surface broken by scoops and hollows; in places drifting snow had formed into hardened dunes. The light was dull, a blanket of cloud obscuring the scene and casting a watery grey sheen over the land. There seemed to be no definition in place, as if the entire scene had been sculpted from dirty bits of old cloud.

'You must be mistaken,' Murdo told her. 'I thought you

said this thing had a flag on it? Surely we'd be able to see it straight away?'

'Not necessarily. This ground is more uneven than it looks. Give or take a few hundred metres, it has to be here,' Lauren insisted. 'Let's rest for a while, then get a search pattern organised.'

'How are we going to conduct the search?' Sean asked her.

'We'll measure a straight line of five hundred metres and spread out twenty metres apart. We walk that transect, then move down one hundred metres and start again.'

They rested their exhausted legs for a while, each locked in a private world of misery as they sat back to back on the ice. No one talked about the unthinkable—about what would happen if they couldn't find the depot.

'It's lunchtime,' Richard said at one point. 'They'll be eating scampi and chips and ploughman's lunches in every pub in Britain.'

In the first days of the trek such a statement would have been met with howls of outrage and pleas to keep his fantasies to himself. Now no one had the energy to tell him to shut up.

Frank began his singing again, this time an Irish tune that Lauren recognised but could not name. It made her want to cry. Periodically he would screw up his face as a wave of pain ran through his infected hands.

At length, Lauren got them onto their feet and the search began.

For two hours she kept them looking, urging them to try and concentrate even as the afternoon wind began to rise. Initially, they were enthusiastic, excited even at the prospect of the hot food and supplies that the barrel would bring. But, as the day stretched interminably on, morale began to slump.

A gnawing sensation of despair began to eat away at Lauren. How long could they continue to search? she asked herself. When would the weaker team members begin to collapse if they didn't get food? They would survive another night, she surmised, but not much more.

After a while the tight discipline of the search broke

down, each of them moving off and wandering in aimless patterns as they looked for the elusive barrel. From time to time, Lauren reminded herself that it was dangerous for them to be separated in this way . . . that Fitzgerald might have followed them, might be waiting for a chance to stalk up and . . .

'I had the same thought,' Sean told her, 'and I've been keeping a good look-out behind us. So far nothing.'

'I just don't want anyone to stray too far,' Lauren told him.

But she didn't have the energy to try and regroup the line and continued her own meandering search as her mind wandered erratically from one thought to another.

The mood when Lauren finally called them back together was one of unmitigated depression. No one, not even Lauren and Sean, had anticipated that the barrel would prove so difficult to find.

'Maybe it got blown away,' someone said, flatly.

'Or Fitzgerald got it.'

'Or we're looking in the wrong place. Your calculations might be wrong.'

Lauren turned to Sean, the frustration clearly written across her face.

'Come on, Sean. Think! What are we doing wrong?'

'Well, the first thing we have to realise is that the flag obviously isn't upright any more. If it was, we'd have found it by now.'

'Correct. But what about the barrel? Why can't we see it? It's a socking great bright blue barrel in the middle of a vast white wilderness, and we can't see it!'

'Maybe the answer is . . . it's not blue any more. We've told everyone to look out for something blue, but what if it got completely coated in ice during a storm? That could happen, right?'

Lauren thought about it.

'You think it could be that simple?'

'Yes, I do. It's the only reason I can think of that we might have missed it. It's camouflaged. Everyone's so damn tired someone might have walked right past it!'

'So we're looking for something white. Everyone got that?' Lauren told them.

'Something white?' Murdo pointed out glumly, waving his arm to encompass the uniform white terrain that surrounded them. 'That narrows it down nicely.'

Nevertheless, after they had rested for an hour the team began the search once more, fanning out again in pairs, continuing a rough search pattern even though most had lost hope they would ever find the depot.

Suddenly, a shout went up to the south of the camp position. It was Sean, waving his hands in the air about four hundred metres off.

'Got it!' the others heard. 'Here it is!'

The barrel was on its side; one of the anchors which had held it upright had been ripped out of the ice in a gale. The flag was long gone, nowhere to be seen, and—as Sean had predicted—the blue plastic was completely obscured by a coating of ice . . . and by a drift of snow which half covered it.

The team gathered round the barrel, elated and relieved that it had finally been found. Frank was the most emotional, gently touching the plastic as if he feared it was not real, then promptly breaking into a fit of unrestrained sobs.

Lauren hugged him until he stopped crying, while the others chipped the plastic object free from its mantle of ice.

'You see that?' Sean pointed to a set of tracks which passed a few metres to the west of the barrel. 'I was right. Someone did walk right past it on an earlier search and never saw it!'

As they broke open the barrel and began to sort through the contents, Lauren walked over and inspected the tracks, her cheeks burning as she recognised the tread. She never told the others that those boot prints were hers.

70

Fitzgerald had driven like the wind, pushed the snowcat so hard the exhaust glowed red hot in the night. He didn't dare sleep, knowing that if he could only get to that depot first . . .

It was a dangerous business, driving at speed across the plateau in the dark, but Fitzgerald was oblivious to the risk, pushing the machine harder and harder until the oil pressure gauge was high up in the red, the engine screaming as it powered onwards, eating up the miles to the target.

The explorer was not frightened of missing them in the night, he knew they would have been able to cover at least eighty or ninety miles by now if they'd been going strong.

He guessed he would make contact sometime in the afternoon, and, sure enough, just after three p.m., he saw the line of black specks on the horizon. There they were, crossing and recrossing an area perhaps a half-mile in width.

Fitzgerald parked the snowmobile behind the cover of a pressure ridge and began his observation. They were distracted. He was confident they would not be looking for any sign of him.

They were searching; he realised that straight away.

So there was still hope! Maybe they wouldn't find the depot after all. Perhaps they were looking in the wrong place.

What had Sean told him about the depots? The explorer had been sifting through his memory, frantically trying to recall. How many were there? Two, perhaps four. And *where* were they stationed along the route to the crashed plane?

Fitzgerald remembered the milometer on the snowmobile, perhaps that would hold a clue. It read ninety-seven miles. That was it! He felt a wave of satisfaction at the discovery, pleased he had thought to zero the gauge before pulling away from the base on the northwest heading.

The depot was one hundred miles from base. Simple, really.

As he watched them, he saw the team come together to a specific point. They were more animated now, the dejected stance of the search replaced by more activity.

They'd found it. Fitzgerald cursed his luck. An hour or two earlier and he would have been there first.

But at least he'd found them. He had to be grateful for that.

The position of the next depot wasn't hard to fathom; logic told him it would be placed an equal distance from the base, at the two-hundred-mile point, on the other side of the Heilman range.

He could overtake them whenever he chose.

Fitzgerald mounted the snowmobile and pressed the starter. The engine coughed once or twice but failed to start. He pressed again, realising now that he might have pushed the engine too hard on that hundred-mile dash from the base.

This time it started, but it didn't have the crisp note of before. Fitzgerald frowned as he engaged the gear. If he was honest, the whole machine felt a bit sick, like the belt drive wasn't engaging properly.

He lurched off to find a place to camp—a place where he

could rest in safety. He hadn't slept for three days now, and he was tired to the bone.

The snowmobile coughed again. Damn this machine, the explorer thought, if it lets me down . . .

71

No child ever ripped open a Christmas stocking with more delight than the Capricorn team exploring the contents of that barrel. Seven days without eating a scrap had driven them to the point where the mere sight of so much food was enough to make them weak at the knees.

Dried fruit. Tea bags. Biscuits. Glucose energy tablets. Pre-packed foil sachets of bacon and beans, beef stew and dumplings, goulash. There was chocolate, sugar, tins of coffee and ham.

'I hope you put a bloody tin opener in here, Frank!' Murdo told him.

Almost as precious as the food was the medical box containing antibiotics, bandages and painkillers which—crucially—included morphine. Mel took charge of the kit and immediately began to treat Frank's infected hands. Within a matter of minutes, she was cleaning and disinfecting the wounds.

Deeper down, packed tightly beneath the food and med-

ical supplies, was cooking equipment, two tents and three
sleeping bags. Lauren almost wept when she saw them. She
walked over to where Frank was lying flat on his back on the
sledge for his treatment.

'You did a great job when you packed this depot,' she told
him. 'Thank God you thought this one out properly.'

'I never dreamed we'd end up using it.'

'How are his fingers?' she asked Mel.

'The infection doesn't seem much worse than yesterday. I
think the spell on the sledge did him good. This clean-up is
exactly what they need, and I'll put him on a strong course
of penicillin after he's had some food.'

Next the team made a careful stack of the provisions so
that Lauren could compile a list of what they had. 'By my
calculations,' she told them, 'we've got enough for six to
eight meals each. If we take care we can eke this out so that
we can eat at least one meal a day each until the next depot.'

'Don't forget the next depot's a much tougher walk with
the mountain range,' Sean reminded her.

'Screw the calculations,' Murdo said. 'Let's eat.'

They erected one of the tents, and Sean soon put the
cooker to work, melting down ice and handing out a steaming plastic mug of cocoa to each of them. After seven days
of tepid meltwater, the taste of the chocolate was exquisite.

Then each was allowed to choose one of the pre-cooked
foil sachets of food—a process they undertook with elaborate care, comparing the contents and discussing which had
more calories to offer.

Lauren chose beans and bacon and waited her turn for the
sachet to be warmed in a pan of boiling water. When she
placed the first spoonful in her mouth, it created an explosion of warmth and taste which almost took her breath away.

Normally, Lauren disliked fatty foods, but now she relished the chunky pieces of salted bacon, chewing the gristly
meat over and over so as not to waste a single particle of
taste. Every bean got the same treatment, the sweet tomato
paste savoured for long moments before she reluctantly
swallowed the food.

When she had demolished every last morsel, Lauren ripped the sachet open and licked it clean.

Afterwards came a handful of dried fruit (each apricot counted out individually so no one got more than anyone else), three squares of chocolate and a few boiled sweets.

'We'll have to get a rota system going,' Lauren told them. 'Four people will sleep while two keep watch. After two hours, the ones on watch go into the bags and another two come out to take their turn.'

'You still think we need to mount a watch?' Mel asked her. 'We haven't seen Fitzgerald since we left the base.'

'We keep the watch,' Lauren told her. 'Imagine how it would feel to come out here in the morning and find Fitzgerald had stolen all this food and the sledge during the night.'

They agreed to the plan, and, desperate for the warmth, the first four volunteers were inside the tent and into the sleeping bags within minutes of finishing the meal. The tent was designed for two, but four could jam in—head to toe—at a pinch. The comfort level was low, but no one had the energy to put up the second tent, and the tight conditions generated a few more degrees of heat.

Out on the glacier, Lauren and Sean took the first watch, sitting on the sledge and staying close to the heat of the fire.

'You must be proud, getting everyone to the first depot,' Sean told her.

'Proud of the team. I haven't done anything special, but I appreciate the thought. Not many people thank the leader.'

'Well, all the more reason to do it. You did a great job to get us here . . . and you were right about keeping everyone together when Murdo wanted to make the break.'

'Thank you, Sean.'

'You think they've got it in them to get over the mountains?'

Lauren let out a long sigh. 'They have to. There's no other way down onto the glacier. But I must admit that frightens me a lot.'

'It's Frank we'll have to watch. He's definitely the weakest link. Richard's a bit wobbly too, but he'll pick up now we've got some provisions.'

Gradually, they fell silent, awed by the millions of stars which the clear night revealed above them. Every few minutes a shooting star would race across the night sky.

'You think Fitzgerald's on our trail?' Lauren asked him.

'I hope not.' Sean peered out into the night. 'But even if he is, maybe we got lucky and he's hit a problem with the snowmobile. Maybe he had a spark plug crack, or threw a belt. I don't know what kind of mechanic he is, but I sure wouldn't want to be on my own out there with a dead machine.'

Lauren looked out into the darkness.

'Maybe he's keeping just out of sight. He wants us to think he's lost us.'

'So we let down our guard?'

'Precisely.'

When their two-hour watch was over, Lauren and Sean took their turn in the tent while Mel and Murdo took over the watch. Crawling into the protection of the sleeping bag was a sublime moment of luxury. To be out of the penetrating wind seemed to Lauren to be the greatest pleasure she had ever experienced.

Her belly was full, her mind relaxed now the tension of the search for the depot was over. Lauren let the glorious warmth of the duckdown fold around her and nestled down to sleep as the snores of her companions filled the tent.

'Sean?' she whispered.

'Yep?' His reply showed he was right on the edge of sleep.

'I wanted to tell you something about what happened between us at the base . . .'

Sean turned towards her, his face so close she could feel his breath on her cheek.

'Don't you mean what *didn't* happen between us?'

'Yeah. It's just that it happened to me before, on another base. I got involved with someone, and then it all went sour. Then we had to spend the entire winter living under each other's skin, and it was a total nightmare.'

'I think we would have been cool.'

Lauren leaned forward and kissed him softly on the lips.

'I think so too. And maybe we still will be.'

'If we get out of this alive.'

They were silent for a while.

'There's still two hundred miles to go,' Lauren whispered, her heart full of fear as she lay there awake, listening to the sound of Murdo and Mel talking softly outside the tent.

72

'One and pull . . . and two and pull!' Lauren called the moves as they hit the lowest flanks of the Heilman range, the sledge graunching across the rough ice in fits and starts as the incline began to work against them. It was day eight of the trek.

'Keep it coming! One and pull . . . and two and pull.'

'You were born in the wrong century,' Murdo muttered. 'You sure you weren't a slave driver in a former life?'

There were four of them on the harness now, Lauren and Sean at the front, Mel and Murdo at the back. Richard brought up the rear, his damaged feet counting him out of the hauling duty even though he desperately wanted to help.

It was the first morning after finding the depot, and they were better fed and rested than they had been at any point since the fire. That was why Lauren was pushing them so hard. They'd slept for a straight ten hours, and Lauren had let them eat their fill at breakfast, knowing that they would need every precious calorie for the trial of hauling Frank over the range.

Frank had fought to stay off the sledge, had insisted he was strong enough to walk, but a quick test stroll had revealed the truth—he was still feverish and weak from the infection. He had reluctantly taken his place, lying in a sleeping bag for extra warmth.

Lauren was sure of one thing. They had to cross the range in a day. One extreme burst of energy while they still had the reserves. If it took them longer and they got stuck on the higher slopes in a storm, there was little prospect of finding a safe place to pitch the tents.

She had them awake at six a.m. By ten they were navigating their way onto the first of the steep glacier ramps which had seemed so easy with the snowcats. They worked on foot; without skins, the skis were as good as useless.

'Don't let the momentum stop,' Sean yelled as the sledge jammed in a crack. They heaved extra hard to free it, thigh muscles straining as they leaned forward to win a few more inches of the slope.

'Keep it coming!' Lauren urged them on as they paused to rest. 'Another twenty minutes before we stop!'

Somehow they did as she asked, leaning forward and straining in unison, the sledge grinding reluctantly up the ice for a couple more paces before they rested, gasping for breath. With every metre of height, it seemed the sledge was gaining weight.

'Are you carrying rocks in there?' Murdo demanded of Frank. 'Or do you just weigh a bastard ton?'

Midday. They hauled the load up a particularly steep rise then eased back on the makeshift harnesses, appreciating the relief as the constant strain on their backs was relieved.

'Take a break,' Lauren told them. 'Ten minutes.' She gave them a boiled sweet each and a swig from a water bottle containing powdered orange drink.

'It's the harness that kills me,' Murdo said, sitting heavily on the sledge.

Lauren knew what he meant. Hauling Frank up the range was proving a backbreaking task, and one which wasn't getting any easier as the hours crawled past. The harness was Sean's design, a simple series of loops twisted into their only rope.

As a means of towing the dead weight of the sledge, the system worked fine; they could harness four pullers at the same time, arranged in a fan formation in front of the sledge. It reminded Lauren of old black-and-white photographs of Scott's expedition, in which his team had manhauled provisions in the same way.

But on these punishing slopes the disadvantage was a serious one: the rope had no padding, the nine-millimetre cord cutting ever more insistently into the flesh of their waists and hips as they fought to gain altitude. They tried wrapping pieces of clothing around their waists, hoping to alleviate the pain, but the constant motion of the rope would inevitably dislodge them, sawing its way steadily into the soft tissue around their waist until the skin broke.

As the ascent went on, these erosions became blisters, then the blisters became sores. Within a few hours, every member of the team was suffering from open, weeping wounds around their hips, one more ailment to add to the chronically blistered feet and the problems of burns from the fire.

'Can't we camp?' Mel begged after five hours of hauling. 'I'm really in pain here.'

'We keep going,' Lauren insisted. 'We can make it in one hit. Another few hours and we'll be at the col.'

An afternoon squall whipped across the mountain, slowing their progress as they contoured around one of the major peaks. A boulder bounced down the slope just a handful of metres ahead of them, crashing quickly out of sight into the cloud.

For an agonising hour, as the visibility continued to fall, Lauren feared they had lost their way; it would be all too easy to head up the wrong arm of the glacier and find themselves in a dead end. She kept to the compass bearing, trusting the instrument to keep them on track; it was essential they followed the same route they had found with the snow-cats.

Then they came to a feature Sean remembered.

'That's the cliff!' he reminded her. 'This is where we stopped to refuel.'

They shared a can of tinned fruit, broke open a packet of chocolate biscuits and ate two each, their bodies greedily absorbing the sugars they contained.

There was no conversation now, just the deep panting as they fought against the incline.

A short while later the squall blew away, taking the dense clouds with it and revealing their position. The col was above them, they were right on target.

'Remember that last section of ice?' Sean reminded Lauren. 'We'll have to think about that one.'

They pulled in a zig-zag pattern, exploiting the easiest angles of the slope, traversing back and forth, gaining a few metres of height on each pass.

'One and pull . . . two and pull . . .' Lauren's throat was sore from the shouting. They were sweating with the effort now, a dangerous state to be in as the moisture froze as soon as they stopped to rest.

Then they came to the final obstacle, the sheer sixty-degree slope which guarded the col. To try and tow the sledge across without the protection of a rope would have been inviting disaster.

Sean derigged the harness and anchored one end of the rope to a big boulder. He inched across the slope and tied the other end off on a shard of rock on the far side. Then he returned and rejoined the group.

'We'll use the rope as a handrail,' he told them. 'Keep the sledge on the uphill slope.'

'Are you sure?' Frank was eying the dizzy drop beneath them. 'What happens if you can't hold it . . . ?'

No one replied.

'Let's get on with it,' Lauren said.

They each took a hold of the sledge and started to move,

unsteadily, out onto the slope. Murdo fell twice, but he managed to regain his position both times and didn't let go of the sledge. Frank's eyes rolled with terror as they hit the steepest section; he was clinging to the side struts, his knuckles white.

'Keep your eyes on the far side,' Lauren told them, 'and for Christ's sake don't look down.'

They hit the easier ground, and Sean returned to retrieve the rope.

Forty minutes later, with a last collective heave, they hauled the sledge over the remainder of the pressure ridges and made the final col; they had gained two thousand feet of altitude in nine hours of ascent, and now the Blackmore Glacier was below them.

'Jesus Christ,' Murdo gasped as he saw the view, his legs giving way beneath him even as he spoke. 'Is that where we're going?'

73

Lauren had focused her mind so sharply on what it would take to get the team up on to the high col that she hadn't even thought about the descent which waited for them on the other side. Now all sense of exhilaration faded fast as she considered what lay between them and the flat terrain of the next glacier.

It wasn't that the terrain was terribly steep, the height fell away in a gradient not much greater than the lower slopes of an average Scottish mountain. But it was complicated territory, riven, as is always the case where unseen forces are colliding beneath the surface, by the dissecting fissures of crevasses and crunched-up ice.

Lauren cast her mind back to the snowmobile descent she had made of this same route with Sean, remembering now the many dozens of times they had made a route-finding error, piloting themselves into a dead end where they were blocked by an uncrossable crevasse. With the machines, rectifying such a mistake was simple and painless, just a question of turning the thing around and letting the engine power back up the slope to try another possible route.

But how would it be on foot? How many times could she ask her team to backtrack—always the most demoralising action under any circumstances—particularly as she would be asking them to backtrack *uphill*?

'Sean, how much do you remember of the descent?' she asked him.

Sean looked down at the slope.

'I think we tried to go through the centre of that ice fall.' He pointed to the feature which dominated the middle distance. 'But we couldn't find a way through that. As I recall, we came back up a-ways and ended up scooting over to that far right wall and going down that gully.'

Lauren followed the line of his outstretched hand.

'You're right,' she confirmed. 'Do you think you could find the same way again?'

Sean considered the question for a while, trying to spot any familiar landmarks which would guide their way.

'I can try,' he told her, 'but it was a hell of a maze.'

By midafternoon they were penetrating the fractured terrain, weaving a trail beneath intimidating blocks of ice. One was shaped like a sail, another a soaring arch like a killer whale's fin. The team passed as quickly as they could beneath these obstacles, knowing that they could fall at any moment.

There was no conversation between them now, no room in their minds for anything but the total concentration needed to prevent a slip. Without crampons, the terrain was hazardous, each of them having to think twice about each footstep, searching for the crimps and rugosities in the surface of the ice which would give them purchase against a fall.

Good though Sean's navigation was, they twice ran themselves into a dead end, having to turn and tediously retrace their steps back up the slope to try their luck on a different line. But little by little they made a safe descent, Sean lowering the weaker members of the team by rope where the ground was too steep to tackle on foot.

By this process they reached the gully Sean and Lauren had remembered from the first time, a kilometre-long ice chute leading in an almost straight line down to the glacier. Here Sean checked his watch and called Lauren over.

'We're too slow,' he told her. 'We'll never get down onto the glacier before dark. You think we can glissade down this?'

Lauren looked down the smooth expanse of ice. 'It looks OK here, but what about the bottom end? What if it ends up in a crevasse?'

'It doesn't,' Sean said with certainty. 'We took this whole section at about twenty miles an hour when we came down on the snowcats. The bottom runs off gently onto the glacier.'

Now Lauren recalled. 'You know, I think you're right. I think we could try it. Like Shackleton on South Georgia.'

'He did the same?'

'When he crossed the interior. 1916. There were three of them, with few supplies and just a short length of rope. They had to cross the mountains to get to the whaling station at Grytviken. If I remember rightly, they ended up glissading down a huge glacier—it saved them half a day.'

'If it's good enough for Shackleton . . .' Sean said, with a smile. 'I think we should try it. It's about fifteen hundred feet from here to the glacier. We'll never get there by dark if we carry on at this pace.'

'What about Frank?'

'He can stay on the sledge. I'll sit on the back and steer it with my feet.'

Once they understood the principle, most of the team were prepared to throw themselves down the slope; anything was preferable to the pain of trying to descend on blistered feet. They followed Lauren's example, sliding on their backsides, using their feet to brake by jamming their heels into the compacted surface when they felt themselves going too fast.

After six days at walking pace the sensation of speed was breathtaking, the wind-polished walls of the gully shooting past at a tremendous rate. The sledge was fastest; bearing the heaviest load, it shot past the others at breakneck speed, Sean whooping with excitement on the back, Frank white-faced and looking anything but happy at the front.

Less than five minutes of exhilarating slide put the team at the foot of the gully, where they were spat out onto the flat surface of the glacier. Lauren ended up in a deep bank of drifted snow, the powder penetrating every gap in her clothing.

They regrouped, smiling foolishly at each other after the excitement of the glissade, a quick head count confirming that everyone had made it down safely.

'Let's get the tents up,' Lauren told them. 'We're running out of light.'

With just minutes to spare, they had the tents erected and the stoves lit. It was Sean's turn to cook, but no sooner had he got the first of the pre-packed food sachets lowered into the boiling water than Lauren was calling him from outside, her voice hissing at him through the tent fabric.

Sean poked his head out of the front flap.

'What is it?'

'I think I saw a light.' Lauren was pointing up to the high col, faintly visible in the moonlight as a looming mass of snow way above them.

'You serious?' Sean was out of the tent in a moment.

'Yes . . . at least I thought I did . . .' Now Lauren was uncertain.

'What was it?'

'Could have been a headtorch. It was only a flicker, nothing more.'

Then they both saw it, the briefest pinprick of artificial light, glimmering in the darkness.

'You were right,' Sean whistled. 'That's Fitzgerald, he's camping up on the col. How the hell did he get on our trail?'

Lauren turned to him, her face drained of all blood.

'He didn't fall for the false note. He knows we're heading for the plane.'

'Shit.'

'My thoughts exactly.'

'We've got to stop him,' Sean said. 'If he gets to that second depot before we do, we're as good as dead.'

'But how, Sean, when he's so much faster than us?'

'Let me sleep on it,' Sean told her. 'If I come up with something, I'll let you know.'

'Don't tell the others,' Lauren begged him. 'They've got enough problems as it is.'

74

The moment came just past nine a.m. on the tenth of September—the eleventh morning of the trek. They stood there together, watching the yellow blaze of light breach the horizon for the first time in six months.

'Hallelujah!' Sean cried. 'Where've you been all my life?'

The grey ice of the glacier—the half-lit world they had become so used to—was suddenly alive with colour, the ice dancing with blues and radiant whites as the rays painted light and shade. Suddenly, there was texture and depth where previously there had been monotone uniformity, the bright colours of their clothing picked out in brilliant detail.

It made them smile, turning their faces to bask in the sun's rays, even though there was no perceptible heat to be felt.

'I always wondered about the guys who built Stonehenge,' Mel said. 'I mean, I never thought of the sun as such a big deal. But I won't take it for granted again.'

All too soon, the sun sank beneath the horizon once

more, returning the glacier to the dusk-light of winter. But— Lauren and her team knew—tomorrow it would be back for longer, then the day after it would appear for longer still.

The arrival of the sun, even if it was only for a quarter of an hour or so, was the final confirmation that winter was drawing to an end. But it still wasn't fast enough for Lauren's liking. The lack of full daylight was still a serious handicap, and by three o'clock each afternoon they were stumbling in the dark.

On the easier terrain, where no crevasses threatened them, the team could continue for a few hours with the occasional use of a headtorch or by using the faint light of the stars. On more dangerous ground, there was nothing to do but pitch the tents, a big frustration on the days when the team was going well and might have continued for a couple more hours.

The long black nights created a problem of their own: the tedium and depression of fifteen hours spent in total darkness with little or no torchlight to relieve the gloom. On a good night, eight or ten of those hours could be spent in sleep, but that still left plenty of down time, most of which was spent in silent contemplation of their miserable situation, bodies throbbing from the demands of each daily trek, minds struggling to cope with the uncertainty of their fate.

'We have to talk,' Lauren begged Sean and Frank, 'distract ourselves, or we'll go crazy here in the dark.'

'Fairy tales?' Frank said quietly.

'Anything.'

'Only one type of story I want to hear,' Sean said, 'and that's stories about people who were in more shit than we are . . . and lived to retire to a life of obscene comfort on some beach somewhere.'

Lauren thought for a while. 'How about Franklin?' she offered. 'The man who ate his boots.'

'I like him already. He sounds like my sort of person. What's his story?'

'We're talking about the early part of the nineteenth century, the 1820s more or less. His mission was to fill in some of the gaps in the Arctic. Like, for example, how did Canada end up in the far north.'

'And don't tell me . . . he'd never been anywhere cold before?'

'Good guess. In fact, on paper he was totally unqualified.'

Sean gave an amused cough. 'I like that about the British. How come you guys always choose such *duffers* for these gnarly trips?'

'National characteristic, I suppose, but I wouldn't call Franklin a duffer . . . more a big softy, a sort of wholesome, mild-mannered giant if you like.'

'Cut to the drama,' Frank told her. 'Where did it all start to go wrong?'

'Oh God, it's years since I read the book, but if I remember rightly it actually started going pear-shaped right from the start. They had about seventeen hundred miles to complete across the wilds of Arctic Canada, but as bad luck would have it the weather was dead against them.'

Sean sucked in his breath in mock sympathy. 'Weather against them, eh? Who would have thought that in Arctic Canada . . . I'd have taken my Bermudas myself.'

Lauren ignored his sarcasm. 'Their plan wasn't that bad . . . to hire native Indians as guides and to hunt food.'

'And don't tell me . . . no one checked if the native Indians actually *wanted* to do this?'

'Right. In fact, most of them mutinied. By that time, they were skin and bone. Their supplies ran out and they were down to eating lichen from the rocks to try and get some sustenance.'

'*Lichen*,' Frank whistled. 'That's a bit rough. Couldn't they shoot anything?'

'I think they got the occasional deer, but I seem to remember most of their protein in the winter months came from a couple of wolf carcasses they found.'

'Great stuff! Sucking the marrow out of a wolf carcass. Those guys were pretty macho, I guess.'

'I suppose they were. But they were literally starving to

death. At one point they were squeezing the maggots out of infested animal hides and eating them like grapes.'

'So how did it wind up? Did they get to eating each other?'

'Strangely enough, there's some evidence to suggest they did, at least some of the corpses showed signs of having been chopped about. There's no doubt that at least a couple of them went stark raving mad . . . they were shooting each other in the end.'

'And Franklin? He survived?'

'He survived the first expedition . . . that was the one where he ate his boots. When he got back he was a national hero, his book a bestseller, made for life. That was despite the fact that eleven of his expedition wound up dead.'

'Wait a moment . . .' Sean was laughing in the dark. 'I get the strangest feeling about this, but would I be right in thinking that after surviving that disaster by the skin of his boots, your jolly Mr Franklin went *back* to the Arctic and did it all over again?'

'Uncannily, you're right,' Lauren confirmed, laughing herself now at Sean's infectious humour. 'He did exactly that.'

'Lauren?' Sean asked.

'Uh-huh.'

'How come all your national heroes screwed up? I haven't heard about a single one that didn't get themselves in all sorts of shit. Have you got one that, like, went out, completed the expedition and didn't have to eat his boots to survive?'

Lauren thought about this for a while, amused to realise as she sorted through her mental list of childhood heroes that Sean was pretty well right—the people the British admired the most *were* the ones who had got themselves into desperate predicaments.

'It's not the getting into trouble I admire,' she told him after some thought, 'it's the getting out of it.'

'Amen to that,' Sean told her. 'You get us out of this one, you can put your own name on the list.'

All was silent for a long while as they listened to Frank's unsteady breathing. He had fallen asleep near the end of the story.

'You think I can do it?' Lauren whispered.

'I reckon, but promise me one thing. If we get to the boot-eating stage, don't make me eat my own. Those babies stink like a couple of skunks crawled in there and died.'

75

'You know what we should try?' Sean was sitting next to Lauren during one of the breaks. The team was shattered, spread around the ice, lifeless and despondent on this, the fourteenth day of the trek. Progress that day had been grotesquely slow, their pulling power reduced to just a few hundred metres before they were forced to rest.

'No. Surprise me.'

'We should rig up one of the flysheets and try to sail the sledge. This wind is running about twenty knots from the south, right? And this surface is the best we've seen . . . look at it, it's like marble here, we haven't crossed a crevasse or a sastrugi for miles.'

Lauren scrutinised the surface, shielding her eyes to look ahead, checking for the telltale wrinkles in the glacier surface which would indicate turbulence below.

'Like Scott?' Lauren recalled the photographs from *Scott's Last Journey*, in which the British explorers had rigged a sail to help them manhaul.

'Like almost everyone,' Sean told her. 'Messner, Fiennes, they all made big gains using sails when the conditions were right.'

'You think the flysheet can take it? We can't afford to rip one.'

'I've been thinking about it,' Sean reassured her. 'Those flysheets are guaranteed by the manufacturers to withstand a wind up to force ten or beyond. It's a brand-new tent without much wear and tear. Plus we can rig it in a way that will minimise the strain.'

'What would you use for a mast?'

'We don't need one. We'd attach it at two points to the front of the sledge and use it like a spinnaker.'

'I'm warming to the idea,' Lauren told him. 'Let's take a look at the fly.'

They unpacked the tent from the sledge and brought out the flysheet. Lauren ran the fabric through her fingers, trying to assess its strength.

'If there's a danger point, it's at these attachments,' Sean pointed out, 'but look how well it's been done. This is a thousand-dollar tent; it can take a lot of punishment.'

'Will it have the pulling power to drag the sledge?'

'Let's try it and see.'

Sean handed two of the guy ropes to Lauren and took the other two himself. He opened the flysheet to the wind, seeing with satisfaction that it plumped out smoothly in the air.

The pull was surprisingly strong, strong enough in fact that the two of them were immediately dragged forward several metres until Sean could collapse it again.

'It can pull all right.' Lauren was astounded by the power the simple sail had exhibited. 'But it could still break,' she worried. 'How can we justify the risk?'

'It's worth the risk because I don't think we'll make it without some help. Look at them, Lauren: they're absolutely spent. How many more miles do you realistically think we can haul Frank today?'

Lauren considered the team and had to admit that Sean was right. The lack of food had reduced them to the point where they could barely walk for themselves, let alone with Frank's weight holding them back.

'We'll give it a go,' Lauren told him, 'but I want someone ahead at all times to check out the terrain for crevasses and holes.'

Thirty minutes later the sledge was underway, utilising windpower for the first time. Sean and Murdo ran the operation, Sean on the front of the sledge to ensure the sail was filling out correctly from its attachment points on the front strut and Murdo at the back, ready to brake.

Frank lay with his head buried in his sleeping bag, preferring not to think of what would happen if they came up too fast to a crevasse.

The sledge ran beautifully on the silky-smooth surface, the sail comfortably generating enough pull to transport the three of them at roughly twice the speed they could achieve on foot. Once they had the system going, they found they were easily outstripping the pace of the others as they tried to follow. A new sound filled their world, the satisfying swish of the runners as they ate up the distance.

Then, a shadow dead ahead.

'Brake!' Sean would shout, as soon as he saw danger.

Murdo would hang off the back of the sledge, hacking a metal spike into the ice and digging it as deep as he could until Sean could get the sail collapsed. Then they would dismount, haul the sledge around the obstacle and rig it to sail again.

They found the technique was not without its problems; a fickle blast of extra-strong wind could cause the flysheet to rear up above the sledge, from where it would fall back onto Frank. Sean would have to patiently disentangle him before rigging the sail again. Sometimes the wind died completely for ten or fifteen minutes, the flysheet flapping redundant on the ice. But then it would pick up again, fifteen, twenty knots, giving the sledge a good five or six knots of headway.

The wind rush was another danger, the relatively high speed creating a wind chill of its own. Sean found his eyes watering, the tears quickly freezing as he peered around and under the sail, looking for trouble ahead.

Soon the foot party were miles behind and Sean called a halt so they could catch up. 'There's enough pull on this that we could take a skier on the back,' he told them.

With the success of the sail clear to all, there was no shortage of volunteers, and for the rest of that day the team took it in turns to be pulled behind the sledge. The extra weight pulled the speed down considerably, but it still beat hauling.

By five p.m., the wind was getting too strong to handle, and Sean once or twice lost control of the flysheet completely. He pushed a little further, but within an hour one of the guy ropes had broken.

'OK,' Lauren said when the damage was inspected, 'that's the warning sign. Can it be fixed?'

'We can splice it back together,' Sean told her. 'It won't be like new, but it will still hold.'

'No more sailing,' she told Sean, 'but, I have to admit, that was a hell of a good day's progress. Worth three days on foot at least.'

As it happened, the smooth conditions they had chanced upon that day were never experienced again. Instead, within a very few miles they were back in the familiar chopped-up chaos of the crevasse fields, in which they would never have dared to try the sail in any case.

That night, Lauren wrote in her diary:

> Luck was with us today. But tomorrow back to the sledge hauling. Frank now on third day of antibiotics but showing very little sign of improvement. He's still getting weaker every day, and the infection in his hands is not healing as it should.

76

The miles were ticking off on Lauren's hand-drawn map. Fitzgerald had not been seen for forty-eight hours. By her calculations they were just three days from the second depot, but the closer they got, the more nervous Lauren was becoming.

'He's got to pass us,' she told Sean as she checked behind them for the hundredth time that day. 'So where the hell is he?'

'Just out of sight, I imagine,' Sean told her, 'keeping on our trail and waiting.'

'But waiting for what? Why is he shadowing us?—that's what doesn't make any sense to me. Why doesn't he make for the crash site as quickly as he can?'

Sean gave a bitter laugh.

'Because he has to *know* we're dead, and know *where* we die. That way he can bend the story any way he likes. And if we start abandoning bodies, you can bet he'll be dumping

them into the nearest crevasse. He can't take the risk that
any of us will ever be found.'

'Jesus, that is so sick.'

'Also, this way he doesn't have to think about navigation
or anything, he can just follow our tracks and know he's on
the right trail.'

'And what about the second depot? You think he'll have
figured where it is?'

Sean sucked on his teeth. 'I'd love to say no, but, if he
saw us at the first depot, the chances are pretty high he
knows that the second one is at the two-hundred-mile point.'

'And he'll find it . . .'

Sean didn't reply.

They picked up the compass bearing again and set out for
the afternoon session, four hunched figures hauling at the
sledge, Richard trailing far behind.

For the hauling, much depended on the precise nature of
the surface the team happened to be crossing. When the going was rough, it was hell all round: hell for the haulers
when they couldn't find a satisfactory rhythm to move to,
hell for Frank as he was jerked and rocked from side to side
and hell for the sledge as the frame twisted and strained with
every jolt.

Sometimes the obstacles were extreme, for the best part
of that day, the team found themselves in a region where the
pressure ridges came thick and fast—and two to three metres high. With no hope of manhandling Frank over these
whilst still on the sledge, they had to coax him onto his feet
so he could make his way across as best he could.

'No problem,' Frank would assure them. 'I can make it
over that little bastard, you'll see.'

They held his arms as he hobbled bravely onto the pressure ridge, only the sharp intakes of breath hinting at the
pain he was experiencing in his hands.

Having made it to the other side of the ridge, Frank
would take his place on the sledge once more while the
haulers waited in their makeshift harnesses for the command
to begin pulling again.

'Start off gently!' Sean would take the lead, easing his strength against the rope, biting his lip against the pain from the sores on his waist as the rope began to burn into his flesh. 'Now, on the count of three . . . one, two, three, pull!'

Often, in this highly stressed part of the glacier, they would make just two or perhaps three hundred metres before the next pressure ridge would rear up and the whole process would start again.

Without a target, Lauren thought, they simply wouldn't have had the strength.

The second depot, the second barrel; the target became so central to the thoughts and desires of the team that scarcely a minute went by when one of them wasn't talking about it, thinking about it or fantasising about what it might contain.

Every step was a step closer.

Their food was running low, low enough that they were down to starvation rations again. The second depot; what would it contain?

Most nights, Lauren dreamed about it, her mind warping the fifty-gallon barrel into something the size of an aircraft hangar as she saw it beckoning across the ice. It was so vast it had doors, huge sliding blinds which rolled back to reveal a treasure house of edible wonders. The interior was like the food hall of Harrods, with smoked hams hanging from racks and vast display cabinets of cheeses and fruits.

Lauren dreamed her way along the aisles, scooping up handful after handful of the delicacies until her mouth was so full she could no longer swallow. There were truffles, baskets loaded with different types of breads, a whole vat full of butter—the fat she craved more than any other. Then she would wake, her heart racing, fighting to breathe, knowing as the dream receded that the reason she could not swallow was that her tongue was now continuously swollen . . . one of the first signs that malnutrition was becoming a serious threat to her body.

That barrel *had* to be there. And it had to be intact.

In three days, they would be there.

77

Son of a bitch!' Fitzgerald collapsed onto the snowmobile seat, his clothes sticking to him where he had begun to sweat.

What the hell was wrong with this damn machine? Forty-five pulls and the engine still refused to fire.

The explorer dismounted and delivered a vicious kick to the drive belt. 'Bastard!' he screamed.

It was the mountain crossing that had done it, even a mechanical ignoramus like Fitzgerald could recognise the rapid deterioration of the snowcat since he had pushed it hard into that steep ascent. Now the infernal machine was paying him back by refusing to start.

He pulled on the starter again, despairing as no answering spark came back at him. His arm was aching, his right hand a little frostnipped after he had made the mistake of touching some of the engine's metal components in a futile attempt to explore the fault.

He had left some skin behind, stuck to the aluminium.

He stared to the north, into the light fall of snow which was obscuring the glacier. What would it mean if the machine really was dead? Fitzgerald could hardly bear to contemplate the consequences.

He would have to manhaul . . . but the sledge would be punishingly heavy with the tent and all that food . . . perhaps too heavy for one man to move. And how many miles? Maybe one hundred and sixty to go to the plane. Christ, that was going to be a test.

He still wasn't back to full fitness after the original crossing attempt.

Worst of all, it would reduce him to an equal footing with the others . . . that was the most frightening prospect of all. This game of cat and mouse—this game which the explorer had begun to enjoy thanks to his mechanical advantage— would suddenly transform into something very different.

They were ahead. Maybe they could stay ahead. And if they knew his snowmobile had given up, would they not come and hunt him down? Six against one.

The explorer shivered, then took the starter cord in his hand and gave it one final yank.

The engine gave a faltering stutter, then roared into life. Triumphant, he twisted the throttle hard, watching the revometer creep up to five, six, seven thousand revs.

'Mess me around, would you?' he muttered, gunning the throttle harder until the engine was screaming at high pitch. In the explorer's mind he imagined it might clear the blockage, if a blockage it was.

He eased himself onto the seat, feeling frighteningly cold where the sweat was freezing under his clothes.

Right. Which way had they gone? Just a simple matter of following their tracks. Fitzgerald drove to the north for a while until he picked up their trail.

The engine continued to trip on itself, the steady throb cutting out intermittently, only to catch again as the motion refired the cylinder.

What about tomorrow? Would it start again? The uncertainty was beginning to wear Fitzgerald down.

78

Sean fixed his eyes on the horizon, looking for the tell-tale dot.

'I thought of an alternative,' he told Lauren. 'Another way of . . . of solving our problem.'

Lauren looked at him without any vestige of real hope in her eyes.

'Try me.'

'How about Deep Throat?'

Lauren screwed up her face as her exhausted mind tried to make the connections required of it.

'Deep Throat . . . ?'

'It's between us and the second depot. Don't you think it would make a perfect trap?'

Lauren got it.

'Oh my God, Sean—you think we can do that?'

'I think it's worth a try. I'll do it alone if you have a problem with it.'

Lauren stared at him intently, doubt written now in her expression. 'I'm not sure . . . it takes us into new territory . . . dangerous territory . . .'

'Just the two of us, Lauren. Really clean.'

'I don't know. I've never . . .'

'And you think I have?' Sean protested.

'No, just that there might be questions. Later. We might have to tell our story . . . and . . .'

Now Sean got really close to her, his voice changing gear, becoming dispassionate, unconnected.

'It's him or us, Lauren; we already worked that one out, remember?'

Lauren backed away, the palms of her hands raised towards him.

'Give me some time, Sean. I need to really consider this. This is big; it's going to change plenty of things if we do it.'

'Yeah. Like give us a fighting chance.'

Lauren retreated to the sledge and sat thinking as Sean and Mel began to put up the tents. Her head was throbbing with a rhythmic ache, the debilitating pangs of hunger nagging at her more urgently now that the food was getting so scarce.

Sean had put the unthinkable into words, and now the idea was sitting there, ugly, tangible, frighteningly real.

They really couldn't do that. Could they?

79

Heavy snow had fallen, compounding the problems for the team. Every ten minutes or so the runners would clog up, making it virtually impossible to tow the sledge.

'Runners!' someone would call, and they would come to a halt.

The runners were another of Sean's responsibilities; keeping them clear was now virtually a full-time job. Under normal circumstances he would have polished them with wax every morning and night, to get the best passage across the ice, but since they had no polish he was forced to carry out improvised maintenance on the trail, mainly consisting of cleaning them as often as was necessary.

As usual, everything depended on the quality and texture of the snow they happened to be crossing; where it was granular and dry, the runners could pass without clogging up, needing only a quick going-over with a knife every hour to expose the smooth plastic surface. When the snow was wet, however, or, worse still, sticky, the runners would very quickly lose their efficiency, balling up with many kilos of congealed ice and minimising the efficiency of the sledge.

'We're not crossing Antarctica,' Lauren observed one morning as she looked back on the two deep furrows the sledge was etching into the soft snow, 'we're ploughing it.'

When it got to the point where they could barely make any headway, they would go through the tedious process of scraping the runners clean. Frank would be offloaded, along with the rest of their equipment and the remaining stack of wood, and the sledge would be turned over to reveal the undercarriage. Sean would take his knife and hack the ice away, taking great pains not to add to the nicks and scores which had already accumulated on the plastic runners.

When Sean was satisfied, the sledge would be turned, loaded, and the grind would begin again. For a few wonderful minutes the sledge would move freely, almost feeling to the exhausted team that the runners were coated with grease, there was so little friction. Then the balling would start anew, the runners growing 'feet' of ice which inexorably increased the drag to the point where even the hardest pull of all four haulers could achieve just a foot or so of progress.

'Did you know the Eskimos have more than two hundred words for snow?' Mel commented.

'That's bugger all,' Murdo told her. 'The Scots have more than a thousand, and every one of them is a swearword.'

Keeping the sledge intact was also occupying their thoughts. The aluminium frame had already been weakened and damaged in the fire, and, after three weeks of hauling, it was showing signs of metal fatigue.

'This sledge isn't really built to take this sort of punishment,' Sean explained to Lauren as he showed her the problem areas. 'Frank's a hell of a weight to be carrying, and we've already got hairline cracks starting to appear at these joints. This is where the frame takes the most flexing.'

'Is it going to break?'

'One or more of these struts might go. If they do, we'll be in trouble. Once one part of the structure starts to crack up, the rest won't be far behind. Then we'll be dragging Frank along on his arse.'

'What can we do about it?' Lauren asked him.

'Best I can do is to try and tie up the joints with some cord, but that's just a temporary measure. If the aluminium tubing decides it's going to snap, then there's not much we can do about it.'

Sean sacrificed his bootlaces to the cause and tied them in a series of cleverly devised knots around the worst-affected parts of the frame. For the time being it would suffice, but Sean wasn't at all confident that the sledge would survive the journey to the crashed plane.

The question of what would happen to Frank then was one that he chose not to dwell on.

For Lauren, the stop-start day passed in a haze. She pulled on her harness, pushed her legs into the endless cycle of push-rest-push, but her mind was fixed on Deep Throat, on the dilemma that Sean's proposal had opened up inside her.

Lauren knew that whatever happened the decision would divide her permanently in some way—a tear in the fabric of her own morality, a rip, with edges that were not clean. The type of wound that gets infected easily.

But Lauren was in the grip of the most powerful force any human being can experience—the imperative which has no equal: to survive.

Later, as they prepared one of the tents together, Lauren found a chance to speak with Sean. 'I thought about it,' she told him quietly, 'and I think it's worth a try. But the others can't know about this. They absolutely mustn't.'

'You're in?'

'Yes, Sean. I am.'

Sean showed no sign of surprise; he took her decision as a matter of fact.

'We'll do it tonight when they're all asleep.'

far behind. They, we'll be dragging there

80

At eleven p.m., Lauren followed Sean's dark shadow away from the tents, keeping her footsteps in the tracks of the empty sledge he was towing. Sean waited until they were out of earshot. 'Let your eyes adjust,' he whispered to her. 'We can't risk the headtorches.'

There was a sliver of moon burning through the cloud that night, the ridges and folds of the glacier gently illuminated with a weak cast of blue light.

'This is crazy, Sean,' Lauren told him. 'It's like Russian roulette wandering around this crevasse field in the dark.'

'Most of these slots are pretty obvious,' he replied. 'I'll use the flag pole to probe in front.'

They set out, Sean in the lead, testing the terrain for sudden holes as they pushed deeper into the most heavily crevassed area. Lauren concentrated her attention on his footsteps in the snow, the shadow-filled holes guiding her forward.

Thanks to the moon, the crevasses were not difficult to

see. They bypassed the bigger ones and jumped the more slender cracks at their narrowest point.

Then Sean was moving with more caution. Lauren could not imagine how he knew he was close—there were no clues that she could see.

He stabbed the pole into the snow, then got down carefully to his knees.

'OK,' he told her, 'I think this is it. I'm pushing into thin air just in front of us.'

'How can we be sure it's the one?'

'I'll take a look with the light.'

Sean punched a small hole in the snow bridge which lay before him, then placed the headtorch inside it. Switching it on, he saw immediately that they had found Deep Throat, the feeble beam hinting at the great depth of the crevasse beneath him.

'It's even more awesome in the night,' he whispered. 'Want to take a look?'

'No.' Lauren shivered at the thought. 'What about the tracks? Even if he's tired, he'll notice them disappear.'

'Don't forget he's on the skidoo. He might be moving too fast to stop. Besides, we have this.'

Sean pulled a length of cord from his pocket and cast it out onto the snow bridge. Then he dragged it back. After a dozen or so casts, Lauren could already see the faint lines in the soft snow, stretching out for metres in front of them.

Sean flashed his headtorch onto it for a second, revealing the marks and scratches.

'That's not very convincing,' Lauren told him. 'What about the footprints?'

'You're right. Let's try something else.'

Sean took a gloveful of snow and squeezed it in his hand until he had created a hard ball. This he threw out onto the snow bridge as a test.

A dark hole appeared where it had sunk a little into the soft surface.

'It's not perfect, but I can't think of any other way.'

Lauren joined him, and for some minutes they were busy

moulding handfuls of snow to create small craters out across the snow bridge.

Sean risked another quick glimpse with the torch.

'That's better,' he said. 'It's never going to bear close scrutiny, but hopefully by the time Fitzgerald works out that something weird's happening it'll all be over.'

They retraced their steps, concentrating hard so as not to lose their trail back to the tent. Then they walked back to Deep Throat one more time, both stumbling with the utter fatigue of that long day. The end result was a confusion of footsteps and sledge tracks which certainly looked like it had been made by the whole party.

Then they returned to the tent a final time.

'That's it,' Sean whispered, 'trap set. Now it's down to Deep Throat to do the job for us.'

They crept into their sleeping bags, intensely grateful for the warmth they offered from that bitter night air.

'We'll sleep for a few hours,' Sean said, 'but we have to be out of here before first light.'

But Lauren could not sleep. She lay awake, tense and uncertain. In her mind she could see nothing but the elegant blue glass walls of that monstrous crevasse, so fatally smooth and uncompromising, leading down . . . and down . . .

81

At five a.m., they woke the others, rousing them with some difficulty from their sleeping bags. They stumbled out of their tents onto the glacier, sleep-filled and shocked by the brittle intensity of the cold.

'We're breaking the routine today,' Lauren told them. 'We've got to get out of here right away, but we'll stop for breakfast after a couple of hours. Try and keep as quiet as you can.'

No one questioned her; there was something in the clipped urgency of Lauren's tone which did not invite further enquiry.

In less than thirty minutes they had the two dome tents and the sleeping bags packed onto the sledge. Lauren and Murdo took the harness between them as Sean led the team away, finding a route further to the east of their nocturnal trip into the crevasse field, a route which skirted the hidden depths of Deep Throat entirely.

After a short distance, Sean left Lauren to continue with

the route-finding and made his way back to the camp site. Using a ski pole, he smoothed over the trail they had just made, continuing until he had obscured some thirty or forty metres of their progress.

When it was done, Sean flashed his torch, seeing with satisfaction that his work had virtually covered up the tracks of their recent departure. Now the heaviest trail leading from the tent site was the false one he had marked up with Lauren the previous night.

He hurried back to the others, catching them easily with his faster pace.

Not long after daybreak, the team reached a large depression, a scoop in the glacier guarded by a low pressure ridge.

'This is a good place,' Sean told Lauren. 'Let's park the crew here.'

Lauren looked about, realising the location was perfect. Fitzgerald would not see the team huddled in here—and, perhaps just as importantly, the team would not see the drama unfolding back at Deep Throat, which was now a good mile behind them.

She took off her pack. 'Let's stop for some food,' she said.

They didn't need to be told twice, within a few seconds their loads were scattered around the ice, the team resting gratefully on their packs while Lauren took out the epigas cooker and began to melt down some ice.

'I'll keep an eye out for you-know-who,' Sean told her quietly. 'Join me when you can.'

Once she had the first litre of water boiling, Lauren let Mel take over the preparation of the food. Then she slipped away to join Sean, sure that the team were so tired they would barely notice their absence.

'Let's move fast,' Sean told her. 'We don't want to miss the main event.'

Quickly, they made their way back up the glacier. The adrenaline was pumping so hard inside Lauren that the distance meant nothing to her.

As she walked, her mind began to play; the main event, Sean had called it. Murder, in other words. Lauren was beginning to feel physically sick at the thought of it. Was there no other route?

'Sean?'

'What?'

'I'm still not sure. Maybe we should be thinking about this another way. He's out here all alone, perhaps he's sick or hypothermic—we don't know what state he's in. Maybe the two of us can get close to him somehow, overpower him?'

Sean stopped dead.

'Can I remind you of something? He's killed already, and he'll kill again without any qualms. We're unarmed; he's got an axe and God knows what else. We've been on starvation rations for a two-hundred-mile trek, and he's been eating as much as he needs every goddamn day. We wouldn't stand a chance.'

'But what if the rest of the team find out what we've done? That scares me, Sean . . .'

'You know the only thing about this that worries *me*?' he replied. 'It's the fact that in eliminating Fitzgerald we're going to lose his snowmobile. That's where I am, Lauren. I'm at that point, OK? The point where I'm regretting that a by-product of killing him is that we're going to forfeit a useful piece of machinery.'

'Well, I'm not in the same place as you then,' Lauren told him. 'I don't know if we have a right to do this.'

'So go back and wait with the others if you want.'

Lauren shook her head, and they continued in silence.

Not far from Deep Throat—a hundred metres at most—they found a prominent block of ice which was big enough to hide behind. From that vantage point they could see the trap clearly, safe in the certainty that Fitzgerald would not spot them.

They sat there with their backs to the ice, waiting for the telltale buzz of the snowmobile to come across the glacier towards them.

One hour. Two hours. Time crept slowly by. Lauren and Sean began to freeze into their positions, their muscles cramping as the cold began to bite.

'There's something wrong,' Lauren said, her teeth chattering as she checked her watch. 'Where the hell is he?'

'Relax,' Sean reassured her. 'He's probably just having a hard time getting the snowmobile started.'

Suddenly, he stiffened as he spotted something. 'Speak of the devil; I think that could be him.'

Away in the distance, the unmistakable black profile of the snowmobile was just coming into view.

'Here we go.'

The minutes ticked past as Fitzgerald weaved a steady route through the crevasse field towards them. Now they could hear the engine, shockingly loud in the still air of the glacier.

'He's lost his silencer,' Sean observed. 'That's why it sounds like a pig.'

After what seemed to Lauren to be an age, the snowmobile arrived at their camp site of the previous night. Fitzgerald slowed perceptibly as he scanned the clues left on the ice, and for a few seconds he seemed to pause, distracted by something away to his right.

'Come on, come on,' Sean muttered. 'Take it. Take it!'

Then Fitzgerald was accelerating once more, driving confidently down the trail Lauren and Sean had laid towards Deep Throat.

'Oh yes!' Sean couldn't hide the excitement in his voice. 'Now just build up a little more speed and everything's going to be over real quick.'

Lauren could taste blood on her tongue where she had bitten into it. 'This is so wrong, Sean,' she hissed. 'There has to be another way!'

'Not now there isn't,' Sean told her. 'He's halfway to hell already.'

The snowmobile rounded a small crevasse and continued on track, close enough now that they could see Fitzgerald's ice-encrusted beard beneath his ski goggles.

'We can't do this! It's not right. I'll never forgive myself if we don't try and talk him round.'

'Lauren, no!'

Sean lunged forward, but he was too late. Lauren had left the hiding place and was already stumbling across the glacier towards Deep Throat.

'Stop! You have to stop!'

Fitzgerald could not hear her above the noise of the engine. He was fifty metres from the edge of the crevasse.

Lauren was running now, waving her hands frantically in the air. She was approaching the far side of Deep Throat.

'Stop!' she screamed.

Fitzgerald glanced up, his attention caught perhaps by the movement in front of him, by Lauren's dark clothing contrasted against the ice.

Lauren was so close to him she could actually see his jaw drop down in astonishment. Then he slammed hard on the brakes, slewing the snowmobile round in a clumsy arc and bringing it to a halt just half a pace away from the place at which the solid ice he was driving on became the wafer-thin snow bridge of Deep Throat.

Fitzgerald took in the scene: the clumsy fake tracks which petered out midway across the snow bridge; the sag in the middle which hinted at the drop below.

For a while they were both silent, the only noise the brittle crackle of the snowmobile engine as it ticked over.

'You can see what we wanted to do,' Lauren called out across the crevasse, 'but I think there's a better way.'

She paused, expecting a response from Fitzgerald, but he made none.

'Two of my team are sick, Julian; they're really sick. If you help us with the snowmobile, maybe we can sort things out between us. You'll have to answer for what happened at the base when we get back to civilisation. But if you help us . . . and we all get out alive, we can make things easier for you.'

Fitzgerald said nothing, just continued to stare directly at Lauren. She thought she could see him shivering, but it might have been her imagination.

Then he revved up the engine, turned back on his tracks

and drove away, the snowmobile bobbing and tilting as he navigated the route back through the crevasse field.

Then Sean was standing next to her.

'That was our chance, Lauren,' he said quietly. 'And you threw it away.'

Lauren turned to him, her eyes filling with tears which straight away began to freeze.

'I had to try.'

'But what did you think? That you could talk him round to *helping* us? You're crazy if you thought that!'

Lauren could not find the words to reply. Soon Sean turned his back on her in disgust and began to walk back to where the group was waiting.

Lauren stood for a while longer, lost in her own misery. From time to time she could see Fitzgerald in the distance, driving erratically back and forth on the glacier.

'You won't win.' She spoke beneath her breath. 'I still won't let you win . . .'

Snow began to fall as she wearily turned back to follow Sean's tracks, her feet like lead as she dragged them through each step.

Thirty miles still to go to the second depot. The thought of all that distance in front of them was beginning to eat into Lauren like a cancer.

82

Fitzgerald creased over and retched his breakfast onto the ice. It formed a little puddle at his feet for a few seconds before freezing hard. He breathed in deeply, trying to regain control, to recover from the shock.

So close. He'd been a hand's-breadth from death. And he'd been right all along. They *had* been plotting to kill him. They *did* know he was following. Secret meetings had discussed the best way of crushing him, of sending him to hell.

Oh, they'd relish that. The unyielding ice beating his destiny out of him as he cartwheeled down into depths where light had never penetrated. How long might he have lain there in that crevasse . . . wedged and trapped, watching his lifeblood seep away as the vice cracked and tightened in on him?

And then . . . The explorer frowned. Had it really happened? He ran it back through his mind. Lauren had run to warn him! In fact, she had saved his life. Why had she done that? Fitzgerald climbed off his snowmobile and stood uncertainly. He began wandering at random through the ice pinnacles that surrounded him. It was like a maze, this place; you could so easily get lost.

He took off a glove, ran his bare hand across a blue shard of ice, savouring the bite as it stuck and peeled.

Lauren had been weak. It was her first mistake. But there was no longer any doubt about the team's intention to kill him.

Fitzgerald returned to the snowmobile and sat on the seat. He wiped the snow from his goggles. Far off, he could see Lauren and her team picking their way through the crevasses of the glacier, a weaving line of dark figures heading off into the darkening void.

Things would be different from now on, Fitzgerald promised himself. So far he'd been passive, content to follow, to watch.

Now that time was over.

83

Lauren scraped the stubborn layer of ice off the face of the compass and checked the bearing, turning the plastic bezel until north was aligned. The red needle was sluggish and slow to swing round, the fluid inside the case close to freezing now the temperature had dropped so low.

They were seventeen days into the trek, and for the last twenty-four hours a dense low cloud had enveloped the glacier, reducing visibility to just fifty metres or less. It made progress more dangerous for the team and made navigation even more critical for Lauren; without the compass bearing, they would be stumbling in circles, hopelessly lost.

The fog was all-embracing—it felt like a blanket, like a shroud. It deadened all noise, muffling the metallic clinks of equipment, dulling the crisp swish-swish of skis sliding over ice, confusing the sense of orientation so that it was impossible to say which direction a shout had come from.

Psychologically, the fog was bad for morale, increasing the team's sense of isolation, enhancing the growing conviction amongst them all that this desperate trek might end in disaster. Mariners through the ages have experienced the same despair encountering fog at sea; there is nothing quite as effective as an impenetrable mist at imparting a sensation of impending doom.

Lauren's tactic in these conditions was the only one she could adopt—keeping the team as closely packed as she could, encouraging the stragglers to keep up at the tail of the group.

'No one loses sight of the person in front,' she told them. 'That's the rule. We can't be sure of finding you again if you get separated from the group.'

The team, utterly terrified at the prospect of becoming lost in the whiteout conditions, did as she asked, bunching into a tight unit, the stronger members dropping their pace to allow the weaker ones to keep up.

As night encroached, they made camp for the seventeenth time.

'We can forget about the watch rota for tonight,' Lauren told them as they settled in for the night. 'Fitzgerald couldn't find us in this stuff even if he wanted to.'

'We should get the food inside us now,' Sean said, 'while we've still got the energy.'

They melted down ice and drank lukewarm tea, bitter to the tongue without sugar, and ate a half-cup of muesli each. The muesli had to be portioned out in advance, mainly because the raisins were so sought after that they had to be counted out individually. Where there was one over the odds, Frank would invariably be offered it. They melted down yet more ice and added warm water to the cereal, the gritty sweetness of the grain putting welcome sugar into their stomachs. They all saved the raisins in the bottom of their mugs, placing them one by one in their mouths only when they could resist the temptation no longer. Each hard nodule of the dried fruit was chewed over and pulped against the roofs of their mouths until the juices began to flow.

Next morning the fog was still with them, but at least there were fewer crevasses to worry about. They set out at dawn, making steady progress for five hours or so, bringing them to the area in which Lauren calculated the second barrel should be found.

They pitched camp and ate a miserly lunch, just half a granola bar each, washed down by a third of a mug of watery cocoa.

'What can you remember about this place?' Lauren asked Sean.

'It was close to a boulder,' Sean recalled, trying to picture the terrain, 'a boulder the size of a car. If we had good visibility, we'd see the damn thing from ten miles away. That's why we chose it.'

'Why don't we wait for tomorrow, save our energy?' Mel asked. 'Maybe it'll clear up and we'll see it right away.'

'It could be like this for days,' Lauren told her. 'In fact, it could get worse. We'll just have to go out and search, like we did at the other depot.'

At the first depot, all the members of the team had joined in the search for the barrel. Now, eight days later, only Murdo and Mel were fit enough to join Sean and Lauren in the hunt.

They worked by the compass, following a bearing for ten minutes, then turning as close as they could estimate to ninety degrees for a further ten-minute line. The same procedure repeated twice again brought them full circle, or rather, full square, back to the vicinity of the tent. Having drawn a blank, they would pause to rest, then set out on a different bearing five degrees to the west.

Here and there, criss-crossing the ice in seemingly random patterns, they came across the indentations of snowmobile tracks.

'Fitzgerald has been in this area,' Sean confirmed, examining the indentations, 'and recently too. These tracks would have been blown away within forty-eight hours.'

'You think he was looking for the depot?' Lauren asked.

Sean shrugged. 'We have to credit the guy with some intelligence. If he worked out that the first depot was exactly one hundred miles from the camp, he'd certainly make the two-hundred-mile point a likely place to look.'

Lauren said nothing, but her heart sank a little further every time they found more tracks. Fitzgerald had been shuttling back and forth like crazy . . . his trail was scattered all over the area.

Please God he hadn't found the depot, Lauren prayed; please God he hadn't done that.

After some hours of this, they were all too exhausted to concentrate on such niceties as straight lines. They abandoned the search, retreating, aching and despondent, to the tents, where they ate just a quarter of a tin of processed meat each before huddling close for the night.

Lauren was on the outside, her back against the goretex outer wall of the tent. No matter how hard she tried to ignore it, the penetrating fingers of cold worked their way through the down, eating into her flesh and making sleep an impossibility.

She was losing her insulation layers, Lauren realised; all her subcutaneous fat was being burned up by the trek. She buried her head inside the sleeping bag, letting her breath create a precious pocket of warmth around her face so that at least one part of her would be warm.

The following morning, after one of the most miserable nights Lauren could remember, she joined Sean once more for a foray out into the void. Her warning of the previous afternoon had not been unduly pessimistic, in fact the conditions *were* worse than the day before, with the precious visibility diminished to fifteen metres at most.

'We've got to cast the net wider,' Lauren told Sean. 'I think we're further from it than we realise.'

They began the process again, now going out for twenty minutes on each bearing, peering into the void in the hope of seeing something—anything—other than the spectral swirling of the fog.

They did this many times, so many times that Lauren lost count, pushing themselves to do just one more circuit when their bodies cried for rest.

At last, looming out of the frozen mist, a dark, bulbous shape emerged.

'Is that it?' Lauren asked, hardly daring to hope.

Sean peered through the swirls of fog, trying to find some definition in the shape.

'It has to be.' He took a step forward. 'But . . .'

The boulder was in front of them with the barrel nearby, lying on its side. The black plastic lid and metal sealing ring were scattered on the ice nearby.

Sean pulled the barrel upright. It was empty. For a while they both stood there, staring dumbly into the interior.

'Oh Christ.' Lauren's voice faltered as she realised the full significance of the development. 'He's left us with nothing. We don't even have any drugs for Frank's hands.'

They were paralysed, nailed to the spot.

'How much further can we go, Sean?' she asked him, trying to get her mind round the distance which still separated them from the plane. 'How much further can we go without food?'

Sean leaned forward, looking inside the barrel again as if the empty interior might have somehow magically recharged with the supplies they so desperately needed.

He shook his head as he looked over at Lauren, his face as white as the ice that clung to it.

'And how are we going to tell the others?' Lauren asked him, the tears already welling up in her eyes. 'What can we possibly say?'

84

Back in London, Alexander De Pierman was a worried man.

It was nineteen days since he'd last heard from Capricorn. Now the alarm bells were beginning to ring.

He looked out of his window, feeling tense and irritable. As usual, London was awash with rain, the gutters gurgling, the shop-front canopies sagging fit to bust, rivulets and minor streams coursing through alleys and thoroughfares as the drains flowed over and spilled. The doorways were filled with trapped shoppers, looking out into the sheeting downpour, wondering bleakly how they'd let themselves get caught without an umbrella again.

At first, the radio blackout from Capricorn had been a blessed relief for Alexander De Pierman and his public relations team at Kerguelen Oils. Dealing with the media had been time-consuming and fraught, and Lauren's satellite gremlin was a fast and effective way to turn down the heat.

Once the media realised that they could get no further

news from Capricorn, or from Fitzgerald, they quickly lost interest in the story. The twenty or thirty calls a day to De Pierman's press office rapidly fell off to five or ten, and within a week the telephone traffic was down to a couple of calls a day.

Breathing an inward sigh of relief that the whole affair had not reflected too badly on the company, Alexander De Pierman turned his attention back to the business of running one of the world's biggest oil companies.

He flew out to Venezuela for five days of negotiations with the Minister of Energy, then on to Borneo to sign an exploration deal for a new field in Sabah. The following week he was in Riyadh, then back to London to supervise the takeover of a small prospecting operation he'd been admiring for a while.

The days ticked by; one week stretched into two, De Pierman expecting to hear from Lauren at any stage. When no call came from Capricorn, he told himself they must still be having problems with their satellite gear.

Dr Michael Collins, the director of the Scott Polar Institute, who were also part sponsors of Capricorn, called on day thirteen. He too was beginning to be concerned at the duration of the blackout, and wondered if De Pierman had any news.

But there was none.

As the days went by, and the radio silence continued, Alexander De Pierman was getting increasingly concerned . . . and so was the Scott Polar. It wasn't like Lauren to leave them in the dark, they agreed. She would know they would be itching for news of the drilling project, which would surely have produced some results by now.

'Any call from Capricorn?' De Pierman would ask his office every time he called in. But the answer was always the same. No call. No call.

'What's the longest you've ever known a base to be out of touch?' De Pierman asked Collins in one of their now daily calls.

'A week, maybe ten days. But never longer.'

A week. Ten days. But now it was the fifteenth day since anyone had heard any news from Capricorn. It didn't feel right.

Day sixteen. Relatives of the Capricorn team were beginning to contact De Pierman's office, disturbed that they had heard nothing for so long. Frank's mother was particularly concerned, insisting on talking to De Pierman even though he was in Sulawesi at the time.

'Last Thursday was my birthday, Mr De Pierman,' she told him. 'Frank has never, ever missed wishing me a happy birthday, no matter where he is.'

De Pierman began to explore other means of contacting Capricorn. He got radio hams to try to raise the base on different frequencies. No response. He asked a Chilean base—the nearest to Capricorn—to try them in case bad atmospherics were disrupting long-range communications to the South American relay station. Again, no response at all.

Capricorn wasn't just quiet, it was downright dead. De Pierman was beginning to lose sleep.

Day nineteen. He consulted with the Scott Polar, and they decided to give it a couple more days. If there was no news by the end of the week, they would consider funding a flight to find out what the hell was going on down there.

85

Misery wormed its way into their souls like a parasite setting up home in a gut. The deepest depression had struck them, a sense of exposure and helplessness as solid and intractable as the two kilometres of ice beneath their feet.

Even the weather conditions seemed to have renewed the battle against them, the cold so invasive it actually froze them in their sleeping bags. Lauren had to dig deep to conquer her own apathy as she crawled out into the wind-scoured world of ice which surrounded their two lonely tents.

'What's the point?' Murdo snapped at Lauren when she tried to rouse him from his sleeping bag. 'We lost the battle, and we're going to die. Better to die in a sleeping bag than slogging our guts out there in the deep freeze for nothing.'

'I'm taking the tents down in five minutes,' Lauren warned him. 'We'll leave you here alone if you don't get up.'

Lauren hated to play the bully, but this was really the only way.

Murdo groaned, and Mel joined him.

'My back . . .' she pleaded with Lauren. 'I can't tow the sledge any more.'

The medic rolled up her clothing to reveal a bloodied mass of blisters virtually covering her entire back.

'We're all the same,' Lauren told her firmly. 'I'll show you mine if you want . . .'

'Give me one reason . . .' Murdo mumbled from his bag. His head was turned away; he didn't want to look Lauren in the eye. 'One good reason to carry on.'

'Because if we quit now, we definitely can't win. There's still a chance, Murdo, that we can get to the plane before Fitzgerald. His snowmobile might break down . . . he might get lost in a storm . . . fall down a crevasse.'

As she spoke the words, Lauren was painfully aware of how thin they sounded.

'He's got all the food . . .' Murdo sulked. 'That was *our* food . . . you promised it to us, remember?'

'I know . . .' Lauren placed a hand gently on Murdo's shoulder. 'But we can still survive. You *can* get to the plane if you really want it.'

'I don't care about the plane. The whole thing is shit.' Murdo burrowed his head even deeper into the bag as Mel and Richard reluctantly began the process of sorting out their gear ready for the departure.

Lauren returned to the other tent and found the biscuit she'd been saving. It was a custard cream, the soft filling frozen hard. She waited until Mel and Richard had left Murdo alone in the tent and took the biscuit to him.

'Breakfast,' she told him, placing the precious object next to his head. 'But only if you get your ass out of that sack and come and join the rest of us.'

Murdo unfolded the sleeping bag, his mouth filling immediately with saliva as he saw the biscuit.

'Where the hell did you get that from?'

'Saved it,' Lauren told him, 'for a moment like this.'

'I can't eat that,' he told her. 'You should give it to Frank.'

'It's yours. It'll help get you going. The others won't know.'

Murdo couldn't resist the food. He placed the biscuit in his mouth, chewing it hard. In a few moments it was gone.

'Now will you get out of the tent?'

Murdo nodded, feeling suddenly ashamed of his greed.

'We should have kept it . . .' he started. 'Maybe someone else is going to need it more . . .'

Lauren left Murdo to extract himself from his bag and went to help Sean with Frank. The radio man was now incapable of using his hands at all. Every zip, every button had to be fastened for him; they helped him out of the tent and pulled him clumsily to his feet.

'I need to piss, Sean,' Frank said. 'Would you be so kind?'

Frank stumbled a short distance away, and Sean helped him to piss.

'Do you want Mel to take a look at your hands today?' Lauren asked him when he came back.

Frank shook his head violently. 'No, no.'

'Is it my imagination,' Lauren asked Sean when they were out of earshot, 'or are Frank's fingers beginning to smell real bad?'

'They sure are,' Sean agreed. 'I never smelled an infection like that before.'

'We should watch him carefully today. I think he's sicker than he's letting on.'

After a long struggle, Lauren finally had the team out on the ice, the tents packed and loaded. Richard was strangely silent, rocking slightly on his feet, his hands placed gingerly inside his wind jacket.

'How are your feet?' Lauren asked him.

Lost in a world of his own pain, Richard didn't respond.

'Richard?'

'I'll walk,' he told her quietly. 'The hurt keeps my mind from thinking of food.'

Richard pulled down the hood of his jacket so Lauren couldn't see his eyes.

The temperature was breathtakingly low, somewhere down in the minus fifties, Lauren estimated. It paralysed them; the severity of the cold seemed to turn them to statues where they stood. The very idea of walking fifteen or twenty miles that day, with nothing to eat, seemed so ridiculous it almost made Lauren want to cry.

Murdo suddenly threw back his head. 'I hate this place!' he screamed into the air. 'I hate this fucking place!'

His shout echoed back from the ice.

No one said anything, but Mel put her hand behind Murdo's back and gently pushed him to make a step.

'Jesus. Has anyone any idea how my feet feel?' Murdo was close to tears as he shuffled onwards.

Lauren was biting her own lip as she forced herself to take a step. The rope began to build pressure against her hips, the familiar deep-set pain of the friction burns reigniting again.

Sean pulled next to her, as strong as ever, his body leaning into the work as the first seconds of the shift passed in a blur of agony. 'How many miles to the plane?' he asked her quietly.

'Ninety. Plus.'

'Frank's not going to make it. He's going down fast.'

'I know. And so is Richard,' Lauren replied. 'You reckon we can pull him *and* Frank on this thing?'

Sean did not reply.

86

Frank had a fever when he woke the next day and complained that his fingers were feeling worse.

'Not that I want to get a reputation as a whinger,' he told Lauren, 'but I'm beginning to feel a little rough.'

He was beginning to look a little rough too; in fact, Lauren had been alarmed at the permanent green tinge to his complexion and the sweat which was beginning to plague him in the night. His eyes had become bloodshot as the days had worn on, and his brow was deeply creased with the habitual frown of an individual who was in constant, severe pain.

He finally agreed for the medic to examine his fingers. Mel winced when she peeled back the bandages; the smell was absolutely putrid, the skin black and obviously decaying.

'Well, we've certainly had a deterioration here,' she said as she examined the tissue. 'These have to hurt like hell. Can you bear me to touch them?'

Frank nodded as she took a sterile swab and began to clean away the weeping fluid which had congealed around the burned tissue of his fingers, the only indication of his acute discomfort the occasional sharp intake of breath.

When she had finished the task, Mel looked at Lauren, her eyes conveying the bad news that was about to come. She took a deep breath.

'I'm going to be honest with you, Frank. You've got the first indications of gangrene in three of these fingers.'

Frank was distraught. 'Oh Christ. What about the antibiotics? Aren't they clearing it up?'

'No. A broad-spectrum antibiotic like amoxycillin can keep the infection at bay, but it can't beat something this strong. Also, as the days go by, your own body defences are getting weaker with the lack of food and the general conditions.'

'When does the course of antibiotics run out?' Lauren asked.

'In two days. And that's it. We only had the one course packed in the first barrel. This infection will probably progress very rapidly without the curbing effects of the antibiotics.'

'And the long-term prognosis?' Frank's voice sounded so thin and frightened it brought a lump to Lauren's throat.

Mel sucked her cheeks for a while, plucking up the courage.

'We're talking about amputation,' she said, finally. 'In the end, that's really the only sure way to sort this out.'

87

'Get up, Richard; it's time to go.'

The journalist buried his head further into the warmth of his sleeping bag, murmuring incoherently.

'Richard! Get out of the bag!' It was a woman's voice, but he was unsure if it was Lauren or Mel.

Getting out of that bag was the last thing Richard wanted to do. This was his healing time, time to devote to thoughts of home, time to teleport his mind back to the life which had once belonged to him—if that really had been him at all. He wouldn't be the same person now, he was sure of that, if he ever got out of this alive.

He rarely thought of his fiancée any more. And all thoughts of sex had weeks ago disappeared as his body had degenerated. No, now it was curious things which drifted into his mind—drifted the way that dreams did just before the waking moment, more vivid somehow, and leaving him wondering if they were dreams at all.

Sometimes he imagined himself driving his car, not go-

ing anywhere in particular, but just driving along a motorway with the heater turned on full. Other times he was standing in a lift, the lift that took him to the fifth floor of the
office block in which he worked. There were other journalists around him, joking as they discussed the breaking news
stories of the day. It was real, real enough that he could smell
the start of day scents of deodorants and dry-cleaned
clothes.

A hand pulled at his shoulder, followed by the sound of
the sleeping-bag zip being unfastened. Richard groaned,
then reluctantly sat, the stiff muscles in his shoulders and
stomach sending dull shivers of pain through him as he
moved.

He found Lauren squatting in the entrance to the tent.

'The others are already out there,' she told him. 'We've
got miles to kill.'

Richard heard himself laugh bitterly, a laugh that turned
immediately into a racking cough.

'Miles to kill?' he spluttered weakly. 'That makes me
laugh for some reason.'

'I know how much you're hurting,' Lauren told him gently, 'but we really are getting closer to the aircraft, I promise
you . . . and I know you can make it. You've done two hundred and thirty miles, Richard; you've been brilliant. Now
just a few days more.'

'I think you're lying,' he said. 'You know we're all going
to end up like Scott, dead in our tents. So let's get on with it.'

He tried to fall back, but Lauren had his shoulders
pinned. There was a pause as Sean's voice came from outside the tent.

'Sledge loaded.'

Lauren scraped some of the frozen condensation from
Richard's hair and found the two pairs of gloves which were
down inside the sleeping bag for warmth. There was no
need to dress him, apart from the gloves, he was wearing
every stitch of clothing he had. Lauren unzipped the bag all
the way.

'There's a pizza place near my flat,' Richard mumbled.

'They do a quattro staggioni. The artichokes are all chopped up, swimming in olive oil . . .'

'Shut up. Swing out your legs,' she ordered him.

The journalist tried to get his legs to work, but they felt as lifeless as wood. He could feel the muscles contract slightly in his thighs, but they were so weak he could not lift his lower body out of the bag. Lauren did it for him, placing both her hands underneath his calves and swivelling him into a position where she could get at his feet.

She pulled at the laces in his boots, creating enough slack to open them up a little, then slid them over his bandaged feet and tightened them up as gently as she could. Richard couldn't help a whimper as some of the blistered flesh was pinched.

Sean poked his head into the tent and gave Lauren some help to get Richard out by sliding him on his backside. He set about packing up the tent with Murdo as Lauren tried to persuade the journalist to get up and walk.

'I don't want to stand,' he told her.

'You have to.' Lauren stood behind him and hauled him to his feet. Richard felt the tears come to his eyes as his pulped flesh began to pulsate and flare. This moment was always one he dreaded: the rush of blood to his inflamed feet as he put his weight on them.

Richard took a few panting breaths and waited while Lauren slid the skis into position beneath his boots. She helped him to snap the boots down into the autolock fastenings—another explosion of pain his reward for this simple act—then they set out together towards the north.

Richard did his best, he really did, but his speed was a fraction of what the others could achieve. Sean and Murdo, harnessed to the sledge and pulling Frank's weight, overtook them rapidly. Richard stared at the sledge longingly as it passed. Was there room for two on there? he wondered. And could the others pull it?

Lauren stayed by his side, supporting him as best she could and keeping up a rolling conversation to which he listened with only half an ear.

'Seventy miles,' she told him. 'A car can do that in less than an hour. It's less than thirty per cent of what we've already done.'

For much of the morning they stumbled along together, sometimes with just Lauren giving him support, other times with Sean coming back to lend a hand when the ice got bad. Richard was suffering so much with the pain from his feet that he could barely pay attention to what Lauren was saying. Somewhere through the fog he did hear:

'That's a mile done.'

Then later:

'Kick through the pain barrier.'

'It's *all* the pain barrier,' he muttered angrily.

Late in the morning they came to a pressure ridge blocking their path. It was a big one, some two metres high, chaotic blocks of ice all jumbled on top of each other and, Richard could see, a real epic to cross.

And that was the moment. The end of what his body could do. Now he didn't care how many miles there were to go; he had given all he had to give.

Richard felt his knees buckle as he decided to quit this game. That was when he discovered that the only thing which had been keeping him upright was his willpower. As for the sinews and muscles of his legs; well, they weren't going to be taking him anywhere soon . . . if ever again.

Lauren stood over him, her face resigned.

'That's it,' he told her. 'I need the sledge.'

88

'Pull . . . and rest! And pull . . . and rest.' Lauren was still calling the shots, but the load, and the pressure, had doubled.

It hadn't taken long to discover that it took all four of them to tow the two men. Previously, Lauren and Sean had done most of the hauling, but now there was no escape for Murdo and Mel. The conditions were soft, the snow deep enough to make progress abysmally slow.

They tugged in unison, pushing forward on their skis and swearing bitterly as the rope sliced a little more into their backs with each jolting movement. They completed four miles on the day that Richard threw in the towel, and now were into the second day of the extra load—one which Lauren was determined would tick off ten or more miles.

Lauren wondered how many pounds they were pulling; was it two hundred and fifty? Three hundred? Whatever, it might as well have been a ton for all the pain it was giving them. Lauren had never asked her body to do more, and the only thing which was keeping her going was the knowledge that Murdo, Mel and Sean were suffering the same.

On the sledge the two men lay side by side, saying little as they were pulled along. Frank was now profoundly depressed, the gangrenous state of his fingers dominating his thoughts. He didn't complain, but Lauren could see he was hurting bad. Once in a while he would mutter: 'I'm so sorry . . . so, so sorry . . .'

But then Murdo screamed at him to shut up, and he said no more.

Richard was also sinking ever deeper into depression, his blistered feet showing no signs of healing, and still grotesquely swollen. Lauren knew there was absolutely no chance they would ever get his boots on again—not until he could get hospital treatment at least.

'Pull . . . and pull . . .' Lauren's voice was down to a hoarse whisper, her vocal cords strained and sore.

At midday Lauren finally called a rest stop, the team falling to the ice just where they stood, without the strength to prop themselves up against a sastrugi or to sit with their backs to the sledge.

Mel was lying next to Lauren, and she spoke to her quietly as she recovered her breath.

'You've got to come up with an alternative,' she said. 'Murdo and I aren't as strong as you and Sean. We can't pull that thing much further.'

Lauren was sympathetic.

'I know how you're feeling,' she said, 'but what do you think we can do about it?'

'There must be something . . .'

'Like what? Leave one of them behind?'

'I don't know . . . Maybe you and Sean should go ahead to the aircraft, leave us here, and we'll wait for you . . . I know you didn't want to split the team up before when Murdo asked, but now . . .'

'The team stays together,' Lauren told her. 'That was the way we began this, and that's how we'll continue.'

'But . . .' Mel began to cry, a quiet sobbing noise coming from deep within her.

'You've got it inside you,' Lauren told her gently. 'Take it one step at a time.'

'I haven't . . . I can't pull that bloody sledge another foot . . .'

Sean interrupted them.

'What about the food?'

He handed Lauren the supply pack, and she took a look at the meagre collection of tins they had left, making her choice quickly.

'Starvation rations,' she said grimly. 'Two cans of sardines.'

Lauren peeled back the lids of the sardine tins, inhaling the aroma of the fish as she did so. Normally, sardines turned her stomach, but now the mere sight of the oily fish had her taste buds sizzling with anticipation.

She divided the contents into six tiny piles, and they ate them in ritualistic silence. All too soon, the food was gone.

They rested for an hour, no one exchanging a single word. Then a hailstorm whipped up from nowhere, the stinging pellets of ice bouncing off their goretex clothing with a pattering sound, the hailstones collecting in small drifts against their legs and boots. Still no one said a word or even moved. Anyone stumbling across the scene could easily have imagined that they were all dead.

The hailstorm moved on across the glacier, a grey mass of cloud hurrying away to the north. Then the moment that Lauren dreaded; the moment she had to motivate them to begin again, to bully them onto their feet and get them into the hated harnesses ready for more hauling.

'How many miles?' Mel asked as Lauren helped her to her feet.

'About sixty.'

Mel hung her head, shaking it gently from side to side.

'It's OK.' Lauren put her arm around Mel's shoulders, holding her close. 'We're all going to make it.'

'That's the mantra,' Murdo said bitterly, 'but does anyone here still believe it?'

No one replied.

'So why won't you answer?' he demanded. 'Because no one believes that bullshit any more . . .'

Lauren crossed to him and tied the rope around his waist. Then she did the same for Mel and finally herself. Sean was already tied in, and slowly, with muttered gasps of pain as their already depleted muscles creaked into movement, they began the endless haul towards the north.

'It's not just a mantra,' Lauren said as they pulled away. 'It's the truth. We're all going to make it. No one's going to die.'

But for the first time her words sounded hollow, and Lauren knew why. She was no longer one hundred per cent certain, not now they had so much extra weight to haul. The grain of doubt had taken root, had sent up a shoot and was choking off her previous optimism like a fast-growing weed will choke a rose. Having two men on the sledge might easily tip the balance, she knew, and there was still so much distance to travel . . .

'Pull . . .' she gasped, 'and pull again . . .'

Deep in her heart she was no longer sure. But something inside her was still going to try.

89

It was twenty-three days since Lauren had informed her sponsors of her radio problem, and De Pierman and the Scott Polar were now at the point where they knew they had to act. The absence of any signal was downright bizarre—the base had been out of contact for way too long—and the possibility that something had gone terribly wrong at Capricorn was becoming a real concern.

The Antarctic winter was coming to an end; the ambient temperatures might just allow a plane to land. Antarctic Air Service promised to give it a try.

There was a weather delay—De Pierman was beginning to understand that with Antarctica there was always a weather delay. But finally the Twin Otter managed to set out for the Capricorn location.

The following day, De Pierman got the news on a crackly telephone line from Tierra del Fuego. Capricorn was completely gutted by fire. The AAS pilots had been able to land and confirmed that there were no survivors.

'Did you find any bodies?' De Pierman asked them, distraught now his worst fears had been realised.

'It looked like the main fuel tanks exploded,' one of the pilots told him. 'There was almost nothing left to see and certainly no bodies to be found. Most of the base was covered in a deep layer of snow and we had no time to dig.'

'You saw no human remains?'

'It is doubtful there would be any. Even the metal was melted.'

De Pierman knew enough about rig fires to know what they were saying. A human body is organic and will crumble to dust given enough temperature. Even the enamel of the teeth will shatter and explode if the fire is intense enough.

'How about transport?' he asked them. 'Could you see if any of their snowmobiles were missing?'

'We found the remains of a vehicle shed,' the pilot told him. 'There were definitely the remains of snowmobiles in there, but as for how many, it was hard to tell . . . two or three at least.'

De Pierman was shattered; his one foray into scientific sponsorship had ended in total disaster, and the negative backlash would have far-reaching repercussions both for him personally and for Kerguelen Oils. More importantly, he felt a genuine sadness at the loss of so many talented people, and particularly for Lauren, who he had come to like and admire.

De Pierman knew he would have to go public with the disaster, but his first call was to the Scott Polar to break the tragic news to Michael Collins. The director took it badly, breaking down in tears on learning that Lauren—whom he'd worked with on several field projects—was lost.

'But is there any chance,' De Pierman asked him, 'that they might somehow have survived? I don't want to go public on this until we're absolutely sure they're dead.'

'You'd better talk to John Gresham,' Collins advised him. 'He'll be able to advise you on that.'

Long ago, the Scott Polar had realised the importance of understanding the limitations of the human body in polar

environments, and Dr Gresham—an eminent physician—
had been drafted in to head the study.

Gresham was one of the old school, a scientist with eighteen Antarctic seasons behind him, still an important figure in the world of polar science even though he should have retired years before. Diligently, he had worked through the existing data, run endless experiments in the cold rooms at the British Army Polar Warfare unit at its Farnborough base and produced a computer program which was as close as anyone had ever got to predicting how a human body would react given a specific set of cold-weather conditions.

De Pierman made contact with Gresham, who, once he understood the context of the call, immediately agreed to see him. De Pierman was driven up to Cambridge and escorted into Gresham's cluttered office, the scientist brushing a teetering pile of academic papers aside to give his visitor a chair.

'May I start by saying how utterly sad I am to hear this news about Capricorn base,' Gresham told him. 'Dr Burgess was one of the finest research scientists in the world, and I was personally very fond of her and several other members of her team.'

'It came as quite a shock, I can tell you.'

'It was a fire, you said?'

'Yes. It seems the base was razed to the ground. Nothing left, and no human remains visible.'

Gresham gave a deep sigh. 'Fire. It has killed more people in Antarctica than anything else. But when did you get this news?'

'This morning. Two Argentinian pilots landed at the base and carried out a search. They found no survivors.'

'And how can I help you?'

'I want to know one thing,' De Pierman told him. 'Assuming that one or more of the team survived the fire, what would they do?'

'There's no doubt about that,' Gresham answered emphatically. 'They would have stayed by the base and awaited rescue. That's the standard textbook response to such an emergency.'

'And Lauren Burgess would know that?'

'Without any doubt. So would anyone else at that base.'

'And if there was nothing left to sustain human life? If all food and available shelter had been completely destroyed in the fire? What would they do then?'

'They would still stay at the base location.'

'And how long would they last?'

Gresham turned to his computer and inputted a series of commands.

'Here we are,' he said, jotting down some notes. 'The answer to your question is this. At minus fifty-five degrees . . . and that, as we know, has been the ambient temperature across Antarctica in recent weeks . . . a fit individual with minimal shelter and no food could theoretically survive for up to seven days. More likely they'd be dead within three.'

'And what would kill them?'

'Exposure. And dehydration. If they had no means of melting ice, they would have no access to water. Of course there are other factors which may be working against them: one or more of them may be injured as a result of the fire. Then there would be the shock of the disaster itself . . . that would exacerbate the effects of hypothermia and cut their survival time by quite a bit.'

'Dr Gresham,' De Pierman said, 'there was another factor in all of this. Capricorn's radio system was down . . . Lauren had contacted us to say they were having problems and not to worry if we didn't hear from her.'

'Oh dear.' Gresham tapped his yellowing teeth with the chewed end of a pencil. 'That does confuse the situation somewhat. How long was the anticipated blackout?'

'Well, that's the problem: she couldn't tell us with any accuracy. In her last radio call she mentioned a week to ten days before restoring normal communications.'

'So she *knew* that no alarm would be raised for at least ten days . . . and probably more?'

'Exactly. By which time—given that they had no food or shelter—according to your calculations, they would almost certainly have perished.'

Gresham nodded sadly as De Pierman continued.

'Do you think it's feasible they might have set out for the nearest base?'

'To get to the Chileans?' Gresham took a quick look at his wall map. 'I doubt it. That would have meant an overland journey of more than seven hundred miles . . . much more than any human being could do without provisions.'

'But perhaps they *did* manage to rescue some supplies. Maybe they had a snowmobile too.'

Gresham thought about this for some time before replying.

'If we apply logic to this situation, there really is only one scenario. *If* anyone had survived the fire, they would certainly have been found at the base.'

'How can you be so sure?'

'If they had no provisions, they would have stayed at the base because they would have had no choice . . . there simply wasn't anywhere for them to go. And if they *had* had the means to sustain life, they *still* would have stayed at the base . . . knowing that rescue would eventually come, albeit after a delay. They certainly wouldn't have risked a long overland journey—with all its attendant hazards—if they didn't need to.'

'Just for my own interest, if someone *had* tried to make a break for it, to walk out, how far do you think they could get?'

Gresham entered more data into the computer, his bony fingers tapping against the keyboard as he waited for the result.

'If they were very determined, Dr Burgess might get her team one hundred or perhaps one hundred and fifty miles before they would start dying. But that would be the limit.'

'So there's really no hope.'

'I fear not.'

'I had a feeling that would be your response,' De Pierman told him, 'but it's obviously not what I wanted to hear.'

'That is my professional response, Mr De Pierman; my

personal response is one of great sadness at the loss of so
many friends.'

De Pierman left the Scott Polar in a bleak depression. He
called the relatives to give them the news, then rang his secretary to arrange a press conference in London for later that
day. By five p.m., he was addressing more than a hundred reporters, giving them the news that Capricorn was destroyed
and with no realistic hope of any survivors.

Lauren Burgess was dead, he told them, and so was
Fitzgerald and his team mate, the *Daily Mail* journalist and
all the rest of the Capricorn crew.

The response to the disaster was electric, the stunned
journalists running to their mobiles to reserve the front page
for this sensational new twist.

After the press conference, De Pierman went for a walk
in Hyde Park—the place he habitually turned to when he
needed to resolve a problem. As he strolled, he went back
over his conversation with Dr Gresham, unsure as to why he
was still uneasy about writing off Lauren and her team so
fast. He knew that Dr Gresham's scientific analysis had been
accurate and based on a wide range of experience, so why
was this stubborn insistence still ticking away somewhere
inside him? The ridiculous feeling—a hunch, maybe—that
somehow, against all the evidence, Lauren and her team
might still be alive.

Again and again that night, De Pierman pored over the
Antarctic pages of his World Atlas, trying to come up with
the one factor which they might have missed. When no further revelation came, he abandoned the struggle and fell into
a shallow sleep, plagued by a series of nightmares in which
Lauren appeared, her arms outstretched in a plea for help as
flames erupted around her.

90

They operated on Frank the following morning, after a night in which he tossed and turned in agony.

'Do it today,' he urged them. 'I really can't bear this any more.'

'We'll use the other tent for the operation,' Mel told Lauren. 'We'll have more room to move in there.'

Lauren and Mel prepared the instruments for the operation, laying them out on a clean handkerchief, which someone had found in an untouched pocket. There was a Swiss army knife, a syringe full of morphine, a small phial of iodine and what remained of the first aid kit which had been in the first barrel. Nearby was the gas cooker and the pot they would use to boil up water.

'Thank God we've got the morphine and the sutures,' Lauren said, looking at the meagre supplies.

'Not exactly what the medical textbooks would require for surgery,' Mel said grimly as she examined the knife. 'This is one operation I hope I never have to repeat.'

'Which blade are you going to use?'

The medic flicked open the multibladed device, selecting the saw attachment.

'This one. It needs a cutting edge to be able to get through the bone, you see,' she said.

Lauren began to feel sick.

They fired up the gas cooker and began to melt down chunks of ice to create a supply of water. When it boiled, they sterilised the Swiss army knife by the simple expedient of immersing it in the pan for ten minutes.

'We're ready,' Mel told Lauren at last. 'Bring in the patient.'

Lauren walked to the other tent, where Frank was waiting. His fever was still raging, his hair plastered to his head with sweat even though the temperature was down to twenty degrees below freezing.

'It's time, Frank. Are you ready to do this? Do you want us to carry you?'

'No, no. I'd rather walk. I need the bloody exercise, let's face it.'

Lauren smiled as she recognised the humour for what it was: an attempt to cover up his fear.

Frank let Lauren dress him in the warmest clothes she could find. She managed to get him out of the sleeping bag and, with the sick man's arm around her shoulder, escorted him to the tent where the operation would take place.

The others were sitting around the camp, awkward and frightened to look Frank in the eye as he passed, now they knew what he was about to endure.

'It'll be OK, Frank,' Murdo called out to him. 'They've got the morphine.' Frank looked at him, wild-eyed, an expression of gratitude passing for a moment across his racked features.

'I know,' he said. 'I'm sure it'll be fine.'

'Good luck, Frank.'

In the operation tent Mel took the iodine and cleaned the wounds as best she could, trying not to gag as the rancid smell of the decomposing flesh filled the tent. She noted that the gangrene had spread another half a centimetre down towards the knuckle. This operation was only just in time, she thought, or Frank was going to end up losing the hand.

'I'm going to inject half of the morphine now to alleviate the pain of the operation,' she told him. 'This is going to hurt a bit now. We'll save the other half for later.'

Frank screamed as she injected the painkiller directly into the infected fingers.

'All right, that's going to deaden the feeling.'

Mel waited five minutes while Lauren talked soothingly to Frank, holding his good hand for reassurance.

'Let's see if that's taken effect,' she said. 'Can you feel anything when I touch here?'

'Nothing,' Frank said. 'For Christ's sake do it now while that stuff is still working.'

He fainted as Mel began to work with the tiny saw, as she had warned he might. Lauren held his head up so his airway was clear, and by the time Mel had the operation complete he was just coming round.

Mel stitched the wounds, then cleaned them with iodine once more and dressed the hand to stem the blood loss. 'Now he needs to rest,' she told Lauren. 'There's no way we can move him today. We'll let him sleep this off, and I'll give him another shot of morphine when he comes round.'

The team carried Frank back to his sleeping bag, and Mel and Lauren stayed with him in the tent through that long day. He wavered in and out of consciousness as the hours went past, helped into a befuddled oblivion by the effects of the morphine.

The crisis came at about three a.m., when it seemed his fever was set to return. His temperature rocketed as his immune system fought back, his cries terrible to hear in the stillness of the night air. But by dawn he was clearly recovering, the fever subsided and his skin colour looked relatively normal for the first time in days.

'I think he's winning,' Mel told Lauren. 'Everything should go fine now, so long as the infection doesn't return.'

At first light they managed to get a cup of sweet tea inside the patient, and by ten a.m. he was sitting up and sipping the cup of asparagus soup which they had prepared for him. He drank it down appreciatively, savouring every last morsel of vegetable it contained.

'There's no more morphine,' Mel told him. 'We're down to paracetamol now, and nothing else, I'm afraid.'

'No matter. This pain is nothing compared to the gangrene,' Frank told her. 'And by the way, shouldn't we be getting underway? I wouldn't want to hold anyone up.'

Lauren looked at him with astonishment, amazed at the resilience of the man.

'You think you're well enough to get back on the sledge?'

'I wouldn't want to let you down,' he said.

'I think,' Lauren told him, 'that I've never been prouder of anyone than I am of you at this moment. Not many people would bounce back after what you've been through.'

When Frank emerged and took his place on the sledge next to Richard, he got a rousing chorus of cheers from the rest of the team. They gave him an extra sleeping bag to lie in to ensure that he kept as warm as possible.

Thirty minutes later they were packed up and pulling away from the camp, inching their way slowly towards their objective.

91

Lauren had assumed—and it had frightened her greatly—that Frank's operation would mark a downward shift in the spirit of the group. She could not imagine that morale would do anything other than plummet once the battle to save his fingers was lost.

To her amazement the opposite had occurred: on the day after Frank's operation, the team had had their best day of progress since Richard had taken his place on the sledge—a full nine miles of distance travelled across the glacier before dark, sustained on a diet of just two water biscuits each and a sliver of spam so slender it was almost transparent.

At one point Frank had even got them singing his old favourite, 'The green, green grass of home', directing them from his prone position on the sledge, laughing as they strained to pull him over the bigger bumps and drifts.

The question of why the team had reacted in this way was one which interested Lauren greatly. She let the theories run slowly through her mind as the soul-destroying process of hauling towards the north continued for hour after hour.

Ultimately, she suspected, the knowledge of what Frank had suffered had pulled the team into a mind set in which every individual had realised that whatever their privations—and there were many—they were better off than him. It was Frank's incredible courage that had re-energised the team when they should have been on their last legs.

As they pitched the two tents that night, Lauren felt her heart bursting with pride. 'We did nine miles today,' she told the team. 'I think we should split open one of the chocolate bars to celebrate.'

She supervised the cutting of the bar—one of only three left from the first depot—each precious square taken with glee by the grateful recipient, cupping their gloved hands so as not to lose a single microscopic crumb.

No one mentioned that the knife used to cut the chocolate was the same one that had been used to amputate Frank's fingers just twenty-four hours before.

Frank got a bonus in addition to his square—the silver paper filled with fragments of chocolate, a gesture which had him beaming from ear to ear as Mel checked his fingers.

'No infection,' she told him. 'Looks like you're going to keep your hand.'

That night Lauren wrote in her diary:

> Anything is possible when the human spirit wants. Frank has reminded us that we are all lucky to be alive. I feel right now that we can overcome anything.

Lauren had saved her chocolate, wanting to delay the ecstasy of the moment when its taste would be hers. As soon as the last torch was turned off, she placed it in her mouth, using her tongue to position the softening square against her palate for what seemed to be hours. Long after the actual square had dissolved, she held a mouthful of the chocolate-flavoured liquid in her mouth, remembering how she had done the same thing eating pieces of Easter egg in bed as a child.

Two bars left. And a handful of cans. Some biscuits and a few packets of soup.

Forty-five miles to go.

92

The front left strut of the sledge broke the following morning. There was no particular knock or movement which precipitated it—it just snapped without warning while they were traversing a smooth piece of ground.

The effect was instant and dramatic, the broken strut causing the collapse of the front of the sledge, which dug straight into the ice, where it acted like a brake. The two occupants were tipped to one side, only just managing to hold onto their positions.

'Hold it there!' Frank called out. 'Problem.'

They carefully lifted the two men from the sledge while Sean inspected the damage.

'Metal fatigue,' he announced. 'Cracked straight through the tube. We got to think of a solution to this one or . . .' Lauren flashed him a warning glance—it wasn't going to help to frighten the two incapacitated men any more than necessary. 'Well, we've got to think of a solution, and we *will*,' he finished lamely.

'I had a feeling this would happen.' Frank's voice was fearful. 'How bad is it?'

'It's a setback,' Lauren told him, 'nothing more. This is the type of problem Sean and Murdo solve for breakfast.'

'If we had any breakfast,' Murdo added despondently.

'Well . . . my magic carpet ride had to hit the buffers somewhere along the way.' Richard lay back against a convenient ridge of ice and closed his eyes, as if by blacking out the scene he could make it disappear.

Murdo came to Sean's assistance as he struggled to remove the broken strut; the others left them to it, taking the chance to rest.

'What do you think?' Sean asked him as they looked despairingly at the fractured metal.

Murdo shook his head. 'This is finished. Even if we could drill a hole in the tube, we wouldn't be able to fix it back onto the frame.'

They lifted the top part of the sledge up.

'Trouble is,' Murdo observed, 'without the left strut the whole platform is going to be tilted on an angle. And the right strut will be taking all the stress.'

Sean nodded in agreement. 'That won't last long. We have to prop up the left side. But with what?'

They considered the various items that had been salvaged from the fire, aware as they did so that their options were frighteningly thin.

'How about this?' Sean proposed, holding up a piece of door frame they had rescued from the base for firewood. 'This has the rigidity for the job. If we saw it to the right length and bore a couple of holes at each end, we can wire it to the frame.'

'We can give it a try.'

Using all the tools at their disposal, they took it in turns to saw through the door frame. The saw was blunt, making the job a tedious one as the cutting edge bit toothlessly into the hardwood, but by persevering for an hour or more they had a section of wood which matched the missing strut.

Next they began to bore a hole at each end of the new

strut, again sharing the work as their fingers froze after ten minutes of handling the knife. The corkscrew was found to be the most effective attachment, combined with a bit of judicious probing and trimming with the small knife blade.

'Let's put it into position,' Sean suggested, 'see how it's going to work.'

They raised the damaged section of the sledge until the new upright could be slid into place. A bit of jiggling to and fro had it more or less in the right position.

'You think we can attach it well enough?' Murdo asked. 'I get the feeling bootlaces are going to wear through mighty quickly.'

'I've got some wire,' Sean told him with a smile. 'Been saving it.'

'You got some *wire*? Where the hell did you get that from?'

Sean slid off his goretex outer coat with the air of a magician about to reveal a favourite trick. He held the hood out for Murdo to feel.

'Check it out,' he told him. 'I had some wire put into the rim around this hood; helps keep it in shape when the wind's really going.'

'You did? I wondered how come your hood was never flapping in your face.'

Murdo ran his fingers along the seam, feeling the stiff cord of metal which ran inside. He had to smile at the luck which had given them this break; that tiny piece of attention to detail—an equipment customisation Sean had had carried out in the States before leaving—was about to give Frank and Richard another chance on the sledge. The strut would never have held with a bootlace alone.

Sean nicked the edge of the seam with the knife blade and carefully pulled the wire from the hood. He handed it to Murdo to test its strength.

'Perfect,' he smiled. 'This could almost have been made for the job. What other secrets you got tucked away?'

'Just a small modification,' Sean shrugged it off, but the others could see how pleased he was to have come up with the solution.

They threaded the wire through the lowest of the two holes and wound it several times tightly around the frame so that the base of the door frame was bound tightly to the runner. Then they ran the wire up the outside of the new strut—to avoid having to sever it—and repeated the procedure at the top.

When they had finished, the wood was secure enough that Murdo couldn't budge it by hand.

'It's not very aesthetically pleasing,' Sean told Lauren, 'but I think it will resist for some time.'

'Can I sit on it?'

Lauren lowered herself cautiously onto the sledge, letting her weight press down on the frame. The strut held its position perfectly, absorbing the weight and keeping the front of the sledge true.

'Lie down,' Sean told her. 'Let's see if it'll tow.'

They dragged Lauren back and forth for a few minutes until they had satisfied themselves the repair hadn't caused some unforeseen towing problem; then it was time for Richard and Frank to be helped back on.

As they pulled away, Lauren thanked Sean and Murdo profusely. She was acutely aware that without their shared genius for improvisation the sledge would have probably remained where it had broken . . . and the two patients with it.

The two men were pensive as they bounced and rocked on the back of the sledge, no cry of protest coming from either even though Richard's legs and feet were now so swollen he had to be physically lifted on and off his transport, and Frank's hand was still giving him hell.

They had got away with this one, Lauren mused, but what if another strut failed? Her mind began to chew away as they strained at the ropes. What if a runner snapped?

Lauren's heart skipped a beat at every groan and creak from the sledge, fearing with almost every bump that metal fatigue would render another vital part of the structure useless.

One thing was for sure: there was a limit to how many times Sean and Murdo could pull off the impossible.

Forty miles to go . . . Lauren knew it would take a miracle now.

93

A big storm was coming, Lauren was sure; their weather luck couldn't hold out for ever.

The first signs were small ones, the tiny clues which don't mean much on their own, but which collectively add up to a big flashing warning light.

'You might think this is a bit crazy,' Richard told Lauren as they set out on their first hauling session that morning, 'but I think there's about to be a shift in the weather. My legs ache like hell when the pressure drops. Right now, they're both throbbing like a bastard.'

Lauren viewed the horizon, wishing for the hundredth time that she had managed to rescue her binoculars from the fire. As yet she could see no evidence of any dramatic shift in the weather, but something told her, as she breathed the bitter morning air into her lungs, that Richard was right. There *was* a detectable change in the air, a pressure shift which could only add up to bad news.

'We could be heading for some serious weather,' she

warned the team. 'Let's get some miles ticked off while we still can.'

Obediently, they put in an extra effort, covering almost two miles in the next hour. The light conditions were extraordinary, with no sign of the sun, but a luminous, almost green glow bouncing off the ice around them. Huge snowflakes fell, dancing like thistledown from the sky, so big they seemed artificial.

'Hollywood snow,' Sean called it, holding out his hand and admiring with wonder the feather-sized flakes which landed on it. 'If you wrote it into a script, no one would believe it.'

The gentle snowfall stopped by eleven, giving way to an altogether less attractive bombardment: pea-sized granules of hail raking down from charcoal-grey clouds which were now scudding past with alarming speed.

Way out to the west, perhaps as much as one hundred miles off but already visible, Lauren could just detect the telltale black line of the incoming storm where it was playing on the horizon.

'Shouldn't we camp?' Mel asked Lauren as they took a break. 'We won't be able to get the tents up if this wind gets any nastier.'

Lauren considered the terrain. 'I'd agree if this wasn't such an exposed place,' she told her. 'We're on relatively high ground. See where the glacier dips down a little over there, about a mile away? Let's get there before we camp.'

The team knew it was a device, Lauren's tactic to get them to put in that extra mile—that there was little more protection where they were going than the place where they stood. But, nevertheless, they still did it, putting their backs into the business of hauling the sledge, biting their tongues to prevent themselves from crying out loud as the hated harness dug its way ever more deeply into the sores on their hips.

Lauren called a halt. The wind was force four to five, not unusual for any Antarctic day, but right on the edge of feasibility when it came to putting up a dome tent or two.

'Let's do it fast,' she ordered, one eye on the scudding clouds, hoping she hadn't left it too late.

As they removed their outer layers of gloves to handle the fiddly components of the tents, the storm made its preliminary introductions, a harassing wind springing up, twisting and shrieking through the ice towers which stood around them.

Lauren and Sean pulled their goretex tent from its stuff sack, the fabric immediately coming alive and threatening to rip itself out of their hands.

'One person on the guy rope at all times!' Lauren called over to the others. 'You let go of that tent and it'll be blown a thousand miles.'

Lauren handed the vital guy rope to Richard, the only role which he could usefully perform given his lack of mobility. He held it tight, still sitting on the sledge, his hood pulled down low around his face to give some relief from the pounding hail.

.Sean screwed the kevlar poles together and began to thread them through the eyelets on the strengthened ribs of the dome. It was hit-and-miss work with the tent billowing and flapping fit to rip, but in ten minutes or so they had the main poles in place and the fabric arched into the characteristic igloo shape which gave it its phenomenal strength.

As soon as the tent was shaped up, Lauren got the front zip undone and began the task of transferring Frank from the sledge into the interior. Trial and error had taught her that this was the only practical way to weight down a dome tent while the crucial task of fitting the flysheet was being completed.

In other parts of the planet a rucksack or two would suffice; here it had to be twice the weight or the tent would simply take off, contents and all.

'Help me get Frank in there!' she called over to Mel and Murdo, seeing they were struggling to hold the tent down.

'What?' someone screamed back, the wind had blown Lauren's words away.

Sean rushed over to help them, joining them just as a particularly vicious gust whipped the guy rope through the air. It lashed across Mel's face, drawing the hardened nylon across her skin with a stinging impact which felt like she had been bullwhipped.

'Shit!' Mel fell to the glacier as the whiplash of intense pain seared into her.

Sean took her place on the tent and put all his body weight onto it to keep it in one piece as Murdo shuffled forward to try and open the zip. Crouching over the tent, he was blown onto his side by another evil gust as he tried, and failed, to jiggle the zip tab up its track.

Sean looked over at Mel, who was still sitting on her backside after the shock of the impact; red spots of blood were seeping through her fingers, even now beginning to stain the perfect white surface she was sitting on. Another gust; now the tiny drops of red were no longer falling straight down but shooting off horizontally in a fine spray.

'It's OK,' Mel said shakily. 'It missed my eye.'

Sean's heart went out to her; to suffer an injury like that was just too much bad luck.

'Stop dithering!' He suddenly felt a wave of frustration at the clumsy Murdo, pushing him aside so he could free the zip himself. His fingers, much stronger than Murdo's, achieved it first attempt.

'Get in!' He took Frank by the scruff and thrust him into the tent, where at least he could perform the useful function of weighing it down.

He put a protective arm around Mel, pulling her close. 'You OK?' he asked her. 'That looked really bad.'

'It got me just below the eye. Stupid of me . . .' she said tearfully. 'I couldn't get out of the way . . .'

'You'll be OK. Let me get you inside the tent. Come on, before you freeze your ass to the ice.'

Sean escorted Mel into the tent and then helped Lauren and Murdo to fix the flysheet in place. They piled up a small drift of ice above each tent peg to freeze it better into place, then went across to put the final touches to the other tent.

The camp was made—and not a moment too soon. Just as Lauren and Sean zipped themselves into the second tent, the leading edge of the storm surged across the glacier. The previous gusts had been innocent by comparison, outriders of the real event.

Lauren knew, as she watched the dome roof of the tent begin to shudder with the impact of the wind, that they were now at the mercy of whatever the Antarctic chose to throw at them.

If one of these tents is destroyed tonight, Lauren told herself, the fear taking control of her no matter how positive she tried to make her thoughts, we won't survive.

94

For twenty-four hours they lay in their sleeping bags, hanging on desperately to the fabric of the tents in the fight to keep them from blowing apart.

The storm had not abated as Lauren had hoped; if anything, now into the second day, it was increasing in intensity. Katabatic winds off the higher plateau of the ice cap had merged with the original front, creating a chaotic vortex, which seemed to blow alternately from the south and then from the west.

There was little dialogue between the two tents, even the loudest shout could only barely be heard above the turbulent roar of the wind.

At three a.m. on that second day, Lauren noticed that the central seam of the tent was beginning to split. It was a minute tear—just a centimetre or so in length—but she knew if the wind got into it the tent would be turned inside out in seconds.

'We're going to lose the tents,' Lauren yelled to Sean as

she showed him the rip with her headtorch. 'We have to give ourselves more protection.'

'How?'

'We've got to build a wall. If this storm keeps blowing for another twenty-four hours, there's no way we can keep the tents up without a wind block.'

They fought their way out of the tent and into the teeth of the storm. Working with the headtorch, Sean set to with Lauren, using their basic tools to hack what chunks they could out of the frozen glacier. It was testing work, with the savage wind snapping in their faces, but one hour of shared labour created a pile of irregular-shaped blocks with which they managed to construct a sheltering wall about a metre high.

Then it was back into the tent to wait.

'What would I give for a piece of bread?' Sean groaned as a cramp creased his stomach. 'Some fruit. Anything fresh.'

But all they could eat was a handful or two of dried porridge, their thirst slaked with mouthfuls of snow.

The next day dragged unbearably, the wind picking up a gear as night crept over the wasteland. Sleep was an outright impossibility, the sheer volume produced by the storm was enough to keep them awake despite the deep vein of exhaustion which ran through them all. Living conditions were miserable, made worse by the fine layer of powder snow which was constantly blasted through the entrances; it was fine, as fine as talcum powder, and able to penetrate even the tiniest gap in the fabric of the tents.

The snow melted on contact with the heat of the human body, so that their necks and faces were constantly damp and chilled. Movement around the tent created a further discomfort—any powder which was allowed to creep into a sleeping bag would slowly defrost as they tried to rest, fostering an environment which Sean described as 'Like trying to sleep inside a giant frozen slug, but a darn sight less comfortable.'

As the evening progressed, so the wind increased again, passing storm force ten and touching hurricane force as it raced uncontested across the icy wilderness. The tents were holding up, but only thanks to the wall; to be inside was like being in the interior of a punch bag, the blows coming thick and fast as the shell of the tent deflected them one after another.

Lauren detected a rhythm in the chaos, a cycle which was terrifying in itself—a calmer pause, the dome regaining its igloo shape as the wind eased off slightly, then a far-off whistling sound, a rushing howl as the tumbling mass of energy gathered for the next attack. Seconds ticked by; the tent would begin to quiver, then shake as if the very ground beneath it was in the grip of some violent earthquake. Before long, the kevlar poles which held the shape would bend to the point where Lauren was sure they would splinter, then, unleashed, the full brunt of the storm would smash into the dome, compressing the structure until Lauren could feel the fabric against her head.

The wall was demolished by the wind at about one a.m., the blocks of ice crashing down onto the front of the tents. The first they knew about it was Frank's scream of pain as one of the blocks crushed his feet. Unrestricted, the wind now had full play on the two domes, twisting and distorting the structures so dramatically that the occupants were terrified that their weight would not be enough to pin them down.

'What happened?' Lauren could just hear the muffled shout from the adjacent tent.

'The wall came down!' she called back, repeating herself to make sure she was heard.

Sean and Lauren quit their sleeping bags and took a fast trip outside to make what repairs they could to the wall. The wind chill was intense—stronger than either of them had ever known. Lauren could feel the heat draining out of her body faster than it could be replaced. They worked by the light of the single headtorch, the driving grains of ice shooting past at phenomenal speed in their small pool of vision.

'My feet are going!' Sean shouted after just five minutes of rebuilding the scattered bricks of ice.

Lauren put a final block on top of the ramshackle pile; the

wall wasn't even half the height it had been. 'That's all we can do,' she said.

They re-entered the tent and collapsed into their sleeping bags, wearing every scrap of clothing. Lauren couldn't make the shivering stop.

By four a.m., another problem began to manifest itself: the snow was beginning to drift, the weight pressing down on the occupants of the tents until it threatened to suffocate them. Lauren and Sean went out into the whiteout every hour to shovel the stuff away with their hands, but each time were forced back in by the cold before they could completely clear the tents.

Despite their gloves, these excursions cost them dear. The pain of defrosting their fingers was unspeakable, the tears welling in Sean's eyes as he placed his ice-cold fingers in his armpits and waited for them to recover.

And so that second night passed, a trial of cold, of damp, of pain for Frank with his mutilated hand. A thin cast of light announced a tentative dawn, at least allowing them to see the anxious, grey faces of their tent mates. But still the wind blew.

At about eleven that morning the storm finally decided it would take some time out, the wind dying off to a modest force three or four, the driving snow tailing away in a succession of last-gasp flurries.

Lying in the tent, Lauren could feel the conditions begin to change, sense the way the goretex of the outer wall was easing off as the wind started to let go. Gradually, the cracking of the fabric diminished, the whipping of loose guy ropes less frequent until, finally, it was possible to fall into an exhausted sleep.

95

It was twenty-nine days since the team had left the base; now every step was punctuated by a long pause to rest. The soft snow dumped by the storm meant that the runners of the sledge clogged up with infuriating regularity. Sometimes, even with all four of them pulling with all their might, they achieved just a few inches of progress before the sledge ground to a halt.

The weather was still unstable, one small blizzard after another sweeping across the glacier and plunging them into whiteout conditions for hours on end. It made route-finding a nightmare, costing them time and precious energy as they were forced to detour and skirt the countless crevasses and faults.

Some of the crevasses were so big that they would be forced to halt while Lauren and Sean split up to see which way provided the shortest route towards the north. Then they reached the biggest gulf yet, a crevasse which looked—from the fresh blue colour of the interior—as if it had only recently opened up.

'This one could be miles wide,' Sean said gloomily. 'I can't even *see* the other side.'

They sat on the sledge for a rest, everyone locked in their own thoughts as the wind and snow played around them. Finally, Lauren spoke.

'You take the east,' she told Sean. 'I'll recce this way.'

Lauren checked her compass and slowly walked west for some ten or fifteen minutes, keeping the crevasse edge on her right side. The driving snow was thickening with every passing moment, and visibility was alternating from a couple of metres to ten at most. Looking back over her shoulder, she could see no sign of her team. She walked steadily, scanning the crevasse continually for a snow bridge they could use to cross, her eyes stinging from the hard pinpricks of frozen flakes as they spun through the air.

The crevasse was beginning to narrow, and for a while she was optimistic that this would be the breakthrough to the north. Then the blizzard lifted for a few moments, and she could see yet another large crevasse dissecting it at an angle.

Lauren cursed and stood shivering for a while as she considered what to do. There was little doubt the weather was worsening yet again, and by rights she should return to the team and order them to pitch camp. She decided to go on another ten minutes; in her mind was the fear that, if they pitched camp in this trap, they would never again have the physical strength to get out. She prayed that Sean was having more luck in the other direction.

She carried on into the whiteout, veering slightly to the south again as the new crevasse decided—infuriatingly—to force her to the south alongside what seemed to be a ten-metre-high ice cliff.

Then she paused. Through the wind rush she could hear the sound of someone coughing. It was regular, coming every few seconds. She rubbed the ice from her eyes and took a few steps forward, straining to see something—

anything—through the snow. She checked her compass, thoroughly confused. Could she have turned a full circle? Was that noise the sound of someone where she'd left the team? Or was it Sean?

She advanced a few more steps. The coughing continued. Except now she realised it wasn't coughing at all.

It was more mechanical. More metallic.

Now she could see a dark shape through the swirling snow. It seemed to be red, but what could be red out here? There was someone next to it, stooping with his back to her.

Then she got it. Holy shit, it was Fitzgerald. Lauren froze to the spot, her heart thumping like a jackhammer in her chest as she stared in terror at the explorer's back.

What if he heard her? What if he turned and saw her? She was too far from the others for them to hear a scream.

But what was Fitzgerald doing here? Lauren's exhausted brain took a few frozen seconds, watching him pull the starter cord, before she realised his snowmobile had broken down. The coughing noise was the starter cord as he pulled it back. She could see that the fully laden sledge was still attached to the snowmobile. There was all the food . . . all the medical supplies . . .

Lauren ducked back behind an ice tower and tried to control her breathing.

This was their chance.

Would she have time to go back and get Murdo and Sean? Or would Fitzgerald get the snowmobile started and leave the location completely?

Pull. Pull. The engine almost fired.

Then she saw the axe. It was lying against the sledge, placed between her and the explorer.

Now the adrenaline was pumping harder than Lauren had ever known before.

A moment in which to act . . . or to flee? Then an image of the empty second barrel flashed into her mind . . . and the expression on Frank's face as he watched his fingers being sawn off with a blunt penknife, and she knew there *was* only one way to resolve this now.

Lauren moved carefully forward, placing her boots as silently as she could on the ice as the explorer continued his efforts to get the engine going. She was close enough to hear his curses, the swearing constant and enraged. She picked up the axe, felt the smooth wooden handle, surprisingly warm, in her hand. The head was forged from the finest steel, the haft painted red.

Only one thought was running through her mind: to disable, or to kill?

Not much competition there. Kill. Now.

Lauren raised the axe and aimed for the back of the explorer's head.

Her movement caught Fitzgerald's eye, a reflection in the snowmobile mirror perhaps as she prepared for the blow.

'Wha—?' He began to rise, turning abruptly as he did so, his cry of surprise cut off midword.

The axe struck a vicious but glancing blow into the shoulder, right through his goretex clothing, deep enough that Lauren could feel it hit bone.

Fitzgerald turned, the shock of the impact sending his face into contortions as it seemed his eyes would pop out of his head.

'But . . .' He took a step towards her, both hands held out as if to reach for her neck. 'But . . .'

Lauren retreated a few more steps, the axe raised for a second blow, watching in appalled fascination as Fitzgerald reached up and felt the wound. He stared at his fingers, examining the blood as if he couldn't quite believe it was his.

Lauren cursed herself inwardly; that injury wouldn't kill him. The wound would give him plenty of problems, would likely become infected, but she had missed the vital organs.

Fitzgerald made a lunge for her, a roar of pain and anger coming from his mouth as he snatched at the air. Lauren turned, ducking to avoid his grasp, then she was running, into the whiteout, dodging between ice pillars and scattered blocks, until she was sure she had lost him.

96

Fitzgerald gave up the chase and returned quickly to the snowmobile, his body surging with adrenaline and the after-shock of the completely unexpected attack. He could sense that the wound in his shoulder was serious, but there would be time for that later.

For now he had to move fast, away from this place on foot.

But what could he take? And what would he have to leave? The wind howled around one of the nearby pillars of ice. He spun round. Was that them? Perhaps they were closer than he'd thought. Maybe within minutes they'd be back, Sean and Murdo, to finish off what that bitch Lauren had started.

Leave them nothing. Take as much as you can tow, but leave them nothing else.

Fitzgerald started with the two remaining jerrycans of fuel, unsnapping the elastic bungee cords which held them in place and carrying them to the edge of the huge crevasse.

He peered over the edge, checking that it really was deep enough, then he lobbed the two jerrycans into the abyss.

He ran back to the sledge, ripping into the provisions and medical supplies which were stashed on the back of the sledge. How much could he tow?

Frantically, he began to dismantle the contents of the sledge, tossing packets, tins and containers of rice and pasta into the crevasse until the load was roughly half what it had been. With the drugs he was more selective, tossing out several of the individual emergency first aid kits the barrel had contained but keeping the morphine, antibiotics and syringes.

He gave the sledge a tug. It was heavy, but he knew he had the strength to move it.

And the snowmobile? That fucking machine. If it hadn't given up on him, he'd never have got into this mess. No way was he going to leave them that little toy. He couldn't get it going, but that was no guarantee that Sean couldn't.

Fitzgerald got to work, unhitching the sledge from the snowmobile and turning the towing platform aside. He placed his hands on the handgrips and tried a push. But the dead machine was heavy, much heavier than he had anticipated. It wouldn't budge an inch.

The explorer swore. He was running out of time. He had to be gone by the time they came back, gone out into the blizzard which up until now he had been cursing. Now it would be his shield, would cover him from sight until he could get enough distance under his feet.

He bent a little lower, dipping his good shoulder down and levering with all the power in his legs to try and get the machine to move. It slipped a few inches. He heaved again, panting with a mix of exertion and fear as he looked once more out into the void.

Was there someone hiding behind that pillar? How long would they be?

Fitzgerald had it moving, a few inches at a time, the iced-up skis graunching reluctantly along the ice, the ribs of the rubber drive belt snagging on small protrusions. Within a couple of minutes he had it at the edge of the crevasse, where a mighty shove tipped it over the lip.

Hurrying back, he took a length of rope and tied it off around his waist. Then he looped the free end in a bowline around the front of the sledge frame. It wasn't an ideal towing harness, but for the next few hours it would suffice.

Fitzgerald snapped his boots into his skis and moved away into the safety of the blizzard, navigating by his compass and changing direction with a zig-zag every time he found polished ice. Leave no tracks, he told himself, or they'll be able to follow you.

As he got into his stride, he tried to pull his mind together. It was roughly forty miles to the crashed aircraft; he could do it in three days, maybe even forty-eight hours at a push.

And he would have to push. The others would be right behind him, encouraged by the knowledge that he was no longer on the snowcat. Fitzgerald upped his pace a little, consulting his GPS navigator for direction through the blizzard.

He could afford little rest now; he'd have to keep going virtually nonstop. This was going to be a race, he realised, a race right to the end.

Fitzgerald winced as a sudden surge of pain cut across his chest. He stopped, doubled up with agony as the shoulder wound throbbed, then stood upright and continued, the half-laden sledge running smoothly behind him.

97

Lauren led the way quickly into the blizzard, Sean and Murdo following fast on her heels. She knew it was un-likely that Fitzgerald would still be at the same place, but they had at least to try.

She concentrated on the compass, desperately trying to remember the bearings which had taken her to the spot where the explorer had been working on his machine. Ten minutes passed, quick progress alongside the crevasse, then veering south, their lungs working hard as they pushed their speed.

Suddenly, they saw red blotches of frozen blood spotted on the ice, a few items such as tin cups, tent poles and straps scattered around. Lauren picked up a butane gas canister and shook it—it was full.

'This is the place,' she told them. 'He must have got the snowmobile started.'

'Shit.' Murdo cursed as he looked out into the blustering storm. 'How much of a head start has he got?'

'Twenty minutes at least. Maybe thirty.'

'Then we've lost him.'

Sean was crouching, examining twin grooves in the ice. He followed the tracks across to the crevasse and leaned carefully over the edge.

'Hey!' he called. 'Come and take a look at this.'

Lauren moved to join him, staring down into the darkened ice cavity. Immediately, she realised that Fitzgerald had not got the snowmobile running at all, that he'd dumped it into the nearest crevasse in an attempt to destroy it.

But the configuration of the crevasse had conspired against him. It was not sheer-sided; it was more like a series of steps going down, each huge jutting shelf created perhaps from the remains of snow bridges which had collapsed in the past.

The snowmobile had plunged, nose-first, into a ledge of soft snow and was sitting not thirty feet beneath them. And around it were numerous small dark objects.

'Are those what I think they are?' Lauren asked, squinting as her eyes adjusted to the low light levels of the cavity.

'I can see cans!' Sean exclaimed. 'And that's one of the personal medical kits! Fitzgerald was in such a hurry to get away, he didn't do a very good job of disposal.'

Lauren straightened up, thinking rapidly.

'Can we get that snowcat out of there?'

'We've only got the one rope,' Sean said, doubt filling his voice, 'and that machine weighs four to five hundred pounds.'

'But we can try, right?'

'Sure. But maybe it's really bust. I might not be able to get it going.'

Lauren was already heading back into the blizzard, the compass in her hand.

'Come with me,' she told Sean and Murdo. 'We've got to make this our base while we retrieve what we can from that crevasse. Every second's going to count now. Let's go and get the others.'

98

Fitzgerald checked the illuminated dial of his wristwatch. It was almost midnight and time for a two-hour break. He had been moving nonstop for almost ten hours, pausing only to eat a few snacks from the mound of provisions on the sledge.

The GPS gave him the good news. He was already twelve miles into his march. This was where his superior strength and fitness would win out . . . there was no way the others could match his pace.

Physically, he was feeling more together, although the wound in his shoulder was throbbing vigorously every time he breathed, but emotionally he was still in turmoil.

His mind kept replaying the moment when Lauren had attacked. If he hadn't seen that telltale movement . . . if he hadn't slipped just those few inches to the side . . .

He would be lying dead, or paralysed on the ice, at the mercy of the others.

A volley of questions was flying round his head, each looking for an answer where none was to be found. Had they planned it all along? Had they planted the idea inside her in case she got close enough? A pressure headache was building inside the explorer's skull, a nagging, pulsing nodule of pain.

He managed to get the tent up, taking twice as long as usual to complete the task. He crawled inside and took off his jacket and shirt. He wished he had a mirror to see the damage.

How deep was the cut? And what had the blow destroyed? Fitzgerald couldn't see the wound, but he could feel the way the muscles near the shoulder blade had been sliced. His left arm was not so effective now, just to clench his fist caused him a flood of searing pain.

And if it got infected? Fitzgerald shuddered to think what the complications might be. There were still days, even weeks to go before he would be out of Antarctica.

Fitzgerald lit his gas stove and watched the blue flames for a while. The light was comforting, cosy almost, as it played around the tent interior. He took the knife with the eight-inch blade and began to twist it in the burner, watching as the stainless steel began to glow dull red and the plastic handle became almost too hot to hold.

Then he took the knife and, reaching over his shoulder with his right hand, placed the blade as firmly as he could, sizzling and spitting, right into the wound. One. Two. Three. Four. Five. He moved the blade, it would be a mistake to miss some of the damaged flesh. Six. Seven. Eight. The tent was filling with the nauseating stench of burned skin and fat. Nine. Ten.

He removed the knife and let his teeth ease off where they had bitten into his tongue.

Fitzgerald was not in the mood to eat or drink. He lay with his eyes wide open, staring at the tiny ring of blue flame until the gas cylinder emptied and the flame petered out.

Then he packed up the tent, hitched himself to the sledge and continued his trek into the night.

99

Sean wrapped the rope around his waist and abseiled backwards into the crevasse. The drop to the shelf was a short one, and a few seconds later he was kicking gently into the deep snow next to the snowmobile.

'Is it damaged?' Lauren called down.

Sean gave the machine a quick inspection by the light of his headtorch. The steering column looked a little bent by the impact of the drop, but the soft snow seemed to have cushioned the fall and there was no other visible damage.

'Seems all right.'

Sean rocked the vehicle a little, hearing the reassuring slop of fuel in the tank. There was no point in busting their guts to get the machine out of that hole if they had no fuel to run it.

'Stop screwing around with that buggy,' Murdo shouted. 'Send up the food.'

Sean began to scout around the shelf, picking up the odd items of food that Fitzgerald had failed to throw far enough to confine to the depths. There was a fruit cake in a tin, a whole carton of dehydrated mashed potato, bags of sugar, tinned spam, and—Sean was tempted to rip into this one and consume the contents right there and then—a whole kilo of the same muesli that had been so critical for energy back at the first depot.

Fitzgerald's logic had been to get rid of the heaviest stuff, Sean reasoned; that was why there were so many tins down here. He carried on building up the stash, placing the booty in a sleeping bag and tying it to the rope for Lauren to haul up.

There were shouts of delight from above when the team spilled the food out onto the ice.

'Hey! Been nice knowing you, Sean,' Murdo called down. 'One less mouth to feed.'

Sean smiled. It was amazing how quickly the presence of a little food had lifted the spirits of the team. That was good, he reasoned, getting that snowmobile out of the crevasse was going to take every ounce of strength they could muster.

The rope snaked down.

'We'll haul you up,' Lauren shouted. 'We should all get some food inside us before we start work.'

'Good call,' Sean agreed. He tied a loop at the bottom of the rope and stepped into the cradle until the rope supported his weight. The others hauled him up, inch by inch, until he was able to flop over the lip onto the glacier.

'It's gonna be a bitch getting that cat out of there,' he said, looking at the weary state of the team. 'If we can do it at all, that is . . .'

They fell on the food, each devouring half a tin of spam and a handful of crackers. Then Mel pitched a tent and heated up some of the powdered milk they'd found.

Lauren checked her watch. 'It's just gone midnight,' she said. 'We've got enough moonlight to work with. I suggest we get going.'

The team gathered; everyone bar Frank, who was obviously in no condition to help pull.

'What's the breaking strain of this rope?' Lauren asked Sean.

Sean ran the nine-millimetre cord through his gloved hands.

'It's designed to take the shock loading of a climber falling twenty-five metres.'

'How does that compare to the weight of the cat?'

'It might hold it,' Sean told her, 'but, with these abrasions, it might not. It's on the limit.'

He abseiled down into the crevasse once more and tied the rope off at two points on the rear of the snowmobile.

'We'll try and bring it up backwards,' he called. 'Take up the slack.'

Sean watched with his heart in his mouth as the rope began to tighten, the fibres protesting as they stretched into the load.

100

Fitzgerald noted the coming of the dawn and decided it was time to take a break. The night had been more of a trial than he'd predicted, with numerous crevasse crossings across snow bridges which were impossible to judge properly in the dark. Still, he'd taken the risk, and come through it intact.

He removed the rope harness from his waist and sat on the sledge for a timed ten-minute rest, pulling out the GPS unit to check on progress. The LCD readout was showing encouraging news: he was now over halfway through this load-haul, with the crashed aircraft just fifteen miles away.

The explorer broke a couple of bars of chocolate out of his provisions and ate them as he watched the light play above the horizon. The storm had blown itself out, ushering in a day which, for Antarctica, was remarkably calm. Normally, Fitzgerald would have welcomed the arrival of the dawn, knowing that with daylight came greater safety, that he could all the better find a way through the maze of crevasses. But this dawn left him feeling curiously exposed, easy to spot as he made his way north.

He unpacked his binoculars and took a long hard look back to the south, screwing up his eyes as he searched for any sign that the others were in pursuit. He was ninety-nine-per-cent certain that no one in that team could match him for speed and fitness . . . but you could never be sure.

And the snowmobile? Was there a chance they could retrieve it? Fitzgerald dismissed the idea as soon as it came, sure that the machine was even now lying many hundreds of metres beneath the ice, smashed to so much scrap.

Gratifyingly, there was no movement to be seen, and the explorer relaxed for the remaining moments of his rest break, moving his arm in circular patterns every now and then to prevent the muscles around his shoulder from seizing up. The wound continued to be painful, but the imperative of reaching the target was such that the explorer was able to put it out of his mind.

All too soon, the ten minutes was over. Julian Fitzgerald popped a handful of dextrose energy tablets into his mouth and sucked them as he continued the trek.

101

The team was in a line, hauling at the rope like it was a tug of war. Even Richard had been persuaded to join them, his weight at the back needed even if the state of his feet meant he couldn't stand.

'Give it another go!' Lauren called out from the front. 'On the count of three . . . one, two three!'

Down in the crevasse, Sean pushed from below with all his might, his arms drained of blood and strength by the hours of work which had already passed. But the snowmobile slid just a few precious inches up the glassy wall before slumping back down again as soon as the team relaxed.

'Hold it there,' Sean called up, his voice hoarse from shouting commands. 'We're never going to do it like this.'

Five hours of soul-destroying labour had proved one thing beyond any equivocal doubt: hauling five hundred pounds of inert metal up thirty or so feet of an almost sheer crevasse wall was no mean feat . . . particularly when the top section of the wall was slightly overhanging.

And even more so when the team of individuals attempting it were suffering the effects of malnourishment and frostbite, let alone the rigours of a two-hundred-and-fifty-mile winter trek across the ice cap of Antarctica.

They'd hauled it roughly twenty-five vertical feet, up to the edge of the lip. Then the overhang had come into play, leaving the machine swinging in free space, the rope which held it stretched right to its breaking point and creaking ominously with every fresh pull.

Sean clambered out of the crevasse to join them, but, no matter how aggressively they pulled on the rope, the inertia of all that dead metal was more than a match.

'How about a counterweight?' Frank suggested, ever the boffin.

'Such as?'

'You need some weight on the other end of the rope,' he continued. 'Give you some leverage.'

Once the team had got the concept, they quickly set to work, the idea giving them fresh energy. They found that the rope was long enough to reach a second crevasse, running parallel to the one the snowmobile was stuck in.

'If you can get a few hundredweight on the end of that rope, you might just crack it.'

They used a tarpaulin that Fitzgerald had left behind, flattening it out on the glacier and filling it with snow and whatever ice blocks they could find. Then they brought the corners together and tied them off at the top, creating, in effect, a huge bag of snow weighing—Frank estimated—around three hundred pounds.

They attached the counterweight to the loose end of the rope and pushed it into the parallel crevasse, then resumed the process of pulling up the snowmobile.

Almost immediately, they felt the benefits of the extra weight, the force from behind them equivalent to two or three extra hands pulling. The snowmobile rose another foot, then a few more inches. But that was as far as it got, still snagged beneath the overhang, and resisting every attempt to get it higher.

Night was falling. The team was running out of ideas. The counterweight had seemed such a strong solution—and had taken them so long to rig up—that its failure had left them in despair.

'It's so close!' Murdo raged. 'Just a few feet beneath that bastard lip.'

They tied off the rope and took a rest, the sky sprinkling them with a fresh layer of snow as they lay there in a state of total fatigue.

'There's only one way to achieve this,' Lauren told them. 'We'll have to cut away the edge of the crevasse, create an easier angled ramp to drag it up.'

Sean walked wearily over and appraised the lip.

'What with?'

'Fitzgerald's axe.'

'That,' Sean said, 'is a ball-breaking job. It could take us all night.'

But Lauren had picked up the axe and was already chipping at the ice, each blow sending a handful of shards into the air.

'We'll take it in turns,' Lauren said as she worked. 'Fifteen minutes each.'

'We'll have to shift a couple of tons of ice to do this,' Sean said, utterly dismayed.

Lauren stopped for a moment, her face calm, resolved.

'This is what we have to do to stay alive,' she said, then began again.

102

With a final shout of 'Heave!' the team fell back as one, the snowmobile slipping up and finally breaching the crevasse lip. They stared at it, scarcely able to believe they'd finally achieved the objective, most without enough energy to pick themselves up from where they'd fallen on the glacier.

'That,' panted Lauren, checking her watch, 'has just taken us the best part of twenty hours.'

'Have we still got time?' Sean asked. 'Can we still beat him to the aircraft?'

'That's down to you,' she replied. 'If you can get this baby started, then maybe—just maybe—we still can.'

Sean stepped over to the familiar snowcat and pulled on the starter cord. Immediately, he noticed the irregular stutter to the engine as it failed to fire. A thick plume of blackish smoke ran out of the exhaust in an apologetic cough. He tried again, letting the starter cord rest in his fingers, pulling gently until he felt the tension of the pressure building in the cylinder block.

He pulled back smoothly. Again, the engine did not cooperate.

'This baby is sick for sure.'

Sean tried more than forty pulls, but he still couldn't get the engine to fire. 'You think you can fix it?' Lauren asked him.

'Not without tools I can't.'

Sean pulled back the velcro strips which held down the foam seat cover. Beneath it was a recess in which a small tool roll was sitting. He untied it and revealed a number of screwdrivers and spanners.

'Bet Fitzgerald didn't even know that was there,' he said with a smile.

Sean flipped back the rubber ties which held the cowling down and exposed the 500cc engine to view. Set on either side of the cylinder head were twin carburettors, both relatively easy to get to. He used the screwdriver to unclip the fuel lines and unbolt the two units from their base.

In less than ten minutes he had both units stripped down and examined, quickly determining that both had problems. Problem one was in one of the float chambers, where the constant battering of the journey had simply thrown one of the float levels out of true.

That was easy to remedy; by bending the bracket which held the float in place, he could put it back in the correct position.

Problem two was one of the jets—Sean guessed a piece of dirt in the fuel had blocked it. He unscrewed the brass thread, raised the jet to his lips and blew sharply through it, sensing the resistance of a blockage in the pin hole. He spat to clear the taste of fuel from his mouth and blew from the other end. He felt the air pass through in a rush as the obstruction cleared.

'That jet was full of gunk,' he told them. 'No wonder this thing won't start.'

Sean reassembled the carburettors and replaced them on the head, taking care to position the gaskets correctly beneath them. He clipped the fuel lines back on and tested they were secure. Then he ripped back the pull start, grunting with satisfaction as the engine fired first time. Even in the first few seconds it sounded like a happy machine.

The team was jubilant.

'That's more like it,' Sean said. 'Now let me check the belt.'

He selected a sixteen-millimetre spanner from the tool kit. He loosened the four securing bolts which held the seat on its frame and pulled it off to reveal the top side of the transmission belt beneath.

A brief pull on the drive mechanism confirmed what he'd suspected: that the belt was running loose.

'I haven't got a spanner big enough for this,' he told Lauren. 'I have to adjust the tension on the belt.'

'Can't you improvise?'

Sean considered the tools available. 'There's only one thing'll get those bolts free. I could cut a notch in the side of the two bolt heads with the chisel and try and knock them round with that heavy spanner.'

'Do it. And make it fast.'

Sean got to work, and soon the noise of hammering filled the air, the clean sound of metal on metal as the spanner hit home.

'That's shifted one!' he told them, pulling on the belt as he retightened it, then a few minutes later: 'And the other.'

Sean got the engine started and took it for a test drive. The belt wasn't perfect, he knew, but it was a lot better than before.

'Pack up the sledge,' Lauren told the others. 'We're leaving right away.'

'One more thing.' Sean unscrewed the petrol filler cap and beckoned for Lauren to look inside. 'We've only got half a tank of fuel.'

'How far will that take us?'

'Hard to say. How many miles to the plane?'

'Thirty-five. Maybe a bit more.'

'It's going to be tight. It's going to be really tight.'

103

Fitzgerald heard it before he saw it, the thin, high-pitched note of an engine carried to him on the wind. It hung in the air for a few moments and then vanished. He stopped dead, his heart pounding with shock as he turned to look back in the direction of the sound.

Silence. Seconds ticked by.

He must have been mistaken, the explorer decided; there *could* be no engine running out here in this wilderness. Unless . . .

His hands suddenly shaking, he reached into his pocket and pulled out his binoculars. There it was again, that engine sound once more.

He scanned the glacier with the glasses, panning from left to right, then back again, as he searched for the source of the noise. But, looking back, the glacier was undulating like a series of sand dunes, the machine—whatever it was—was hidden from view.

Then it emerged from a dip, and Fitzgerald saw it as clear

as day. Just a couple of miles behind him, a fully laden snowmobile was picking its way steadily through the glacier, a sledge running behind it.

He picked out the figures, could see Sean in the driver's position, Lauren sitting behind him.

But *how*? Fitzgerald had been so certain he had destroyed that machine. He felt a wave of panic wash over him as he watched them bearing down on him. They would kill him, he was sure of that.

Fitzgerald looked quickly over to the wreckage of the crashed plane, expertly drawing down the distance. Less than a mile—twenty minutes if the ground was good. Could he beat them to it? Without the sledge, maybe, but to leave the sledge was as good as suicide anyway.

Fitzgerald whipped the harness around him and set out for the remains of the aircraft, moving faster than he'd ever moved on ice before, the sledge bumping and tilting in his wake as he pushed his legs towards the objective.

104

Lauren was the first to see him.

'There he is!' She had glimpsed the explorer just a few hundred metres in front of them. Not far ahead of him, large shapes were dark against the ice. The remains of the aircraft, Lauren realised; they were almost there.

'I can see the wreckage,' Sean confirmed.

Then the snowmobile juddered slightly, the engine noise dying away for a few beats, then picking up again and continuing.

'The tank's just about empty!' Sean yelled.

Oh no. Just a few more minutes, Lauren prayed; please God, don't let the engine die. Not when we're so *close*.

The machine gave another lurch, the sledge bucking violently behind it as the engine coughed. Then the last drops of fuel trickled through the carburettors and the snowmobile coasted to a halt, the front runners sinking into the snow as the engine died. They could see Fitzgerald looking back towards them as he appraised this new development, then he continued his trek towards the aircraft wreckage, moving like a man possessed.

Instantly, Lauren dismounted, snatching her skis and sticks from the sledge and setting out in pursuit. Sean was right behind her, his breath coming in short, explosive bursts as he pushed himself to more speed.

105

Fitzgerald could hear them gaining on him, the sound of their skis against the ice. *Did they have the axe?*

He knew he didn't have the time to look back.

Fifty metres. There was the aircraft wing, partly covered in snow, big pieces of engine and gearbox strewn here and there.

His legs were beginning to cramp, he could feel the muscles starting to knot as they reached their limits. The great crevasse was in front of him, the one the aircraft had fallen into. On the other side was the remains of their camp, the tents no longer standing but the fabric still visible poking from the winter drift. Inside one of those collapsed domes would be the emergency transmitter, but if the others reached it first . . .

The explorer thought he would have to skirt the crevasse, a detour which might mean at least an extra mile on foot. Then he saw that a snow bridge had built through the winter. It looked fragile, but now there was no choice. Fitzgerald committed himself to the thin span of ice, feeling sick as he felt it slump in the middle, the weight of the sledge threatening to drag him down into the void which fell hundreds of metres deep on each side.

But the snow bridge held.

Fitzgerald reached the other side, turned, saw that Lauren and Sean were just seconds from crossing the crevasse.

Next to him was a mass of metal. He saw rubber, aluminium struts: the remains of one of the Twin Otter's wheels. The explorer reached down and pulled with all his might, wrenching the forty or so kilos of wreckage free from its icy grip and hoisting it above his head.

With a roar, he threw the metal remains out onto the snow bridge, the weight crashing with a muffled crumping noise into the midsection of the bridge and collapsing it into the depths.

106

Lauren and Sean came to an abrupt halt, just before the edge of the monster crevasse. In front of them, huge fragments of the snow bridge were tumbling down into the dark interior of the ice cap, and, not twenty metres in front of them, Julian Fitzgerald was standing, triumphant and untouchable.

Lauren tried to scream something at him, to vent the fury and despair that welled up inside her. But she didn't have the breath. Instead she bent over double, winded and desperate for air after the chase.

They had failed. For the sake of a cupful of petrol, a few metres of distance, they had failed. Lauren could feel what remaining vestige of strength was left inside her ebb and fade as she watched the explorer walk over to the remains of his old camp.

'We can work our way round the crevasse . . . maybe we can still catch him up . . .' Sean began, but his voice faltered as he saw how far the fissure stretched across the glacier. Even if they had had a reservoir of strength left to get around the obstacle, he knew that Fitzgerald would be long gone, the headstart enough that he could now never be caught.

Sean knew it was over; his body had given up the fight.

Close to where they stood was one of the wrecked engines—a mess of mangled pistons, valves and pipes. Sean helped Lauren to take the few steps, and they collapsed with their backs to the hulk of metal while they struggled to catch their breath.

Some distance behind them Lauren could see Mel and Murdo towing the sledge—plodding so slowly along they hardly seemed to move as the minutes rolled past.

On the other side of the crevasse Fitzgerald was busy digging at the collapsed tent, searching for the transmitter.

Lauren turned to Sean, her face puffy and swollen from wind blisters and solar radiation.

'Is there *anything* we can do, Sean? Think one last time. Once he's gone, we'll never catch him again. How can we stop him?'

Sean turned to consider the engine, pulling absently at the twisted metal. One of the broken fuel lines was jutting from the wreckage, and as he tugged at it, a thin trickle of avgas trickled from the metal line.

'There's still some aviation spirit in these fuel lines. If we could get enough out of this thing, we could fill one of the cans with it, use it as a weapon . . .'

Sean's voice petered out as he watched the pathetic trickle running from the slender fuel line.

'Shit.'

He crimped the aluminium fuel line to stop the flow and slumped back against the engine.

'It'd never work anyhow,' he concluded wearily.

Soon Sean wandered off to help Mel and Murdo drag in the sledge, leaving Lauren on her own, leaning against the shattered engine.

'Think,' she whispered to herself, the scientist in her not quite ready to concede defeat. 'There has to be a way.'

Lauren turned her mind one more time to the problem, knowing that, if she couldn't work out a solution, all six of them would die in that godforsaken place.

107

Fitzgerald stood on one side of the crevasse, Lauren and her team on the other. He was no more than twenty metres from them, but in that moment, those unbridgeable metres were the gulf between the living and the dead.

'I found the transmitter,' Fitzgerald told them, gesturing to the yellow object strapped to the back of his sledge.

'So why don't you activate it and we can all go home?' Lauren asked him.

Fitzgerald laughed.

'Actually, I admire what you've done,' he conceded. 'I thought you'd lose most of your team on the way. Three hundred miles on those resources was a hell of a feat.'

'Save your compliments,' Lauren told him. 'It makes no difference now.'

'No . . . I suppose not. No one's going to stumble across you by accident, and there's nothing here to keep you alive.'

'Our bodies will be found,' Lauren told him bitterly. 'We'll make sure the truth will be known in the end.'

Fitzgerald laughed. 'How? By leaving a note? Who do you think will ever come to this place to find it? And how do you think they'll find you under the three metres of new snow which will fall in the next couple of months? Besides, I'll tell the world you all died a hundred miles from here.'

'Where are you going to call in the plane?' Sean called. 'Just out of curiosity.'

Fitzgerald thought carefully for some moments. 'I don't suppose it would hurt to tell you my plans,' he said. 'Actually, I'm going to continue down to the coast before I put in the mayday call.'

'Eighty miles? Why go so far?' Sean asked in surprise. 'All you have to do is get out of this crevasse field and find a nice flat piece of ice. Ten miles would be enough. You know we haven't got the strength to follow you.'

'Oh, I just want to put a little distance between us,' Fitzgerald replied. 'I don't want the pilot to be tempted into a quick overflight of this place, for one thing . . .'

Suddenly, Lauren gave out a bitter laugh.

'And for another thing,' she said, 'you'll get to the coast and claim you made it across the continent on foot just like you originally planned. That's about right, isn't it?'

Fitzgerald made no response to this but merely glared at her across the gap. Then he turned away and prepared to leave, tying bits of gear onto the back of the sledge.

'One more thing,' Lauren called out, her voice weak now and barely able to project.

Fitzgerald paused in his packing. 'What is it?'

Lauren fished in her pocket and brought out the titanium tube she had so carefully guarded through the trek; she held it high in the air so he could see what it was.

'The sample from the lake,' she told him, the words heavy with resignation. 'Will you take it with you and see it gets to my sponsor, Alexander De Pierman at Kerguelen Oils?'

Fitzgerald laughed. 'And why the hell should I do that for you?'

'Because there are species in this sample that are new to

science. It's my last request, if you like. We know we're going to die here now. The least you can do is let me die in the
knowledge that something came of this.'

Fitzgerald's first inclination was to tell her to go to hell,
but as his mind ticked over he saw another possibility.

'Species new to science? I'll do it. Throw it over.'

Lauren gave the sample tube to Sean.

'Will you . . . ?' she asked him. 'I'm not sure I have the
strength.'

'You want to do this?' Sean looked at her in amazement.
'He'll take the credit for it, Lauren; you know what he's capable of. It'll be another Fitzgerald scoop—"How I saved
the vital specimen from destruction." He'll probably end up
naming one of these life forms after himself.'

'Do it, Sean,' Lauren told him. 'That sample has to be
properly analysed and recorded, or it's all been for nothing.'

'Well, if you're sure . . .'

Sean reluctantly took the tube and walked to the very edge
of the crevasse. Then he threw it, underarm, across to Fitzgerald's side, where it plopped unharmed into the soft surface.

Fitzgerald plucked it out and looked at it closely.

'How do I know you haven't put a note inside?' he demanded suspiciously.

'Unscrew the top,' Lauren called out. 'The titanium tube
is just an insulating outer shell. The sample is inside in a
glass tube.'

Fitzgerald did as she said, removing the top and sliding
the glass test tube out. It was immediately obvious that there
was no note inside—the tube contained only clear fluid.

'Good enough.' Fitzgerald placed the glass tube back into
its snug titanium protector and carefully put the phial in the
breast pocket of his windsuit.

'Anything more?' he called back sarcastically.

Lauren and Sean said nothing.

'Then I'll be gone.'

Fitzgerald flicked down his ski goggles and hitched the
harness around his waist. Then, without a backward glance,
he began his trek towards the coast.

PART 5

The Hero Returns

108

Alexander De Pierman was sitting in heavy London traffic on his way to a meeting when the call came through.

'I've got Irene Evans on the line for you,' his secretary told him.

'Who?'

'Julian Fitzgerald's logistics manager. Says it's top urgent.'

De Pierman was perplexed. He'd had a few dealings with Fitzgerald's team during the press annnouncement to break the news of the loss of Capricorn and its crew, but he could not imagine what Irene Evans was calling for now, so many weeks later.

'Put her through.'

'You're not going to believe this,' Evans told him, her voice alive with excitement. 'I just got the most extraordinary news from Ushuaia. Fitzgerald's emergency transmitter was reactivated yesterday. Someone out there is still alive.'

De Pierman paused a moment while the information sank in.

'Alive? But how can they be?' he asked.

'I have absolutely no idea. But it's definitely Fitzgerald's transmitter. An Antarctic Air Service flight is on its way to investigate.'

'But after all this time . . . ?' De Pierman was struggling to comprehend what he was hearing. 'How the hell has anyone survived? And where's the signal coming from?'

'That's the bizarre thing; in fact, I had to question AAS to make sure that they understood the coordinates properly. But they're adamant there's no mistake: the signal's coming from the coast—on the *edge* of the continent, about four hundred miles from the Capricorn base.'

'The coast? Where exactly?' De Pierman opened his notepad and jotted down the figures as Irene gave him the coordinates. 'When will we know more?'

'In the next few hours. As soon as the flight gets there, we'll get a radio call to say who it is.'

After his meeting De Pierman went back to his office and pulled his world atlas from its shelf. He turned to the Antarctic double page and consulted the coordinates on his notepad to find the location of the transmitter. How on earth had any survivor ended up in that position? Surely, if anyone had survived the fire, they would have stayed at the Capricorn site?

By midafternoon Irene Evans was back on the line.

'I just got the call from AAS,' she told him. 'They picked up one survivor. It's Julian Fitzgerald.'

'Did he give any news of the others?'

'They're all dead. I'm very sorry to have to tell you that.'

'Oh. Well . . . I . . .'

There was a long pause as she waited for De Pierman to respond.

'Mr De Pierman? Are you still there?'

'Oh, I'm still here. I just don't trust myself to speak right now.'

'I'm so sorry. I expect there was something inside you believed that Lauren and her team might have survived?'

'Call me an old fool,' De Pierman told her sadly, 'but you're right. All the experts said it was impossible, but you

always come up with a way to convince yourself there might
have been a factor they'd overlooked.'

'Well, there obviously was something they overlooked or
Fitzgerald wouldn't have lived to tell the tale.'

'How did he do it? And how did he end up where he did?'

'We'll all know soon enough. He's sent me a message to
connect him straight through to London and to get a press
conference fixed up.'

'My God, he must have a story to tell . . .'

'That's what the rest of the world has realised. There's
going to be quite a reception committee waiting for him
when he gets back to civilisation. I'll arrange the press conference at Heathrow. I'll call you when I know the timings.'

De Pierman terminated the call and stood, lost in thought,
as he considered this startling piece of news. Fitzgerald
alive? But how had he survived where Lauren and the others
had died?

And by what set of circumstances had he ended up on the
edge of the continent, in the very opposite direction to the
nearest base?

Whichever way De Pierman looked at it, not a single as-
pect of this new development made any sense at all.

He consulted the atlas again, considering Fitzgerald's position, drawing a mental line from the place to the location
of the Capricorn base.

In a flash he had it.

The plane. The crashed plane. Fitzgerald's route would
have taken him right past it. Of all the factors he had so
painfully run through, De Pierman had never thought that
the crashed plane might have offered salvation to the Capricorn survivors. Perhaps the transmitter had been left there?

Next, De Pierman made a rough calculation of the distance from Capricorn to the aircraft; it was about three hundred miles. That was well beyond Dr Gresham's estimate of
what a survivor could achieve on foot . . . so how had
Fitzgerald done it?

Like the rest of the world, De Pierman would have to wait
for the answers.

109

Julian Fitzgerald refused all interviews to the local press at Ushuaia, knowing he would get far more attention from the international press in London.

He transferred to the first available 747 flight out of Buenos Aires, and, by the time the Aerolinas Argentinas jumbo put the wheels down at Heathrow, the airport press room was packed with news crews and reporters. CNN, Reuters, Associated Press and the BBC had all devoted crews to cover Fitzgerald's miraculous reappearance from the dead, and they'd been joined by a host of local and other news agencies.

As the frail, frost-ravaged figure of Fitzgerald was escorted into the room, there was a collective gasp from the reporters. Could this really be the renowned explorer? He looked like he'd aged a lifetime in the last six months. Cameras flashed as he held the side of the table for support.

Alexander De Pierman was also present at the conference, as was Irene Evans. They sat uneasily behind the press-briefing table and waited while Fitzgerald lowered himself painfully onto a seat.

Quickly, the volume of the shouts rose. For a while it seemed the press mêlée was going to turn into a fistfight as reporters jostled elbow to elbow in front of the explorer. Fitzgerald tried to talk but no words could be heard. Gradually, the row began to diminish.

Someone handed Fitzgerald a plastic bottle of water.

When the explorer finally managed to moisten his lips enough to speak, his words were not much more than a whisper. The press pack fell absolutely quiet as dozens of microphones were thrust towards him.

'Mr Fitzgerald,' one of the more strident reporters managed to ask, 'what happened at Capricorn base?'

'The fire?' Fitzgerald said. 'It was an electrical fault, something wrong with the wiring in the base. There was a strong wind, the flames took hold faster than we could fight them . . . Then the diesel tank exploded and destroyed everything.'

'How many people survived the fire?'

Fitzgerald took another swig of the water.

'One died immediately, my team mate Carl Norland. Others were burned and died later.'

'What happened after the fire?'

'We had no food and no transport. We realised there would be no rescue, and we knew we could never make it to the nearest base. So we headed for the plane which crashed on the Blackmore Glacier . . . we knew there was an emergency transmitter there . . .'

He stopped as he was hit by a violent coughing fit. The surrounding reporters let him recover before firing the next question at him.

'How did you survive?'

Fitzgerald looked into space for a long moment before replying; when he turned his attention back to the reporter, his stare was terrible, the blood-red eyes mesmerising as they fixed on the questioner.

'There were depots with food and equipment,' the explorer said. 'Two of them, one hundred miles apart, heading towards the crashed plane. Dr Burgess had put them in place when she came to rescue me at the beginning of the winter, and they were still there.'

Sitting next to the explorer, De Pierman cursed himself quietly as he heard this news. So *that* was the missing factor that they hadn't built into the equation. Lauren had put down depots which could keep the team alive. Now it was all beginning to make a type of sense.

'How did your companions die?' the reporter asked.

Fitzgerald paused once more.

'We got them all to the first depot,' he said, 'but there wasn't enough medical equipment to keep the injured alive. They were burned, you see, in the fire. They died of the infections . . . one after another . . . and there was nothing we could do. We buried them in the crevasses . . .'

Fitzgerald's face crumpled as he wept, the reporters keeping a respectful silence as he struggled to regain some composure.

'Dr Burgess was the last,' he continued. 'My God, she was strong. But even she didn't get much further than the second depot. Then it was just me and the fight to get to the crashed plane.'

'Why didn't you call in the rescue right away when you got to the transmitter? What made you keep going to the coast?'

Fitzgerald took a deep breath.

'There are two types of people in this world. There are starters. And there are finishers. I made a solemn promise some time ago that I would become the first person to cross the widest point of the Antarctic continent on foot. And I kept that promise by crossing those last eighty miles to the coast.'

There was a murmur of admiration from the gathered reporters.

'One more thing.' Fitzgerald reached into his top pocket and brought out the titanium sample tube.

The cameramen shuffled and bumped each other as they tried to focus on the phial.

'Most of you will know,' Fitzgerald said, 'that Capricorn was a scientific base, but not many of you will know what its true aims were. In fact, Dr Burgess's objective was to examine a subterranean lake ... a lake which she suspected would contain life which had never been encountered on earth before. The day before the fire, the team drilled into that lake and retrieved this sample. It was Dr Burgess's dying wish that this sample be delivered to her sponsor for analysis, and I honour that wish now by handing this test tube to Alexander De Pierman.'

Fitzgerald handed the sample over to De Pierman with a flourish, the oilman nodding his thanks. Then the explorer broke off the interview and was escorted, with a policeman on each arm to support him, into a waiting ambulance. De Pierman left too, brushing the reporters' questions aside and climbing into his limousine for the journey back to London.

The last hope had died; De Pierman had to be realistic: there was no hope for Lauren and the rest of her team now. Fitzgerald had seen them die with his own eyes, and you only had to take one look at the man to know that he too had been through hell and back.

De Pierman couldn't help but feel that he'd failed Lauren in some crucial way. Why hadn't he raised the alarm earlier? Why had he waited through more than two weeks of radio silence before wondering if something had gone badly wrong at Capricorn? How might this have ended if he'd been more alert?

De Pierman buzzed his secretary.

'Jane, will you come and pick up the sample from Capricorn? I want it taken in for analysis right away.'

He held up the sample tube and shook it gently. From within he could hear the faint sound of liquid sloshing around. There'd better be something good in that tube, he mused, or Lauren had given her life for nothing.

110

Alexander De Pierman came out of a meeting at the Sheraton Park Lane and checked the LCD display on his mobile. There was one message waiting, a number he did not recognise.

'Mr De Pierman,' the voicemail ran, 'this is the Cowley Laboratory. I have some bad news for you regarding the specimen from Capricorn base. Can you get over here right away?'

De Pierman had himself driven to the laboratory, the manager meeting him at the door and escorting him through to the analysis room.

'We got the equipment all sterilised,' he told De Pierman, 'worked out the correct procedures to deal with the sample, but I'm afraid you're going to be very disappointed when I tell you what we found.'

De Pierman was perplexed.

'There was no life in the specimen?'

The lab manager gave a brittle laugh.

'I'm afraid we've all been the victim of an elaborate hoax. What's in that test tube will never hold life.'

'How can you be so sure?'

The lab manager held up the test tube and pulled out the rubber bung from the neck.

'Take a smell,' he said. 'You'll see what I mean.'

De Pierman put his nose to the glass phial, pulling back a little at the pungent aroma that assaulted his nostrils.

'I haven't run any tests yet,' the lab manager told him, 'but we have a pretty good idea what it is.'

De Pierman took another sniff to make sure he was not mistaken, a bewildered expression crossing his features as he did so.

'Oh, I know what this is all right,' he said, 'but how did it come to be in this test tube? Has there been a mistake?'

'No mistake,' the lab manager confirmed. 'That is the sample Fitzgerald handed to you earlier today.'

'But Lauren wouldn't have given him the wrong tube. How could she? That sample was everything to her . . . It doesn't make any sense at all.'

The lab manager shrugged. 'We're as much in the dark as you are. Someone's idea of a joke, maybe?'

De Pierman chewed it over in his mind, his sharply analytical brain trying to make some sense out of this bizarre development.

'Unless . . .' he said, 'unless this isn't a sample at all. Maybe Lauren was trying to tell us something. Perhaps it's a signal of some sort.'

'I'm sorry, I don't follow you.'

De Pierman checked his watch.

'If I'm not mistaken, Mr Fitzgerald is meeting his adoring public as we speak. If I'm lucky, I can just catch him. I think he has some questions to answer.'

111

Alexander De Pierman's chauffeur-driven BMW pulled up outside the Royal Geographical Society just after eight p.m.

'Wait here, please,' he instructed the driver.

De Pierman made his way through the plush corridors to the lecture hall, where he gently pushed open one of the side doors and found a standing place in the crowd. Fitzgerald had become front-page news all over the world, and the room was packed with hundreds of people.

The explorer stood before them as he reached the end of his address, emaciated but poker-backed, his face pock-marked with the ravages of frostbite.

'And so to conclude.' He wiped a tear away from his eyes with his bandaged hands. 'I would have to say that a journey to hell itself would scarcely have held more horrors. To watch Lauren Burgess and her brave team die one by one, to know that there was nothing more that I could do other than share my last few crumbs of food with them . . . those were moments which will live with me for ever. When I reached the crashed aircraft I managed to find the transmitter, but something inside me—call me stubborn if you like—prevented me from calling in help at that stage.'

Fitzgerald gulped, seemingly overcome. There was not a whisper in the auditorium, a dropping pin would have sounded like a scaffold pole.

'I decided to carry on my original quest. To walk from one side of the Antarctic continent to the other . . . at the widest point. Seven days later I made it to the sea, where I finally set up the radio and called in the air rescue. But my greatest satisfaction was not from my own humble achievement, it was to be the bearer of a vital test tube from Capricorn base. I gave that test tube for analysis today, and I believe the results will prove the whole enterprise worthwhile.'

The hall erupted into a thunderous roar of approval, hundreds of people cheering and clapping. Cries of 'Bravo!' were ringing out; many of the women were in tears. On the stage, Julian Fitzgerald stood modestly behind the lectern, waving occasionally with his bandaged hands to acknowledge the crowd.

After some minutes, the President of the Society took the stage, raising his palms to quell the applause.

'My lords, ladies and gentlemen,' he began. 'It has been our pleasure over the years to witness some remarkable stories of human courage within these four walls. Extraordinary stories of triumph over adversity. But I believe we have seldom heard a story to match that of Mr Fitzgerald. Faced with one setback after another, and often with his own life in danger, he struggled to preserve the lives of his companions in one of the most hostile environments on earth. When they were lost, he struggled on, becoming the first man . . . the *first* man, mark you, to make a complete crossing of the Antarctic continent at its widest point.'

There was another ripple of applause around the hall.

'And not only that,' the President continued. 'In addition, he preserved the one precious scientific sample which had survived the catastrophic fire at Capricorn base. A sample which may, we understand, change the fabric of biology as we know it. Not since the days of Livingstone, Stanley or Scott have we been blessed with such a stirring national achievement. We salute you, Mr Fitzgerald, and may I say we will be forwarding your name to the committee to receive the Founder's Medal!'

More great cheers rang around the hall.

'And now, if anyone has any questions, I'm sure Mr Fitzgerald will oblige.'

A hand went up at the front.

'What can you possibly do next? After this stupendous achievement, is there anything left for an explorer such as yourself?'

Fitzgerald took the stand again. 'There is always another challenge,' he said, 'and that is why this is an auspicious moment to announce that I will be setting up a scientific institute called the Fitzgerald Foundation. The objectives will be to pursue challenging scientific projects in the polar regions of the planet. I will be looking for subscribers and benefactors for the foundation in the near future.'

The audience showed its appreciation again. There were calls of 'Here, here!' from some of the older members.

Then a voice rang out from the back.

'I have a question for you,' it said, 'but I'm not sure you'll want to hear it.'

The applause died down as Fitzgerald squinted into the dark recesses of the hall, half recognising the voice but not quite sure.

'That sounds like Mr De Pierman?'

De Pierman stepped forward to the front of the hall.

'It is. Perhaps you would be kind enough to introduce me to the audience?'

'Alexander De Pierman was the sponsor of Dr Burgess's Capricorn base,' Fitzgerald told the crowd. 'One of those rare industrialists who put their money into the world of scientific research.'

There was a polite scattering of applause.

'Do you have news of the test-tube analysis?' Fitzgerald

asked him. 'Perhaps there are some results we can share with the audience here and now?'

'I have more questions than results, Mr Fitzgerald.'

Fitzgerald could not mistake the undercurrent of hostility in De Pierman's tone.

'How so?'

'Are you absolutely sure that that sample was given to you by Lauren Burgess?'

Fitzgerald licked his blistered lips, giving the audience a quick, exasperated glance.

'Of course,' he snapped. 'How could I be mistaken on that?'

'And that sample never left your possession from the moment that Lauren gave it to you until you handed it to me?'

'Absolutely not,' Fitzgerald spluttered indignantly. 'I was well aware of the vital importance of what that test tube contained. It was Lauren Burgess's dying wish that I guard that test tube with my life. And that was what I did.'

The lecture theatre was quiet now, the many hundreds of people uneasy at the exchange they were witnessing.

'So there is no way at all that anyone could have switched the contents of that test tube after Lauren handed it to you?' De Pierman asked.

'Correct.'

De Pierman took a few steps onto the stage, where he positioned himself next to Fitzgerald. A low muttering began to sweep through the hall, there were a couple of cries of 'Shame!' from some of the audience.

De Pierman referred to the huge map of Antarctica which was projected on the screen behind Fitzgerald.

'Would you be kind enough to show me where Lauren died?'

Fitzgerald began to redden with anger. 'Sir! I no longer see that your questions are relevant. Kindly leave the stage.'

'Show me where she died.' De Pierman was insistent.

Fitzgerald glared at him and took up a pointer. He tapped it on a midway position on the Blackmore Glacier.

'As I have already said, Dr Burgess died here.'

'And the location of the crashed aeroplane?'

Fitzgerald moved the pointer, tapping impatiently again.

'Here. About one hundred miles away. Now, will you kindly let me continue with my lecture?'

'So, Lauren Burgess never made it to that aeroplane?'

'She certainly did not. I was the only one.'

'What did Lauren tell you that test tube contained, Mr Fitzgerald?'

'I already told you. It was a sample of fluid from the lake they had drilled into. It contained microscopic species new to science.'

'Then perhaps you can help me with one perplexing thing. That test tube contained no life, Mr Fitzgerald. What it actually contained was avgas. One hundred per cent aviation spirit.'

There was a collective gasp from the audience as his words sank in. Fitzgerald rocked visibly on his feet, clutching for the side of the desk as the blood drained from his face.

'I checked the Capricorn base inventory,' De Pierman continued. 'There was no avgas there at all. The only place Lauren Burgess could have got that aviation spirit was at the site of that crashed plane. That proves she was there and filling that sample container was a way of telling us that.'

Fitzgerald said nothing.

'So. One more question.' De Pierman spoke quietly in the hush which had descended. 'If you are lying about this vital piece of information, Mr Fitzgerald, how are we to trust a single word of your story?'

Suddenly, Fitzgerald was sweeping up his notes from the lectern.

'I don't need to listen to this . . . this rubbish!' he exclaimed, and headed out of the door.

112

De Pierman strapped himself into the front seat of the chartered Agusta 109 and watched as the lights of Battersea heliport dropped away beneath him. Twenty-one nautical miles to the north, his personal Gulfstream jet was already being wheeled out of the executive hangar at Luton Airport, ready to be fuelled.

If there was one thing De Pierman's lifetime in the oil industry had taught him, it was the art of moving fast across vast swathes of the planet. He was on a mission, and he wasn't going to waste a second he didn't need to.

The Gulfstream was ready to roll as soon as De Pierman took his seat, the pilot reporting a strong tailwind to assist them on the southerly route. The stewardess served De Pierman smoked salmon and his favourite Sancerre as they tracked at a shade over six hundred miles an hour across France and the Pyrenees.

The Gulfstream touched down at Madrid Barajas Airport at eleven fifteen p.m. De Pierman paid for a VIP limousine transfer directly across the tarmac and took a first-class seat on the midnight Aerolineas Argentinas flight to Buenos Aires. He could have taken the Gulfstream across the Atlantic, but it would have meant a refuel at Dakar and a subsequent loss of time.

While De Pierman slept, his London office was already on the phone to South America, sorting out the next leg of the journey, a chartered Learjet which would take him down in a single hop to Tierra del Fuego.

The connection was smooth, and by eight a.m. local time he was in Ushuaia, where the Antarctic Air Service operations manager greeted him and took him for a briefing. Also present was the local medic who had been alerted by De Pierman's office. For a modest fee, he had agreed to accompany the oilman on the flight, ready to treat any survivors they should find.

'We were surprised to get the call from your office,' the operations manager told him. 'May I ask what the purpose of this flight is?'

'If my hunch is right, we'll be picking up survivors from Capricorn at the site where your plane crashed some months ago.'

'On the Blackmore Glacier?' The operations manager was perplexed. 'But how could they be there? And more to the point, perhaps, how could they still be alive? As I understood Mr Fitzgerald's account, all of the other Capricorn team members died as they crossed the ice.'

'I really don't know,' De Pierman had to admit. 'But I owe it to the base commander to check this out. It's their last chance, and I wouldn't want to deprive them of that.'

'You have dollars?'

De Pierman flashed him a credit card, the limit on which would have enabled him to buy the aeroplane if he'd so wished.

'You realise, Mr De Pierman,' the operations manager told him regretfully as he swiped the card, 'that your journey will probably be a wasted one. It is a long way to fly for such a disappointment.'

'I appreciate that,' De Pierman told him, 'but I think—no, I *pray*—you may be wrong.'

De Pierman signed the credit slip and was escorted to the waiting plane.

113

L auren was dreaming, just as she seemed to have been doing for every moment of the weeks they had been waiting. Or were they hallucinations? In these days of wasting
away it was difficult to tell.

Frank and Sean were still by her side, but they might have
been ghosts for all the conversation they offered. Maybe
they *were* ghosts, Lauren sometimes thought; they could
have died without a sound. Frank's breathing was now so
light his chest barely rose and fell. Days were passing without a single word being exchanged between them.

Sometimes Sean held her hand, radiating heat and care
into her by some magic force.

It was a gentle experience now the pain had receded, dying little by little like this. Lauren almost found it fascinating, the way her body had metamorphosed. She'd always
been good at endurance; she had little doubt she would be
the last to go.

Her world was green, a calming enough colour, the dome

above her head creased and rucked where the wind had stretched and tested it. In the early stages the tent walls had become a cell, a prison, a tomb or worse. Hope was hanging on in there, but by such a slender thread it might have been spun from gossamer.

But then Lauren learned to relax. Their fate was no longer in their own hands but in the hands of Alexander De Pierman and a titanium tube filled with aviation spirit which he might or might not have received. Would Fitzgerald have destroyed it? Maybe he had thought twice about delivering it. And even if he had handed it to her sponsor, would the oilman recognise the cry for help it contained?

Then it happened, the noise of the approaching Twin Otter as it flew towards them across the glacier. How many days had they waited? How many countless, sleepless hours had they wished for that very noise?

Lauren thought her heart would burst.

She tried to speak, but her lips and throat were so blistered she could not form a single word. Instead she just squeezed Sean's hand, the answering pressure telling her that he too was still alive and that he too had heard the sound and understood it.

Lauren now knew for sure what heaven sounded like. In heaven, two 578-horsepower Pratt & Whitney turbo-props were swooping out of the sky, buzzing low over the tent and fading off once more into the distance. Lauren prayed there would be a medic on board, she knew that Richard and Murdo were both close to death in the next-door tent. It was at least two days since she had had the strength to visit them, and Mel too had been almost incoherent with starvation and dehydration when she had seen her last.

She knew that the aircraft could land; their last actions before their final retreat into the tents had been to recce and mark a new landing strip a short distance from Fitzgerald's original—and deadly—choice.

Next to her she sensed that Sean was trying to say something. But his words, like hers, could not be formed, and they came out as a series of murmured gasps. Then the engine noise increased to a roar, and through that echoing chaos in her head her mind exulted in the knowledge that her message *had* got through. That someone out there in the world beyond *had* cared to discover whether or not the Capricorn team was still alive.

Lauren tried to lift her arms out of her sleeping bag, but found she did not have the strength. Shadows merged at the front of the tent, then, astonishingly strong hands helped her to undo the zip. She was carried out onto the ice where the bright red aircraft sat, as unexpected and surprising in that place as an alien spaceship.

Things went weird for a while, and somewhere in that black spell Lauren was dimly aware that she might have passed out. She came to in the recovery position, her head cradled on her arm, but tried to raise herself up, wanting to know who was still alive. Had Frank died? Was Richard even now cold and lifeless in that tent?

A face loomed over her, and she had to concentrate hard to recognise who it was. Her vision was blurred, the edges fuzzy and lacking definition. An echoing voice called to her as if from a great distance.

'Lauren? Can you understand me? Do you know who I am?'

Lauren wondered why the face above her seemed so shocked. She could not know that her appearance was terrifying, that she looked to be little more than flesh and bone, that she had aged beyond belief. Nor could she know that her face was almost black, stained by months without washing and by the rigours of the solar radiation from which they had had no protection.

Lauren's lips tried to form the 'A' of Alexander, but then a new face took over and Lauren felt herself lifted onto something hard. It felt like canvas . . . a stretcher, she thought. Then the sharp point of a needle penetrated her arm, and she was lifted into the cabin of the aircraft.

There was activity around her, and she began to be more aware. The drug, she thought; whatever it was that they injected me with, it's starting to take effect.

'Take some tea,' a voice said. Someone unscrewed a flask and offered her the piping hot fluid. She sipped minute quantities through blistered lips.

A figure was carried past her on another stretcher, she recognised Frank's face. Minutes later, others were placed in the spaces on the floor.

She managed to grasp a hand which was nearby, pulling weakly at it until De Pierman's concerned face came close to her.

'Are they all . . . ?' she managed to croak. She could tell De Pierman was crying.

'They're all alive, Lauren, and they're going to be fine. You're all going to be fine.'

De Pierman, the medic and the pilots loaded the last of the Capricorn survivors and closed up the door of the Twin Otter. Then the engines were powered up, and the aircraft bounced round in a tight circle as it taxied to the end of the makeshift strip. Lauren felt the airframe shuddering as the engines revved strongly, then the brakes were released and the plane accelerated fast before biting into the frigid air and gaining height.

That was when Lauren knew that this was no dream, that they really had made it and that she really had brought her team through it all alive.

She tried to raise her head to look out of the small aircraft window but could not muster the strength. De Pierman realised what she was doing and gently cupped his hand behind her neck to support her.

Lauren found herself gazing out of the window as the Twin Otter banked round in a big arc and began to head north. Beneath her she could see the creased surface of the glacier, the interior of each crevasse coloured a delicate powder blue. Far, far away, she could see the mountain range they had crossed, the peaks only just visible against the darkening sky.

Beyond that range was Capricorn, gone for the moment, but not from her heart. Lauren knew that one day she would be back.

POSTSCRIPT

London

Billy Fraser parked his battered old Escort van beneath one of the railway arches to the south of Tooley Street and took his bag out of the back. He slung it over his shoulder and made his way across the busy street to the network of cobbled alleyways running through the old wharves and warehouses of St Saviour's Dock.

He kept close to the dripping walls, his head down, his sharp features obscured by the soiled tweed cap he habitually wore.

Anyone observing him might imagine he was a fisherman perhaps, with his rod bag slung over his shoulder. In his worn green oilskins he certainly looked the part.

But Billy Fraser wasn't a fisherman . . . he'd never cast a rod in his life. He was actually a mudlarker, one of the many dozens of Londoners who scoured the low-tide mudbanks of the Thames in the search for old coins, discarded trinkets or anything else which could be sold.

Most were part-timers—weekend treasure hunters dreaming of the big haul. Billy treated them with contempt. Not many of them lasted more than a few weeks, digging up a few hundred bottletops was enough to see them off. But Billy was different—one of the diehards, out there at every low tide almost every day.

In the bag was the tool of his trade: a state-of-the-art metal detector powerful enough to pinpoint a button-sized sliver of Roman silver—a denarius perhaps—even if it was two feet under the mud.

He'd had his successes, had Billy, all of them in the East End. In his early days he'd occasionally tried the western reaches of the river—Hammersmith, Putney and beyond— but the regulars up there hadn't looked kindly on an interloper from Bermondsey, and in the end he'd stuck to the pitches from Tower Bridge to Greenwich.

It was dirty work; Thames mud stinks of rotting fish in the summer and in winter it freezes your feet to blocks of ice. There were hazards—the rusting needle of a drug addict's syringe had once slid easily into the sole of Billy's rubber boot, missing his flesh by a whisker. There were knives hidden in the glutinous slime, sharp fragments of broken glass waiting to slice into an unwary hand.

The worst thing was the bargekeepers' dogs; bull mastiffs and sometimes Rottweilers roamed around the exposed shorelines every time their floating homes were grounded. Billy had lost track of the number of times he'd had to fend off dog attacks, beating back flashing teeth with the blunt end of his metal detector.

The river could turn on you too. Billy had friends who had been so engrossed in digging up a find that they'd neglected to watch the incoming tide. The Thames moves fast, its churning, silt-laden waters coursing faster than a man can run. Leave it a few minutes too long and you could find yourself cut off by a fast-rising channel, unable to reach the steps or ladder which lead to the safety of the embankment. Billy had had a few close shaves himself.

Mudlarking was not a pastime for the faint of heart, but,

as Billy had found to his gain, there were compensations for the many thousands of hours spent in fruitless toil.

The Tudor sword was a good one. 1978, that find had been, Billy's first 'big one', as he called it. Four hundred and eighteen pounds from a military museum in Lambeth. Not bad.

Roman coins? By the bucketful. Billy sometimes wondered if all the Romans did all day was stand on the banks of the Thames throwing their denarii in for luck. He must have made a good two or three thousand out of them in his time.

Then there were the oddities. A cash box containing a loaded revolver, the keys to a Bentley, a silver picture frame holding a photograph of a young girl, an artificial arm, sucked down into the mud.

Oh, the river had secrets all right; that was part of the charm. Billy really didn't know what curiosities it was going to throw up from one day to the next.

That was what had kept him mudlarking for more than twenty-five years.

Today his plan was to sweep the muddy banks at the river end of St Saviour's Wharf. The slime was a good foot deep there, but he had his thigh-high waders on, and the pickings could be rich. Only the most dedicated mudlarkers chose these more difficult spots, and for that reason Billy was sure there would be something waiting for him.

The day was overcast, dull and cold. Billy checked his watch: six fifteen a.m. He clambered as quietly as he could down an access ladder on the side of the dock, his sharp eyes glancing to and fro for any early risers who might be watching him. It wasn't exactly illegal to roam on these mudflats, but it wasn't exactly legal either. The river police routinely turfed mudlarkers off the flats, and he'd been arrested once or twice.

He picked his way past a few lumbering steel barges, their hulls streaked with rust. There was a dredger tilted on its side, the muffled sound of an angry dog barking from within.

He was just thinking about switching his metal detector

on when he saw it, the shape lying amongst a few rusting pieces of debris by some rotten old pilings.

At first he thought it was a dead seal; he knew they sometimes swam into the river by mistake, only to die from starvation and the effects of the toxic soup which surrounded them.

Billy looked around him once more, craning his neck to see if anyone was watching him from the top of the barges. But there was no one. The dog had stopped barking; the only sound now was the throaty chug-chug of a tug in the middle of the river.

As he got closer to the shape, he realised with a sudden shock that it was a human body. Billy knew mudlarkers who had found corpses before, but this was the first time such a thing had happened to him.

The smell was strong, the rich odour of decomposition mixing with the silty aroma of the flats. It was a man, middle-aged or perhaps older, bearded. The upper torso was half naked where the victim's shirt had ridden up, exposing a back which was strong and broad. One foot was bare; the other wore a dark blue sock. His trousers were black, the belt still in place.

Billy's first thought was of foul play; perhaps this was a victim of some gangland vendetta? He wedged his boot beneath the corpse's chin and rolled the head sideways, half expecting to see a bullet hole through the forehead, or a severed windpipe. But the face was intact, with no sign of trauma. A suicide, Billy decided, or a drunk who had had one too many and decided to try and swim the river in the dead of night to impress his friends.

Billy knew what to do. He bent down and slipped a hand into one of the trouser pockets, grunting with a tut of disappointment when he found it empty. He rolled the body slightly to one side to search the other pocket. Again nothing. Billy cursed his luck. The least he could have expected was a slender leather wallet, a few notes, soggy but retrievable, inside.

A sudden movement caught his eye: a City worker pedalling his mountain bike along the embankment above him.

Billy kept still, and the cyclist passed on, not noticing him where he crouched among the wooden piles.

Time to go. The last thing Billy wanted now was the river police dragging him in for a statement. He'd move on to another pitch; perhaps Tobacco Wharf would be a good choice.

Then he noticed the hand, the way it was clenched so tightly. That was odd; it looked like there might be something inside. Whistling lightly beneath his breath, Billy tried to prise open the corpse's fingers, grunting with frustration as he found them locked into a fist by rigor mortis.

On an impulse he switched his metal detector on, sweeping it over the hand in a quick pass.

The bleep was unmistakable; there *was* something metal inside that hand. Billy bent once more, his fingers sliding under the clenched fingers of the drowned man, prising harder and harder until they finally gave with a brittle cracking sound.

The glint of gold. Billy's heart skipped a few beats, then he took the medal into his hands, feeling by the weight that this was the real thing. He wiped the cloying mud from the surface, squinting to read the inscription etched elegantly into the precious metal:

THE POLAR MEDAL.
PRESENTED TO JULIAN FITZGERALD
BY HER MAJESTY QUEEN ELIZABETH II.

Billy felt the weight once more, trying to estimate its value. It had to be a good few ounces, even on the quiet it would be worth a pretty penny.

He wouldn't waste any time. The gold markets of Hatton Garden were only a fifteen-minute walk across Tower Bridge. Billy knew plenty of jewellers there who would buy with no questions asked. He'd take some breakfast in a transport café he knew just off Chancery Lane and wait for them to open at nine.

The gold would be melted down within minutes, and Billy would be a few hundred pounds richer.

He pocketed the medal and moved away quickly, his

boots making small sucking noises as he lifted them from the mud. At the ladder he looked back one more time at the body, lying so pathetically amid the styrofoam burger cartons and other waste.

The tide was already lapping at the man's heels. Billy knew that sometimes bodies were swept right out into the North Sea and never seen again.

He climbed out onto the embankment where the early commuters were now beginning to emerge. He slipped off his waders and placed them with the metal detector in his bag. Soon he was just another anonymous figure amid the bustling crowds crossing Tower Bridge.

A good morning's work, Billy reckoned; one of the more interesting he could recall.

As for the drowned man, well, Billy had already forgotten the name.